MRS DYMOND

ANNE THACKERAY RITCHIE

MRS DYMOND

Introduction by Esther Schwartz-McKinzie

SUTTON PUBLISHING

First published in 1885

First published in this edition in 1997 by
Sutton Publishing Limited · Phoenix Mill
Thrupp · Stroud · Gloucestershire · GL5 2BU

British Library Cataloguing in Publication Data
A catalogue record for this book is available from the British Library

ISBN 0 7509 1411 4

Cover picture: detail from A Labour of Love *(1892) by Alfred Glendenning (1861–1907) (photograph: courtesy of Sotheby's).*

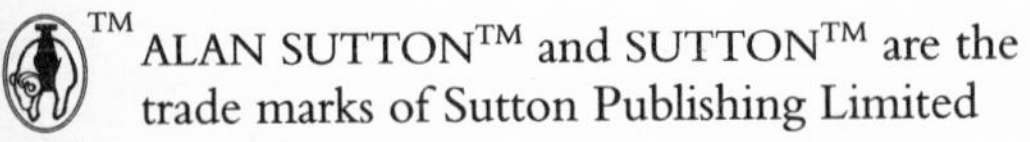

Typeset in 10/11 pt Bembo.
Typesetting and origination by
Sutton Publishing Limited.
Printed in Great Britain by
The Guernsey Press Company Limited,
Guernsey, Channel Islands.

CONTENTS

BOOK IV

SUSANNA'S CONCLUSIONS

INTRODUCTION

Reflecting on her long experience as a woman of letters in 1908, Anne Thackeray Ritchie acknowledged the often fleeting nature of literary success. Many 'worthy books', she lamented, undoubtedly 'pass away' with time. 'But sometimes after a century or two, such books are called back into existence and raised from the dust. Their hearts seem to beat once more; the time has come for their reincarnation.'[1] This seems an apt opening for the reintroduction, after over one hundred years, of Ritchie's *Mrs Dymond* (1885), the last of her five novels and, in the analyses of her biographers, her best.[2] Certainly Ritchie, who had lived at the centre of England's literary milieu for some seventy years – first as William Makepeace Thackeray's precocious eldest daughter, later as a celebrated author in her own right and finally, as mentor and adviser to a younger generation of writers including Meredith, Swinburne and James – knew something about this kind of quiet 'passing away'. In particular, she knew what it meant for a woman artist to stand in the shadow of a great man, and though she had earned her own writerly laurels, she was, in the later years of her career, very much aware of her status as Thackeray's 'living representative'.[3] Finally submitting to the pressure to produce a biography of her famous father in 1894, she negotiated the parental veto on such a project by writing the first of a series of biographical introductions to his *Collected Works*, later expanded and revised to commemorate the centenary of his birth in 1911. Producing what Swinburne called 'the most perfect memorial ever raised to any great writer on record',[4] Ritchie in effect subordinated her identity to his, and despite her earlier accomplishments, she has been remembered primarily as a dutiful and affectionate daughter.

Being the child of a literary luminary had both its advantages and disadvantages. Thackeray took special pride in 'Anny', and he provided her with a remarkably liberal education that included extensive novel reading. In her youth, she met and formed many intimate friendships with the most interesting personages of Thackeray's generation, including Dickens, Tennyson and the Brownings, connections that would later ensure her notoriety as a biographer of the Victorian era. For exactly this reason, however, critics have tended to dismiss her as a passive 'insider', whose memories were more compelling than her oeuvre. Listing her under her husband's name, the *Dictionary of National Biography* glibly asserts, 'it is in social life rather than in literature that her position was unique',[5] and until recently, readers have had little opportunity to challenge this assumption. Fortunately, scholarly interest in Ritchie over the past decade has begun to raise her from the dust, and rereading her work, it is possible not only to credit her with the success she earned during her lifetime, but also to recognize and value her efforts (quite apart from her relation to Thackeray) to emphasize the importance of *women's* lives, struggles and accomplishments in a world that relentlessly associated greatness with masculinity. These efforts included documenting the lives of women artists (Mrs Barbauld, Amelia Opie, Felicia Felix, Fanny Kemble and Angelica Kauffmann), who otherwise faced obscurity; reintroducing the works of her literary foremothers (Mary Russell Mitford, Elizabeth Gaskell and Maria Edgeworth); and, in her essays and novels, calling attention to the destructive consequences of the marriage market, and of women's subjective position as wives and mothers with little or no legal or economic power.

Though born in London in 1837, Ritchie spent most of her childhood in France, where she and her sister Minny lived with their paternal grandmother, Ann Carmichael-Smyth, a Calvinist whose inflexibility fostered the young girl's spirit of rebellion. The death of another infant sister and the permanent institutionalization of her mother, Isabella Shawe Thackeray (who became depressed and attempted suicide after Minny's birth in 1840), made for a large share of early sorrow, but by all accounts Ritchie's personality was resilient, and Paris (which would become the setting for much of her fiction) made a strong impression. Nurturing and warm-hearted by nature, she easily slipped into the roles of surrogate mother and 'little wife' after Thackeray reunited the family in Kensington in 1846. At fifteen she became his 'secretary amanuensis', entrusted to record his dictation as well as to offer insight and critique. The exchange fostered Ritchie's creative self-confidence, and she wrote 'several novels and a play'[6] while still in her teens. Her first essay, a description of her visit to a London poor school, was submitted to *The Cornhill* (Thackeray's magazine) in 1860, and was soon followed by other essays and a short novel, *The Story of Elizabeth*, in 1862. Published anonymously, *Elizabeth* was hailed for its psychological realism and was even recommended by George Eliot, whose usual antagonism towards contemporary fiction made this high praise indeed. However, Ritchie would not bask long in the joy of this independently won success: within a year, Thackeray died suddenly without leaving an inheritance, thus making her, at twenty-six, financially responsible for herself and her sister.

With the positive reception of her second novel, *Village on the Cliff*, in 1867, Ritchie's future as a professional writer was well assured. Over the next half-century, her essays, journals, short stories, memoirs and novels would become an acknowledged 'foundation'[7] of *The Cornhill*, and other periodicals, including *Macmillan's* and *Fraser's Magazine*, were eager to get work from her. She was known for her 'distinctive style',[8] alternately impressionistic or 'diffuse' and realistic and precise, that in the estimation of numerous critics, conveyed 'deep veracity'[9] and created a felt sense of life as lived. In this, Ritchie's fiction contrasted sharply with the dominant tone of the 'sensational 60s', and offered relief, as one critic described, from 'the falsehood in art which is so prevalent among the novel writers of the present period . . . the falsity of extremes'.[10] In fact, Ritchie felt a responsibility to portray heroines with whom readers could easily identify and whose triumphs over adversity made them meaningful role models to young women. Howard Sturgis, eulogizing her in 1919, summarized the effect of her prose style on two generations of readers: she possessed a 'great gift of genuine sympathy' – a 'sap-stirring, life giving' quality that inspired empathetic connection with her subjects.[11] This particular talent, considered rare and valuable in the genre of biography, partly explains why Ritchie turned almost exclusively to memoir writing after the publication of *Old Kensington*, which ran through three editions in 1873. Another explanation, however, may have to do with the circumstances of her life during this period.

A woman who – like many of her female subjects, real and fictional – had early on become a nurturer and caretaker, Ritchie now filled these roles for a large extended family, including Minny's bereft daughter and husband (after her death in childbirth in 1875), her own mother (whose care was literally and emotionally costly), and her governess' two orphaned children. Given the emotional and financial commitments here entailed, novel writing may have simply become too onerous. Additionally, Ritchie occasionally suffered from bouts of depression and illness that eclipsed her usually optimistic perspective and made it difficult for her to work. Support would come from an unexpected source, however, and she dealt a blow to the English sense of propriety when, in 1878 (though she had already long been considered an 'old maid'), she announced her engagement to her second cousin, Richmond Ritchie, sixteen years her junior. Though the marriage caused a flurry of excitement, Ritchie remained unruffled professionally, and it was when her cup was fullest, after her daughter's birth the following year, that she began *Mrs Dymond*. Soon distracted by the arrival of a second child, a move to a larger house and several urgent commissions (including a memorial of Elizabeth Barrett Browning for the *DNB*, and a book-length biography of Madame de Sévigné, 1881), Ritchie postponed completion of the novel until 1885, when it was serialized by *Macmillan's*. Despite its obvious merits, it seems to have received less attention than her other novels, and after her death memorialists recalled her primarily as the author of *The Story of Elizabeth* and *Old Kensington.*

Like these earlier novels, *Mrs Dymond* focuses on a young, powerless heroine who is gradually matured by her experiences and learns to exercise some control over her world. Fascinated, as always, by women's relationships with one another, Ritchie here, more pointedly than in these other texts, interrogates the ways in which women are wounded by a social system that defines them (and requires them to define themselves) through their relations with men. All three plots involve women who are prevented, either by their preoccupation with or subjection to authoritative men, from pursuing key female relationships. Perhaps a reflection of her own feelings of 'motherlessness', Ritchie's dramas highlight the intense longing of daughters for mothers, and this is especially so in her portrayal of Susanna (later 'Mrs Dymond'), who helplessly witnesses her mother's emotional and physical abuse by a smooth-talking second husband. Even more surprising than Ritchie's graphic depiction of wife-abuse is the still resonant psychological realism with which she conveys Mrs Marney's self-deception ('It is not the same to you as to me . . . you cannot understand how long we have loved each other . . .'), and Susanna's 'mental suicide' when she attempts to squeeze her personality into the narrow mould made for her by her own husband. Colonel Dymond's good intentions underscore a somewhat radical argument: that in the best of situations, women are cramped and debilitated by their relations with men, who are their social, economic and legal superiors. Set in part against the backdrop of the Paris Commune in 1871, the novel implicitly equates Susanna's release from her mould, and her gradual sexual awakening, with revolution.[12]

In the *Times Literary Supplement*'s obituary for Ritchie, Virginia Woolf, for whom she had been a valuable example of a literary daughter and woman artist,[13] expressed surprise that her aunt's fame was already fading, and mourned the passing of 'a woman of genius', an artist 'faithful to her vision'.[14] Later writers, including Ritchie's own daughter, would express similar surprise and dismay. Calling her book 'back into existence' now repeats the service she performed for other female artists; this edition, the republication of *The Story of Elizabeth* and *Old Kensington* by Thoemmes Press in 1995, and Lillian Shankman's 1994 *Anne Thackeray Ritchie. Journals and Letters* all testify to her enduring worth as a writer who possessed originality of style, as well as keen insight into issues and dilemmas that continue to be part of women's lives.

Esther Schwartz-McKinzie

NOTES

1 Anne Thackeray Ritchie, *Blackstick Papers* (New York, Putnam, 1908), p. 4.
2 Ritchie's two most recent biographers base their evaluations on the 'structural soundness' of *Mrs Dymond*; however, readers may want to think about why her contemporary audience found Ritchie's 'diffuseness' and 'impressionism' appealing, and to consider how her work is part of an alternative literary tradition that need not necessarily be evaluated according to traditional standards of merit. Winifred Gerin, *Anne Thackeray Ritchie, A Biography* (Oxford, Oxford University Press, 1981); Lillian Shankman, *Anne Thackeray Ritchie. Journals and Letters* (Ohio, Ohio State University Press, 1994).
3 Constance Cary Harrison, 'A Visit to Anne Thackeray Ritchie', *The Bookman*, vol. 1 (1895), 164.
4 Algernon Charles Swinburne, 'Charles Dickens', *Quarterly Review*, vol. 196 (1902), 39.
5 Lord Blake and C.S. Nichols, *Dictionary of National Biography* (Oxford, Oxford University Press, 1990), p. 463.
6 Hester Thackeray Ritchie, *Thackeray and his Daughter, The Letters and Journals of Anne Thackeray Ritchie, with Many Letters of William Makepeace Thackeray* (New York, Harper & Brothers, 1924), p. 124.
7 'In Memoriam, Anne Thackeray Ritchie and Henry Charles Beeching', *The Cornhill Magazine* (1919), 447.
8 Howard Sturgis, 'Anne Isabella Thackeray (Lady Ritchie)', *The Cornhill Magazine* (1919), 455.
9 Margaret Oliphant, 'Novels', *Blackwood's Magazine*, vol. 94 (1863), 176.
10 'Miss Thackeray's "Old Kensington"', *Edinburgh Review*, vol. 138 (1873), 166.
11 Sturgis, 452.
12 This equation is, however, not altogether positive, as Susanna's late understanding of passion finally reveals 'the secret' of her mother's life to her, and suggests that women in love with men are always alike in vulnerability.
13 Carol Hanbury McKay, 'The Thackeray Connection; Virginia Woolf's Aunt Anny', *Virginia Woolf and Bloomsbury*, ed. Jane Marcus (Bloomington, Indiana University Press, 1987).
14 Virginia Woolf, 'A. Lady Ritchie', *Times Literary Supplement* (1919). Reprinted in Gerin, 279.

BOOK I

SUSANNA

AN INTRODUCTION

Not mine own fears, nor the prophetic soul
Of the wide world dreaming on things to come,
Can yet the lease of my true love control

CHAPTER I

EMPTY HOUSES

The lark, that tirra-lyra chants,
With heigh! with heigh! the thrush and the jay,
Are summer songs for me and my aunts,
While we lie tumbling in the hay . . .

Jog on, jog on, the footpath way,
And merrily hent the stile-a:
A merry heart goes all the day,
Your sad tires in a mile-a.

WINTER'S TALE

Before the game of chess begins to be played, the heroes and heroines of the coming catastrophe are to be seen in orderly array. There is nothing to tell in which direction the fortunes of the board will drift. The kings sit enthroned by their spirited partners; the little guards of honour are drawn up in serried lines, prepared, if necessary, to fall for their colours; the bishops are in their places, giving the sanction of the Church to the dignities of State. The impetuous knights are reining in those fiery steeds that are presently to curvet, in wayward leaps, all over the field; the castles, with flying flags, flank the courts at either end. And so in story telling, when the performance begins, the characters are to be seen, quietly drawn up in their places, and calmly resting before the battle. There are, as we all know, four castles to every game of chess. If I look at my chequered plain I see on one side a grey fortress standing in its wide domain, guarding the lands that lie between the hilly lake country and the Scottish borders. At the other end of my story, where the red court is assembled, a shabby little strong-hold is standing in a walled garden, not far from Paris. As for the other two castles, they are both empty ones. They belong to Colonel John Dymond of Wimpole Street, and of Crowbeck Place in Lancashire.

What a strange, indefinable feeling there is about empty houses. The London house was blind-drawn, dingy, and in order. The portrait of the late Mrs Dymond hung in the drawing-room, with the shrouded candelabra; she was painted full length, in blue satin, going to a ball. In the back drawing-room – fitted with its many couches, faded cabinets, brass rails, screens, Parian statuettes – hung the Colonel himself, in his uniform. It was a half-finished picture, in water-colour, begun by Mrs Dymond many years ago. The drawing represented a good-looking man with black moustachios which have since turned grey. She had left it behind when the family went off to the Colonel's country-house one summer, and the poor lady never came back to finish that or any of the other things she had begun. She had been a feeble, incapable woman, nervous, and jealous by nature; and her death was more of a shock than a sorrow to her husband. The children cried, and then wiped their tears; the Colonel looked very grave, went abroad all dressed in black, and sent Jo and Tempy, his son and daughter, to Bolsover Hall, their uncle's house, for a time; and then the town-house and the country-house were shut up both together, instead of alternately as heretofore. The Colonel often went abroad. He found his homes very sad.

But when the country-house was closed, it never seemed quite so deserted as Wimpole Street. The echoes were less startled; the doors did not creak so forlornly. Crowbeck Place was not far from Mr Bolsover's more stately hall, where the young people were staying. They often liked to go over and stray about the Place garden and eat the unripe fruit and pick the flowers; and Mr Bolsover used to fish in the grounds, and Miss Bolsover, the late Mrs Dymond's sister, used occasionally to spend a day opening old cupboards, examining drawers and store-closets, and seeking for mysterious articles, which she wished to put by for her niece, she said. She also read any letters that happened to be lying about for the Colonel.

Crowbeck Place stood on the slope of a meadow shelving to the lake. Jo and his sister liked it ever so much better than the Hall; they delighted in the silence, the liberty, the sense of ease that seemed to meet them at the very gates of the old Place. At the Hall everything was fenced, and clipped, and boxed up, including Tempy and Jo themselves; whereas here they were free – the land, the sky, the sunlight, the water, each element seemed a new happiness to them. Their Aunt Fanny discarded the elements altogether from her system of education: for her water meant eau de Cologne; land was the family estate; air was what came in through the carriage window; and fire, if it shone in the shape of sunlight, was to be carefully fenced off with spotted net and parasols.

Their aunt, Mrs Bolsover, was the very contrary to her sister-in-law, Miss Fanny. She loved exercise, she liked it straight and serious, a waterproof and a road by an iron railing suited her temper best; she was grim, but the young folks had more sympathy for her than for Miss Bolsover with all her graces.

'I wouldn't be Aunt Fanny not for a thousand pounds,' says Jo. 'She spends her life screaming, spying, making mischief, and writing poetry, and she would like you and me to do the same.'

'How can you exaggerate so!' said Tempy.

Tempy was very serious, and never laughed. Jo was a lanky boy, with red hair and an odd humorous twinkle in his face. Tempy was a Dymond, people said, and took after her father's family. As for Jo, nobody could tell exactly what he was; *he* was not a Bolsover, nor was he like the Dymonds; and he certainly took after nothing that anybody held up for his edification.

Families are odd combinations; they seem to have an existence which is quite distinct from that of each individual member of which they are composed. We know of enthusiastic families, of grasping families, of matter-of-fact families, of others desponding, cheerful, noisy, fanciful. There is also a family standard of right and wrong and of discretion and indiscretion which is quite independent of private feeling and conscience. Some families will talk where others preserve an absolute silence, some families make jokes where others weep.

The Dymonds were by some people called a cranky family, they went their own way, they were precise and confiding, serious and discreet; the Bolsovers, with whom they had intermarried, were people of the world, more easy-going, and more conventional too. A Dymond might do wrong, but he would not call it right. A Bolsover, at the worst, made things pleasant with a laugh, and so got out of the difficulty. Colonel Dymond's wife had been a Bolsover, Mr Bolsover's wife was a Dymond. The unmarried Miss Bolsover remained; at one time she was living not with her own brother who rarely left the Hall, but with her brother-in-law, the Colonel, who spent eight months of the year in London and four more at the Farm, or 'Place,' as it was called by the country folks.

Tarndale Water is not the least beautiful of the Cumberland lakes, although it is comparatively little known. The swallows have found it out, and dart hither and thither along the banks; tourists come there from time to time, not in shoals, but sparingly and by chance; now and then a solitary figure toils round the head of the lake by the Hall. A little pathway across the sloping fields leads from the Hall to Crowbeck – an old building, made green with delicate ivy and frothed with the white spray of the convolvulus; its porch is heavy with purple clematis. The brother and sister as they talk are travelling along the sloping field early one summer morning. Fragrant woods and meads and hedges seem trembling with life and song. The whole place is athrill: the swifts go darting hither and thither; thrushes and larks are singing their summer jubilee; beetles, gnats, midges, are buzzing in the air and droning in chorus; the fishes are darting among the brown shallows. The encircling hills seem nearer now than later in the day. Everything is awake and astir and alive with that indescribable life of the field and the waters: the cows are cropping the long grass down by the water-side; the dew is shining on the delicate leaves, one single drop is brimming in each emerald trefoil cup, the white and lilac weeds are sparkling in the sunlight; the banks cast long shadows into the water; the queen-of-the-meadows is scenting the air with her fragrant white blossom, a great honeysuckle head rises above the hedge. Jo and his sister go struggling across the long grass, following each other. Jo climbs a stile built according to the fashion of the country, where slabs of slate are let into the wall. The little calves in the adjoining field start off running, with their long tails arched as they fly past. Tempy screams like her aunt, and stands, hesitating, on the top of the stile.

'Don't be afraid, Tempy,' says Jo; 'you are much more likely to eat the poor little calves than they are to eat you.'

Encouraged by this assurance, Miss Tempy jumps and goes plodding after her brother towards the old boat-house, whither they are bound. It stands among pines on a narrow tongue of land jutting out into the lake.

'We are late,' says Tempy, 'there will be a scene!'

'Let them rave,' says Jo, sententiously.

'Jo, I can bear it no longer,' says his sister. 'I have written to papa. You may read my letter if you like,' and she pulled a paper out of her pocket and put it into his hand.

'Bolsover, July 24, 18——.

'My Dear Papa,

I am afraid it will be a disagreeable surprise to you to get this letter. It is to implore you to send for us at once. I thought you were coming home, and I waited patiently, but now that you have put us off again, I can be silent no longer. We do *so hate* being here. Aunt Car would be kind enough if Aunt Fanny would let her, but she never lets any one alone. She watches us, and suspects us of I don't know what, and never believes a word we say; she burnt some verses only yesterday that poor Charlie Bolsover had written for me; she reads all our letters; she is having him sent away again in fresh disgrace because he played cards down at the hotel. I would scrub, I would eat dry bread, I would do *anything* to please you, if only you will send for us at once, but I will not submit to Aunt Fanny; indeed, this is no childish outburst. I cannot bear injustice, no more can Jo, and we long to come to you. Please write at once, and we might come by the next train. – Your miserable

'TEMPY.'

Jo whistled and pulled a long face as he read. 'Is not this rather strong?' said he doubtfully. He was not without some admiration for his sister's style, but he felt that the Colonel might justly expect some more definite grievances to justify him in sending for them.

'It is only the truth,' says Tempy, 'and papa will understand. I have a great mind not to go to the Vivians to-day, Jo,' she said gloomily and walking as fast as ever she could.

'You can do as you like,' said her brother, stooping to drag up the old boat, that was disporting itself in the sunshine tethered by its chain. 'Hullo! she is full of water. Give me that tin kettle, Tempy.'

A tin kettle was lying in the dew-spangled grass, and Tempy flung it to her brother. He began baling the water with great energy, the water splashed into the shining lake, the boat rocked, the fishes fled in shoals, alarmed by the disturbance. A few minutes more the little boat was zigzagging across the lake in very workmanlike fashion. Jo was rowing, Tempy sat steering; when the boy looked up he could see his sister's red hair and round pink face against the soft landscape. Jo himself, in his ragged straw hat and flannel shirt, was not an unpicturesque figure. He was pale, and slight, with very speaking blue eyes under shaggy eyebrows. He had heavy red locks, that he sometimes tossed back with an impatient jerk. By degrees Tempy forgot her grievances.

A worse humour than Tempy's might have been charmed to peace by the sweet sights of that early morning; the heavens and the earth were shining and astir, a thousand ripples were flowing in from the far end of the lake; the sunny slopes were dotted with farmsteads, stretching up, on one side, to where the long moors rolled purple with the heather, while on the other, behind the sweet pastoral country, lay, like dream-land itself, the long line of the mountains, quivering through veils of light, in that region where heaven and earth meet, the boundary, not of one horizon alone, but of all we hope to see in life. Lovely, indefinite, beyond our reach, those distant crests speak of more than all the summer glory round about.

After a time they come to a little landing-place, green and overgrown with ivy; one or two boats are floating there among the weeds and clanking their rusty chains; an owl-tower had been converted into a boat-house, towards which Jo paddles, skilfully steering the old punt to the steps. The sound of a distant bell comes floating along the water.

'Late!' says the boy. Then he leaps to shore, leaving his sister to follow, and they hurry off as hard as they can go to breakfast.

They meet a bronzed figure coming along the gravel drive, with a post-bag slung to its shoulders, and a battered straw hat. This is Mrs Wilson, the postwoman of the district.

'Good-day, Mr Dymond! good-day, Miss Dymond! there's a letter for ye up at t' Hall: a furren stamp letter fra the Cornel.'

She trudges on, Jo sets off running towards the house, Tempy hesitates for a moment, and then calls after Mrs Wilson –

'Here is a letter, Mrs Wilson; will you post it for me?'

''T'woan't go till the night, miss,' says the postwoman.

'Never mind, take it,' cries Tempy hastily. 'To-night will do.' The deed is done.

Aunts, breakfast, letters, Uncle Bolsover, the *Times*, were all to be found in the big dining-room at Bolsover Hall punctually by nine o'clock every morning. Jo and Tempy are ingredients less accurately to be counted upon. To-day, they find Aunt Fanny, as usual, reading her own and everybody else's correspondence. Her head is a little on one side, she is softly preoccupied, and her white fingers beat a gentle tattoo upon the papers. Aunt Car is pouring out strong tea with a serious countenance. Uncle Bolsover seems absorbed in the local paper, of which he actively climbs column after column every morning; there is a dead silence as the young folks come in; evidently something is amiss.

Tempy opens her eyes, looks round, says, 'Good-morning,' in a loud inquiring voice.

'Good-morning, Tempy,' says Aunt Bolsover, dryly.

'Good-morning, my dear,' says Aunt Fanny, with a sort of 'what next?' intonation.

'Where is my letter, Aunt Fanny?' says Tempy, aggressively. 'Mrs Wilson told me there was one from papa.'

'Here it is,' says Aunt Fanny, daintily turning over the heap before her, 'I opened it by mistake,' and she looked full at her niece as she spoke.

'I wish you wouldn't open my letters by mistake,' says Tempy, throwing the envelope back. 'Since you have read it, Aunt Fanny, you can answer it and tell papa why.'

'I opened it by accident, Tempy,' says Aunt Fanny, with a musical laugh; 'you need not look so tragical. I have *not* read your letter.'

'Dear, dear,' says Uncle Bolsover, looking very red. 'Don't let us waste time over discussion; we ought to be off at ten, and you, none of you are dressed.'

'I suppose you have been to see the Charlieboy off,' says Miss Bolsover, still daintily dealing out her papers. Her reticule was a sort of lion's mouth into which they disappeared by degrees – announcements, warnings, denunciations; no one ever measured the contents of that velvet maw.

'Do you mean Charlie? We drove part of the way with him,' said Jo. 'We didn't want to miss the lunch, so we came back. I say, Tempy, it's half-past nine. It's time to get ready.'

'Poor boy,' says Tempy, gloomily, pushing her cup away. 'It is time for us to amuse ourselves, and for him to go off alone to that horrid place.'

'Well, well, let us hope Charles will like his tutors when he is used to it,' says Uncle Bolsover the mediator. 'I was at a private tutor's once myself; sent there in disgrace, too. I assure you I never was happier in my life. We had some capital fun at Tickle's, I remember.'

'My dear Fred,' said Aunt Fanny, 'we hope for something better than *fun* for our Charlie.'

Uncle Bolsover's remark was deemed inappropriate by Aunt Fanny, but it comforted Tempy, who got up with a dramatic toss of the head and left the room to get ready.

The more angry Tempy seemed, the more sweet and silvery was Miss Bolsover; she undulated up the broad staircase after her niece, who bounced up to her own room, banged the door, burst into tears, rang violently for her maid, wiped her eyes, and then proceeded in hot haste to put on a very smart, tight, braided costume, which distracted her by degrees from her troubles. When she appeared ready to start, with an ivory parasol in her hand, it would have been difficult to recognise the calico nymph of the lake in the fashionable young person bustling along the passage on high heels. Jo was also completely transformed – not for the better – and Uncle Bolsover had assumed knickerbockers for the occasion. The carriage was ready to take them to the station, the train was waiting to convey them to the feast; it was a long journey thither, to the place where a hospitable old castle opened its ancient halls once a year to the neighbouring villages. As the train flew along, Tempy's spirits improved, and Aunt Fanny herself became less irritatingly amiable. Aunt Bolsover, bolt upright, sat looking through the window. Uncle Bolsover ran his usual comment upon things in general, addressing an old gentleman, the only passenger beside themselves in the carriage –

'Very fine, but very flat all about here, sir – very flat indeed.'

CHAPTER II

IN A GIG

I saw her, upon nearer view,
A spirit, yet a woman too,
Her household motions light and free,
And steps of virgin liberty,
A countenance in which did meet
Sweet records, promises as sweet.

The North of England is essentially a romantic country. To a southerner, used to narrow enclosures, to thick-grown hedges, to close-packed villages all peaceful and economical of space and emotion, there is something very impressive in widespread chases, in horizons that heave mile beyond mile, in great moors and fells, cloud-swept perpetually. These moors stretch for miles on either side of the long lines of railway, hiding away many a secret. There is a mystery of sylvan life, a treasure of rushing waters, of deep glens and valleys, a whole hidden world concealed below the surface of these plains that spread flat, unbroken to all appearance as far as eye can strain. If you cross them you become intimate with their secrets, unsuspected depths of green and rocky terrace open at your very feet, you look down into beautiful chasms swept by slanting light and shadow; a tumult of waters echoes from the green depths, a sweet overflow of vegetation droops to meet the spray, flowers and ferns start from the shining rocks. These wild glens and plains, at once tender and austere; all these places, in their loneliness and beauty, seem to me to express the very spirit of endurance and romance which exists in some people who certainly would not consciously seek a reflection of themselves in the rocks and plains which delight them.

While Jo and Tempy were scudding along the iron rails, a country gig had been driving for miles across great grass fields, where young colts were galloping in the sunshine, and inside the gig were two people, a little man with a long nose, and a girl in a white dress and straw hat, making her happy discoveries – exclaiming delighted, beshaken, perched so high up that she could see into the first-floor windows of the little towns as they drove through them, and look for miles and miles across the country they had crossed.

'Shall we soon be at the station, cousin John?' said the girl. 'I hope grandpapa won't have to wait. How beautiful everything looks.'

She leant back as she spoke, the horse swerved, and a whole horizon of clouds, of far-away Cumberland hills, seemed to revolve before her eyes.

'We shall be there in ten minutes,' said cousin John. 'Can you make out the sea, Susy? Look, there it is shining in the hollow. Yes, you have seen something of the country at last, and you'll like to be able to say you have lunched at the Castle.'

Susy looked doubtful.

'*Must* we go on there?' she said, hesitating, and anything but enthusiastic.

'Dear me; not go,' answered cousin John, 'why they sent a telegram to ask us. I knew Mrs Vivian would be glad to see any friends of mine. Look, Roman remains,' continued the Doctor, pointing with his whip handle, and doing the honours.

Susy looked as she was bid, and while she looked the horse kept on its way. It did not take ten minutes to travel past as many centuries of time, and to pass from the handiwork of the Roman to the great tower of the old abbey church sunning itself in the morning light. The delicate high arches were casting their shadows on a placid sward of green, where sheep were browsing. Then they came to a bridge which crossed the stream beyond the valley, and the Doctor's whip now pointed to a wooden height beyond the bridge.

'The Castle is over there,' said he, 'but the road winds round by the station.' And then in four minutes more they had reached the station, not of Roman legions, but of civilisation in its progress.

A train had just come in, and some people were getting out of the carriages on to the platform.

'There he is!' said the Doctor, with a cheerful wave of the hand. 'Pretty punctual, eh? Jump down, Susy, don't be shy; walk him up to the Castle. They quite expect you. I will join you there as soon as I can.'

Susy gathered her white skirt together and jumped as she was told; for a minute she stood in the middle of the road, then she turned, nodded good-bye to cousin John, and with a bright look ran to meet her grandfather, who was standing at the far end of the platform. He was a tall, handsome old man, dressed in a clergyman's black flapping coat; he stooped a little as he walked. Susy was a slight, bright-looking girl, with a dazzling complexion, and a round innocent-looking face; she did not stoop, but walked straightly and freely, looking like some young nymph from the plains below; as she passed, some people standing by made way. The old man seemed not a little perturbed as the girl came up, and kissed him with a 'Here I am, grandpapa!'

'Are you alone, Susanna? where is cousin John? what are we to do now? where are we to go? which is the way?' said he nervously.

'Cousin John showed me the way, grandpapa. He is coming back for us,' said Susanna, speaking more confidently than she felt, and pointing vaguely up a road. 'There are some other people going to the Castle; we can follow them, you know.'

Susy and her grandfather did not hurry to pass the people who were walking ahead; they were glad to be preceded by so imposing a party whose presence seemed to shield their own insignificance. Susy admired the important air of the two splendid ladies in brown and crimson, of the fashionable young lady with the pink parasol. There were also two gentlemen of the party: one was a short, fat, good-natured-looking little man, in knickerbockers; the other was a pale, very young man, who whirled an umbrella as he walked along. Susy might look with vague admiration at the prosperous presentable set of people who seemed so used to the world, to great houses, to open-air festivals; she did not know how far more sympathetic a sight to world-worn eyes was the fresh young apparition of the smiling, wondering girl as she advanced with her gentle, old protector. The two came together, crossing sunshine and shadow, the deer scarcely fled at their approach, the whole summer world was alight. There was a stirring of birds in the air, a far-off shout of children's voices, then the sound of the clock came up the avenue to meet them striking clearly.

'The school-children must be there, already, grandpapa,' said Susy; 'is it one o'clock?' and Mr Holcombe pulled out his old-fashioned silver watch, and said –

'Yes; I suppose so, my dear; my watch is a little slow; I thought it had been earlier.'

Everything was so sweet, so silent, so splendid in the sunshine that both Susy and her grandfather by degrees forgot their shyness. The two lingered for a minute to look, through an open door, at an old-fashioned garden of lilies and yew hedges, to stare back at the solemn old chase, beyond which the Cumberland hills were floating; then they reached the moat, flooded with shining green leaves, and Susy stopped again, ivy-charmed. Perhaps some spell left long years ago by belted Will himself, the once owner of the old keep, had reached her. Meanwhile the fashionable figures of to-day had disappeared through the gateway, and when the two inexperienced visitors came up in turn, the company had vanished utterly, no one was to be seen anywhere. They now had come to a low archway leading to the Castle court. There was a bell swinging on a long iron chain, which Susy boldly pulled, but no one answered; no one was to be seen in the court-yard; it was all enclosed by old walls and latticed windows and paved with flagstones and soft green turf – once Susy caught sight of a rosy little child's face at a lattice, but then it vanished. A scent of jessamine was everywhere; it seemed as if the very stones gave out a perfume. Some great Scotch deerhounds were lying asleep upon the turf, and came slowly trotting up to the strangers to be petted, then they turned and lay down to sleep in their sunny corner again.

'But where are we to go?' said Mr Holcombe again.

Susy looked at her grandfather, and seeing his distressed expression, began to be a little bit frightened too.

'Can this be the right Castle?' said the girl, half laughing still. 'I wonder where those people went to; where can all the school-children be? I think this must be the way, grandpapa,' and she turned under a second gateway, where a scutcheon of carved stone hung among the rose sprays.

Grandpapa stooped his handsome old head, and followed her. They passed up a narrow passage, the adventurous Susy pushed a swing door, crossed a small ante-chamber, and suddenly stopped short. A sudden blaze and clatter met them – they had come wrong – and wandered into the great Gothic kitchen of the old Castle, reflecting fire and sunshine and brass saucepans, full of people and preparations. Women were busy, chopping and thumping, men with trays were passing busily across the flagged stones; the fires burnt as if it were December instead of August; long processions of eatables stood ready on the dressers, jellies in shining armour, creams propped by gabions, fierce stacks of serried pastry, cairns of buns. All these preparations did not seem incongruous with the solemn old arches overhead, or the great oriel window shining down upon the busy scene. Beautiful things are like beautiful people, and rarely out of harmony with their surroundings. Susy might have been amused, if it had not been for her grandfather's nervous look; she had never before realised his terror of strange sights and places; but if she was dismayed, she did not show it, she stood a composed white figure in the midst of the carnival, turning round as if to protect her dear old protector, and at this moment a serious-looking man, who might have been the master of the place, so dignified and urbane was he, came forward –

'Excuse me, you have taken the wrong turning,' he said; 'will you kindly follow me?' and he led them across the kitchen, and opened a side door, and from thence ushered them into a great vaulted hall. It looked as big as the cathedral itself, to Susy, with arches and windows, with pictures and armour everywhere, with people sitting at distant tables at the farther end, and the sound of voices echoing from arch to arch. The trophies of armour were stacked at intervals, iron knights stood with steel legs propped on to pedestals, wielding battle-axes in their iron hands; there were portraits of warriors who wore frills upon their mail, of statesmen in puffed sleeves, of ladies with high heels and coronets. It was a very noble gathering all along the wall, a company whose coronets on earth had long since, let us hope, been exchanged for coronets in heaven.

Some of the people sitting at table looked up and saw these two strangers come in suddenly among them. Susy and her grandfather seemed like figures out of some old Scotch ballad, so quaint, so shy, so unconsciously dignified were they, with something not of everyday life appertaining to them. Their clothes were country clothes, their faces looked calm and tranquil as country faces do. They advanced, looking neither to the right nor to the left, and sat down in the seat the butler pointed out. Susy was an undoubted presence; you could not pass her over although she had scarcely been beyond the yew hedges of her grandfather's rectory until now. She had some beauty, though she thought herself so plain, for her round face did not please her own taste, nor did her hazel eyes so liquid, so prominent – they could laugh, they could call, they could weep on occasion, or they could become stone and seem asleep for days together.

Susy found herself sitting next to the party of people they had followed up from the station. The young lady was at the head of the table; the young man, looking very small, was between the two grand ladies; and the fat gentleman in the velveteen costume was next to Susy herself. He looked very friendly, made way for her, turned about to see what there was for them to eat, drink, and be merry with.

'Cold grouse,' said the gentleman. 'Excellent salad; I can recommend the cutlets. Tempy, can you hand me that dish of mayonnaise? Our hosts are in the tents,' he explained, 'but they wish us to help ourselves. You went wrong, I'm afraid; I had half a mind to come back, and look for you. I sent the butler to find you.'

'Thank you,' said Susy, opening her eyes; and Mr Holcombe bent forward, and said in his pretty old-fashioned way –

'It was truly kind of you, sir, to concern yourself on our behalf. My granddaughter and I are strangers here; and have indeed no real right to be present on this occasion.'

'Oh, we have all a right to be here,' said the gentleman, 'since our hosts are hospitable people. I don't know if I can be of any use, showing you over the grounds. I am sure I shall be very glad. Here is my niece, she has seen nothing yet;' and he looked at the young lady who was munching away with a hearty appetite, at the head of the table.

'Don't look at *me*, Uncle Bolsover,' said the niece, in a loud voice; 'I'm not near ready yet. I'm perfectly ravenous.' Tempy, as she predicted, had recovered her temper and her appetite too. Leaning forward to Susy, she said, 'What time did you leave home?'

'Not very early. We are staying at Carlisle,' said Susy, shyly. 'I drove over with a cousin, who brought us here.'

'Well, he should have taken better care of you,' said the young lady; 'and now mind you keep by us.'

'Hush, my dear Tempy, don't speak so loud,' whispered one of the grand ladies, the grimmest of the two, bending forward emphatically.

She was dressed in red and brown and green. She was plain-featured and rather alarming Susy thought. The other lady was plump, fair, affected with a curious little, tiresome, silvery laugh, which went tinkling on perpetually; she had twinkling diamond earrings, a marabout in her bonnet, and a quantity of beautiful old lace round her throat and wrists, and an elaborate manner. As for the girl, she was pink-cheeked and red-haired, fresh and bouncing; she seemed quite used to the world and its ways; she had a loud voice, a military decision and good-natured directness, and gave one an impression somehow of being in uniform. The young man seemed to be receiving a great deal of advice with a great deal of indifference, and with an occasional glance at Miss Tempy, who openly shrugged her broad shoulders. Susy sat wondering at everything in her demure fashion, everybody seemed to her wonderfully kind, from the butler to the invisible hosts; she was fascinated by her new acquaintance, and the fat gentleman's attentions pleased her grandfather too.

Some days have a way of lighting up beyond all others with a peculiar happiness of their own, a bright intensity never to be dimmed again so long as life exists; and this day was one of these; many sad days came for Susy after this happy one, that seemed so warm, so long, so full of enjoyment, the present was better than anything she had ever dreamt of – and indeed, to the young, both joy and sorrow, when they come in their turn, seem greater than they could have ever imagined. Susanna Holcombe was eighteen, the sun was shining, the feudal Castle was rearing its grand old walls – the birds were in the air. Everybody else was happy, and why should not Susy take the delight of the hour? She had established a tacit understanding with the friendly fat gentleman. The young one was so kind as to offer her some mustard; Miss Tempy seemed already a friend for life, so communicative had she become over her chicken. A loud shouting in the court outside put an end at last to the luncheon: they all got up, and went to the door at the far end of the great hall; it led on to a little terrace, upon which they all crowded, for the courtyard below was invaded by a chubby pacific mob which must have surprised the knights in armour used to such a different tradition. The company from the Hall was met by a tremendous cheer as it appeared – which the master of the house, who stood laughing at the head of this invading force, signed to Mr Bolsover to acknowledge; and Mr Bolsover, quite in his element, immediately made a low bow, and began a speech which was more or less appropriate and inaudible.

I am not going to describe at length the programme of the day's festival; for Susy, the story might have been told not in tents and buns, and games in the ring, but from more delightful and less tangible aspects.

Dr John was delighted when he arrived to find his protégés in such good company. Mr Vivian himself was showing Mr Holcombe the old moated garden; and Susy, arm-in-arm with her new friend, met him with a beaming smile.

'Dear me, Susy, has Miss Dymond taken you under her wing?' said Dr John. 'I was unavoidably delayed at the inn by an accident. I am glad to find you have been so well looked after. How do you do, Mrs Bolsover? How do you do, Miss Bolsover?'

The grand ladies acknowledged the little Doctor's salutation with their finger tips, and meanwhile Miss Tempy dragged Susy away and went on cross-questioning her all the way across the lawn; along the terrace, all down the steps.

'Don't you think Tempy an odd name? I am sure you never knew anybody else called Tempy. It was poor mamma's name, you know; she was Temperance, and they christened me Tempy. Those are my two aunts, Aunt Car and Aunt Fanny, brought us up that sort of thing; dragged us along by main force, my brother says. Have *you* got a brother?'

'I have two little half-brothers,' said Susy, 'but I see them very rarely. My mother has married again. I live with my grandfather.'

'Oh,' said the other, 'we don't like second marriages. I should never allow it, nor my aunts either. Papa always consults me – at least, he generally does,' says Tempy; 'but I have had a great deal to try me lately. I can't tell you about it. Never, never allude to the subject, to me or to anybody else. How old are you?'

'I am long past nineteen,' said Susanna, apologisingly. 'I know I look much younger.'

'And I'm not yet sixteen,' said Miss Tempy, with a sudden explosion of laughter; 'who would ever imagine you so many years older than me? But you don't know me yet. Miss Martin often says there is a great deal more in one than people have any idea of at first. I suppose you think me plain, don't you?' says Miss Tempy, blinking her blue eyes. 'It is a pity, isn't it? – one doesn't do oneself justice, though, of course, looks don't matter.'

'I don't think you plain at all,' said Susy laughing, 'looks do matter a little, I suppose; but a great many ugly people have been very happy, and good.'

'Well, papa likes my looks,' said Miss Tempy, only half satisfied, 'and of course I care more for his opinion than for anybody else's.' As they talked they were walking along a beautiful fern-grown pathway that led towards the gorge, where the waters were tumbling over the stones. To Susy every commonplace word was idealised by the rushing of the waters in the gully below, by the stately 'vanguard of pines' that ruled the summit of the hill. Some of the children had straggled up into this beautiful wild grove, and were gathering the bluebells that grew among the ferns. The light was turning yellow, and the shadows were beginning to grow long.

Before parting, Susy's new friend, in return for so much confidence, had made her describe her home, old Betty the cook, the tranquil rectory by the churchyard, the old yew-tree by the church door.

'And what is your mother like?' says Tempy.

'My mother,' said Susy, and her whole face brightened, 'she is very beautiful and very very dear and gentle. She has brown eyes and a lovely face. I'm like my father, people say. Nobody ever could be like mamma again.'

But here cousin John came running after them, calling out that it was time to go.

'Take your grandfather back to the train, or we shall have him climbing the Maypole, or running in a hurdle race. Was not I right to make him come?'

Susy thought she had never seen her grandfather look so well and animated. He had charmed the whole party by his gentle, old-fashioned grace; he laughed, his cheeks were flushed, his eyes looked bright. He looked ten – twenty years younger than when he arrived.

'It has been a happy day, a very happy day, my dear,' he said, as they were both going back together by themselves. The Bolsovers were in another carriage, and Susy and her grandfather were alone.

'Mr Vivian knew your father, my dear, he had a brother in the same regiment. He was kind enough to ask us to return on some future occasion; if we revisit our good cousin, I certainly hope to see those kind people again.'

All the way back Mr Holcombe sat up, talking very brightly. Susy was even surprised at her grandfather's audacity in venturing to laugh when she talked of her new friends. 'They amused me, my dear,' said the old gentleman, 'the ladies were not without pretension, but I am glad you got on with them.'

They found the Doctor's wife and her little girls looking out for their return. The curtains were drawn, the supper was laid, the little parlour looked home-like and comfortable; a fire was burning in the hearth, and it was reflected in the round glass that hung on the opposite wall.

'I thought you might be cold after your journey,' said the Doctor's wife, in her usual querulous tone. 'What an expedition you have had; will John be back to-night?'

'He won't be long, cousin Ellen,' said Susy. 'It has all been perfectly delightful, and grandpapa is not a bit tired.' As she spoke her grandfather sank down wearily into a seat.

'A long day, my dear Ellen, but a very pleasant one,' said grandpapa. He sat with his arms resting on the arms of the chair. He had lost his bright look, and was paler than usual.

'Well you must rest to-morrow, before your journey,' said the Doctor's wife. 'I'm sure I can't think why you don't stay longer, cousin Edward.'

'I'll take a good rest to-morrow,' said cousin Edward. 'It is very good of you and John not to be weary of such a cranky old fellow as I am; but I want to get home, Ellen.'

Ellen, who was a good soul at heart, though a grumbling friend, now began ringing the bell and preparing Mr Holcombe's supper, telling him that he must not think of waiting for her husband. 'Don't you marry a doctor whoever you take, Susy: morning, noon, and night there is never an hour one can count upon them. Well, who was there, and what was it all like?'

While Susy chattered on of castles, drawbridges, knights in armour, the old man drank his hot soup, broke a bit of bread, and tasted a little wine. Then Mr Holcombe got up, saying he was tired and should go to rest. 'Good-night,' he said, and he kissed Susy very tenderly. Afterwards she remembered that he raised his hands and put them on her head, as if in benediction.

'Your grandfather's tired to-night; but he is a young-looking man for his time of life,' said cousin Ellen, as he left the room. 'We are a young-looking family, Susy, what age should you give me?' The Doctor's wife did not wait for an answer, to Susy's great relief, but wandered on. 'Lou and Bessie don't look their age, either,' she said. 'Poor girls, they are disappointed to think you won't stay a little longer now you are here: why, you have seen nothing yet.'

And this was true enough; except for that day's expedition, Susy's *impressions de voyage* had been confined to the smoky cathedral tower, the statue in the market-place, and the hucksters crying their wares all round about it, to the Doctor's laborious home, where the wheels of life turned, but certainly were not oiled.

'I don't take to strangers,' said the mother of Lou and Bessie; 'but I don't look upon you two as strangers, though you have only been here a week. Do you know your mother stayed with us over a fortnight once? It was before that foolish marriage of hers. No, my dear, you needn't look so black. We none of us ever liked him, and she was a foolish woman.'

'Mr Marney makes my mother very happy,' said Susy, blushing, and drawing herself up.

It was a relief to her that the Doctor came in just then brisk, shivering, in good spirits, hungry, and talkative, and changed the thread of his wife's comments.

'Where's your grandfather – gone to bed? Well, children, well, Ellen, here I am. Susy will have told you all about it. We have had a lovely day, and I wish you had come with us.'

'You really seem to think, John,' said the Doctor's wife, 'that I have nothing to do but to drive about in a gig, and praise the weather. I should say it had been a very usual sort of day,' then she stopped. 'Was that your grandfather's bell, Susy? I wonder if he has all he wants;' and Susy jumped up.

'What can he want?' said the girl, running out of the room.

The Doctor helped himself to a glass of claret. His wife got up and went to make up the fire; and then in another minute they heard the bell ringing and ringing again, and Susy's voice overhead calling passionately, 'Cousin John! cousin John!'

Cousin John turned pale, some instinct told him what had happened.

Something that all his good-will and long experience could not help, nor Susy's piteous terrified prayers and tender tears. She sat on the bedside with her sweet face bent to her grandfather's pale lips, holding him up with all her anxious strength; but the dear old man lay at rest, and they could not disturb him any more to life.

Very late at night the Doctor's wife came, and put her arms round the girl and led her away. 'John is writing to your friends,' cousin Ellen said; 'would you like any one to come to you?'

'Oh, mamma; I want mamma,' said Susy, bursting into tears; and she asked for a pencil and paper, and wrote a few words: 'Darling mamma, they are so kind, but please come, please come to your Susy.'

And the Doctor enclosed the note in his own more formal letter.

CHAPTER III

COFFEE

Oh! Friend, I know not which way I must look
For comfort, being as I am oppressed.

W. WORDSWORTH

Shall we follow the letter? A villa once stood on one of those long roads that lead from the Arc de Triomphe, at Paris, to its dependent villages. These long, dull roads are planted with poplars and lime-trees, and seem to become straighter and more dreary with every succeeding revolution. The villa itself was in a garden green and roughly tended, that put out its straggling shoots, and blazed with marigold heads. The four walls were white and green, and sweet with vines within, sun-baked without, and stained with the dust that skirted the highway. The gates opened upon the boulevard: they were painted green, faded and blistered by the sun; the white-washed wall was decorated with a half-defaced inscription, in straggling black letters: – '*Villa du Parc. Appartement meublé. Parlez au Concierge, S. V. P.*'

The house had been named after its original proprietor, whose widow made a living by letting her two pavilions to persons in want of '*salubrious and furnished apartments, ornamented with beautiful mirrors, in the vicinity of Paris.*' So ran the advertisement. 'I am of Scotch origin myself, and I have an English connection,' little Madame du Parc used to say. 'The Miss O'Sheas have been with me these five summers; Madame Muldoon and her niece come to me every winter season: they have now sent me *la famille* Marney, who inhabit the North Pavilion. The South Pavilion is very well let to a patient attending Doctor Pujat's water-cure. There is no house more sought after than mine,' says Madame du Parc, looking round with pride at the signs of habitation. 'There is no room empty, but my son's, in all the house.'

The house stood in a pleasant place, overrun, as most French gardens are, with straggling beds of nasturtiums. There were pansies, very purple and splendid, and snap-dragons, and lupins, and white and lilac floxes, sedulously flowering in odd corners; the paths were roughly laid with stony gravel and sprinkled with fallen leaves; iron chairs were standing here and there under the trees. There was a plaster statue in one corner, and an iron table. The air came fresh from the *bois* and the open spaces at the back, and of evenings and mornings the garden seemed full of voices and the scent of flowers, while the echoes of the rumbling and itinerant life in the highway outside would be sometimes enlivened by music of soldiers marching past. One evening a little company of people sat drinking coffee in the garden of the villa, looking like any one of those groups which you may see assembled behind the railings which divide French interiors from the outer world. It was after-dinner-time, and the coffee-cups were set out on the little iron table by the plaster Mercury. Two boys were rolling on the grass, at play; a little girl was stooping to caress a dog; an elderly gentleman, with a grey moustache, sat at the table, occasionally talking to two ladies, with work-baskets; while another man, younger and more portly, stood with his back against a tree, discoursing in a monotonous voice. Some faint clouds were slowly trailing their lonely rose-coloured vapours across a serenely burning sky. There seemed to be perfect peace in the silence overhead: a peace sometimes dreamt of by tired people resting for a while before becoming again tired.

The orator under the tree went prosing on. He discoursed, warming to his subject, at great length and with some monotony. The old lady, at the iron table, had been briskly exclaiming for the last ten minutes and trying to interrupt the orator, pishing, pshawing, waving her arms: she had sparkling black eyes and a shrill voice which was to be heard all over the house. Having said her say to the ladies, she now swiftly turned upon the gentlemen.

'Don't listen to him, Colonel,' cries the old lady to the good-looking elderly gentleman who had been submitting, with a somewhat dissentient expression, to the harangue. 'Mr Marney, he write for journals, and his business it twist everything round *de haut en bas*, or he having nothing to write about. My son write for journals sometimes, but he never show me his articles. He is too much ashamed of himself and those friends – liberators and agitators. They are a good-for-nothing set, who won't work, and like talk and to talk. I tell Denise to shut the door on their noses——'

'You must not confound every man who loves his country in the same category with your son's friends, madame,' said the orator, concealing his annoyance at the old lady's interruption. He spoke with a slight Irish accent. 'Here in your fair France questions are complicated. I allow that it is scarcely possible to foretell from one day to another what the consequences may be of giving supreme authority to any one party. But with us in Ireland it is not so. It is not a case of brother's hand red with a brother's blood; but of a country groaning under the rule of the Egyptian,' says the gentleman, talking louder and louder, for he saw the old lady preparing to interrupt again. 'Yes, Colonel, the sorrows of my most unhappy country,' and his voice toned to a different note, 'are the sorrows of a whole nation crying aloud for a tardy justice. These I feel from my very inmost soul: my heart bleeds when I hear those in authority speaking lightly of wrongs such as ours, and I do not exonerate you, Colonel Dymond, honourable gentleman as you are, from the charge.'

'*Venez,* Fox,' said the little girl, who had not been listening; and as she moved away, the little dog set off scampering after her, and the boys with a shout ran after the dog.

'Your country! my country! Patriots, patriotism, I don't care one *sou* for your patriots,' cried the old lady shrilly. '*Le pays des honnêtes gens*, that is my country.'

'Do not let us wander from the point, my good lady,' said the orator, impatiently waving his hand; 'personalities have nothing to do with a great idea. When the wrongs of a generous race rise before our legislators in their seats in Parliament crying aloud for justice, it is the duty of every man to give them a hearing. You, Colonel, are not one to turn aside from the cry of the helpless.'

Mr Marney paused for an answer; the Colonel started, somewhat confused. He had been disturbed by the barking dog and the boys' stampede, and he had lost the thread of Mr Marney's remarks.

'Oh! ah – certainly not; but I didn't get into Parliament, you know. It cost me a great deal of money,' said the Colonel, recovering himself; 'I have not paid it all off yet.'

'Michael takes it all to heart, as very few people do,' said Mrs Marney proudly, looking up from her crimson bale of wool. 'If everybody did as he wishes, things would be very different.'

'Mrs Marney thinks that, as the wife of a political writer, she has a right to her say,' said the orator good-naturedly, and loftily accepting the tribute. 'I won't engage to maintain *all* your opinions, my dear; but as to making a pudding or darning a stocking, I don't think there's many could give sounder advice.' He said it in a jaunty affable way. Mrs Marney's dark eyes brightened with pleasure; the Colonel made a courteous little bow.

It was at this moment that the children came scampering up with the evening post; the faithful little dog barking at their heels as usual.

'Here's a letter for you, mamma,' said one little boy, 'what a funny black letter.'

'And here's a letter for you, papa,' said little Dermot the youngest.

'I've two, I've two pretty letters,' said the little girl, in French, dancing after them, and she gave them both to the old lady, who pulled out her glasses to read the addresses.

'Why, you silly little child, that is for Monsieur le Colonel. Ah, here is Max's writing, this is for me. What a shocking hand he writes, *pattes de mouche*.'

'Please remember the postman,' said little Dermot, holding out his cap.

'Be off,' said his father, crossly; and he flung him a penny out of his pocket as he spoke.

'Little boys shouldn't ask for money,' said Madame du Parc, looking up before beginning to read.

As for Mrs Marney, she had torn her letter open and was so utterly absorbed in it that she did not heed anything that was going on round about her. Another time she might have anxiously followed her husband, when he suddenly walked away crumpling up his correspondence and thrusting it into his coat-pocket, but she did not heed him, nor Madame du Parc's vehement exclamations. 'As usual!' said the old lady, 'Max, he put me off. There is his room ready, water in the jug, clean sheets on his bed, Denise 'ave been all the morning clearing out the potatoes. We take all this trouble, and now he write that he will not come till next week. I shall turn him out when he come. Oh, it is too abominable. Come, Marie, come with *marraine*, let us go and tell Denise that she need not give herself any more trouble;' and the old lady took the little girl's hand, and hobbled off talking through the darkling garden, and disappeared. Her voice died away scolding in the distance.

Mrs Marney sat on, with her head resting on her hand and the tears in her great eyes. The Colonel had pulled out his glasses and was also too much absorbed in his correspondence to think of anything else. It was a disastrous post. Mr Marney's tailor's bill was the least unwelcome letter of the four. The pencil lines written by poor Susy in her sorrow had reached her mother; Tempy's indignant protest was in her father's hands.

The poor Colonel read it, re-read it; he could not solve the riddle, nor make up his mind what was to be done. 'Tut, tut, tut!' he said, beating his foot in perplexity. He had himself a great admiration for Fanny Bolsover, she had ruled his wife and she now ruled him, it was unlucky that she had not got on better with the young folks. Tempy, he feared, was vehement, and yet he could not quite disregard all she said. He folded the letter with great exactitude, and put it carefully away in his pocket, then he took it out again and unfolded it once more. The evening was closing, and he could not see Mrs Marney's troubled face, nor the tears which dropped quickly on the paper that was lying in her lap – tears do not show in the dark as they do in the sunshine, and men do not guess as women do at the things which are not put into words.

The unlucky Colonel in his perplexity suddenly determined to appeal to Mrs Marney for advice – she was a kind woman, she had children of her own. She would understand a girl's feelings where he was at fault. It was an inopportune moment that he chose, poor man, to open his heart to his new-made friend. He began, deliberately at first, and speaking, I fear, to very inattentive ears – 'Mrs Marney! may I have a few minutes' conversation with you? I ought not, I know, to trouble you with my affairs, but perhaps you, who are kindness itself, will excuse. . . . I have, alas! no right to ask any one to advise me *now*,' he continued in a plaintive voice. (He forgot that the late Mrs Dymond had been the last person he ever applied to in a difficulty.) 'You,' he went on, 'are a mother, a good, devoted mother. . . .' Then he stopped short, quite frightened by the sudden outburst he had unwittingly called forth; he looked up, and the words failed him, and he saw for the first time that she was in distress.

'Oh, do not speak to me like that. No, no, not that, not that,' she said, with a sudden irrepressible flood of tears. 'Oh! do not say such things to me. See, Colonel Dymond, my child wants me, and I cannot go to her, she is in trouble and I can do nothing to help her;' and the poor overwrought woman hid her face in her two hands that were trembling.

The Colonel was startled; he was a kind-hearted man, he was quite taken aback by such trouble.

'Oh, it is a cruel thing to part from one's children,' she went on, choking her grief and recovering herself little by little. 'Everything comes in to divide one in after days. . . . How can I go to my poor darling? Where is the money to take me? How can I leave my home? Oh! Colonel, I sent her to her father's people, thinking I had done for the best; but it is never the same, never the same.' And she looked up piteously, with dark eyes shining through her tears.

The Colonel sat listening and very confused, and yet not unsympathising in his confusion; he began gently patting the iron table by way of soothing the poor lady; two trains of thought were going on together in his head, an unusual thing for the simple-minded man. In all his sympathy for her he was still pondering over his own perplexities. Yes, she was right about the children. She had helped him unconsciously to make up his mind, and he now began to wonder if he could do anything to help her. . . . He wanted to see her face smiling and unruffled as usual, not all changed, stained, suffused as now. He felt very shy for a Colonel, but he presently began – 'Will you excuse me, Mrs Marney, if I speak plainly to you. I can unfortunately do very little for anybody. I seem to be always going to others for assistance, and you have helped me more than you have any idea of; but there is one way, at least, in which, perhaps, you would let me simplify your difficulties, and if – if a small advance, say fifteen or twenty pounds, would be convenient for your journey, would you give me the pleasure of feeling that for once I have been of some little use to a friend?' He laid his hand on hers as he spoke, and she with a sudden grateful impulse caught it and raised it to her lips.

'Oh, how good you are!' said she.

'Don't! don't, my dear lady,' said the Colonel, 'I have a daughter myself. . . . Here is Mr Marney coming. I will go for the notes at once,' he added, 'and I beg you will not say another word, *indeed* the obligation is mine.' He hurried past Mr Marney, with a friendly sign, as he walked towards the house. Mrs Marney's grateful eyes seemed to look into his; her grateful voice to be in his ears.

When the Colonel returned, with the notes in an envelope, he found Mr and Mrs Marney still standing together where he had left them; they were waiting for him and talking eagerly. He had hoped that she might have kept the transaction to herself, but she had evidently been telling her husband.

The Colonel was shy and held back for a moment, but Marney certainly, perhaps from habit, was equal to the occasion, and made things easy for all parties.

'Colonel!' he said, with emotion, flinging back his coat, 'I am a man of few words, but as long as I live I shall never forget your goodness to my poor wife and her girl. Thanks to you, we shall *both* be able to hurry over to our poor child in her trouble. You have done a noble action, sir, and one that you will like to remember when you are yourself upon your – a – looking back at your past life.'

Whatever his future reflections might be, the poor Colonel seemed very uncomfortable at the present moment; when Marney held out his hand, he did not immediately put the money into it, but merely shook the outstretched palm. Then going up to Mrs Marney he said 'Good-night and thank you' in a low voice, and raising in turn her hand to his lips, he respectfully kissed it, leaving the paper in her fingers. She did not speak – she looked at him with a curious, puzzled, grateful expression in her beautiful eyes, and he walked quickly away.

'There goes a good, honest, well-conditioned old gentleman,' said Marney, approvingly. 'How much is there, Mary, and where are you going to put the money?'

'I shall take care of it, you may be sure,' said Mary, smiling, and slipping the envelope into her pocket.

'You had better let *me* keep the notes for you,' said Marney (and he spoke in perfect good faith); 'perhaps there may be more than we shall want for the journey. How much did he promise you, Polly?' She hesitated still.

'I think he said ten or f-fifteen,' she answered, looking at him in doubt. 'Why do you want the money now, dear?'

Marney turned, with a sullen stare; 'Make haste,' said he. 'Don't keep me waiting.'

'Let us go to the light, dear, and count them,' she said tremulously, still feeling in her pocket.

When they got into the room, Mrs Marney, with a pale, face, gave the envelope to her husband, who exclaimed cheerfully – 'The old fellow is better than his word – there are four hundred-franc notes, Polly – 16*l.* – hurrah for the Colonel!'

And then, when she was alone once more, poor Mary, still with a pale face and feeling as if she were a thief in the night, pulled out one last hundred-franc note, which she had kept back from her husband, and she looked at it, and hid it away carefully between the leaves of her Bible. Later in the evening, she went upstairs to the bare room where her two boys lay sleeping,, and sat down by the big bed, looking wistfully at the little round brown chubby heads. They were like their father, and yet they reminded her somehow of her own people too. Little Michael turned and opened his brown eyes wide, smiled at her, and then dropped to sleep once more; little Dermot lay sunk warm in the pillow. Oh, might they grow up good men, upright, truth-fearing men, not as she was, not as their father was; her husband whom she loved with all her heart's passionate devotion, but whose faults were clear to her aching eyes. She prayed for commonplace things for her children, not for heroic achievements, but for daily virtues, hard work, truth, uprightness. 'Mamma, mamma,' said little Michael, struggling to break through the spell of sleep that divided him from her.

'My darling, my darling,' answered the poor mother softly, so as not to arouse him, and she bent over him, and once more her tears flowed, but they were gentle and more happy.

Then she went downstairs to make her arrangements with Madame, and the two stood talking on the landing, and recapitulating all the details of the daily history, the soup for the little boys, the directions for the washer-woman, the girl who was to come in during Mrs Marney's absence. Mrs Marney fetched her hundred-franc note; it was to pay for these necessary expenses, and also for a certain proportion of rent that was owing. The moon rose, and the two dark figures prosed on and on in the moonlight.

'Well, I would not cross the sea, not even for my good-for-nothing Max,' said Madame, 'but you are right to go; and do not be uneasy about your children. Has Monsieur Marney gone to the station to make arrangements? I will not wait up any longer; at my age one is weary when the night comes.'

'I wonder he is not back,' said Mrs Marney.

'It is a long way to the station,' said Madame. 'Good-night and good-bye.'

Mrs Marney said only 'Good-night,' and she went and stood at the window, watching. The moon was streaming, and the dark clouds were drifting and hurrying along the sky; the clock struck eleven. She went and fetched a shawl and wrapped it close round her and sat down at the window again; after a time she fell asleep and woke up as the clock struck one, and hour after hour passed and struck as she waited.

And then in the early morning Marney had come home, declaring he had been robbed; he had been cheated, he said, and then suddenly he became piteous, contrite, abject in his entreaties for forgiveness. On his way to the station he had turned into a café, and there met a patriotic acquaintance who, alas, persuaded him to look in for an hour at a place not far off where, unluckily for Marney, one of those fatal green plains was spread where dice are sown and bitter crops are reaped. He was tempted, and, as usual, instantly succumbed. When he came away in the early dawn one five-franc piece was all that remained of the Colonel's advance.

And then, as usual, Mary, after being angry, forgave him, making some absurd excuses to herself; and having forgiven him, the next thing was that she tried to console her heart-broken husband as he lay with his head comfortably buried in the sofa cushions. Poor thing! what a life would hers have been had she not been able to forgive. He was ruined, he said. It had been of vital importance to him to get to London; he deserved it all, he sobbed. As he became more desperate she was more pitiful. Would he go even now? Would he fetch Susy away and bring her back? There were fifty francs still left, which she had kept back for the children's expenses. Madame had the money, but she would get it back, and so Marney allowed himself to be consoled and sent off on his way.

CHAPTER IV

'TELL ME WHY SUSANNA'S FAIR'

Making a poet out of a man,
The true gods sigh for the cost and pain.

E.B. BROWNING

The Colonel meanwhile had passed a good night, he woke up thinking with pleasure of the chance by which he had been able to come to the help of this worthy couple. Marney made too much of a very simple action, but, after all, gratitude was a rare commodity. The Colonel had written a letter to his children, in which he had tried by dignity of language to conceal what some people might deem weak compliance. It is often difficult to tell why one does one thing more than another, or to realise what slight impulses drive the whole fabric of existence in one or another direction. A chance question or association, one person or another coming into the room, trifles scarcely to be weighed in the balance of daily life, seem to lead to such unexpected conclusions. It was the tone of Mrs Marney's voice, more than anything she had said, which had brought conviction to the Colonel. He went back to his comfortable room, sat down in his arm-chair, re-read his letters with great deliberation, and all the time he seemed to hear her plaintive voice, 'Others may do their best, but it isn't the same.' The Colonel was a serious man, who always took things seriously; he paused for a minute and then he began to write.

'My Dear Tempy,

I was painfully surprised by the contents of your letter of the 24th, which I have received only this evening. You write, my dear girl, as if you were not aware that my chief object in life must be to promote my children's welfare, as far as in my power lies. My health required change, and I hoped it might have been a pleasant arrangement for all parties, for you and your brother as well as for your aunts, if I asked Bolsover to receive you both during my absence. That this arrangement should have resulted in dissatisfaction on your part greatly disappoints me. Your aunts are not aware of your painful feelings, and write of you both with the warmest affection. They are very superior women; your poor mother had the highest opinion of them and of your uncle Bolsover. I should be indeed grieved if any estrangement arose in your minds towards such near relations. After some deliberation I have come to the conclusion that it will be best, under the circumstances, that you should not wait for my return, which may be delayed, and that you and your brother should join me here. A better acquaintance with French will be of use to Jo when he goes to the University. I am writing to your Aunt Caroline by this post, to tell her of my change of plans, and giving no special reason beyond my protracted stay at Paris. My present landlady, Madame du Parc, has not room to take you in, but a suitable apartment will easily be found. I need not add that I should not require you either to scrub or live upon dry bread, though I have less pleasure in welcoming you, my dear child, than I might have had if you had earned this "treat," as I think I may call it, by cheerful acquiescence in my wishes. Nevertheless it will be a real pleasure to me to have you with me again, and I trust that no more occasion for complaint will arise – either on your part or that of

'Your affectionate father,
'JOHN DYMOND.

'P.S. – I am sorry for poor Charles's troubles. A young man cannot be too careful in the choice of his associates. I have no doubt that it is a wise plan to remove him at once from evil influences. Let us hope his muse will not permanently suffer from the loss of the verses.'

The Colonel was pleased with his composition, and had taken it to the post, and was coming back in a cheerful, well-satisfied frame of mind, when, to his surprise, he met Mrs Marney, whom he imagined far away on her way to Paris, quietly walking under her big sunshade up the village street with her little boys on either side of her. She was dressed in black; she was carrying a letter; she looked very pale, but she suddenly flushed crimson when she saw him, and stopped short, waiting for him to come up to her.

'Not gone!' said the Colonel. 'I thought you were off this morning early.'

'No, Marney is gone,' she said, faltering and very much agitated. 'He could not – we could not. . . . Oh, Colonel Dymond! how can I explain? There was so much to be done – more than I can tell you – more than I knew of yesterday. I gave up my share. It has been a cruel disappointment,' and her eyes filled up. 'He is gone – alone; he will bring her back to me.' Then she said, 'Don't think me ungrateful; please say this much, though I feel as if we had ill requited your goodness;' and she stood confused, and, with her beautiful eyes cast down, she did not seem able to face the Colonel's gaze.

Colonel Dymond was easily led, but he was also a strict-minded man, and he answered dryly, for he was disappointed –

'I am sorry you were not able to carry out the purpose for which I advanced that small sum, Mrs Marney; it was intended for your convenience. You owe me no account;' and then, without another word, he walked stiffly away along the hot sunshiny road, while poor Mrs Marney, still holding the boys in each hand, passed on, chilled and with a heavy heart.

Poor soul! for her was the shame, for her the bitter disappointment and the brunt of opinion. It seemed to her like some dream of something that had happened before.

Mary during all those hours saw that the Colonel avoided her more and more. When she met him in the garden he wished her a cold good-morning and went on his way, instead of establishing himself by her side as he had done hitherto. The poor soul felt as guilty as if she herself had been to blame, as if it was her fault that her husband had failed her. She had little by little grown to confide in her new friend, and she missed him sorely. When she met his averted looks it gave her a pain in her heart; she felt as if Mick was more to blame in some way because the

Colonel was angry, and once, seeing him turn up a side path to avoid her, she sent the little boys running after him to beg him to wait. He waited, and allowed her to come up to him. He could not help admiring her, even then, vexed as he was; she looked so beautiful, so beseeching, as she advanced along the straggling little walk.

'I can't bear it any longer, Colonel,' she said, half laughing, but bitterly in earnest. 'You have been such a true, kind friend that your displeasure is a load on my heart, that is all I want to say. Believe me, I would have given twenty pounds, twenty times over, had it been mine, that this should not have occurred.'

He was somewhat mollified, but he did not quite relent. 'You owe me no account,' he repeated.

It was all she could get from him, and yet she was glad she had tried to set matters right, when next day he came once more and walked by her side for a few minutes, talking more like himself. Mary, too, was more like herself.

'I have heard from them,' said Mrs Marney, with a happy face. 'They will be here this morning. Madame, I am expecting my daughter.'

'So much the better,' says Madame, dryly. 'I hope she will not behave in the way everybody else does and change her mind at the last.'

Madame, too, had frozen ever since that unlucky night when Mrs Marney had taken back her fifty francs and given up her journey so mysteriously.

But an hour or two later, when the travellers arrived, Mrs Marney's delight and happiness were irresistible. This was no culprit asking forgiveness, but a proud and happy woman claiming their sympathy. Mrs Marney met them at the gate where the railway omnibus stopped in the sunshine, and then the mother and daughter were tight clasped in one another's arms.

Madame was at her window; Colonel Dymond was smoking under the acacia-tree as the Marneys passed by. He thought he had rarely seen a prettier sight than the little procession. The mother and daughter were walking arm-in-arm, looking so entirely united and one, that he wondered that they could ever have been apart. He thought the girl looked perfectly charming; she had a certain prim delicate grace in place of her mother's somewhat easy-going manner. She was sad, and her black dress told its story, she was dusty and tired after her night's journey, but all this could not alter her sweet triumph of girlhood, her complexion was dazzling, her bright eyes were alight.

She was looking up with that perfect trust and reliance which a child feels for its parent, and the mother was gazing into her sweet face with the proud confidence a mother feels in her child. I do not know that these two loved each other more than most mothers and daughters, but their often partings and long separations made their feelings more evident when they met at last.

'Here she is, Colonel Dymond,' said Mrs Marney, stopping short when she saw him. 'Susy knows all your kindness to me.'

'I am very proud to be so introduced,' said the Colonel, with a smile and a bow.

And so Susanna had got her wish, and was at home, and Mary Marney could watch her with loving eyes as the girl came and went about the place. It filled the elder woman with strange pride and delight to see how pretty her child was grown, how charming she was in all her ways. Sometimes, when Mary smiled at her and Susy smiled back, the two faces looking at each other might have been the same face softened and reflected in the waters of a pool. A sudden brightness would come into the girl's eyes as she met her mother's look, and she nodded with a pretty little spontaneous gesture. She was a little sallow and sleepy when she was not speaking, but then again, when the people she cared for came to her and the things she liked, her face would light up and her eyebrows would arch into new expression. She seemed a different person touched to a different life. The mother was the handsomer of the two, but she had not the sweet expressions and tones of the young girl.

This was the conclusion Colonel Dymond came to next day when he met them all in the garden as usual. After a very few minutes' talk – so it seemed to him – Miss Susy started up and announced that she was going down to the village with Mikey and Dermot.

'Are you going down to the village again, Susy?' said the elder lady. 'You must be tired, you have been about all day, and all yesterday you were travelling.'

'I'm not a bit tired, mamma,' said the girl. 'I wish you would come with us.'

'I can't come. I – I have some letters to write,' said Mrs Marney, who had as yet tried to conceal from her daughter some of the makeshifts of the establishment.

'You have always got letters, mamma,' said Susy, smiling; 'who do you write to?'

The mother sighed and then smiled – she was, in truth, an impatient woman drilled to patience by long habit. The daughter had lived peacefully hitherto among peaceful people in a distant place; her gifts, such as they were, had come to her from nature, not from that cruel second nature which is the experience of life.

'Well, then, I'm tired,' said Mrs Marney, laughing. 'I wonder you are not, Susy.'

'Ah, *she* don't want to sit and rest,' said Madame du Parc, who had come out for ten minutes' chat with her lodgers. 'My dear madame, she won't demand stools or arm-chairs for thirty years to come. They are for decrepid old *patraques*, like myself.'

'*You*, madame! What do you call me, then?' said Mrs Marney, smiling and looking very handsome.

'I must beg that you, Polly, will keep about long enough to see to your duties,' said Marney, by way of a joke; 'or I shall have to look out for your successor, my dear.'

Susanna's cheeks were burning, her soft hazel eyes were looking indignation. To hear her beloved beautiful mamma, the goddess of her girlish imagination, so spoken to, filled her with a strange intolerant anger. She had scarcely known her stepfather until now, and the more she knew him the more she shrank from him and his ways and his speeches. Her mother had always come alone to Crossham, where Susy's early years had been passed with the kind old grandfather who was gone now: sometimes Mr Marney had appeared for an hour to fetch his wife. Mr Holcombe's old-fashioned dignity and distance had overawed him on these occasions. Susanna had been sorry for him. He had seemed stiff and shy, but more to his stepdaughter's fastidious taste than now when he was 'at home,' as people say, and all restraint was gone. Susanna had been brought up in a somewhat rigid school. She could have grown accustomed in time to his smoke, his free and easy ways; but what she could not get used to was the tone which he used to her mother, – her sweet beautiful mother, for whose presence she had longed ever since she was a little child first parted from her side. Mary Marney had always seemed like some angel to her young daughter. Susanna had inherited from Mary herself a turn for hero-worship, a certain faith in those she loved which idealised them and made them more than mortal. Now she was living in a daily bewilderment. It was but a few hours since she had first come, and already a hundred doubts were in her mind. She was not disappointed in her mother; but she could not understand her: she loved her more than she had ever done, but she was not satisfied, and she seemed to know her less.

'Is mamma happy?' she asked herself; 'can she be happy? Ah! now that I am come to her, my love must make her happy.' This, at least, might be granted.

It seemed so little to ask for, but that little was not in her life's conditions; other and greater blessings might be Susanna's, but not this one.

She wanted all her mother's heart, and there between them stood Marney with his odious blinking handsome face, his free and easy ways; there scrambled the little boys with their wild heels and clamour, there came the daily cares, the hours crowded with sordid laborious tasks. Was this the life her mother had been leading all these years – the life that absorbed her so utterly? Poverty was nothing: Susy had been used to simple ways in her grandfather's house; but these shifts, these insincerities, these unpaid-for luxuries, the duns, the bills, the expedients which had never been dreamt of until now, all these things were now to be a part of Susy's daily experience. All this was in her mind as she turned away from the group under the acacia-tree. There they sat: there was the sky again all peaceful as if no ache existed beneath its *couleur de rose.*

CHAPTER V

THE ATELIER

I had a little chamber in the house,
As green as any privet hedge a bird
Might choose to build in, tho' the nest itself
Could show but dead brown sticks and straws.

AURORA LEIGH

Susy's room was over the sitting-room, and looked towards the garden. It was a narrow, little whitewashed slip. The bed was hung with yellow curtains, that were fastened to a gilt crown suspended from the ceiling; there was a marble washstand, with a looking-glass with one Cyclops eye reflecting the light; there was a wooden chest of drawers, and a trunk containing her modest possessions; and a peg or two, from which hung Susy's cloak and her black bonnet with its long veil; as the breeze came blowing through the open window the veil gently floated. There was also an arm-chair with four straight legs and a huge yellow paunch; a little pair of red slippers stood against the bed. The walls were quite bare, except for a little pencil drawing of the dear old rectory. The room itself opened upon a wide landing, which was used for many purposes, as a store for washing lines, for potato sacks, piles of firewood, and besides all this it contained various ladders and trap-doors and long poles. Susy, who had got up early one morning soon after her arrival, was startled by a faint scream, and, opening her door, found an unexpected pair of neat black legs suspended mid-air from a ladder which had been let down from the ceiling.

''Elp! 'elp!' says Madame's voice, somewhat muffled, from above. 'Denise, *venez!* I am lost; I cannot get down. Ah! who is it – is it you, Miss Susy? Come up, careful, and guide my feet. Ah! that is right. Thank you,' says Madame, once landed from the ladder, panting and shaking herself. 'That good-for-nothing Max, it is all 'im. He will not 'ave the apples in his *atelier* – such fancies! I went up to see if there was room in the *grenier*, and I lost my poor old head.'

'Had you been there long?' said Susy.

'An age,' said Madame mysteriously. 'I have scream for an age. You 'ave save my life.'

Madame must have had good nerves, for she soon recovered her breath and her composure, and she invited Susy to accompany her on her explorations. Madame led the way downstairs, the neatest imaginable little Rembrandt-like figure in her white cap and black skirts. 'Was it not a well-built handsome house?' she said. 'Her poor 'usban' had planned it all.' – It was hers now; it would all belong to Max some day, he was her only son.

'Is he a painter?' said Susy.

'No; he is a graver on steel. This is where he work,' said Madame, as she opened the great door of the *atelier* with pride and led the way into a huge room with a big window, built out into the garden. It was more like a barn than anything else. It was furnished in the simplest, roughest way; but there was something which gave a touch of life and of romance to it all, to the odds and ends, the plaster casts, the photographs upon the walls; to the old orange curtain swinging across the window; it was the something which belongs to all that concerns those mystical worlds of art, those dreams, eternal, of life which passes away.

Madame, who had some perception under her frilled nightcap, secretly wished for Max to make a drawing of the young Life now walking into his great shabby *atelier*. The slanting stream of morning came dazzling from the high window into the girl's face, and as she moved aside she found Madame's blinking eyes approvingly fixed upon her.

'Ah! you should know my son,' said Madame, who did not beat about the bush; 'he want to marry; he is a good boy, very 'andsome, not like me. He take after his poor fazzer.'

'And is your son engaged to be married?' Susy asked.

'No,' says Madame; 'I have not yet found the lady. He say to me, "Mamma, find me a wife if you will, but she must 'ave a *dot*. I 'ave seen you and my poor papa in such torment and difficulty for money that I will not marry without a *dot*. I should wish my wife to 'ave a carriage, if possible. This house is so far from the *barrière*!" It is reasonable, is it not, and well said?'

'Very reasonable, indeed,' said Susy, laughing. She did not take interest enough in M. Max to be shocked by Madame's very matter-of-fact explanations.

'Max he works *à l'eau-forte*,' continued Madame, beginning to dust and straighten. 'He have worked for all the best houses; he have made pictures for Mr Charles Blanc. Look, that is his table,' and she pointed to a business-like-looking table in a window shaded by a slanting frame through which the light came softened by silver paper. All the many murderous appliances of the peaceful art – daggers, stilettos, sharpened blades and piercing points – were heaped in the tray; the dabbers lay together, the oil-pots and acids stood in a row along a shelf against the wall. A sort of iron oven had been erected near the fireplace, to which Madame proudly pointed. 'Those are the hot plates; you could not touch them when the gas is turned on. The extravagant! He buy that pretty piano only last year. He is never here to touch upon it. Do you like music? You can come when you like to play.'

Susy's eyes brighten at this permission.

'You need not be afraid to come – Max 'ave not been near the place for two months. That is his portrait – wicked, good-for-nothing;' and she pointed to a charcoal head curling from the wall where it had been fastened by a single nail. It represented a long-nosed, frizzle-headed person with a sort of grin. 'It is like,' said Madame. 'Ah! you will see he is a 'andsome fellow. There are his portfolios. Look, what he can do;' and while Madame ferreted about with dusters and spectacles, Susy opened the big portfolio on the chair and began turning over picture after picture, not a little puzzled by some, delighted by others. She had absolutely no experience or knowledge of art, but some natural taste. As she stood there, some one came in at the door; it was not the owner of the studio, only the lodger – the Colonel – coming back from his water-cure, who now stood looking in, attracted, as most idle people are, by an open doorway.

'Come in, come in, Monsieur le Colonel,' says Madame hospitably. 'Come and see my son's work. You are rich; you should buy some of his pictures to hang on the walls of your châteaux. Show M. le Colonel what you have in that portfolio, my dear child;' and Susy, instinctively turning accomplice, pulled at the yellow curtain to keep out the dazzling sun, and then began holding up one engraving after another.

The Colonel stood by gravely looking through his glasses. There were pictures of every sort – portraits, fancy pieces, Holy Families, original sketches, and copies from the old masters.

'This is a very pretty picture,' said Susy, holding up a landscape, delicately etched with sunlight and shade, and water reflecting, and April clouds drifting across the sky.

'That is not unlike Tarndale, where I live; where my children are at present,' said the Colonel, wondering what Susy would say; 'it is certainly an admirable engraving.'

'Your children?' said Susy, pausing; 'have you——?'

He interrupted her. 'My children would not seem children to you, Miss Holcombe; my son is seventeen, my daughter is sixteen.'

'And her name is Tempy, is it not?' cried Susanna, clasping her hands, with a look very bright and then very sad. 'Oh, I am so glad. I hoped so it might be you when mamma told me your name.' And then she told him of her meeting at the Castle – of her acquaintance with Tempy – of that happy day, so short a time ago, so long ago. Susy was thankful to speak to any one who seemed interested, not pained, by what she had to remember. Her mother used always to shrink from it all. To Mrs Marney the dear old grandfather had only seemed a judge. She had never understood him. It was a delight and an ease of mind to Susy to talk of him, of his goodness, to so kind and sympathising a listener as the Colonel; and then Tempy, too, seemed a fresh bond between them. Were they coming to Paris? How delighted Susy was! If Susy was pleased, her new friend was not less pleased. The girl interested him more and more. What a friend for Tempy! How glad he should be to bring them together!

'Well, what are you about? you are not looking at the pictures!' cried Madame; and Susy, recalled to her duty, held up a new print.

'Here is a *very* pretty one,' said she. 'I think this must be Ruth and Naomi.'

'Yes, my dear child,' said the old lady, coming up and giving her an approving pat. 'Ah! *that* is the daughter-in-law I should wish to have. Just see how well it is done; look at the veil, Colonel, and the necklace. And the expression! Oh, what expression!'

'But Ruth had no *dot*, Madame,' said Susy, a little maliciously, with one of her pretty bright looks.

'Ding, dong, ding, dong, Soooosy; ding, dong, Sooosy,' comes from the garden outside. One little brother is rattling a stick in a flower-pot, the other is pretending to be a bell. 'Venez déjeuner, Sooos!' cry the children in the jumble of French and English habitually used by those young Anglo-Parisians. They come thumping along the passage to the doors of the studio, peep in, and run away, and Susy turns at the summons.

'Do not forget to come and play the piano,' said Madame, calling after her. 'You shall give my little goddaughter, Marie Pichot, some music lessons, if you like. She is coming to stay here.'

'I should be very glad,' said Susy simply; and, as she spoke, an idea came into the worthy Colonel's head.

The little boys trotted along the passage, followed by their sister. The summons to breakfast was an improvisation on their part. The meal was still frizzling and boiling in the pans and pots through which breakfast is transmogrified on its way to the table. The children burst open a door with an accustomed air; Susy followed, and found herself, not in the dining-room, but in a sunny little kitchen full of fumes and sunshine, where her mother stood bending over the stove. It was a contrast to her last invasion. Mrs Marney looked up confused, somewhat displeased, and blushing crimson, with a spoon in her hand and her dress pinned back.

'Oh! mamma,' cried Susy, 'why don't you make me do this?' and she sprang forward. 'Are these your letters that you write before breakfast?'

'I – I thought you would be vexed, dear, if I told you it was I who did the cooking, not Denise,' said Mrs Marney humbly. 'I know all this is not what you have been accustomed to at home.'

'Don't,' cried Susanna flinging her arms round her mother's neck. 'I have not been accustomed to a mamma.'

Meanwhile Mick and Dermot, who seemed bent upon revealing the family secrets, went on their way through a second door, which led across a passage to the little ante-room where the family met at meals. Through this open door came a sudden burst of anger and impatience. 'Go away, you urchins. Where the devil is your mother?' cries a voice. 'Tell her——'

'Yes, dear, yes,' Mrs Marney calls out, hastily interrupting, and turning back to her eggs again. 'Go, Susy dear, and talk to him.'

Susy, blushing, and with some repugnance, crossed the passage and said 'Good-morning' to her stepfather, who was sitting with a pile of papers at a table where some cups were set upon the oilcloth. He didn't look up, and seemed little inclined for her company, and she went into the sitting-room to wait for her mother's coming. The garden outside looked pleasant and green; the room itself was a scene of confusion. The round table was covered with pens, papers, and ink; a black bottle and a dirty glass stood in the centre, by the lamp, that cloud by day, that pillar of light by night, under which Marney wrote his articles and Mrs Marney patched the family patches.

Opened and unopened a heap of newspapers were flung on a chair by the table; a pair of slippers that Marney had thrown off were lying as they had fallen. There was a sofa with yellow cushions tumbling tipsily about, and a great yellow arm-chair piled with children's garments; the doors of the cupboard were swinging open. It was a dingy, untidy-looking room, and Denise had certainly done little but undo the shutters that morning. Susy, with housewifely instincts, looked round and began folding and straightening some of the disorder into order; she picked up the torn papers from the floor and threw them into the waste-basket. One scrap was written twice, on two different sheets, in Marney's tidy handwriting. Susy could not help seeing it, and wondering what it meant. 'It is with the greatest pain and reluctance that I have written so plainly. Your kind and generous heart will——' Susy blushed, read no more, and threw the paper away with the rest; then she turned to the newspapers – she had laid hands upon one or two of them, and began to pile them tidy when an exclamation from one of the little boys who had come into the room stopped her.

'Mustn't touch,' said the little boy, whipping his top. 'Father will beat you if you touch.'

'I don't think he will beat me, Dermy,' said Susy, laughing; 'but I will leave the papers alone if he does not like them to be touched.'

'He always scolds when mamma touches,' said Dermot. '*Dis donc, ma soeur*,' continued the little boy, 'did the Colonel give you any pictures?' and the child came up and slipped his hand into Susy's. The little bright face looked up quite artlessly. Susy was puzzled. 'He gave me no pictures, dear,' she said, stroking his head.

'Why didn't you ask for some?' said the other little fellow. '*We* always ask.' Again Susy's heart began to sink with vague apprehension. She already felt that there must be much in her new life from which she must turn away, much that she must be content to ignore. A time came before very long when the poor girl could no longer pretend not to see what was passing before her eyes.

Susy used to meet the Colonel constantly after that morning, as people do meet who are living in little suburban boarding-houses. One day he stopped, and looked greatly embarrassed, and finally asked her whether it was true that she had consented to give little Marie Pichot lessons in music.

'Yes,' said Susy, 'I am very proud of earning a little money.'

'It has occurred to me that perhaps you would allow your friend Tempy to profit by your delightful acquirement,' said the Colonel. 'The music-mistress we have been counting upon has just failed us. If you would agree to my daughter's terms, it will be a great kindness on your part.'

'But I couldn't teach well enough,' said Susy, blushing and opening her round eyes, 'and I'm sure if I could, I wouldn't like to – to——'

'I know I have offended you,' said the Colonel, looking so crestfallen that, rather than give him pain, Susy doubtfully agreed.

'It is absurd,' said she, looking up, 'but I know what you have done for mamma. Will you let me try to pay part of her debt to you?'

'We will talk of that presently,' said the Colonel, brightening again. 'I will come and speak to your mother, if she is at home this afternoon.'

A little later in the day the Colonel came as he had promised. Marney was out; Mrs Marney and her daughter were sitting together in the window of the sitting-room. 'Come in, Colonel,' said Mrs Marney, in her friendly welcoming way. 'What is this my Susy tells me?' The Colonel had soon talked Mrs Marney over; she was willing enough that Susy should be paid, and indeed her admiration for Susy's music was unbounded. 'I can't think where the child gets it all; I never could play a note,' Mrs Marney declared. This matter being settled, the Colonel presently found himself with a poetry-book in his hand, reading to the two as they sat at their darns. He had not done anything so sweet and to his taste for a very long time; as he read he looked up and saw Susy's eyes fixed upon him; she had let her work fall into her lap for a moment as she listened. The hoofs of Marmion's charger were ringing on the drawbridge of Tantallon Castle. She seemed carried away far from the little villa, from the green garden, the homely daily toil, the Great Wizard had laid his spell upon her; as for the reader, dry old colonel as he was, the girl's bright look touched him, he went back to his rooms feeling as if they were strangely dull and deserted. And still more so was the grand apartment he had taken for his son and daughter, to which he reluctantly moved next day. All the life and interest in the place seemed to him centred in that bare little parlour, where the two women were sitting at work, hour after hour, while the little boys played in the garden outside. Tempy was a very dear girl, and Fanny was a very superior woman; but they did not seem to make things look so peacefully *home-like* as these two. Tempy would have opened her eyes if she could have read her father's thought. What, *that* a home – that little shabby, untidy parlour, scattered over with scraps? Impossible!

CHAPTER VI

PIANO

The pedal is a good servant but a bad master.

'Musical Birthday Book'

The sound of a piano came through a window that opened on to a stone balcony. The hesitating notes echoed along a street or avenue, which had been lately built not far from the Arc de Triomphe, at Paris. The music struck the stone and reverberated into the dry blazing sunshine, and then seemed absorbed in the dust and the acacia-trees that were planted at intervals along the road, and which cast their dumpy shadows on the ground. Everything was so hot and so glaring that very few people were about; a few par-baked figures went quickly by; the shutters of the houses were closed; the people were hiding inside from the fierce rays. There is a silence about the mid-day sunshine which must have struck us all at times, when the houses are shut up, as if in protest; when the shadows scarcely shade, and the sun burns in fierce intenseness, then it is that the distant piano is heard echoing, whose notes we can all remember in so many places in the hottest hour of the day. A close carriage rolled by, a cat darted across the pavement and ran up a white wall, and then after an interval a drifting figure in black came along the pavement. It stopped at the door of the house from whence the piano had been sounding. The figure was only Susy, who put up a shabby black glove and rang a great bell; and when the door opened stepped from the glare outside into the cool vestibule with its stone staircase and glazed arches. Colonel Dymond's scheme had actually come to pass. Tempy and Jo were established at Paris, and the music lessons and the meetings he had hoped for were realities, serious realities to Susy, who conscientiously spared nothing to fulfil her bargain, and came wearily through the blazing streets day by day, trying to stimulate her pupil into some genuine effort and interest. Tempy looked upon it all as very great fun, she thought it must be of great advantage to Susy, with her shabby gloves, to have her for a pupil. She was as enthusiastic as ever about her, and ready to patronise her to any extent, all the more so that Aunt Fanny, who was for ever surveying the world from her own particular pedestal, had for some weeks past been made uneasy by Miss Holcombe's visits to Tempy. She remembered Susy quite well, Susy and her pretty looks and her sudden blushes, and it didn't seem to Miss Bolsover that this young lady was at all the sort of person who should be constantly an inmate of her brother-in-law's house. Aunt Fanny's tacit objections had, if anything, given extra interest to the music lessons for Tempy. One letter after another had been coming, deprecating, hinting, suggesting a whole series of music masters; there was Pocoforte so well spoken, of, Herr Thumpenau so highly recommended.

On this particular morning Miss Dymond, crossing the hall, had found the usual Aunt-Fanniad lying on the table. This one was more emphatic, if possible, than any which had gone before. Tempy opened her eyes as she read it, it was difficult to forget it entirely. She could not but feel of some extra consequence with such a letter in her pocket. 'You are old enough to know something of life,' wrote Aunt Fanny, 'and I need not say that this is for you alone. Do not encourage that girl too much. You must be wise for others. Jo is young, and even your father is of an impulsive nature, and might not be able to see *as a woman does* by some instinct what secret motives a girl may conceal beneath an apparently *artless* manner.'

When the servant announced 'La maîtresse de piano pour Mademoiselle,' Tempy jumped up from her stool, and came forward even more eagerly than usual, 'How *could* you come through this furnace?' she said. 'How brave of you! How glad I am to see you!'

Miss Tempy was not a little transformed from the wild nymph of Tarndale waters, and even the fashionable young lady at the Castle might seem outdone by the present frizzed, flounced, Parisian belle. Tempy was not unconscious of her elegant appearance; and she occasionally put on a curious starched and mincing manner to match her toilette. Jo used to laugh; but her father was rather dazzled by it, and thought that she now reminded him of her poor mother. But if Tempy was improved, Susy was very much altered by her few weeks' experience of the changes and chances of life. Her innocent beaming look was perturbed, and the clear waters of her eyes were troubled. Her clothes looked shabby and dusty in the hot white glare, and among the gilded splendours of the Colonel's drawing-room, the smart arm-chairs and satin sofas that were sprawling about the room. Great flower-jars stood filled with handsome exotics, and candelabra on the chimneys. The curtains were silk covered with Chinese bridges; the tables were rampant with golden legs. Tempy, radiant in the centre of this shrine, sat, with the pedal down, banging at the piano.

The boy looked up from his book and nodded, without changing his attitude, as Susy came in.

'How tired you look!' says the hostess, helping the black figure off with its black hat and dusty shawl.

'Tempy, do ring for some seltzer-water,' says the boy on the sofa, without looking up; 'one never gets anything in this house without making a fuss.'

Our friend Tempy gave a tug to the great bell-rope, and the seltzer came just as Miss Holcombe, turning pale, had sank wearily into a seat by the piano.

'There, take that,' says Jo, getting up lazily, filling a glass and giving it to the music-mistress; 'one orders things for oneself, and somebody else always wants them.'

Susy was not offended, she laughed and drank, and as she drank the colour came back. Presently the lesson begins. Miss Holcombe can hardly aspire to the title of music-mistress, but she is thoroughly in earnest and doing her very best; Miss Dymond is not in the least in earnest. Conversational, digressive, she attends on and off, makes the same mistakes over and over again, presently begins a discussion about the pedal. 'The passage should be played lightly, not with too much expression,' says Susy, and she bends forward, serious and stern, and plays the passage with a very precise and delicate touch.

'I don't agree with you,' says Tempy, quite unconvinced. 'I like the pedal myself, and I like people to play as if they felt the music all over, not as if they were only listening to it.'

'But putting the pedal down does not always mean that one feels more intensely,' said Susanna; 'it means that one says more about one's feelings.'

'I like talking about my feelings,' said Tempy; 'if I feel a thing, why should not I say it? I like to look at you; I think you perfectly lovely, and I like to tell you so.'

'There goes Tempy's pedal,' said the boy, looking up from his book.

'Papa said so, too,' cries Tempy.

'It always sickens me to hear second-hand conversations about myself,' repeated Jo, turning over a page.

'Whoever would repeat conversations about *you*!' cries Tempy, with a sisterly shriek of laughter.

'G Sharp, G G G please,' says Miss Holcombe, blushing, and striking the note, and once more the two start off on their pilgrimage along the weary pages of the music-book, among the shoals and the pitfalls, the occasional flats and sharps, from level to level, over a mountain pass, and so at last into a wide and lovely plain, easy, smiling, and beautiful.

And then the drawing-room door opens, and the Colonel comes in. Tempy looks round, and leaves off playing altogether. 'Well, papa,' says she cheerfully, 'what have *you* been about?' Jo gets up, somewhat disconcerted, from his sofa, pulls down a blind, pulls it up again, and goes out of the room. The music-mistress glances at the clock; the Colonel sits down stiffly on a chair in the middle of the room. He looks somewhat out of place, though it is his own hired golden chair and his own hired house. He is not an uncommon type of colonel, well brushed and baked, with a brown face and a white moustache and an expression of great seriousness. His manner took people in who did not know him well – even Susy felt a little in awe of him here especially, more so than in the apartment at home; she blushed up nervously to-day when the Colonel turned to his daughter, and said –

'Tempy, if you will put your bonnet on, I will take you for a drive. I have a few words to say to Miss Holcombe first.'

'Have you papa?' says Tempy, looking surprised; then she remembered that the lessons had not yet been paid for, and added, 'Oh, to be sure,' and left the room, banging the door and singing at the pitch of her voice.

'I wanted to ask you a question,' said the Colonel, looking very much embarrassed. 'I can only beg you, my dear young lady, to take it in good part as it is meant,' and he looked away as he spoke. 'You are perhaps aware,' he continued, 'that I am an older friend than I imagined when I first had the pleasure of meeting your mother at Madame du Parc's. I must have known her at Carlisle before her second marriage.'

'Did you know mamma so long ago?' said Susanna, blushing with pleasure; quite young and old people are alike in respecting the past. 'I have lived so little with her that I scarcely know all her old friends.'

'I hope you will always remember me as one of them,' said the Colonel very courteously, and then he sighed a little sadly. It seemed to him so unlikely that this bright young creature should have any constant remembrance or thought for him; as for his own recollections they were of the vaguest description. 'And now,' said the Colonel, looking thoughtfully at the neat reflection of himself in the great gilt mirror opposite, 'I am going to ask you to speak plainly to me as to an old friend and to forgive me for asking you whether your good mother keeps the control of the money which comes to her in her own right. She kindly trusts me, and is good enough to tell me of her affairs at times; and now I find that she is in some temporary annoyance, from which I should most gladly relieve her if——' The Colonel had gone on talking, without looking at Susy, but suddenly some movement reflected in the glass caught his attention, and he turned round in some consternation. The girl's pale face had flushed crimson, her drooping eyes were full of tears of angry shame and vexation; she seemed to shiver with ill-concealed annoyance. The Colonel had given the note into her hand.

'Has mamma been writing this to you?' she said, the first sentence seemed strangely familiar. 'It is with the greatest reluctance,' she read; and then, 'your kind and generous heart' – she had seen it all before. 'Oh, that is his doing; he made her write!' Susy cried, with a sort of passionate choke, starting up and throwing the letter away. It was a most painful moment; the Colonel felt quite bewildered and distressed; he backed his chair.

'My dear young lady,' said he, 'pray, pray, be calm. We are all of us at times accustomed to look for help from those who are interested in us. Literary men, as we know, are not very practical. Mr Marney may have been unfortunate in his arrangements.'

'Unfortunate!' said Susy bitterly.

'Well,' said the Colonel, 'that I will not go into now. We must do the best we can under the circumstances, and see if we can help your good mother.'

'What can you or I or anybody do?' said Susanna, with a fresh burst of indignation. 'Don't help her, don't try to do so; believe me it is the kindest thing in the end; and pray, believe that I come here to give your daughter music lessons, and not – not to beg for money.'

Susy's natural youthful pride overcame her gratitude as she spoke; but she could not but melt again, when the Colonel, looking very kindly at her, said –

'My dear girl, do believe me when I tell you that I look upon it as a privilege to be allowed to – a – participate in your mother's affairs. An old fellow does not want much in life. My children have all they can require, and the one luxury I allow myself is that of feeling that I can sometimes be of use to an old friend;' as he spoke he put out his hand, and Susanna, as suddenly grateful as she had been unreasonably angry, caught it in both hers.

'Dear Colonel Dymond, forgive me; how much too good you are!' she said, and her voice seemed to vibrate, and to fill the room.

The Colonel, who lived a very lonely life, although he was surrounded by many people, felt as if his whole fortune might be well bestowed if it brought forth one such sweet look and tone as this. He was immensely touched and interested; he might have said so if he had followed his impulse; but he resisted it, and only looked very kindly at the beautiful young creature struggling for the first time with the bitter experience of life and its impossibilities. He was still holding her hand, and she was still looking at him with her grateful, speaking eyes, when the door opened, and Tempy walked in ready dressed for her outing, bonneted, jacketed, with her yard-long gloves buttoned tight, and a general air of business-like expectation. The Colonel let go Susy's hand. Susy blushed up, she knew not why.

How often it happens that the great events of life seem to come about by chance, quite simply, in a moment.

It was with Aunt Fanny's letter in her pocket that poor Tempy flung open the drawing-room door and walked in upon the *tête-à-tête*. 'Dear me,' said she; 'how very strange;' and she looked at Susy with a disagreeable stare not unlike one of Aunt Fanny's own glances.

'What do you mean, Tempy?' said the Colonel, firing up. 'Is this the way you dare to speak to me and to your friend?'

When people who love each other quarrel, the absence of accustomed tenderness is almost worse than the super-added anger of the moment. Tempy, strong in her feeling of injured innocence, felt bitterly aggrieved. 'My friend, papa!' said she. 'You seem to have monopolised her!' Then remembering Aunt Fanny's warnings: 'I would not believe it till now; I suppose this is what she has been coming for all this time.'

The Colonel, white with passion, turned from Tempy to Susanna, who was standing scared and holding to a chair. Then he closed his eyes, and the colour came back to his cheeks. There was something pathetic in his momentary struggle with himself, and in the voice with which he now spoke.

'My child insults you,' said the Colonel, trembling very much and turning to Susy; 'and I can only repeat her words, and tell you that if indeed I could hope to monopolise you, to win your affection, I might feel that at last I had a home once more. I am in earnest, Miss Holcombe; old as I am, I can still feel that I have a heart. I might not have spoken, but now I feel it is only fair that you should know the truth, now that others have perceived it. My life would still, indeed, have worth for me if I could ever hope that you would consent to be my wife.'

'Oh, no, no, no!' cried poor Susy. 'You have been so dear, so kind. Oh, I must go back to mamma; I won't come any more. I will try to forget it all.' She looked beseechingly from one to the other. Tempy stood hanging her head; the Colonel's eyes were following her with a sad sort of reproachful look. It was more than she could bear, her only impulse was to escape.

'Papa, papa, what shall I do?' said Tempy, bursting into tears, as Susy disappeared.

The streets were burning still; but Susy scarcely heeded the glare as she flew along, angry, jarred, vexed, and beside herself; she hurried on. It was not her fault, but she felt as if she had done something wrong. She no longer wondered why Tempy had looked so strange. A longing came over Susanna to feel her mother's tender arms round her, to tell her all, to be comforted.

Susy was very tired by the time she got back to the old green blistered gates, and turned out of the straight avenue into the desolate little garden, which felt more home-like than it had ever done before. Dermot's straw hat was lying on the grass; Mikey's wheelbarrow was overturned beside it; the little dog came sidling up to meet her. Nothing else appeared; the garden was silent, and had a look of desertion. The sitting-room was empty, so was the kitchen. Susy knocked at her mother's door, and called 'Mamma! Dermot! Mikey!' but no one answered. In the dining-room she found a solitary plate set ready on the table with some cold meat and a cake, and some fruit in a dish; but no signs of any one.

Denise came in from her marketing with her basket on her arm, filled with green stalks and heads, while the girl was still standing doubtfully gazing at the preparations on the table.

'Well,' says Denise, 'you have found the letter? Madame laid your cover before she went off; they caught the omnibus. There is what she wrote on the stove.' A note lay there with its address 'Susy' in Mrs Marney's writing. The girl had overlooked it: 'Papa wants to give the little boys a treat to St Cloud, but I dare not let them go without me; Dermy knocks up so easily, and Mikey is so wild. How I hope our kind friends may keep you, darling! I hate to think of your long lonely day. Denise has a cream-cheese for your dinner, and you will find the key of the cupboard under the clock. Ever your loving Mother.'

Poor Susy! It was all nothing, but she began to cry. She had been spoilt, she told herself. She had been so needed by her grandfather, so much made of, and now her old home wanted her no more, and her mother had never wanted her. She loved her with all tenderness; only she did not want her as some mothers want their daughters. Another day Susy might not have felt so morbid, nor had occasion to be angry with herself; today she was vexed with everything, with everyone, with her mother, with the Colonel, with Tempy, with herself. It was right enough and natural that Mrs Marney should go; only a sort of lonely feeling came over Susy as she thought of it all. She had so longed for her mother all the way home; it was in vain she scolded herself, and tried to put the thought away; it came back again and again in different shapes and aspects, as persistent thoughts will do. Now wiping her eyes she pictured the little family party to herself: the mother, the little boys, the father; the children's happy laughter. Then she saw another vision of the Colonel and Tempy driving off happily together in their big comfortable carriage; and then she seemed to see herself as she was, in her black gown, in the silent little garden, alone. Her fancies were cruelly vivid that night. Everything seemed touched with a bitter-sweet intensity of feeling. 'It must not be,' Susy told herself; and tried to eat the cream-cheese and determined to conquer her troubles. She was glad, however, to be distracted from them, and to see Madame returning home along the garden walk.

Madame was dressed in solemn 'costume de ville.' She wore a big bonnet and veil. She carried an umbrella, and was neatly looped up in festoons.

'What, all alone?' says the little old lady. 'Oh! it is not convenient – a young girl like you. I have been out to take little Marie home to her parents in the Rue Lavoisier, but it is different at my age. Your mother she should not permit you to go alone. You shall come with me to-night. Have you seen my apartment? Come in, come in; the rooms are well-disposed, are they not?'

Madame's apartment consisted of three rooms, opening into one another, which she seemed to think a singular and admirable arrangement. There was a little ante-room where she dined; then came a salon with four big chairs in striped petticoats, and two huge vases on the chimney filled with red and blue calico cornflowers and roses. Beyond this came the bedroom, where Madame treasured more calico bouquets, and a tall crucifix, where also stood the large bed in which she reposed, with its brown cover and fringes. There was also an *armoire à glaces* she was very proud of, in which she kept her black jackets and white frilled caps, and where she now carefully enshrined her bonnet; reappearing shortly in her usual costume, and prepared for a confidential grumble – there was an endless variety to Madame's grievances – Max's iniquities, the weather, the lodgers, the extraordinary amount of rheumatism in the quartier. It was, however, some relief from Susy's own less tangible troubles. The evening was still further diversified by the appearance of two visitors, who were seen coming in at the garden gate.

'Ah! Monsieur Fayard and Mademoiselle,' says Madame, well pleased; 'let us go out and meet them.'

The visitors were accommodated with chairs and made welcome, and presently Susy found herself one in a sober quartet. Monsieur and

Mademoiselle Fayard were an old brother and sister living together in the village close by. They were good-natured and kindly disposed to Susy, though Mademoiselle Fayard scanned the young lady's toilette with some severity.

'Do you wear your skirts still puckered in England?' says Mademoiselle Fayard, opening the conversation.

'Oh!' says Madame, 'do you not know how eccentric the English are, my dear Séraphine?'

'How long has Mademoiselle been in Paris?' says the little old gentleman. 'What does she think of it?'

'I have not seen very much of Paris yet,' said Susy distractedly, for all the time she was still listening to Tempy's reproaches, the Colonel's voice was in her ears.

'We must see to that. I mean to take her for a day's sightseeing,' says Madame. 'There is to be a grand funeral mass at St Philippe; we can visit the Chapelle Expiatoire on our way home.'

'And Mademoiselle should see the Duke of Orleans' mortuary chapel,' says Monsieur Fayard, adapting his suggestion to what he called the *serious* of the English character.

'Oh, how dull!' says Mademoisse Fayard. 'Take her to the Magazin du Louvre, and let her see the Passages and the toys in the shops; and then there are the environs – she should see the environs. There is St Cloud; we went only last week. It is a most delightful excursion. They make music, and there is dancing too on Sundays; you go half the way in a steamer. That is where you should take her.' Mademoiselle Fayard wondered why Susy blushed crimson. At that very minute the sound of a child's voice crying was heard in the distance.

'Ah! there is mamma at last,' said Susy, starting up, and hastily taking leave she went running to the gate to meet her mother. As she reached the garden end a little group appeared as footsore, as weary as anybody could expect to be after a long day's hard pleasuring. Little Mikey was in tears. Susy had recognised the familiar wail. Little Dermy was in his mother's arms, and the poor woman herself seemed scarcely able to stand.

'Here we are,' she said wearily; 'Mikey has been a wild boy. He has been naughty all the way home; Dermy has been a darling, but he is tired out. You missed nothing, Susy; it has been hot and tiring. I can't think what possessed Marney to start off on such an expedition. We went in the steamer, and dined at St Cloud. I wished myself home all the way. Will sister find the boys some bread and milk? they must get to bed at once.'

'No! no! no!' says Mikey dolefully; 'I won't go to bed. I haven't given sister my flowers yet.'

'Well, child, make haste and give them,' says the poor, tired-out mother. And Mikey holds up his little hot hand, in which he has been tightly clutching for hours past the bunch of clover and dandelions which he had got for Susy.

'Thank you, dear little brother,' says Susy, catching him up in her arms.

Mrs Marney sat on the bedside, undressing the children, while Susy brought up the supper for them.

'We walked all the way from the boat,' says Mrs Marney; 'I thought I should never get home. Marney went off with some friends.'

'Why did you not take a carriage, mamma?' said Susy.

'Marney had got my purse, dear,' said her mother. 'Stand still, do, Mikey! while I untie the strings; and Dermy, drink up the nice milk, like an angel. Is it boiled? – never mind, my pet, it will do you good.'

'Do the angels drink boiled milk?' says Dermy in tears.

'Always,' says Mrs Marney with much conviction. Then the little tired boys are tucked up in bed, and lie side by side with dark eyes following their mother as she comes and goes, folding their clothes, putting one thing and another away. Mikey drops off to sleep first, then Dermy's eyelids fall; and Mrs Marney takes the light and leaves the room.

'How tired you are, mamma! Can't I sit up for Mr Marney?' said Susy, as she followed her mother downstairs. She was almost frightened by the tone in which Mrs Marney suddenly answered: 'Certainly not; that is for me to do, not for you. I shall hear him. Goodnight, my dear;' and she folded her in her arms, as if to make up for her vexed tone.

And then at last Susy's opportunity came, and with an effort she began then and there to tell the strange story of her eventful day. She expected she knew not what, a shocked sympathy, an exclamation of surprised regret and tenderness. 'Oh, my Susy, you never refused him!' cried Mrs Marney in consternation – 'such a kind, good man, so well off, such a gentleman!'

She would have said more but that Susy, shrinking from her mother's arms, ran away suddenly into her own room. She had kissed her mother and bade her good-night; but she was not comforted now. She had longed to talk to her, the opportunity had come, and she felt chilled and lonely; she had so pined to be at home in her mother's arms, and she had reached the place she longed for, but it was hardly home. She went to her room and undressed, and lay down in her little creaking bed with a confused impression of something that she must put away from her mind – of something, of many things, of Mrs Marney's passing vexation, the Colonel's reproachful look, and Tempy's angry stare. Had she been unkind to him? He had been so good, so wonderfully good to her; and so at last she fell asleep.

CHAPTER VII

IN THE DAWN

If thou wilt case thine heart
Of love and all its smart,
Then sleep, dear, sleep.

BEDDOES

Everything was very homely in the bare little room, and quiet as the peaceful slumbers of its young inmate. Her work lay folded on a chair; her black cloak hung against the wall; the nosegay her little brother had picked for her was in a glass upon the window-sill; the window was half open to the garden that looked gold and grey and chill in the faint keen dawn. The shadows heaped in the corner began to tremble as the faint light came creeping quietly. The round eye of the little looking-glass seemed to twinkle and wink; the light spread from ridge to ridge, it reached the gilt crown above the bed at last, which seemed to awaken and to give out faint thrills of light.

Susy lay sleeping, unconscious of it all, and dreaming of the tranquil orthodoxies of her past. The present was too strange and new as yet to dream of. Her mother's face seemed the only familiar thing in its tangled perplexities. There is a picture of 'Sleeping St Barbara,' by Paul Veronese, in the National Gallery, which is not unlike Susy as she was then. The angel appears bearing the cross, and the maiden dreams on with a peaceful countenance, not afraid of that which is before her. So lay Susy, unconscious and tranquil. With the first faint streak of daylight some birds began to awaken in the garden with faint stirrings and chirps; then came a faraway knocking that reached the girl in her dreams as from some other world. Then she started up suddenly, confused; she had heard a step on the gravel just outside her window which roused her. She sat up in bed and listened; everything was very still, very serene; she could see the garden through the half-open window – it seemed asleep still, though the birds in the tree tops were waking. A few white stars were throbbing through the dawning mists.

Susy was confused; when she awoke, some feeling was in her mind that she must get up and let in the person who was waiting outside. Perhaps her mother was asleep, tired out, and had not heard the summons.

She jumped up, wrapping herself in her warm dressing-gown, and slipping on her red slippers. There was light enough for her to grope her way; she opened the door, and came to the head of the stairs and looked over. The little staircase led down by a single flight to the front door; and, as Susy stood leaning over the bannisters, she saw a figure carrying a light and cautiously descending, and with sudden relief (for she had been vaguely frightened) she saw that it was her mother. Mrs Marney was dressed, and she was cautiously unlocking and unbarring the bolts of the door. As it flew open it let in a rush of cool keen air, and then out of the sweet morning, with its thousand delicate scents and fragrances, through the tender light breaking so suddenly into the darkened house, came a figure slouching and heavy-footed, reeling as it advanced – a dark, forbidding figure that Susanna might have fled from had she met it in some lonely place.

She heard her mother whisper, 'Oh, Michael!' and then it seemed to her the heavy eyes were raised and met hers. There came a dull thick utterance – an oath. 'Ar you both watching me? D—— you, is not one enough?' said the voice; and then Susy saw an upraised hand, and heard the sound of a heavy blow and a low suppressed cry.

The girl started forward. She ran half down the stairs, and stood with the dawn in her face like some avenging angel.

'How dare you,' she cried out incoherently; but at that moment she met her mother's appealing glance, and saw the poor hands held up with an entreating sign.

There is some strange intuition which flashes quicker than words or even than looks; and as Susanna stood there, shivering with passionate anger, she felt somehow that her mother's one agonised wish was that she should not interfere.

'Go, please, darling,' reached her in a whisper. For a moment she stood scarcely able to obey, and then with a great effort she turned slowly away; but she could scarcely stand as she went back into her own room, and sank down upon her bed and hid her face.

Such horror, such indignity had never entered into her mind before. The quiet home in which she had lived hitherto had been far removed from such terrors as these. In the holy commonplace of her past life the possibility of such misery as this had not occurred to her; and now the wretched secret was hers, and now Susy knew why she hated her stepfather.

The dawn turned into day. Susy still sat there; she was shivering, but she did not know it; the door opened at last, but she did not look up; some one came in.

'Are you not gone back to bed, Susy?' said her mother in a faint sharp voice. 'It will not help me much if you make yourself ill.' Then, melting suddenly: 'My poor darling! my poor child, I would have hidden it from you if I could,' she said. 'He is not often so, dear, and I'm used to his ways; and oh, Susanna!' said the poor thing, 'there's many a worse man than my poor Michael, with all his faults. You are my own child; but you are not his, and you can't understand how long I have loved him.'

Poor Susy! what could she say? Every word her mother spoke sank into her heart; it did not lessen her loyal trust and tender fealty, but it made her feel more and more as if they were apart.

'Lie down, child,' her mother went on, 'and let me cover you over. Go to sleep, darling.'

And Susy, suddenly yielding and obeying like a child, and feeling by instinct that this was best, did as she was bid, and lay down and let her mother cover her over warm. What could she say? what could she do? The little room was alight by this; the birds were in full song, a distant roll of wheels had begun. There was a sound of people stirring about.

Mrs Marney went to the window and drew the curtain across to dim the light; then she came back and sat by the girl's bedside; and Susy, worn out, fell asleep at last, still holding her mother's hand, and by doing so comforted her more than by any words or tender devotion. The poor much-tried woman's heart swelled with tender maternal pride as she sat watching by the girl. Scheme after scheme passed through her mind, as she sat by Susy's bedside. Tenderly as she loved her, she longed for her girl to go from them. What chance of happiness could there be for Susy in this sad home? For herself at least there existed a reality that carried her through its trials; but for Susy what interest could there be?

Mary Marney was not a bad woman, she was not a very good one; she would do a friend a good turn, she would pluck the feathers from her bleeding breast for Michael and the children. When she sent her Susanna away for the first time it was with anguish in her heart; but it seemed to her that it was best. And now again she could not bear to see her child unwelcome; she could not endure the thought of her Susanna watching day by day that which she herself would fain conceal even from herself, learning little by little the whole miserable gamut of a life such as Marney's The girl's presence seemed to drive him to wilder courses, to irritate him. He seemed scarcely himself at times; or was it that, with Susanna looking on, Mary could the less easily blind herself to the life which Marney was leading?

Then Mrs Marney thought of the Colonel, of his kindness, of his friendliness, of his comfortable home and good connections. Ah! if only she could see her Susy safely landed in such a home! She slipped her hand softly away from the young loving clasp, and crept from the room, closing the door very softly. The girl did not awaken till late in the day, when some burst of military music from the high road recalled her to life and sunshine and the sorrow of the night.

CHAPTER VIII

AFTERWARDS

Nor was this fellowship vouchsafed to me
With stinted kindness.

COLERIDGE

Breakfast was on the table when Susanna came in, looking very pale, and dressed in her black gown. To her relief her stepfather was not there. She did not dare look at her mother at first; and Mrs Marney, too, avoided the girl's looks.

'I have put your coffee to keep warm by the kitchen fire,' said Mrs Marney. 'Dermy, go, like a good boy, and fetch sister Susy's coffee. I shall be very angry if you spill it.'

'Let me go too,' says Mikey, starting up.

'Mikey, don't be naughty,' says his mother, absently and as a matter of course; and Mikey takes this for permission, and off go the little pair. They came back in a minute, with a rocking coffee-cup balanced between them.

Susy sat down to her breakfast. Once she raised her eyes to look at her mother, but they filled with tears; and she had to keep them fixed upon her plate, for fear the children should see and make some remark. In that one glance she had seen, to her surprise, that Mrs Marney looked much as usual, only a little flushed and harsh in manner.

'Now, boys, go and fetch your father's coffee,' said Mary a second time as the door opened, and Marney came in. She spoke in her usual voice. Marney certainly did not look as usual. He was not shaved, his handsome face was blurred, he had an odd bloodshot look in his eyes. Susanna turned her head away.

It is an awful thing to hate another person; and poor Susy, so gentle, so yielding, felt as if she hated Marney with an indescribable loathing.

'Well, my fair Susy,' said he, attempting an uneasy familiarity, and, seeing that Susy did not answer, 'Mary, my head aches,' said Marney, and flung himself into a chair that stood by an open window.

'Stopping at home is the best thing to cure the headache, Michael,' said his wife, with a sigh. She began putting his breakfast things ready, using one hand only.

One of the children started up and caught her by the other arm. Mrs Marney shrank back.

'Take care,' said Susy, involuntarily, with a glance at her stepfather, 'you hurt her.'

'It's my rheumatism,' said Mary hastily; then looking at Susanna, she said imploringly, 'Go, darling, tell Denise I am coming.'

Susy started up. She had to pass close to her stepfather, and as she passed she unconsciously pulled her dress so that it should not touch him.

Marney looked at his wife with an odd fixed glance. 'Did you see that?' said he. 'What have you been whining to her about?'

'Do you suppose I would complain to her?' said Mrs Marney.

'You can, if you like,' rejoined he, sulkily. 'When is that old fool of a colonel coming to the point?'

Mr Marney sat turning over his day's politics. The little boys were building an impregnable castle with their bricks. Susy was standing in the little kitchen, by the furnace where the family meals were cooked. Her mother came in, looking for her; she had been more frightened by the girl's scared looks than by Marney's fiercest outbursts. Susy went up to her mother, and put her two arms tight round her neck. 'Oh, mamma! mamma! I have been thinking. Oh couldn't you come away with me, and bring the little boys? I will work for you day and night. Only come! Only come!'

'Ah! my child,' said her mother. 'Do not say such things. How can I come? I have chosen my own life; I must abide by it. You too must live your life. You might be a happy woman, and help us all,' said her mother, looking fixedly at her. 'And make another person very happy – that dear, good Colonel Dymond, who worships the ground you stand on. Michael saw it from the first.'

'Hush! mamma,' said Susy deeply wounded. 'How can *you*, of all people, urge me to marry? Oh! forgive me,' she hastily added, seeing her mother's pained look, and that her eyes were full of tears.

'Promise me at least, Susy, that if he ever comes again you will not refuse him without reflection,' said her mother, wistfully.

'He said something yesterday about waiting,' Susy answered, 'I don't know what, nor do I care. For it is you, mamma, whom I live for. I will even bear with my stepfather,' Susy added faltering, and looking through the open door towards the adjoining room, 'if it makes you happier.'

'No, no, no! it will not make me happier,' cried the poor woman, torn between her two hearts. 'You must live your own life, my child, not mine. I hoped you would never have found it out. It is not the same to me as to you. We make it up,' she said, with a pitiful smile. 'Sometimes he has forgotten all about it in the morning. The children are accustomed to our ways; you are used to other things. You are my own child; but you are not his, and you cannot understand how long we have loved each other.'

Susy stood strangely silent, watching her mother with dry, wondering eyes. Each word smote her. The poor child's heart was full of pain; it seemed so hard, so very hard, to leave that dear, bent head to bear its burden alone, and yet Susy felt that her mother was speaking the truth.

'I will try and think of some plan,' she said faintly, and as she spoke the brick castle fell over with a crash in the adjoining sitting-room; Dermy began to cry; Mr Marney called out, 'Mother! mother!' and Mrs Marney hastily turned and ran across the passage in through the open door. Susy also passed out into the passage, and then hurried aimlessly into the garden.

It was a lovely day; everything was shining, and yet everything seemed to ache, from the long, green grass at her feet to the sky above; the poplar-trees shivered; the nasturtiums looked desolate. Susy, as she went by, saw Madame at her window making signs. It seemed to Susy as if she was a person looking on at a dream. Was it also a dream that she was alone – that no being in the whole world wanted her or needed her? She only brought trouble upon every one. The Colonel looked at her with reproach; even Tempy shrank from her. The girl had come aimlessly along the shaded avenue which ran by the palings that divided the villa garden from the road; the lilacs grew thick on either side, and their dark green foliage beneath the blue made leafy walls to the little path.

As she hurried along she nearly ran up against a strange young man with a long nose and twinkling eyes, who looked at her curiously and compassionately as she passed. She scarcely saw him, and yet this stranger, as strangers sometimes do, knew the whole story of her troubles. He had come by chance stumbling into the secret of poor Mrs Marney's sorrowful life – the secret she would have hidden from her nearest and dearest. He had returned by some midnight train; reached home at dawn; come out into the garden, hearing Marney's step. He had looked on for a moment at the tragedy; heard the blow fall: hesitated, and while he hesitated the door shut – the tipsy man staggered into the house. It was nothing to him, and yet the actors interested him, as actors do interest those who having seen them stirred by great passions and events now recognise them as they pass by quietly. The young man watched Susy as she brushed past, and walked towards the house again. Madame du Parc was still at her window. 'My son is come! He arrive last night,' shouts the old lady. ''Ave you seen him in the avenue?'

Susanna shook her head; she could not speak. She turned aside, like a poor little hunted hare, to the sitting-room window which was open. Some one called her; the little boys came scampering to meet her; the little dog flew out barking. 'Here she is,' said her mother's voice. 'Ah! Susy, here is a good friend who has come to see you. We have been speaking of you. Dear child, listen to what he has got to say.' It seemed all like some awakening from a miserable dream.

The Colonel, with his neat hat and umbrella, was standing by the window. Marney was gone. Mrs Marney, who looked as if she had been crying, was sitting smiling in the big arm-chair. As the Colonel turned to meet Susanna, he was quite shocked by the scared expression of her face, by the black lines under her eyes. A flush came into his yellow cheeks, and his looks became very wide and bright. Then he came up to her and said very simply, 'My dear, your mother and I have been talking of something very near my heart. I have come to bring you a message from my girl. She wants to come and ask your forgiveness for what she said, she herself sent me to you, or perhaps I should not be here. Susy, I am an old fellow; but you know me and you know my children, and if you could make up your mind to love me a little, and to come to be my wife, I think, I am sure, we could make you happy. Your good mother consents, and thinks she could trust you to me.'

'Indeed! indeed! Susy, I could trust you to him,' cried the poor woman eagerly. 'I could be happy, if I felt you safe in such hands. Ah! darling, if it were only for my sake!'

'You must not influence her,' gravely interrupted the Colonel. He seemed quite clever suddenly to Susy, and able to understand everything – every shade of feeling. 'It would be a cruel mistake for Susy to marry me, or anybody else, unless she could do it for her own sake, and because she thought she could be happy. I dare not think what it would be to me and mine if we could hope to make her so.'

Susanna, in her black dress, stood in the centre of the room, facing the two who wished her so well. She was still holding a sprig of ivy she had gathered. She seemed scarcely to see what was before her, or to be understanding what was happening; but it was not so. She was living too intensely to give much sign of what was in her mind. She looked from her mother, with the anxious, speaking eyes, to the kind face of the time-worn man who loved her. She had never till this moment realised the selfish, human, irrepressible happiness of being another person's happiness. What strange experience the last few hours had brought! She seemed suddenly to have come into shelter, after being in a great storm or battle. An hour ago she had been alone in all the world, her heart had seemed almost dead, and now she was alone no longer, and her pulses were beating so that she could scarcely breathe.

Colonel Dymond waiting for her to speak, thought that her silence lasted a very long time. 'Susy!' he said, almost shyly. Something in his voice touched her – it seemed natural and familiar. She was very young, she was easily touched, easily made grateful. It seemed so natural to say Yes, and to put her future into this good friend's keeping. What this future contained – where it might lead her in its onward course – she knew not. She accepted the present with a true heart, and with a faith and loving conviction, which did not grow less as time went on.

BOOK II

SUSANNA AT CROWBECK

Touch us gently, Time,
Let us glide along thy stream
Gently, as we sometimes glide
Through a quiet dream;
Humble voyagers are we,
Husband, wife, and children three

BARRY CORNWALL

CHAPTER IX

BEACON FIRES

Some say thy fault is youth.

One September evening a bonfire was burning high up near the summit of Tarndale Crag in the Lake Country. The fire burnt clear, with keen flames piercing the dying light. The smoke went spiring gently into the air, the fading sky was wide and tenderly serene above the moor and the lake below, where the waters, still flushed with sunset, came rippling against the rocks and the placid slopes of meadow-land. All about Crowbeck Place the chestnuts and the ash-trees had lit up their autumnal bonfire of yellow and russet flame; was it for the marriage of summer and winter, or in honour of Susanna's wedding-day, that they were flaring? Meanwhile, Crowbeck Place, the white house by the lake, was making ready for its new mistress; it stood with shining windows and new-mown lawns, gleaming between gardens and meadows that sloped to the water-side. Farther on was Bolsover Hall, wrapped in an ivy cowl, and also illumined, with many windows repeating the west; and then in the distant shadow rose Friars Tarndale, the fine old home of the lords of Tarndale, all shuttered and abandoned.

The hills beyond Tarndale were already in purple and shadow; this upper end of the lake was still alight; a fisherman's boat was patiently bobbing up and down, and trying to complete its daily count of fish, doomed from their cool depths into the frying-pans of the neighbouring gentry. But the lights perhaps frightened the fish, for the fisherman pulled grumbling to shore before recrossing the water on his way home to the village.

The people living in the houses along the lake-side came to their cottage doors, and looked across the water towards the bonfire flaming on the opposite moor. 'Twould be for the Colonel's wedding, they said, and they wondered 'what sort the new leddy was like.' Mrs Barrow, the fisherman's wife, standing in her doorway, with the convolvulus hanging overhead and three curly-headed little urchins clinging to her knees, told Mrs Tyson from the Lake Farm, that she wondered to see the lights, for her master told her Miss Bolsover had sent orders from the Ha' to 'do away wi' the bonfires. The squire himsel' had the faggots carted up, but Miss Bolsover said she would na' ha' a bleeze.'

Mrs Tyson, a martial figure with a basket on either arm and a straw bonnet fiercely cocked, replied, with a laugh, 'that it was na' to be wondered at if the family at the Ha' did na' favour the new wife, considering their relationship to the old one.' And so the two voices chattered on, gossiping peacefully to a romantic accompaniment of evening, of distant echoes, to the rush of the stream under the little stone bridge hard by. Mrs Tyson was a sturdy cynic; Mrs Barrow, who was a peaceable woman, taking a friendly view of people and events, tried to find excuses for all 'Miss Bolsover might surely be a bit fashed; she who had been a mither so long to the Colonel's two children at the Place and to Mr Charles at the Ha' as well; it was hard to gi' all up to another – and Miss Bolsover hersel' such an uncommon spirited leddy.'

'Mr Josselin and Miss Tempy will be thinking they've had eno' o' mithers,' says Mrs Tyson dryly, with a hitch at the baskets. 'M'appen Tempy'll be for taking a husband, now her father's bringing hoam a bride.'

'Some fwolk do meak a fuss and a bodderment,' says Mrs Barrow; 'Miss Tempy and the new Mrs Dymond are gran' friends sure-ly. Why, Mrs Dymond is scarce older than Miss Tempy hersel'.'

'More's the pity,' says Mrs Tyson, sternly. 'Many a young lass will tak' an old man for his brass. My Jane would ha' wedded wi' old Roger Hathwaite if it had na' been for our warnings. Her feyther said he wad tak' the stick to her if she had onything to do wi' that old foxy chap.'

'Eh! but the Colonel is a good gentleman and Crowbeck is a pretty place,' says Mrs Barrow, 'wi' flowers in the gardens and ripe fruit on the wa'. Eh! Tim!' And the mother proudly patted one of her curly heads.

'Miss Tempy gied us pearrn and applen out o' t' garrden,' says shrilly Tim, grinning and joining in the conversation.

'And Miss Tempy's auntie cam oop and said we werrn't to have'n,' cries curly Tom, at the pitch of his voice; 'and Miss Tempy she bade us rin heam quick wi' what we gotten.'

'Ah! Miss Tempy is a Dymond, and na' niggard, like the Bolsovers,' says Mrs Tyson, with a last hoist of the baskets. 'I should na' like Miss Bolsover o'er *my* head. My goodness! she will raise a rout to see the fire: I dinna ken who can ha' kinnelled it!' Mrs Tyson's speculations suddenly ended in a sort of gulp; two figures had come up silently, mysteriously, as figures do when darkness is falling.

'It's well for you, Mrs Tyson, that you don't know,' said a youthful voice, speaking in hollow tones.

'Nonsense, Mrs Tyson,' cries his companion. 'Whoever lit the fire will get five shillings by coming up to the Place and asking for me. Good-evening, Mrs Barrow; I hope Tom and Tim have been good boys to-day.' And the two young people walk on – a very young man and a very young woman. The girl kirtled in crimson, active, with a free, determined air; the youth, a slim sandy youth, with a red face and shabby clothes and gaiters. He looks like a gentleman, for all his homely clothes and ungainly ways.

'Whoever ken't Mr Josselin and Miss Tempy were stan'nin thear! I thowt they were goasts,' cries Mrs Tyson, and she strides off to her own home somewhat crestfallen.

Meanwhile the brother and sister had stopped for a minute upon the bridge down below, and stood breathing in the peaceful evening. Even eager young souls just beginning life are sometimes a little tired, and glad of the approach of twilight with her starry steps and resting sights! colours dying, workaday noises silenced one by one, natural echoes sounding clearer and more distinct – night approaching. They could hear the fresh roar of the torrent dashing against the weed-grown rocks below, and then the sleepy chirp of the birds overhead in their nests, and the rustling of branches, and far-away echoes of dogs and lowing cows travelling homewards. The scattered cottages along the stream were lighting up their lattices one by one, the flowers were giving out their last evening perfumes before being blown out for the night. As the sunset died away out of the sky, the distant bonfire seemed to turn brighter and brighter.

'So Mrs Tyson doesn't know who lit the bonfire,' says Tempy with a laugh. 'She generally knows everything. Jo! how could you frighten her so? People mustn't say we didn't want the fires lit. It seems disrespectful to papa and to Susanna too.' Josselin Dymond didn't answer, but hung over the old stone parapet with his hands in his pockets, whistling the hunting chorus out of the *Freischütz*.

'I wish you and Charlie would not whistle from morning to night,' cries the suddenly indignant Tempy. 'You let everything go on; you allow papa to be insulted, you don't interfere when you ought to speak, you leave me to bear the brunt of it all. You never said a word this morning when Aunt Fanny countermanded the bonfire, and you just stand whistling, and think that is all you have to do in life,' cries the sister.

Josselin looked at her with an odd half-amused expression, and a gleam in his blue eyes.

'I'm sorry you ain't pleased with us, Tempy. We quite agreed with you, but you and Aunt Fanny made such a noise it was impossible to get in a word. We did our best, and – and – it wasn't George Tyson who lit the fire. You can give me the five shillings if you like.'

'What, *you*!' Tempy cried confusedly. 'But the fire is over there on Crowbeck Crag, and you are *here*, Jo.'

'I came over in the fisherman's boat just before you met me,' said her brother. 'Look! There's Charlie's beacon lighting too,' and as he spoke another gleam began to shine on one of the further peaks like a bright red star rising against the dark line of the moor.

'Oh, Jo! what will Aunt Fanny say?' cries Tempy, half terrified, half triumphant.

'Uncle Bolsover will catch it,' Jo answers philosophically. 'He always does.'

Jo and Tempy Dymond walked on without another word along the road that leads by the head of the lake to Bolsover Hall and to the Place beyond the Hall. Their steps quicken as they reach the park gates, but they are encountered by a stout, shadowy, agitated figure, evidently on the look out for them.

'Here you are at last! Been looking for you everywhere. Heard you were in the village,' says the squire mysteriously, and hurrying up. 'Terrible upset up here – most distressing. Tempy, you can soothe your aunt; go up at once, there's a good girl – she's hysterical; we don't know what to do with her. My wife has sent me down for Jeffries. That mistake about lighting up the beacons has quite upset poor Fanny. Good heavens! there's another of the d—— things,' cries the poor squire, catching sight of the second illumination.

Tempy, conscience-stricken, turns to her brother. Can he have the face to laugh!

'Oh! Uncle Bolsover, I – I'm very sorry,' says Jo 'You mustn't mind my laughing – I'm really very sorry. I thought my father would wish the bonfires lighted, as it is the custom down here; perhaps Aunt Fanny won't mind so much if I go and tell her it's not *you*. I mean that we – that Charlie and I——' Jo was getting somewhat confused.

The squire stopped short, looked from Josselin to Tempy, buttoned himself up tightly. 'Perhaps you had better let Tempy explain,' says the cowardly Bolsover. 'You – you might come with me for the doctor, Jo.'

'No, I'll have it out,' says Jo, setting off running up the sweep as hard as his long legs could carry him. He did not stop to ring, but hurried in by the back way and by the familiar passage to the door of Aunt Fanny's sitting-room, which Charles Bolsolver used to call the harem. Tea-pots, coffee-cups, liqueur-stands, salts, fans, eau de Cologne, every soothing appliance seemed scattered in disorder about the place. The curtains were drawn to keep out the odious reflection of the lights without. Miss Bolsover was lying back, with her sister-in-law, Mrs Bolsover, and two ladies' maids in attendance.

'Who is it? – what is it? Are you Doctor Jeffries?' screams the invalid, wildly.

Jo walks in, half penitent, half defiant, and without further preamble confesses to his share of the catastrophe. Once more Miss Bolsover goes off into genuine hysterics; to be thwarted in any way always upsets her nerves, she says. All the cats and the dogs join in the *mêlée*. Josselin Dymond at a sign from Mrs Bolsover leaves the room, and as he opens the door the gleams of the bonfires throw the shadows of the hall windows in great chequered squares upon the marble.

'Josselin!' says Mrs Bolsover, following him, 'you had better go after your uncle, and tell him at once of your inopportune rejoicings. You have done enough to upset your aunt, even without the agitations of this ridiculous marriage, and do try and hurry up Jeffries. He is never at home when he is wanted,' says Mrs Bolsover, going back to her harassing duties.

Some very good people have a singular fancy for speaking severely of their neighbours, for whom, if the truth were known, they feel no very special dislike. Mrs Bolsover generally, and upon principle, blamed everyone and everything, and yet it was but a habit of speech; she was one of the meekest of women. Aunt Fanny used rarely to blame, but to praise with many adjectives and exclamations, and yet somehow she was not meek, and they were all afraid of her. Her fat hand ruled Bolsover Hall as well as Crowbeck Place, for Mrs Bolsover, who had married late in life, never assumed the reins of management. At the Place, Colonel Dymond naturally turned to his late wife's sister for sympathy, companionship, and advice. He trusted Mrs Bolsover, who was his own sister, but he was a little shy with her – they were too much alike, both serious, sincere, reserved people, feeling much, but holding back where Miss Bolsover did not fear to rush in. As for the squire, the master of the house, the head of the Bolsover family, he was a Fact rather than a person. He paid the bills, shot the pheasants, went on the box when it was convenient; he turned a lathe, and had also steered a small steamer on the lake at one time, but this was not considered safe by the ladies, and the squire was made to return to the mainland again. He could photograph a little; he was passionately fond of waltzing, the young ladies were still glad of him as a partner in default of younger but not more active men. Mr Bolsover liked dress, he twirled his moustachios, he walked with a curious dancing step. He was called the squire by the country people, Uncle Bolsover by Jo and Tempy, Frederick by his wife and sister, Uncle Bol by Charlie Bolsover his nephew, who was supposed by many people to be the heir.

Perhaps few people in this world had ever given less trouble to others than this kind and friendly little man; many of us may have laughed at him, but all who have known him have had a kindly regard for the squire. And yet it must be confessed that he was a coward, that in the presence of the *Vehmgericht* in the boudoir, he scarcely dared show his own amiable predilections, among which must surely be reckoned the good-will he felt for the pretty young bride now expected at Tarndale.

CHAPTER X

A WEDDING PARTY

The bride she is winsome and bonny,
Her hair it is snooded sae sleek,
And faithfu' and kind is her Johnny,
Yet fast fa' the tears on her cheek.

OLD SONG

While the fires were burning away on Tarndale Crags, and the discussions also flaming up and dying away, as discussions do, while the people at the Hall and round about the lake-side were speculating as to her motives, the bride had turned to her mother with tears and many parting looks of love and farewell. She involuntarily shrunk from her stepfather Mr Marney's embrace, but she held her little brothers close in her kind arms with kisses and promises of happy things, of letters and gifts, of long summer holidays to be spent at Crowbeck Place, all together, with her husband the Colonel's full sanction and approval.

The two little boys had been to the wedding in brand-new jackets and trousers – the gift of their elderly brother-in-law. Except for this unusual magnificence all had been quiet enough. The Colonel's family was in England, as we know, and Susanna had no one to invite. Her mother gave her away. The only other witness was Madame du Parc, looking like a picture out of a second-rate fashion-book, in her *cachemire* and *chapeau-à-plumes* and lemon kid gloves. After long years in France, Madame du Parc had grown to look more completely a Frenchwoman than if her Scottish antecedents had never existed. There is some curious process of amalgamation which makes our adopted habits often seem more marked and individual than those we are naturally born to. Madame's French was more voluble, her English more broken, than if she had been born in the Faubourg, instead of Pollok, N.B.; her clothes, her *chaussons*, and *camisoles* were completely and entirely characteristic of a French *bourgeoise*. The *chapeau-à-plumes* was purchased for the occasion of Susanna's marriage; as for the famous *cachemire*, Madame had worn it at her own wedding some thirty years before, when she had married the mathematical master of the school where she had taught so long.

Susanna was not dressed out of a fashion-book, but she looked very charming. The little brothers opened their round eyes to see Sister Susy a grand lady. 'Zat is 'ow I likes to see 'errr!' says Madame du Parc to the children – '*à la bonne heure! hein! hein!*' The children could hardly recognise their sister in the grand lady in the shining gown, with a carriage waiting and a husband in attendance, who took leave of them in her feathery bonnet; but her kisses and her tears were the old ones all unchanged, and so were her smiles and her kind eyes. How much nicer she looked in her wedding-dress than in the rusty black gown she had worn so long after she came from England! But she had put off her old clothes and her mourning on her wedding-day; and to please the Colonel she had donned her silk attire. At Neuilly, as in Tarndale, it was thought a great match for Susanna, when it was known that she was marrying Colonel Dymond. The *épicière*, the washerwoman, the *mercière* next door, were only translating Mrs Barrow's gossip into French as they stood in the shady avenue waiting to see the carriage drive off with the bride and bridegroom. The difference between their ages was as great as that between their fortunes: she was twenty and penniless, he was within a year or two of sixty and rich enough to gratify all her fancies, as well as his own. One little back room at Madame du Parc's contained Susy's possessions – her work-box, and her desk, and the old hair trunk from her grandfather's rectory, which she had brought with her to Paris. But neither Crowbeck itself, nor the family mansion in Wimpole Street could hold the Colonel's many belongings. It was natural that his relations should be vehement in their exclamations.

Susanna had scarcely any relations to exclaim, except her cousins the country doctor and his family, who were glad to hear of her comfortable prospects. As for her stepfather's cordialities, they were somewhat ominous; and the Colonel, although a simple and unsuspicious person, instinctively felt that he should have to pay a good price for Mr Marney's hearty congratulations. Mrs Marney wept tears of mingled joy and sorrow for parting, and for happiness, and when Susy herself, standing with her husband in the chapel, put her hand into his, it was with grateful trust, it was with tender respect and admiration. The bitter experiences of the last year, during which she had been so unhappy, seemed condoned and forgotten. She felt that it was for himself, for his goodness to herself, to her mother, to all of them, that she was marrying John Dymond, and she vowed to herself to be a good wife to him, to bring a true heart to him and his: a loving home, like that dear old home with her grandfather, seemed hers once more; a happy life, a tender welcome, a good man's honour and love. Her own love for her colonel was made up of many mingled feelings; gratitude, tenderness, glad submission – all had a part. He gave her peace and self-respect, the delight of helping those she loved, a society to which she was glad to suit herself more and more every day, conversation to which she and her mother listened with deep attention, and in perfect faith. Susy was leaving her mother's home; but Mrs Marney and Susy both knew that the secrets of that sad house were best borne unshared and unspoken. Its martyrdom (for martrydom it was) was made lighter, perhaps, by Susy's absence.

No flowers were scattered before the newly-married people as they came away walking across the autumnal garden, followed by the little household of the villa; only the crisp fallen leaves rustled under their feet, a scent of September was in the air, some sudden dry soft breeze shook the branches overhead. Susy came with her hand in the Colonel's arm. He already stooped a little, she walked erect and firm, trying to keep back her tears.

The horses waiting outside in the road by the shabby green gates were already chafing when Susy got into the carriage, helped up the steps by Marney's officious hand. The little boys waved their new caps and raised a sudden shrill shout. It was an unlucky shout, for it frightened some stray fowl that had been perching in the branches of an old acacia-tree overhanging the gate, the bird started up flapping its wings with a loud angry crow, the horses were frightened, and for a minute they were scarcely to be held in.

The Colonel, who had lingered saying good-bye to Mrs Marney, rushed forward greatly alarmed for his bride, but Susy was too much absorbed to be frightened even by the untoward little incident.

'Good-bye, good-bye,' she said, leaning forward, with all her heart going out to the mother she was leaving behind for ever – so it almost seemed to her.

Afterwards Susanna remembered that as the carriage was driving away, a branch from the acacia-tree fell to the ground with a crash, again startling the restive horses almost into a gallop.

Mrs Marney, who was superstitious, turned pale. Marney shrugged his shoulders as he moved away with an odd expression on his handsome face.

'Old branches rot and have to fall when the time comes,' says he, with his Irish accent. ''Twill be a good thing for Susanna if she is left with a handsome jointure, Polly. I wish I could have got the Colonel to sign a proper settlement. I suppose the old fellow was afraid of his family.'

'Oh! It is not good to talk of such things at such moments. Oh, no,' cries Madame du Parc, indignant with Marney for his cold-blooded cynicism. Before resuming her usual domestic *camisole* and ordinary habits, the good lady carefully examined the acacia-tree. The branch, so she observed, had been partially sawn through, and furthermore she ascertained from her son Max, the engraver, on the occasion of his next visit to his home at Neuilly, that he himself had occasioned the mischief.

'The branch was dead, and I began to cut it away,' he said, 'but I was called off to a friend and forgot all about it.'

'You call zose frens! frens, who only interrups, who stops, who smokes,' says Madame bitterly, speaking English as she usually did when she was excited; 'that M. Jourde he was here again yesterday; he came with M. Caron. Does he not know I sees through 'im? Why could you not give up conspirations for once and come to the wedding, Max? The old Colonel he look well considering; and that dear child was pretty like everything. You should pay a visit of felicitation to the new married when you next go to London about your catalogue.'

'I have no wish to see the Colonel look his best or to felicitate any one,' said Max, dryly. 'And, listen, mamma,' he added, with some emphasis, 'if you go on talking like this about me and my friends, you will get me into some serious trouble.'

Max, usually so quiet and easy going, looked vexed and thoroughly in earnest, so that his mother was frightened.

'*Allons donc! par exemple*,' cried the poor lady once more. 'Ah, you joke!'

'I am not joking,' Max answered, gravely; 'these are bad times, and though you may not know it people are ready enough to suspect each other. Monsieur Marney is (so I have every reason to believe) in the pay of the police,' and Du Parc raised his voice and looked towards the door. Was it a sudden breeze? The door which had been half open to the passage leading to the garden creaked a very little and seemed to move.

Madame's bright old eyes darted one quick glance at Max, and then she ran nimbly to the window and threw it up. She was in time to see Marney slowly crossing the grass and lighting a cigar as he went along.

'Boys, where are you?' he called out, with some affectation of loudness. 'Polly! where have ye hidden the brats?'

CHAPTER XI

LONDON CITY

I love the haunts of old Cockaigne,
Where wit and wealth were squandered.

LOCKER'S 'London Lyrics'

After a few days' loitering journey, from Paris to the coast, along a road which is pleasant with limes and poplars, and green horizons, and where (if so inclined) pilgrims may still travel from one shrine to another, and rest each night in a different city, with wonders to be worshipped, and ancient stones still working miracles, the Colonel brought his young bride to England. There had been some talk of a foreign tour, of Italy and the South; but Colonel Dymond longed to be home again by his own hearth with his children and the accustomed faces round about; and to Susy, London was as strange and new a city as Rome itself. She also longed to be at Tarndale and beginning her new life, only she was glad of a little time to get accustomed to it first, to her fresh dignities, her silk dress, her gold ring, her strange golden fate.

Was this Susanna Dymond, this new-born being walking with her husband by her side in dignified ease and sober splendour? She used to glance shyly at the Colonel as he walked along; at the well-preserved grizzled man, the kind brown face, the grey moustache. He was about her own height, well brushed, well blacked, well starched. All was of a piece; decorous, respectable, and Susy began to feel as if perhaps of all things in the world decorum and respectability were the most intoxicating. What a contrast to the life from which she had come away – no bills, no troubles, no seams ripped and opening wide, no storms, no daily struggle for life, no Marney to terrify her, no tears to hide away from her mother. All seemed smoothed, and calmed, and in order. In Susy's pocket was a well-filled purse, and by her side her attentive, courteous husband. Well-dressed people nodded smiling as they passed them on foot or in well-appointed carriages. Susy wondered if at that minute her mother was wearily trudging along the dusty Neuilly road on her way home from market. If only mamma had married another John, thought Susy. The Colonel was not the least of the marvels of this new life in this wonderful London, with its wide garden-like parks, where the trees were scattering their leaves not less freely than at Crowbeck; where the bells came jangling over the housetops and the birds flew across the horizons of the overflowing streets. Susy had never seen London streets, never driven in carriages, never shopped in her life before. How many things there were she had never done! The Colonel, enjoying her pleasure, took her to see the sights, to the Tower, to the Abbey, and to St Paul's, and to the pictures. The Opera was closed, but Susanna went with her husband to the play once or twice, and he introduced her there to some of his friends, who immediately began to call from their clubs and from various resorts, and who all lost their hearts to the gentle and fair young bride.

'Dymond had made a most fortunate choice,' said the old friends, and they left their cards again and again at the door of the little hotel where the new married pair were staying.

The Colonel was pleased with Susy's success, and wrote home long accounts of their visitors – admirals, generals, brigadiers. Susanna's admirers were high up in the service.

'Old bores!' said Tempy crossly as she impatiently tossed one of her father's letters to her aunt Fanny. Jo and Tempy had come over to spend the day at Bolsover, and were sitting with their two aunts in the sacred precincts of the harem. Miss Bolsover was still extended on the sofa, she had not yet recovered from the effects of the Colonel's marriage.

Whatever storms and trials might assail the spirit Aunt Fanny liked her little comforts. The room was sprinkled with many devices, and musical instruments, with footstools, with flowers, and white cats, and Pomeranian dogs, and pugs with silver collars. The sunshine came through muslin of various shades, the whole place was scented with sandal-wood, and faint patchouli, and various drowsy emanations. Jo always declared there was something Turkish in his aunt Fanny's character as well as in her surroundings, and that patchouli made his head ache.

The other prodigal nephew, Charles Bolsover, who did not mind patchouli, though he also rebelled against his aunt Fanny's silken bow-strings, was sunk back in a big arm-chair stroking the Persian cat's tail. The ladies were assembled round their tea-table, Mr Bolsover, in a mountaineering costume, was preparing to walk down to the village with Jo.

'Have you read papa's letter, Aunt Fanny?' says Tempy, jealously taking up her grievance again with the sugar-tongs. 'I can't think why he is so pleased, though I can imagine her enjoying it all. How Susanna must like being flattered!'

'So would you if you could get a chance,' says Jo from his doorway.

'She will never get anything but plainest truths from me nor from auntie either,' says Tempy, helping herself to plum-cake.

'We will let her know what to expect,' says Jo, with a brotherly grimace.

Here Charlie suddenly pulled the cat's tail, and Poussette uttered a miaull.

'Oh de poor litty pitty darling ting,' cries Miss Bolsover, precipitating herself. 'Charlie boy, how can you be such a naughty, cruel uncle.'

'Hey! what is all this?' said Uncle Bolsover, chiming in. 'When are they coming? Where are they staying?'

'They are at an hotel in Piccadilly. I suppose Wimpole Street is not fashionable enough for the bride,' says Aunt Fanny.

The Colonel had not taken his young wife home to Wimpole Street, the house was shut up, and the memories that were locked up in the dismantled rooms were melancholy and seemed to him out of time and place. One day Susanna went with her husband to see her future home. She looked up at the great stone staircase, peeped into the lofty drawing-rooms, with their catafalques of shrouded furniture. She shuddered from the long, black dining-room, into the square, dark study, with its gratings and dingy rows of books, and came away with a feeling of intense relief, leaving the family mansion to its ghosts and cobwebs, and to the care of that forlorn and courageous race of charwomen who dwell in solitude and wander from emptiness to emptiness. From long habit, perhaps, they do not heed their own footsteps, nor look behind them startled when the doors bang in the distance.

The new married pair had settled down in one of those comfortable little hotels which lie in the centre of things and of people, quiet and convenient oases amid the noisy vortex of Piccadilly, Bond Street, and Mayfair. From Eiderdown's Hotel Susy could come and go and receive her husband's friends, and see her sights, and complete her trousseau without effort or exertion. It was indeed a fairy London to the girl; beautiful, expensive bargains were blooming in the windows of the shops all about, arcades close at hand were lighting up and festooned with objects of every shade and fashion; hats and bonnets floated from plate-glass to plate-glass all triumphant with garlands and streaming ribbons; shoes of rainbow colours pointed their silken toes in long procession; delicate kid hands were beckoning from behind the shop fronts; other windows were stuffed with gimcracks and trinkets, nor was she ever tired of the jewellers' shops and the toy-shops which fascinated her most of all. Susy longed for her mother to enjoy all these childish pleasant things with her, and for Mikey and Dermy to exclaim alternately at bonbons and diamonds. There was one of these treasuries which she used to pass every day as she came out for her daily walk with her kind old husband. In the centre of the great pane of glass, amid a shining sea of gems, lay two loveliest opals repeating the lights, in some tender Mozart-like-colour fashion of their own; between the opals lay one bright star of diamonds shining with brave chords of sunshine and flashing beauty.

'Oh! how mamma would like those beautiful opals, John; and how wonderfully that star does shine,' says Susy, lingering, while the Colonel in turn glanced at his wife and then at the star again.

How beautiful she was, how well the ornament would look in her thick brown hair thought the admiring husband, and he sighed with some odd regret and apprehension even in his happiness. There was something almost as pathetic in the Colonel's moderate happiness as in the girl's simple enjoyment.

Susy was not romantic, not touched by any of the greater sentiments, but she was childish and rational, as childhood is, and he was rational and childish as age is apt to be.

September in Piccadilly is a very modified solitude. The carriages roll more freely, perhaps, the pavements are not quite so impassable as later in the year, but if the weather is fine, the parks and gardens are even pleasanter than at any other time. At night Susy from her sitting-room window could see a distant world, twinkling with the lights of the great tumultuous city which was now her home. Paris had been but a sad place to her, burning and garish with pleasures which were not for her, as she came and went sadly like a young postulant in her black gown. But

London was a home, here she had a place, here she felt a certain right to be and to a share in the sumptuous life. It seemed to her as if this too, this right to be happy, was among the Colonel's many gifts to her. So from her windows Mrs Dymond watched the lights by night, and by day she used to look out at the wide horizon, so changing and various where the mists were passing or dividing, and showing the palaces and the workshops, the streets, and the spaces of the mighty city. Beyond the park and the Abbey towers she had seen the river flowing between its banks, and the long lines of embankment and the dockyards, crowded with the life, with the commerce of the world. All these things she enjoyed and noted as she came and went day by day, not alone, but in kind company, not as a wayfarer looking on, but as a sharer in the great feast.

As I have said, she had been taken to the Abbey and St Paul's, and the Tower, and heard the city bells jangling cheerfully, and then one morning before luncheon the bride (always with her Colonel by her side) went to visit the pictures in the National Gallery. They seemed stately to her, somewhat gloomy, but splendid and satisfying all the same.

'It is a very fine gallery, you know, my dear Susy, one of the finest in Europe,' said her husband. 'It is a very great thing for us having such a collection. Let me see, is this Raphael or Michael Angelo? Oh! Carlo Dolce, of course.'

The good Colonel walked on to the end of the long gallery trying to find some picture to show her which he once remembered having had pointed out to him by a painter, and Susy had been standing for a moment before the well-known portrait of 'Andrea del Sarto.' She was not so much examining the picture as trying to remember who it was it recalled to her mind, when she looked round suddenly, feeling a glance upon her, and by some odd chance she found herself scrutinised by two dark, questioning eyes not unlike those she had just been gazing at, and as she looked she knew who it was the picture had reminded her of. It was this very man whom she had scarcely seen and never spoken to, Monsieur Max, the artist, the revolutionary son of her kind old friend, Madame du Parc, who used to abuse him by the hour with motherly pride. During what long afternoons and mornings with Madame du Parc had Susy not listened to Max's many misdeeds and shortcomings, to his aberrations, to his difficulties, his uncertain comings and goings.

Susy was shy, and though she longed to speak to this dangerous character she only stared, smiled, exclaimed, half put out her hand, and then drew it back once more seeing a look of surprise in the living Andrea's face. His frizzed hair was not quite like the picture, and for a moment she was confused between her previous impression and the vivid presentation before her. Du Parc, too, was uncertain, and being also shy, specially of grand ladies, he merely bowed and passed on.

'What is it, my child?' said the Colonel, as she joined him, looking excited, and with blushes.

'I saw some one from Neuilly,' she said, 'Madame du·Parc's son, Monsieur Max. I wanted to speak to him, but he did not seem to know me, and walked away.'

'Perhaps it is as well,' said the Colonel consolingly. 'These sort of people are difficult to shake off again once one happens to get entangled with them.'

'I wanted to send a message to mamma,' said Susy, wistfully looking after the erect figure of the young man as he proceeded with echoing steps down the long gallery.

It must be confessed that Susanna's youthful mind was intent upon something at that time to her more important than her presence in that solemn temple of art among the painters and their works, something nearer to her heart than priceless heritages of light and solemn aspiration, than the signs and tokens of the noble dead who live still for us, as we drift along upon the stream of life. She had a ten-pound note in her pocket, she was pondering upon toy-shops, she was longing to spend it for her mother and the children, and she was ready to leave the gallery at the first sign of weariness the Colonel might give.

As for Max du Parc walking along the great shining halls, he had no thoughts of gold pieces to spend elsewhere. His whole mind and attention were present, riveted, absorbed. He was at home, though a stranger among these old friends and teachers. He had come commissioned to make some engravings for a French dictionary of art, and for the moment his interest and enthusiasm completely overpowered him, and carried him away, even from the thought of the work which had brought him there.

He seemed to be in some Elysium among the gods and goddesses, and their incarnations. The mind of Titian was there in its glory. There were the dreams of Turner breaking and dawning and vanishing into space, while calmly serene the golden illusions of Claude were floating before his eyes; or was it a Velasquez or a Giorgione whose chivalrous, harmonious soul touched the disciple to some ambition beyond the common aspect of things? All about shine together with the noble realities, the golden superstitions of art, of religions, and of pagans, and the truth upbears them fearlessly in its generous train; the mythologies of Greece, of medieval Italy are there; angels sing their shrill songs of praise, wielding their fiery swords and fiddle-bows with a fanciful strength, or gods and goddesses revel under summer skies. A whole revelation of past life, of bygone strength, wisdom, and splendour ever present is recorded for us who pass in turn looking up for a moment on our way at the pictures which remain.

Max looked and wondered and looked again, and then remembering the work for which he had come, began making his deliberate choice, and returning again and again to the types which seemed to him best fitted for his purpose. As he stood half hopeless, half deliberate, before the Giorgione knight in shining armour he heard a cheerful, somewhat husky voice behind him: The Dymond *ménage* had caught him up again.

'Well, my dear Susy, have you had enough of all this?' And young and eager came the answer, 'Oh, yes, thank you, John, I'm rather tired of it, and now will you take me to the toy-shop in Bond Street?'

Max did not even turn his head, a sudden impatient scorn for Philistinism came over this young dweller among tents.

Susy and her husband left the gallery, descending the steps from the great entrance that lead to the stately square, and then went walking leisurely along the streets to the haven of Susy's desires. The Colonel left her there, where she wished to be, absorbed and happy, bending over a counter full of toys, then, promising to return for her in time for luncheon, he walked a little way up the street thinking of the wondrous change which had come into his life, and resting in tender admiration on the thought of this bright star which had risen to lighten his somewhat dark and solitary path. Surely, surely, it must be for the good of all. His dear and excellent sisters would recognise the fact when they knew more of Susy, of her unselfish goodness and sweet happy nature. Tempy, too, would be far happier in the end with such friend and companion at hand, than she had ever been before. Of late her letters had not satisfied her father. He was glad that she should have something more suitable, more feminine than boys' society. Charlie Bolsover was certainly not the companion he should have desired for either of his children. The Colonel had many perturbations on the score of Charlie. Aunt Fanny was naturally carried away by her warm feelings and affectionate nature, the Colonel used to think. She had even on one occasion hinted at a possibility for the future, upon which the Colonel had immediately and most decidedly put his absolute veto. Charlie was the last person in the whole world to make a good husband to Tempy or any one else. The sooner he was started for life, the better for himself and for everybody else, and most especially for Tempy, who was sixteen, and would soon be no longer a child. All these very consequent and rational suggestions were in the Colonel's mind as he walked leisurely along the street. He had given Susanna half an hour by his watch for her shopping. Then the Colonel himself suddenly succumbed to temptation. Susy with all her youthful admiration had never gazed into the jeweller's shining shop front with such covetous eyes as did the grey-headed Colonel now. He had come to the shop window she so much admired. There was the star shining on its blue velvet horizon, the Colonel looked, blushed rather guiltily, hesitated, went in, and presently came out with a little sealed parcel in his pocket, and lo! one more planet had set out of Bond Street. As he walked away he thought of something he should like to have engraved on the back of the jewel, he turned back, not without some confusion, disappeared through the glass door once more, and giving the parcel to the obsequious shopman desired that *Stella mea* should be written upon the ornament with the date of the wedding-day.

CHAPTER XII

'A BOAT, A BOAT UNTO THE FERRY'

Oh where will I get a good sailor
To take my helm in hand?

OLD BALLAD

September is shining upon Crowbeck as upon Piccadilly, glorious September's last golden hours are lingering still; a boat comes peacefully floating on the buoyant waters of Tarndale. A young woman is sculling, her pink dress, her broad back, her bright red curls are familiar to us by this time. She is strong and used to the task, and the boat makes way rapidly. A fat gentleman in knickerbockers and a garb of many colours is steering, while a handsome young man dressed in white with an amber tie and a broad white felt hat is lolling in the bows, languidly running his slim fingers through the water.

'Delightful morning, nothing like a fine September,' says the stout gentleman, heartily, giving a jerk to the rudder as he pulls at his watch with the other hand.

'Take care, Uncle Bolsover, you're running us in,' cries the girl, in her loud, not unmusical voice.

'Take care, Uncle Bol,' says the young man, with a drawl, 'you have been steering quite straight till now, and Tempy too has done very well. I like to float smoothly along with *no* jerks.'

'Don't talk nonsense, Charlie,' says the girl, looking round at him with her bright blue eyes. 'Remember *you* have to scull back all the way.'

Uncle Bolsover has by this time got out his watch with some effort, for it is very large, and tightly wedged into his belt. 'One o'clock!' says he. 'Time's up. By Jove! there's Jo fishing under the pine-trees! Capital! Hulloa, Jo, you are to come back to lunch. Tempy won't stop. She says she has to go home.' And good-natured Uncle Bolsover, with another jerk of the rudder, turns the boat's head to shore with many cheerful signs and halloas.

Jo comes forward quietly from his station under the pine-trees, and begins to wind his tackle.

'Got anything in your basket, Josselin?' asks the languid youth; the words are carried clear across the water.

Jo, for answer, lifts the cover of his shabby basket, which is filled with silver to the brim.

'He was out by six,' says Tempy, who dwells on her brother's achievements with sisterly pride. Then, with a dash of the oars, the girl turns the boat's head in towards the little promontory where her brother is standing. Some charm, delicate, shifting, incandescent, falls upon the lake, and its banks, upon the swallows still darting in long curves along the water, upon the people in the boat, upon Uncle Bolsover and smiling Tempy, and silent Charlie; upon the old Manor Farm across the lake with its spreading trees all changing for September. Everything is lovely on every side. Lambdale is divided into tender shadows, and Crow Crag stands piled between the lights. A thousand, thousand flashing ripples seem floating up to meet the boat from the far end of the lake where the Hall chimneys are to be seen smoking for luncheon, and farther still are the roofs and gables of Friars Tarndale beyond the elms. At the foot of Crowbeck the little promontory is starting out from land, shaded by a grove of pines. Between their straight stems springs a wilderness of flowers and feathery grasses, tangling and delicate, and tasted by the droning bees all the summer long. Here the young fisherman, motionless for hours past, had been established with his tackle, just stepping from light to light into the shadow as it slid from beneath his feet. A little farther on was the landing-place by the boat-house, where the Place boat fastened by a rusty chain was bobbing and basking on the water among a shoal of minnows.

As Uncle Bolsover was carefully steering in, and looking over his shoulder for posts ahead, Tempy rowed slowly and more slowly.

'Oh dear! for the last time, Charlie,' she said, with a sigh; 'you are going, they are coming back; everything is to be different.'

'Not everything,' muttered Charlie in a low voice. 'Some things won't change,' and he looked hard at Tempy's face. It was Charlie's image of home, of conscience, of truth in life, almost the only one he had. She too looked up; she scarcely understood him at first, then, suddenly, the girl's heart began to beat, she forgot her boat, forgot her oars, and Uncle Bolsover; the whole lake seemed flowing, upheaving in some strange sympathy, she caught a crab and would have fallen backwards if Charles Bolsover had not leant forward, seized the oars with one hand, and pulled Tempy back with the other.

'Take care,' cries Jo from the shore. 'What are you thinking of, Tempy?'

'By Jove! that was a narrow escape, my dear,' pipes Uncle Bolsover, starting forward and half upsetting the boat.

In the meadow just beyond the pines, George Tyson, who is at work with his scythe, looks up, hearing the splash of oars, and leaves his gleaming circles of steel and feathering grass, to come down to help to pull them in; but before he can reach the landing-place, Charlie Bolsover, with more agility than might have been expected from such dazzling white flannel, is already out and standing on a jutting rock, holding the boat-chain, of which he throws the end to George.

'Jo, you row back, there's a good fellow,' says Charlie, standing firm on the shore and helping out Tempy. 'I left some books up at the Place; I'll be back with them directly.'

Jo gives one of his shaggy glances, deliberately shoulders his basket, and without more ado steps into the boat.

The squire looks slightly perturbed. 'Thank ye, George,' says he abruptly, in return for George's rustic salutation from the shore. 'Don't be longer than you can help, Charlie,' and Uncle Bolsover again looks at his watch, as if to make up by extra punctuality for any lack of prudence. Charlie's feelings for Tempy have been discussed by the family conclave before now, and indeed Aunt Fanny is not against the match from her own point of view, but they all feel that the Colonel's prejudices are not to be disregarded. However, the squire reflects that this is Charlie's last day, he is going back to Oxford at once. The Colonel himself could not object to his fetching his books. So the two young people are left standing side by side for the last time in the fragrant shade of the pine-trees promontory.

On the opposite shore of the lake, Tarndale village climbs the mountain sides just where they divide into a gorge. Sometimes, as now, this gorge is shining with light and innumerable reflections, sometimes it is covered by mists and silver shadow. In stormy weather waterfalls suddenly stream down the steep sides of the mountain, dashing in white flashing lines from rock to rock. But on fine days the channels are dry, the lake lies calm, the boats put out, the fisherman with his sail floats by on his way to the creek where the trout lie sleeping, the swallows swim in the sweet air, the cows from the Manor Farm come out straggling knee-deep into the water. The sweet, demure intoxication of the place and time seems to reach to the very heart of all things, animate and inanimate. George Tyson, the farmer's son, who is something midway between those two conditions, might have seemed a loutish fellow in London streets, but to-day, as he stands with his gleaming scythe mowing the grass on the slope of the Crowbeck meadow, any painter of dreams might have taken him for a figure of mythology, a young god of country things, a lingerer from the golden age. For a minute he looks up at the two, as they pass along out of the shade of the pines, skirting the meadows, by the path that leads to the Place, and then he goes on with his work. Tempy herself might have stood for some blooming nymph of the hills. Her thick auburn locks were piled and twisted round her head; her dress was of gingham, a rough straw hat shaded her smiling eyes. A greater contrast than the two cousins, who suited each other so well, could scarcely have been found. Charlie Bolsover was dressed in the extreme of fashion, with every charm by which art could detract from natural good looks. He was handsome, dark, slender; he affected a manner even more than fashionably soft and modulated. Jo once said that Charlie's hair was velvet, his eyes black satin, his coat plush, and his manners silky; but such as he was, jewellery, lavender-water, jimcrackery, notwithstanding, he seemed the most interesting person in all the world to the young nymph looking up so sadly with her innocent blue eyes, for the time of parting was at hand.

'I may come up with you, mayn't I?' said Charlie, and Tempy, all changed somehow, gentle and simply yielding, agreed.

When did she not agree to Charlie's wishes? To her cousin she was almost always gentle, though her manner by the rest of the world might have been characterised as bluff.

Tempy, fresh and kind-hearted, conceited and diffident too, as such people are, was yielding enough, for all her decision, to those she loved. She walked on quickly; she did not want to let herself dwell upon Charlie's leave-taking. She forced herself to think of many very tangible preoccupations in the way of those changings and shiftings, flappings and dustings, which in civilised countries herald the approach of new-married and other important people. The girl had, among other things, a general cheerful sense of her own importance; and that the world could not possibly get on without her – neither her father nor her stepmother, any more than the very competent housemaids in charge of the Place. This conviction was a consolation to her in many of the subsequent trials and disappointments of life, although, in her case (as in other people's), these trials and disappointments often consisted in the fact that she discovered that others *could* get on without her better than she expected. Could Charlie get on without her? she sometimes asked herself, as she did to-day again, treading the clover and the meadow-street, breaking the little twigs from the hedge as she passed, and feeling somehow that to-day was not like any other day for either of them. Once she looked up, it was for an instant only; she could not meet the force of the fixed gaze that was turned upon her.

'I'm looking good-bye,' said Charlie simply, seeing her blush up; and then again Tempy raised her blue eyes, and he saw in them something so gentle, so innocently tender, that a sudden conviction came over him, some overpowering sense of her goodness and affection, of the reality and all-importance of her feeling. What was he, to be loved by so true, so dear a creature – he who had no future to bring her, not even a clear past for her innocent eyes to look through? What was he, to dare to love her? And yet, as he looked, he knew, even without words, that she loved him, and this seemed reason enough, even in *his* troubled life, for him to try to win her.

'Tempy, Tempy,' he said, scarcely knowing what he said, 'don't you know what it all means?' He spoke with a burst of strange emotion, triumph, passion.

George Tyson, sharpening his scythe, looked up again from the meadow, and saw them standing side by side near the brown cow in the upper field. From the boat, far away upon the water, Uncle Bolsover could still be heard shouting a cheerful view-halloo. The girl neither heard nor heeded it all; she cared not who was there, she stood passive, stirred by a wonder. Girls think of love as of something all round about in life in the hearts of others; when they first dimly feel that they, too, are touched or swept onward by the great tide, their whole girlish heroism rises to assert their independence. For an instant the lordly Tempy stood with sudden conviction of love in her heart, absolutely sure, outwardly unmoved, silent and still for an instant. Then the whole world burst in upon her senses; the blue sky arching in triumph over her head, the birds flying in the air, the music of life all around, the rustling leaves, the voices floating from the water, all seemed but a part of the great thing which had changed the whole of life for her. Charlie's looks, so familiar, so strong, and so gentle, seemed, like words, to speak, to order, to entreat.

'Tempy, why don't you answer?' he cried.

Then she looked up at last. 'Yes, I know what it means, Charlie,' she whispered; and the young fellow overcome and touched to the heart, shaken from self and from his fantastic egotism and fancies, caught her suddenly for an instant.

'Tempy, you won't let them part us?' he cried; 'we belong to each other now.'

CHAPTER XIII

STELLA MEA

> Gremio. – *Nay, I have offer'd all, I have no more;*
> *And she can have no more than all I have:*
> *If you like me, she shall have me and mine.*
>
> TAMING OF THE SHREW

Charlie was gone, and Tempy remained by the lake-side to prepare for her father and stepmother's home-coming, and to ponder and wonder over the difficulties that lay before herself and Charlie. Would her father ever consent to their marriage? In time, in time, thought Tempy. Jo, her sympathising friend and brother, looked ominously sympathetic.

'If only he had any profession, and if only he hadn't spent so much money,' said Tempy, turning very red. She was too straightforward to disguise the truth from herself, and she began already to feel accountable for Charlie's misdeeds.

'If only he had any prospects at all,' said Jo, gloomily.

For Charlie was not the heir, though Uncle Bol made him an allowance; another uncle somewhere in South America was not the less entitled to his rights because his address was somewhat uncertain. People had imagined that Aunt Fanny's savings would come to Charles, but Tempy knew that most of these moneys had been engulfed in a desperate speculation of Miss Bolsover's, from which the squire had also suffered. This dearly-bought experience had been useful in helping Aunt Fanny to point a moral when not unfrequent letters arrived from Oxford containing expostulations, explanations, and tradesmen's accounts. Charlie had all the Bolsovers' love of cheap finery, and a special aptitude for more expensive amusements as well. He had shown himself a reckless youth, unpunctual, unpractical, experimental, driving up unexpectedly at different hours of the day and night in fresh dilemmas, and without money to pay his cab. On one occasion (just before being sent down from Oxford) Charlie had persuaded Jo to join him in some venture there on a neighbouring racecourse, where Miss Bolsover had miraculously appeared, parasol in hand, and, with great spirit and presence of mind, extricated the two boys then and there from the hands of a couple of sharpers. The Colonel was specially bitter about this affair; with paternal sympathy he considered Jo to have been misled, but he had no excuse for his nephew, and even refused to see Charlie again before he went abroad.

Poor Tempy gave a great sigh as she remembered this episode and its possible influence upon her fate, but she trusted her cousin. He had promised her on that occasion that he would bet no more, and he had never failed Tempy yet.

Tempy had constituted herself Charlie's guardian of late ever since he had outgrown the legal authority of Uncle Bol and of a certain Mr White, his mother's cousin, to whom he still, from habit, used to apply for advice and forgiveness on occasion. The Revd Samuel Wilberforce White was a worthy but preoccupied man, dwelling among the pianofortes in a modest lodging in Soho, and one who, taking life philosophically himself, found it difficult to realise the overwhelming importance of other people's failures and successes in their own estimation. He was a hard-worked man, well on in years, with a bad head, a smiling face, and with so many troubles and delinquencies on his hands that Charlie's particular share scarcely counted so seriously in the incidental confusion all round about the curate's house, as at Bolsover, that decorous and orderly establishment, where life passed to the sound of punctual gongs, docketed, discussed, and labelled for weeks beforehand.

Mr White, from long practice, could grasp the heavier troubles of life far better than its proprieties and social problems, and, being a simple-minded person, he took it for granted that others were like himself. He also remembered what it was to be in love, and could sympathise with Charlie's state of mind when that young gentleman, immediately on arriving in town, poured out his feelings over a pipe by the study fire; and the result of their conversation was that Charles Bolsover that very evening was ringing at the visitors' bell of Eiderdown's Hotel, and was being shown up by a boy in buttons to his fate. Alas! the little page was no cupid in disguise.

The young lover tried to look even more at his ease than usual, but his heart was in his mouth, as the saying is, when he was shown into the room where Colonel Dymond sat reading the paper by the light of two candles in tall silver candlesticks. The blinds were drawn, the room was dark, but the light fell upon the Colonel and his handsome profile and his gold eyeglasses. He looked up when the young man was announced.

'Why, Charles, are you up in town?' said the unsuspicious Colonel kindly, willing to condone the past in his present new-found happiness. 'How d'y do? How did you leave them all?'

This friendly greeting gave the youth some hope.

'Much as usual, Uncle John,' said he, with a faint revival of spirit. 'They are all quite well. Aunt Fanny has set up a guitar and another litter of cats; Uncle Bol has been out sailing on the lake, and Jo has caught nearly all the trout.'

Charlie tried to speak in his usual tranquil drawl. He was wondering all the time how he could best begin upon the subject he had in his mind.

'You must stop and dine with us,' said the Colonel, with a magnanimous effort, 'and be introduced to your – your aunt.'

'I am at Mr White's for a day or two,' said Charlie; 'I am afraid he is expecting me home to dinner, then I go back to Oxford, Uncle John. That last term was very unlucky. It has all been very unlucky,' he added, 'and I'm afraid they will look very black when I first get back, but nothing shall go wrong again if I can help it. Mr White has kindly written to my uncle and made every arrangement for paying up what I owe at present out of the funds still in hand; any future claims I must contrive to meet out of my allowance. I can assure you it is a lesson I sha'n't forget. These sort of difficulties do bring home one's utter folly as nothing else could do,' said poor Charlie with some bitterness.

The Colonel was very much taken aback to hear his nephew, usually so indifferent to reproach, speaking in this practical sensible way. He somewhat mistrusted sudden reforms, and had not yet the key to Charlie's change of mind; he was so used to look upon him as a hopeless young scapegrace, for ever suggesting rebellion to Jo and to Tempy, for ever giving trouble and having to be extracted from difficulties, that he was almost disconcerted to find the youth sitting opposite to him, amber tie, cameo ring and all, talking like a man of forty.

'I – I am very glad you take such a sensible view of the past, and I hope you will remember the lesson,' said the Colonel, somewhat perturbed and still anticipating a demand for money. 'Such reckless extravagance as yours makes everybody else suffer, and most especially your good Aunt Fanny, who has been absolutely devoted to you for years past.'

The door opened while Uncle John was speaking, and a waiter looked in, carrying a small paper parcel, which had just come from the jeweller's.

'Oh, take it to Mrs Dymond, she is in her room,' says the Colonel hastily.

The momentary break gave Charlie courage to go on. After all Uncle John is a kind-hearted old fellow, he thinks. He may be vexed at first, he will be sure to relent in a little time. Charlie seems to see Tempy's tender steady eyes before him and to hear her saying, 'Courage! don't waste words.'

'Uncle John,' he said, when the Colonel looked round again. 'There is something else I want to say to you. I came to London to say it. How could I – when could I see you?'

'See me! here I am,' says the Colonel, in a more natural voice, and not unkindly. 'Well! what is it about? I hope no more——'

Charlie, usually so deliberate, so self-controlled, lost his advantage, and the cruel gods having first taken his reason, now allowed him to rush upon his own destruction.

'I don't suppose you will approve particularly, but it's no new thing,' he says, quickly, and starting up to his feet. 'For years past, and especially this summer, I have known that my feelings, Uncle John – in short, that I have fallen hopelessly in love with Tempy. I don't deserve her, but I love her truly, with all my heart; indeed you may depend on me in future,' says Charlie.

But Colonel Dymond, who was quick tempered, who perhaps overestimated his daughter, who had never liked or approved of Charlie, who had expected some confidence of a very different nature, now blazed up in a sudden wrath, which was all the more fierce because the Colonel was usually so gentle. He dashed away his paper.

'You must be out of your mind, Charles. Do you propose *yourself* as a fit husband for my little girl – you who have given us all nothing but trouble ever since you left school? – you who are the last man in the world I should ever think of, or consent to accept as a son-in-law. Of course you have not spoken to her on the subject, and I beg that you will never refer to this nonsense again, to me, or to anybody else.'

'She knows, of course she knows how much I love her,' said Charlie Bolsover, gravely, turning very white, and putting a strong control upon himself. 'You have no right, it is not fair, to speak to me in this way. I don't pretend to be worthy of her, but if she had not loved me I should certainly not have come to you.'

'I have a right to protect my daughter,' cries the father, in his coldest, hardest tone, also getting up from his chair; 'and I am surprised that you should have spoken to her in this – in this most unjustifiable way without waiting to ascertain my wishes. She is sixteen and romantic; she will get over a girlish fancy, and thank me for what I am doing. As for you' – confound your impudence, thought the Colonel – 'I really need hardly point out to you how undesirable you would be in every way as a son-in-law. Your own fortune is involved, you are past twenty-one, but you have never shown one single sign of moderate application. Your chosen companions are people of blemished character and reputation – the less I say of them the better – and now you come to me, after a whole year of disgrace and – and laziness and – rustication, and ask me to give you my child,' cries the Colonel, relapsing into a fatherly and not unnatural fury.

At that moment, as the two were standing side by side – Charlie still very pale, and with difficulty mastering his indignant protest, though all the time some secret consciousness of justice and right-doing upheld him, the Colonel flushed with suppressed anger, and trembling nervously – at that very moment, the door opens again, a smiling, sweet apparition comes in flying with floating draperies across the room, holding a shining star in one upraised hand.

With a bright, and sweet, and happy face, unconscious Susy stands there. 'Oh, how good of you, how lovely,' cries the smiling young goddess – 'oh, thank you, dear John. How——'

The apparition suddenly stops short, seeing that her husband is not alone. She turns confused from one to the other; looks from the Colonel's flushed face to Charlie with the pale and trembling lips, and finding that something is seriously amiss, the brightness dies away out of her face.

'This is Charles Bolsover, Susanna,' says the Colonel, very gravely, but regaining something of his usual manner with an effort. 'I am glad you like your star, my dear, but will you leave us a minute to finish our business?' And Susanna slowly turns, and, looking rather anxiously from one to the other, leaves the room once more. All the brightness seemed to go with her, but something less angry remained behind. 'I may have seemed hasty,' says the Colonel as she left. 'I beg your pardon, Charles;

but it is truest kindness to speak plainly on such occasions, and not to try to ignore the difficulties – the insuperable difficulties, in the way of such a match. Some marriages are impossible and absolutely unsuitable in every way.'

'Did you find that out when *you* married, Uncle John?' said Charles bitterly. 'It's no use my staying,' he went on. 'All I have to say is that I love Tempy with all my heart, and with all my strength, and that you are doing us both a cruel wrong. I shall not be the only one to suffer, remember that,' said Charlie. 'I shall not change; you don't know me, if you think I shall ever change; and she won't change.'

'And I am not in the habit of changing my mind either,' said the Colonel, dryly. 'If there is any other way in which I can help you at any time——'

'You needn't insult a man,' said Charlie, furious, and feeling that he was losing his head.

He went away very quickly, without taking any further leave. He was dreadfully shaken – bitterly, miserably disappointed. He brushed past Susanna in the passage, and got out into the street he hardly knew how. Susy went back into the room where her husband was sitting; she was haunted by the poor boy's wild looks, she could not forget them.

The Colonel, after a few irritated stamps up and down the room, sat down to his papers again with a final tug at his well-fitting coat collar, and tried to dismiss the disagreeable subject from his mind. He felt perfectly satisfied with himself, and he told himself that he had done his duty as a father and a colonel in the army, and that it was his part to save his child from so outrageous a marriage, and yet he could not prevent an undefined and continuing feeling of irritation and apprehension. What business had the fellow to put him into such an unpleasant position, to throw all the disagreeables of interference upon him? Poor little Tempy, it was a girlish fancy; it would soon pass off. . . .

It ought to have been easy enough to put such an unpleasant subject out of his mind now, with Charlie gone and no Tempy at hand to look reproach, and while so sweet an audience stood beside him ready to agree to every one of his conclusions. To Susy, indeed, the Colonel made very light of the whole affair.

'Didn't you know Charles Bolsover? He has set up some absurd nonsense about Tempy. It is simply preposterous, and out of the question, and I told him so very plainly.'

'Oh! John, didn't you give him any hope?' said Susy, looking troubled.

'What the deuce should I give him any hope for?' said the Colonel, testily. Then he softened again as he read the expression in Susy's eyes; it was not reproach, not even protest, but a sort of diffident sympathy, pity, bewilderment. 'Some day, when Tempy knows more of the world, when she realises what sort of a fellow this is, she will be grateful to her old father,' said the Colonel; 'and she and you, Susy, will do me justice,' he added, with some reproach in his tone.

'We can do you justice now, John,' his wife answered, gravely, raising her eyes to his, and as she looked she saw his grave face brighten up.

Perhaps a juster, less impressionable spirit might have made things less pleasant than Susy could bear to do. For, to tell the truth, though she tried to believe her colonel must be right, she could not forget the poor lover's stricken looks. Hers was not an uncompromising nature, and herein lay the secret weakness and the flaw in her true heart. Some harmonious spirit presided at her birth, and gifted her with qualities perhaps too well suited for this life, so that from her childhood she seemed to fall naturally into her place, into her daily task, to unravel quietly and patiently the tangled skein of other people's wishes and opinions. It was not that she did not feel for herself, but she was slow to express what she felt, diffident to assert her convictions; she could look at life from that wider and less selfish point of view, which helps some people through its chief perplexities, but which also takes away from the useful influence which those exert, who possess the clear unswerving minds, which belong of right to the rulers, the leaders of the world. Susanna was not born to lead; she was a follower for many years. Then came a day, still far away, when she found she must cast away the guidance of others, be true to herself, to her own instincts and nature, or fall utterly in her own estimation.

People like Charlie, all unused to self-control, become immediately desperate somehow, where calmer natures have not begun to give up hope. As he hurried along more than one passer-by was struck by his pale and miserable face; one young man, something older than himself, no other indeed than Max du Parc, on his way to a dining-house close by, stopped short as young Bolsover reeled against him, and took a step after him thinking he was ill, but Charlie strode along the road and disappeared in the crowd. He hardly knew where he went nor cared what became of himself; an excitable, nervous boy, he was overpowered by this new feeling, the most unselfish he had ever known, by this sense of responsibility, and by the knowledge that it was not only his own happiness but Tempy's which was at stake. He was completely over-mastered for the time by the possibility of being irrevocably parted from her. It seemed to him like a death sentence, as if he had seen the Colonel put on a black cap and heard himself condemned then and there. He found himself at the curate's door after wandering about the streets for an hour. The Colonel and his wife at Eiderdown's Hotel were just sitting down to their eight o'clock dinner; Mr White, concluding that Charlie was with his uncle, had long since finished his own modest meal, and had rushed off to a class-meeting. Charlie flung himself into the curate's chair before his hard-working table, and found some comfort in pouring out all his bitter disappointment, misery, indignation, in a long endless letter to poor Tempy, written on the paper of the Society for the Relief of Distress in London. The secretary might have found some difficulty in dealing with Charlie's case. When Mr White got home not long after from his vestry meeting he found the poor boy all changed and disordered, sobbing and broken-hearted, with his head upon the table and the letter lying on the desk ready to be sent to post.

Charlie's head ached, his hands burned, he had tasted no food all day, for he had been too much excited to eat coming up in the train. His smart clothes were dirty and crumpled, his black satin hair was rough, his black velvet eyes were dim and heavy.

'Poor boy!' said kind Mr White. 'Cheer up, Charlie, don't give way like this. The Colonel will relent in time when he sees you are in earnest. Come and post your letter to her and get some supper,' added the curate, not knowing what other consolation to suggest, nor how to provide food for his guest at that time of night. His housekeeper was a punctual virgin who locked up her stores and only kept her lamp burning up to a stated hour. 'There's a very good eating-place close by. I shall be glad of some supper myself,' Mr White continued, and he put his arm into Charlie's and brought him out into the street, still dizzy, but also somewhat comforted by such kind words and sympathies; and he gratefully followed the curate, who knowing the district, led the way to a certain *Café Fourchette* some ten minutes off.

CHAPTER XIV

PRINCE HASSAN'S CARPET

Where, though I, by sour physician
Am debarred the full fruition
Of thy favours, I may catch
Some collateral sweets and snatch
Sidelong odours that give life . . .

C. LAMB

There are places in London where without crossing the Channel, and by merely walking in at a doorway, you find yourself, as in some fairy tale, suddenly whisked off a hundred miles from home into some new world and state. The language is different, the faces are different, so are the gestures and the very clink of the glasses and plates as the waiters come and go. The chickens and vegetables, the fishes and sauces all taste of a different tradition. You are no longer in England, no longer among English people. The guests come walking out of Balzac and George Sand, carrying French newspapers in their hands which they buy at a little shop, close at hand, which also looks as if it had been caught up bodily from some Paris street corner. Monsieur Fourchette's establishment in Kirk Street is to be known by its trim and well-kept appearance. There is a bow window over the low doorway, and various hospitable inscriptions inviting you to enter. The host himself, prosperous and friendly, stands in the doorway and welcomes you. The coffee-room has surely been transported, all complete with its flies and gilt looking-glasses, from the other side of the water. There sits the *dame du comptoir* established behind her piles of oranges and monster pears; the gilt looking-glasses reflect the flies, the people coming and going, and the lovely lady together with the old grey parrot on the counter, perching in his brass cage, and winking his wrinkled eye at the company. A door at the father end opens and shuts perpetually, revealing a glimpse of a white cook over a bright fire, and busy kitchen-maidens hard at work, and you recognise the cheerful sing-song refrain, '*Deux pommes frites, un bifteck, en avant la matelotte*,' &c., &c., varying with the hour, the man, and the appetite. There are English people here, of course, for the little place is well known, and deservedly popular. You may find clerks and their wives dining economically. There sits an Anglo-Indian, home on furlough, and hospitably entertaining his family. There sit Popkins and Tomkins giving themselves airs at an opposite table. The kind little head-waiter can hardly content them or supply their demands. Next to these are two old generals from the Senior Sabretash Club sharing a bottle of port; but a considerable number of the guests seem to have come from across the water with the rest of the establishment, there are solitary individuals with moustachios out of the Louvre, Henri IV, Henri III, Francis I are all to be seen in turn; some study the *carte* with a lordly air as if it was the Magna Charta, others read their newspapers folded into neat squares like napkins, while others again, *habitués* of the place, fat men chiefly with chains and prosperous waistcoats, settle down leisurely, nod to the waiters, and order their meal with intelligence and deliberation. There are sometimes strange aspects of life to be seen at Fourchette's establishment, tragedies among the champagne bottles and the comfortable clatter and overflow of good things. Yonder is a woman with death in her face, she laughs and quaffs, her cheeks are painted red, but her hollow eyes haunt one across the cheerful place.

Presently enter two male beings with mysterious strides, cloaked, and with sombrero hats which they fling aside as they throw themselves down in tragic attitudes at the first vacant table. Fish-salad and an omelette seem the results of their sombre consultation. At the adjoining table sits a neat little old man, the very contrary to the eccentric type, with a blue wandering eye, a high forehead, and a well-kept grey beard, who has ordered a cutlet and a cup of coffee, and who seems absorbed in a packet of MSS while he waits for his meal. He is soon served, his requirements being small, but the next dinner is laid for two and claims much more of the waiter's attention. Glasses of different shapes, bottles of various sizes are already set out, the champagne stands ready in its ice. The donor of the feast, one of the stout, middle-aged men I have already described, sits impatiently awaiting his guest, who arrives at last, coming up the crowded room with a quick swinging step, looking about as he advances. The guest is Max du Parc, who walks in with a certain air inherited from his grandfather, the tanner at Avignon, which makes people look up and remember him. He stops short for an instant with an exclamation as he threads his way, for he catches sight of the quiet old man with the MSS who has already finished his cutlet and is leaving the place. In reply to Max's greeting the old man puts out his hand with a smile, says a few words and goes his way, while Max at last joins the impatient host, whose temper is bubbling over like the champagne, and who receives him with a 'Late, very late, the wine will be too much iced.'

'Pardon, sire, pardon,' cries Du Parc, gaily, quoting from some opera then in vogue. 'I have been at work until the very last moment upon your business; I wanted to bring you my calculations completed, and——'

'First of all let us dine,' says the fat man relenting into a confidential imperative, as he tucks his napkin neatly into his coat, talking his native French mean-while. 'I have ordered *bisque, saumon, fricandeau à l'oseille*, champagne. Help yourself Monsieur du Parc.'

'With pleasure,' says Max, looking round, 'especially now that M. Caron is gone. He does not approve of champagne.'

'Was that Caron! Jules Caron!' interrupts the fat man with some interest. 'The impossible philanthropist – *l'homme aux moulins à vent* they call him – the vind-mill man. Hein?'

'Yes, that is Jules Caron,' said Max, laughing. 'I suppose I am one of his windmills. He has spent his money and his time upon me, and I am afraid he has had but small return as yet for his trouble. By the way, there is one thing, M. Hase, I want to say to you, which I may as well mention at once. The more I go into the details of your proposal, the more it attracts me, but the more I feel convinced that you do not calculate upon the length of time required to do any sort of justice to the work. Thank you, no more champagne just at present; it is excellent, not over-iced. I am glad I have nothing to reproach myself with.' And Max finished his glass looking handsome and confident as usual.

'The cooking is good here, the champagne of excellent quality,' says M. Hase. He was an editor and a dealer in prints in Paris and London. 'Now, as to business,' lowering his voice. 'I had contemplated publishing three quarto volumes – of which a certain number are to be printed in bistre ink on old vergé paper – with about forty typical illustrations, some etching, some engraving, in each;' and then followed a long technical discussion of *procès* this, *procès* that – prices, sizes, copper-plates, steel-plates, electro-plates, and the possibility of photographic engraving, which had not then made the strides it has done of late years; all this, enlivened by agreeable interludes of fish, flesh, fowl, more champagne, coffee, *liqueurs*.

The stout editor was anxious to bring out an illustrated catalogue of art treasures in England, which was to take its place with other similar works already published by him in Paris. This catalogue was to include a critical description of the chief pictures in the National Gallery and in certain well-known country houses, with illustrative engravings. The champagne dinner was, perhaps, intended to make up for a somewhat shabby scale of payment, for Max was a well-known and experienced engraver, and an etcher of some mark. 'I am ready to offer you the preparation of two of the volumes,' said M. Hase, with a flourish, as he insisted on filling up the young man's glass. 'You have a delicate hand, a pronounced taste. If I tell you in confidence that certain persons in high quarters at the Tuileries have interested themselves personally in the production of these volumes, you will understand that I am anxious to see the undertaking carried through well and honourably; and I need not add that I know you will do us credit.'

'Of course I can do you credit if you make it worth my while,' says Du Parc; 'but I must live, I must earn my living. The work you suggest represents, at least, two years' hard labour. Such work must be up to a certain standard, and unless it is carefully done it is worth nothing at all. I could not live for two years on the sum you offer, much less treat myself to such good champagne,' he added, smiling.

'But why not have two standards?' said the stout man, more and more confidentially. 'Finish up certain favourite pictures likely to take the public, which could be put forward as examples – say the "Venus" of Correggio, the "Ariadne" of Titian, &c., &c. As to the others, we must not be too exacting or too severe in our criticisms.'

Here the conversation was interrupted for a moment by some new-comers arriving and sitting down at the table which Caron had left vacant. One of them called for soda-water and brandy, and some cold meat and bread. Max looked round, then he looked again. He recognised the pale young man whose face had impressed him so sadly in the street an hour before. It was a strange chance to come across him again, and he was glad to see him with a friend, 'a respectable reverend,' as Max in his mind called all clergymen in black waistcoats. The waiter brought the brandy and the soda-water and poured it out, and the new-comer eagerly drained the glass, but in a minute he started up, crying out that 'the room was too hot, too crowded; was there no cooler place to be quiet in?'

The waiter looked round, and pointed through an open door to another room just across the passage.

'Come along, Mr White, come along,' cried poor Charlie, excitedly, rushing to the door, and followed by Mr White, who took up his friend's hat and stick and hurried after him.

'In short, make up your mind,' continued the editor, who had been talking all this time without noticing Max's distraction. 'There are plenty to undertake the work if you will not.'

'I tell you my feeling frankly,' said Du Parc, again returning to his own affairs, 'I like your proposal. I have spent the whole day in the Gallery, and I am simply lost in admiration at the marvels it contains; but,' continues the young man, who has a dogged matter-of-fact conviction that a workman is worthy of his hire, 'I feel I cannot give up so much of my time at the price you offer, and, as for sending out half-finished engravings, it is against my conscience. Imperfect etchings are bad enough, where the workman himself undertakes the responsibility of his misdeeds, but to turn out a bad engraving, a scamped mechanical copy, to traduce a Titian or a Velasquez, it is like a blasphemy against the spirit of art. Here is the list I made out to-day,' he continued, 'and the time which each picture should take at the rate at which I can work. Look it over, and see if any compromise occurs to you. I will call upon you in the morning, and, meanwhile, Monsieur Hase, many thanks for your excellent hospitality.' And Max gets up, and, to M. Hase's unconcealed annoyance, shakes hands warmly, takes up his hat, and wishes him good-night.

'He is evidently in earnest. That old fanatic Caron has put him up to all these absurdities,' thinks the ill-used Hase, while Du Parc, unconscious of offence, nods once more, and turns away.

As he turns, he sees a letter lying by the chair where Caron had been sitting. Max picked it up. It was not, however, as he had for a moment feared, part of Caron's usual correspondence, suggesting gunpowder and plot and police intervention with every dash of the pen. This was an envelope belonging to the Society for the Organisation of Relief, sealed and stamped, and directed, not in Caron's careful calligraphy, but in an unknown scrawling English handwriting to 'Miss Dymond, Tarndale.'

A waiter came up as Max stood reading the address.

'The monsieur who has just gone must have dropped the letter. He is in the other room,' said the man, 'you will easily find him.'

There was, alas! no difficulty in finding poor Charlie. He and his friend were standing in the doorway, surrounded by a knot of wondering people. Mr White, annoyed, perturbed, was trying to lead Charlie away;

the poor boy seemed almost in hysterics. The brandy had been too much for him; acting on his excited brain, it had completely upset him. He had suddenly burst out laughing incoherently, and talking nonsense, he was bewildered, giddy, irritated at being followed by waiters, napkins, remarks. 'He has been drinking,' says one of the two generals, who was finishing his bottle of port.

'I seem to know his face,' says the companion general staring through the open doorway at the showily-dressed, dilapidated-looking youth.

'He is ill, he has *not* been drinking!' cries poor Mr White, emphatically addressing Max, who came up at that minute, holding up the letter. 'Oh, thank you! it is ours. Just post it, will you? and can you help me to get him out? Come along, Charlie; you will be better outside,' said the kind man, still holding him up. Max quickly came to their assistance, and between them they got the poor fellow safe down the passage, out into the street, with its cool night sky. 'Thank you, I shall take him home,' says the breathless curate, as he beckoned to a passing hansom. 'He has been upset and in trouble. It is nothing serious. Good-night,' cries Mr White, regaining his composure. 'Cabman, drive to 36 Jubal Street,' and away rolls the cab with the pastor and the troublesome sheep inside.

As the cab starts off, the generals, having paid their bill, come away, lighting their cigars.

'I remember that young fellow now,' says one of them. 'It's young Bolsover; I've seen him at his uncle's in Wimpole Street. Are you going on to the Sabretash to-night?'

Needless to say the generals were both going on to the club, where they told the story, and where in due time it reached the Colonel's ears. He was less annoyed than usual by his nephew's escapade. He was more and more satisfied in his own mind of the wisdom of his own decision, and not sorry that his decision should be so satisfactorily confirmed.

CHAPTER XV

MONSIEUR CARON'S HISTORY OF SOCIALISM

Thanks to the human heart by which we live.
W. WORDSWORTH

Meanwhile Max du Parc is walking along the dark streets that lead from Soho into Piccadilly. Late as it is, little children are still out and about, staring at the gas-lights in the shops, sitting on the door-steps. A little girl comes up shyly with flowers to sell, another with matches; a man goes by with a truck, shouting out pine-apples in the darkness; squalid people walk up the middle of the street boldly, for the night clothes their rags; then, finally, Du Parc reaches Piccadilly and its blaze of lights and rush of flourishing life. He passes the corner of Eiderdown's Hotel, where Susanna dwells. The Colonel comes out at the swing-door, on his way to the club, and Max recognises him and passes on. He could almost have laughed out, suddenly remembering the worthy couple's pottering progress among the pictures that morning.

There is a certain similarity in the dry, independent humour of French people and Scotch people. Max inherited, together with his father's gaiety, a certain grim, sarcastic turn from his mother and the Forgies, her ancestors. Madame had but little now to remind her of the Forgies and her early days at Pollok, N.B., except indeed the faithful memories she still retained of her youth. She had christened her only son Maxwell, after the laird of the village where she was born, for although Madame du Parc had never seen Pollok again, and the good laird was gone to his rest, the Scotch lady still looked upon him as a person of European importance. It was after over twenty years' work as a teacher in a provincial school that Madame, with infinite condescension, had accepted the hand of the arithmetic master of the establishment, on his promotion to a small appointment at one of the colleges in Paris. Their united savings were judiciously invested in the villa at Neuilly, and it was a just cause of satisfaction to Madame du Parc to reflect that this 'pretty propriety,' as she called it, would eventually go to her son, who also, on his mother's side, enjoyed the privilege of the ancient blood of the Forgies flowing purple in his veins. The late Monsieur du Parc was from the South of France and of very humble extraction. His parents had worked in a tan-yard at Avignon; his blood was not blue, but of the ordinary colour; nevertheless it was to the Du Parcs that Max, as they called him, owed his good looks, his dark eyes, his frizzed black hair, his well-cut limbs, and marked features. The nobler Forgies, as represented by Madame his mother, must have been squat and sandy in appearance; at the same time, they were a determined and hard-working race, with a certain wholesome tenacity of life and will, in which the elder Du Parc had certainly been wanting. He had been an honest man, an enthusiast in his youth, almost entirely led by one or two of his friends, chief among whom had been Monsieur Caron, a paper manufacturer in the neighbourhood, with an establishment near Paris, a man of some note, a philanthropist and benevolent experimentalist, belonging to any number of isms and prisms of fancy. When Du Parc died at Paris, not very long after his marriage, this Caron, the owner of the paper-mills, who was a generous and exceptional person, came forward to help the widow with her boy's education and later on paid the fees for his apprenticeship. Max, by his own wish, was bound to an engraver. His patron would have taken him into his business, but Maxwell had set his mind upon art in some shape. His mother meanwhile kept house, as we know, took in her boarders, gave lessons in English or in French, let the Villa du Parc furnished to families from England and Ireland, to Monsieur Marney, the newspaper correspondent, and his family among others, and made out a respectable living, showing no lack of energy and shrewdness in her arrangements.

So time went on. Max worked hard and with credit to himself and his patron; he made friends, he grew up tall and active and animated, he had plenty of spirit and natural gaiety and *insouciance*, although sometimes of late when he came away from his long visits to his godfather, leaving him absorbed in his dreams of possible truth – for his dreams were of the truth – Max had begun to ask himself more seriously for what did he himself live? Of what did he dream?

Everybody wishes for happiness of one or another sort for themselves, or for other people – for those they love, or for the human race. Caron's heart ached for the human race; his hopeful nature pointed to better things in the future than those which were now past. Max, who was younger and more definite in his desires, might have confessed, had you cross-questioned him, that he still possessed a personality – still wished for as much happiness as ever he could get for himself, for his old mother, for his many friends, as well as for his country. And by happiness he certainly meant success, power, money, luxury, even that tangible sign of comfort and well-being, for the romance of his nature had been somewhat hidden and over-shadowed by constant toil, by a certain loneliness at home, and by its dry economic aspect of things. Max could not help feeling some effort of mind in suiting himself to the worthy people among whom he lived. The necessity for living among them had induced a certain recklessness of acquiescence which perhaps savoured of contempt. As he grew older year by year the high-bred artistic instincts in him put him into a different relation with his natural companions in life; but Caron was the person with whom he used to feel most at ease.

Caron's influence was very great, and the constant presence of that gentle philosophy had ended by strangely impressing the young man, who was the son of an optimist be it remembered, although his mother was a practical woman. The human race is farther away at six-and-twenty than at sixty years of age. Madame du Parc was frightened by her son's enthusiasm. She was grateful for Caron's kindness, she profoundly mistrusted his '*lubies*,' as she called them. 'Yes, *lubies*, that is the word. Listen, Max, do not let him persuade you to leave your work for the good of any of those humanities,' she used to say. 'Humanity is nothing at all – nothing but lazy fellows, who will not work, and are turned off from their *ateliers*.'

Caron, much as he loved Max, his godson, never attempted to persuade him to anything. The old man came and went his own way, busy with his own schemes. He was an excellent man of business; his manufactory flourished, notwithstanding his experiments. Sometimes Caron himself would leave the whole thing and mysteriously disappear for long periods. He would go abroad, or come over to London on errands of his own. To-night, when Max met him at Fourchette's, young Max had not even known that Caron was in England; but his godfather seemed pleased to see him, had given him his address, and told him to come to him in the lodging where he was living, over a little toy-shop in the Brompton Road.

In his lodging in Brompton, by the light of the green lamp in the window, the old man sat, with Max beside him, later into that night, bending across his papers; there were maps of Europe, piles of MSS written in a delicate foreign hand, heaps of letters neatly strapped and ticketed. Everything Caron did was orderly, and, if one may use the expression, respectful. To him nothing was common, nothing worthless. He was an amateur, perhaps a dreamer – but there was a certain gentle magnanimity and method in his visions which comprehended small things and humble as well as great ones. He showed a certain *courtesy* to the troubles and wants of life which is far less commonly met with than the pity they must always inspire.

Max, looking round the shabby room, could not but contrast it with that of his friend the editor's, where, amid disordered heaps, crumpled proofs, and dirty velvet cushions, among gilt confusion and statuettes and vulgar ornamentation, Hase, extended in his arm-chair, sat puffing out the law. Here, in the shabby, orderly room, Caron, with grey hairs, bent at his work, patiently searching for the truth, deferring to others even while he was planning their interests.

What Caron had to propose to Max was also a publication, one which he had at heart. A publication for the people, a book to be illustrated by Max, with lithographs and wood-blocks and engravings and cheap carbon reprints of photographs, on the cheapest paper, to be published at the lowest price – a history of Socialism from the earliest times, a history explaining the real meaning of the word, of that divine theory by which the rich and the good and the capable were to teach their secrets to the poor and the dull and the incapable, to show them how to be self-respecting and respected by others, industrious, and commeasurably rewarded. The disciples of truth, of justice, were to break the bread of spiritual life and dispense it to the hungry multitudes still, alas! fainting in the wilderness. The free were to teach freedom, to teach hatred of wrong, and at the same time just rebellion against unjust oppression. It was to be the modern version of the miracle of the loaves and fishes. Caron's life and heart were in his book. He had worked at it from time to time for years past, writing it down in words, living it in his daily life more eloquently than by any words. The chapters were to begin with the earliest mythologies and dawn of natural science, and travelling on from one age to another, from one mind to another, from law to law, from experience to experience, to record the progress of knowledge, of truth; to point to an ever-continuing faith in the human race, an everlasting hope; to preach the true fusion of interests human and divine, help and love meeting want and callous ignorance, knowledge and justice raising misery and crime. We must not fear, said Caron, to preach the salutary transforming elements which, alas! with pain and violence at times divide true and natural laws from those social phenomena which are nothing, only illusions of men's making. Evil is but a force to be lifted to higher aims; crush it and imprison it by bonds, and sooner or later these will fail to constrain. . . .

Max listened in silence as his godfather talked in his low calm voice, so gentle, so convinced. All his life he had loved and admired the old man, respected his generosity, and trusted it, even though he sometimes smiled at his Utopian dreams. Max knew that Caron, who had been born rich, had spent more than one fortune in his day upon others; he had helped his generation with a liberal hand, and spent hundreds for the good of men who had never benefited by his aid. Max was one of the exceptions to the many who owed so much to him and who had repaid him with failure and lazy ingratitude. This one pupil had honestly and gratefully profited by Caron's past kindness. Du Parc thought, as Caron talked on that night, that he could have made a fine drawing of the eager, delicate, pale face shining in the light of the lamp and of its own hopes. 'This book – this book shall be a Bible to the poor man,' cried Caron: 'it shall show him how to hope, how to work, how to admire those who have gone before – our high priests, our martyrs, our teachers. How many more are there whose names are scarcely known? You, Max the engraver, know poor Meryon's work; he too was one of us. And now,' said Caron smiling, 'though I have promised your mother that I would never try to tempt you from your career and your own work to help me in mine, the moment has come when you can help me materially by your work. Leave that man with the champagne and the shabby offers, and come and labour for me, and for those who want your help. Leave that editor with his low ambitions and vulgar promises.

High quarters! Is this a time when the Emperor should be amusing himself with picture-books? I mistrust that Hase. He wants your name, Max, rather than your talent. But you have a conscience, my son, as your father had before you. Have nothing to do with that shopkeeper; I have better work for you to do.'

'You know very well, Papa Caron, that I should always do any work you wanted,' said Du Parc, laughing. 'I think you are hard on M. Hase. There is no harm in his making a bargain any more than in my refusing it. His offer is shabby, but as times go it is not so bad; before I accept or reject it, tell me exactly what it is I am to do for you.'

And Caron, who for all his dreams was a clear-headed and extraordinarily capable man of business, explained at some length and with great exactitude what it was he required.

What he required was enough to take up the young man's time for many months to come, and consequently it was impossible for Max to hope to accomplish the work which Hase had proposed to him. The drawings from the National Gallery must go to some one else; one of the smaller volumes, that of the private collections in the west of England, Du Parc hoped he might still execute.

It was not without a sigh that he rang at the bell and asked to see M. Hase the next day, and explained to him the reason of his change of mind. In vain Hase augmented his offers. Du Parc would only agree to undertake the one volume. 'Carons wants his drawings done at once. If you have any more work for me later I shall be glad of it,' said the young engraver, 'but I can't fail him.'

'You are wrong, altogether wrong,' cries Hase. 'You are engaging yourself to an old imbecile who has no notion of affairs.'

Max came back early next day to the toy-shop, and for an hour or two the master and his pupil sat together with the first few chapters and elaborate notes of the book of books spread on the table before them, while Caron stood explaining, dilating, planning this illustration and that – symbols, compositions that were to take the working man's fancy, to remain imprinted on his mind, and lead him insensibly to the truth. One picture most especially of his own composition did good old Caron insist upon. There was to be a rising sun; the rays of light were to be shining upon a great globe scattered with the wrecks of past ages, fetters lying broken on the ground, spears and cannon overturned, and the symbols of war rent asunder, the rainbow of peace and universal tranquillity shining in the sky.

'Of course I can draw anything you like, but what do you think all this will do?' Du Parc said, laughing at last almost against his will.

'Men will note this. Those who have not patience to read my words will see your pictures, and will ask what the meaning of the riddle may be. The voice of Truth is not to be silenced, the very stones cry out,' said Caron, gravely. 'All life is a symbol, a secret to be discovered,'

As he spoke, an open carriage, drawn by two livery horses, stopped at the door of the shop below, shaking the low room with its sudden vibration. In the carriage was seated a beautiful young woman dressed in the fashion, and an older man – grey, military, upright – by her side. At the lady's desire the servant jumped down from the box and went into the shop, apparently to make some purchase, and, while the carriage waited, it so chanced that a beggar in many rags came up, followed by a shabby woman with a sleeping child wrapped in a tattered shawl. The window was open, and the two men in the little room which was close over the toy-shop could not help assisting at the scene. The man shuffled up, and in a whining voice began to ask for money to get his tools out of pawn, and somewhat rudely touched the lady on the shoulder, to attract her attention.

'How dare you! Be off, you fellow;' cried the gentleman, starting from his seat with sudden irascibility. 'Take care, or I will give you in charge on the spot;' and he called angrily to the coachman to drive on. The coachman whipped his horses, and one of the wheels just grazed the beggar's foot.

'D—— them!' said the man to the woman, as the two heaps of rags stood side by side on the pavement looking after the carriage.

'I could drive in a carriage too, if I had one,' said the woman, with another oath. Then she looked up, for Caron was leaning far out of his window, and calling to attract their attention. 'Here,' he cried, 'get your tools out of pledge, my friends; do your own work; do not demean yourself to beg of others,' and he threw down a couple of half-crowns, which rolled in different directions across the pavement. While the beggars leapt to catch them, the occupants of the carriage returning on its wheels saw the scene. The young lady looked up in amazement at the eager grey head and outstretched hand, the gentleman pulled angrily at his moustache, the servant came out from the shop with some parcel, the whole equipage rolled away. Du Parc had drawn back into the shade of the curtain. 'I know that girl,' he said; 'she has just married that old fellow for his money. She is a friend of my mother's.'

'She has a candid face,' said Caron. 'Poor thing, she deserves a happier fate.'

CHAPTER XVI

SUSANNA AT HOME

Sweet day, sweet songs. The golden hours
Grew brighter for that singing,
From brook, and bird, and meadow flowers
A dearer welcome bringing.
New light on home seen nature beamed,
New glory over woman,
And daily life and duty seemed
No longer poor and common.
I woke to find the simple truth
Of fact, and feeling better
Than all the dreams that held my youth
A still repining debtor.

WHITTIER

People's lives as they really are and people's lives as (for all their experience of the past) they imagine they are going to be, are very different. And yet reality has often a great deal more spirit and invention in it than the most romantic day-dreams – it is less gracious, less *poseur* than one's own imagination, but at the same time it is a great deal more amusing and original.

When tired Susanna got out of the train and looked about at the sweet country place which was henceforth to be her home, she had a feeling not unlike that with which one imagines a bird flying into the rustling depths of some cool green tree. The Tarndale line stops short in a garden shaded by green, where roses are clustering in the hedge, beyond which shine the sweet evening gleams of Tarndale water. The passengers alight into fragrance among sweetbriar and flower-beds, and disperse by degrees: some cross the lake in boats, some walk away by the lanes that lead to the village, others may be seen disappearing across the moors and uplands, where the roads climb to meet the sky. For Susanna an open carriage was in waiting, a couple of flags had been set up on two poles, and as she alighted she was greeted by a cheer from half a dozen assembled urchins led by a stout foreign-looking gentleman, who came forward, heartily grasped her hand, and finally saluted her on the cheek with a flourish of his hat. Mr Bolsover always looked exactly the same, but his clothes were new for this occasion; he wore a dark green velvet hunting suit, with a horn slung across his shoulders, knickerbockers, green stockings, buckled shoes. He had assumed a general air of gala and cheerful jauntiness to which every possible adornment of button and shirt-stud added brilliance.

'Welcome, my dear Susanna, welcome. Here you are at last among us. Here is my wife come to meet you. You will find the others at the Place all expectant! Get in, my dear, get in,' and her new brother-in-law, replacing his hat carefully on one side of his head, gallantly leads Susanna by the elbow and hoists her up the steps of the barouche, on the back seat of which sits an elderly, bony lady in glowering satin, who shuts her parasol, bends forward, and receives Susy with a kiss not unlike a postman's rap at the door. 'Caroline insisted on coming in Tempy's place' continues Mr Bolsover. 'Tempy, slightly indisposed, is waiting at the Place; get in, John, get in; Car as you know prefers the back seat.'

It was one of Mrs Bolsover's many peculiarities always to sit with her back to the horses, and the Colonel and Susy being placed in the seat of honour, Mr Bolsover leaps in himself, banging the door several times in succession. The porters and the children give a second straggling cheer, the carriage rolls away by the shady road skirting the lake, which is all rippling and edged with reeds and birds, and many starts and plashes among the fringing grasses. Susy, shy, wondering, confused, sat silent, smoothing out her folds and wraps, feeling herself raked by Mrs Bolsover's two steady scrutinising eyes.

Aunt Car was accustomed to Aunt Fanny's gorgeous elegancies, to her fifty years; she cast a disapproving glance at childish Susy's soft flounces and delicate clouds and frills, they seemed affected and airified to the elder lady.

'I remember you at Vivian Castle,' says she in her deepest accents, 'you were there with your grandfather. I hope you will not be dull down here with all of us. I suppose you have always been used to live with old people?'

'Oh, yes, always,' says Susy, rather confused. The Colonel feels vaguely disconcerted by his sister's greeting, but Mr Bolsover has begun immediately pointing out the remarkable objects along the road, the barn and the haycocks and the five-barred gate and other subjects of common interest. Mr Fox's new hotel by the lake, the Fletcher's cottage upon the hill-side, the gates of Bolsover Park with the big trees leading up to the house. It was all new to Susy, but every branch and twig and stone seemed to be a part of the elder people's lives, and as they rolled along by the scenes of his youth, the Colonel forgot his years and his passing irritation in the silent welcome of the old haunts; he could not but contrast this home-coming, with his happiness by his side, with all the gloom and forlornness of the past ten years of his life.

It never occurred to Colonel Dymond that everybody else was not as happy as he now found himself. Now, they, too, would know her, thought the simple-minded gentleman, and to know her was to love her.

His heart was full of gratitude and tenderness, he thought of the green pastures and still waters of the psalm. Surely King David might have had Tarndale in his mind when he wrote his psalm.

Colonel Dymond, so methodical, so deliberate in his ways, so scrupulous in his attire, so hasty at times, as precise people are apt to be, was a true-hearted and single-minded man, strung up just now to some higher mood than was his wont. He had determined when he married to make others as happy as he was himself. When he thought of his sad and silent home, now once more brightened to life by that sweet and conciliatory presence, it seemed to him impossible that those who loved him should not rejoice for him and for themselves as well.

The Colonel took it for granted that Aunt Fanny would be of the same mind as the rest of them, according a benediction all the more valued because it was not lightly bestowed. He pictured to himself Tempy warm-hearted, welcoming, Fanny with accomplished arms outstretched – a prop, a guide, an invaluable adviser. Car might make a few good-humoured jokes, perhaps, but he could trust to Car's kind heart, very soon she would learn to prize his Susy. And then one cannot wonder that John Dymond looked kindly and admiringly at the sweet figure by his side; he could not but note its grace and gentle presence, and the sober girlish expectancy of Susanna's eyes, as he thought with a proud thankfulness of the lovely soul he had discovered in its fair and gentle shrine.

John Dymond felt a better and more important person somehow for his charming young wife, who trusted him, and looked up to him – and who shall blame him if he also felt it was not without reason that she did so? He had been kind to Susanna and to her mother; he was prepared to do more if need be; and of this need be, the Colonel had little doubt in his mind. Mikey and Dermy's education must be attended to without delay. Bohemia is certainly not the place in which to study the rules of the Latin grammar, and the Marneys were, it must be confessed, for the present at least, dwellers in Bohemia.

As the Colonel sat quietly in his place driving along the lane, his mind travelled right away, as minds are apt to do, to a Winchester ball some twenty-five years before, and to the days in which he had waltzed with pretty Mary Holcombe, Susy's mother, less beautiful even then, however, than her daughter was now. All the past seemed like a far-away burst of tears and laughter to the grim sentimental old fellow, only he told himself that now at sixty the present was best.

That candid, grave face, those sweet innocent eyes, that rare smile which delighted him when it came, all seemed like a rainbow after rain, a token of happiness after long trouble and difficulty. The carriage turns in at two wide gates; Susy's heart begins to beat.

The Colonel looks out eagerly.

'Do you see Tempy?' says he. 'Is that Jo?'

A dog barks, the butler and the footman come to the door, the carriage stops, the butler advances, the footman retreats, the dog wags its tail and gambols up and licks the Colonel's boots.

'Where is Miss Tempy, where is Mr Jo? Down, Zillah – down!' says the Colonel, impatiently.

'Miss Dymond is upstairs; you will find Miss Bolsover in the drawing-room, sir,' says the butler. 'She has just ordered tea. Mr Jo was in the 'all a minute ago.'

The Colonel looks somewhat disappointed, the footman throws wide open the drawing-room door, and as the wedding party enters the room, followed by the dog, a quivering pile rises from the sofa where it had been heaped, a trophy of flounced muslin, of ribbons, of yellow ringlets and glittering ornaments. It advances, serious, awful, with an artificial smile, and does not speak.

'Well, Fanny, here we are,' says Uncle Bolsover, with a hasty attempt at a rally. 'Train late, of course. Better late than never – eh, John? I mean, of course, as regards the railway,' says the squire, suddenly confused.

'This was good of you, Fanny, coming over to make us welcome,' says the Colonel, wincing, but following his brother-in-law's lead. 'Here she is come home to us,' and he turned to Susy, who was standing rather frightened in the middle of the room.

'How do you do?' says Miss Bolsover, advancing with a glittering kiss for the bride; then turning to the Colonel; 'I hope you will excuse poor Tempy's absence, John. She has been entirely upset by her letters, by all that has occurred, or she would have met you. I have advised her to remain in her room for the present.' Then, changing with alarming politeness, 'Are you tired after your journey, Mrs Dymond? The servants are bringing the tea; they have been hard at work, poor things, preparing. I hope you will find everything comfortable, but of course we none of us knew what you would wish or what you were accustomed to.'

'I – I am accustomed to nothing at all,' said Susy, blushing up and pretending to laugh, but somehow she felt more inclined to cry. This terrible, ceremonious Aunt Fanny and her cheap scents and furbelows and attentions, Tempy's absence, Tempy, her own friend and companion, whose welcome she had counted upon, who had written so warmly, who now seemed to turn against her; Mrs Bolsover, still staring her out of her countenance – it was all like a frightening dream.

'Is Tempy upstairs?' said Susy, looking imploringly from the grim Mrs Bolsover on the sofa to the still more alarmingly affable Aunt Fanny. 'Is she really ill? May I go to her?'

'Thank you,' said Aunt Fanny, pearling her words, 'you are most kind; but for the present she is best alone. I am taking her back to Bolsover with me for a few hours' entire quiet; it is better for her to be with those she is accustomed to for the present.'

'But she knows me quite well, indeed she does,' cried Susy, longing to escape, to see Tempy, to know what was amiss, to 'have it out,' as girls say.

Aunt Fanny looked at the Colonel.

'Is it your wish, John, that the child should be further upset? We have only been able to calm her with the greatest difficulty. She will see *you*, of course. But give her time.'

The Colonel, feeble-minded man that he was, turned in bewildered consternation, turned from his wife, of whom he was not afraid, to his sister-in-law of whom he *was* afraid.

'Perhaps, my dear Susy, you had better wait a little,' the Colonel faltered. 'As our good sister suggests, I'll go up and see her directly,' and he walked straight out of the room.

Susy flushed crimson, and looked from one to the other; she too was upset, she too was over-wrought; she felt a strange, heavy pain in her heart. Was this her own home, her home-coming; was this her new life? Were these the people whom she had determined to love with all her heart? To love Aunt Fanny! It seemed about as easy to love a muslin toilet-table, pincushions, scent bottles, and all. What did it all mean – why these looks, these reserves? Was it her coming that had brought such trouble? Oh! what business, then, had she there? Even John had turned away. Oh, it was cruel of him. What had she done! what had she done! She looked appealingly at Mr Bolsover, as if he could explain it all. As she looked across the room with a sinking heart, she seemed to see spread out as a picture before her the many years to come, Mrs Bolsover for ever sitting on the sofa with her fixed stare, for ever serious, for ever disapproving; Miss Bolsover, so big, so pink, with her false curls and plaits and heavy playfulness, arranging, marshalling, ordering everyone about. Was this her home? The over-crowded room, with its stuffed birds and gilt frames and stag-horns and sprawling legs, seemed to oppress Susy like some nightmare.

Even the kind old squire, in his fancy dress and Vandyke attitudes, had got upon Susy's nerves; she scarcely did justice to the friendliness with which now he came up, trying to make things more cheerful.

'I see you grasp the situation,' said he jauntily. 'We are all used to do as we are told here – eh, Fanny? – all used to it, and we have all found by long experience it is the best thing we can do,' he hastily added, seeing a pink eye flashing round upon him.

Perhaps Miss Bolsover felt that a crisis had arisen; perhaps she had suddenly realised that a young republic was threatening where she had ruled so long. Her plans were deeply laid, and simple as they seemed, the events had been arranged with an elaborate care, which was almost defeated, however, by a very simple move on Susy's part, for suddenly in the doorway she sees her husband leading Tempy, and followed by Jo, who had been upstairs all this time vainly endeavouring to persuade his sister to come down. But was this Tempy who had come down, and who stood motionless while Jo strode up to meet his young stepmother, with a shy, but friendly greeting? Was this Tempy, with downcast looks and swollen eyes, gloomy, passive, with a dull expression like that of a person half-bewildered and asleep? Her dress was tumbled, her looks were changed, even her curly red hair looked limp and straight.

'Tempy, darling – Tempy, what is it? Is it because I have come?' cried Susy, running to her with outstretched arms, with a sudden rush of natural emotion, so warm, so true, so different from all the hysterical agitation that it carried everything before it; Susy's whole heart was in her kind face. 'I have been so longing to see you,' she cried. 'Your aunt says you are going back to Bolsover Hall. Don't, *please* – don't go away now that I have come.'

Tempy looked softer for a moment, let herself be kissed, but only sighed, and did not speak. As Susanna released her, the Colonel came up.

'I must add my own request, my dear child, to Susanna's. Notwithstanding your good aunt's wishes, I confess your departure would wound me deeply,' said the Colonel, plucking up some spirit at last.

'We will send her back to you in very good time, John,' interposes Aunt Fanny, blandly, taking the girl's hand in hers. 'Tempy only needs a few hours' quiet at the Hall with us, and she will come home braced and prepared to do her duty, and to accept your will – and Mrs Dymond's,' adds Miss Bolsover, with an odd intonation. 'You, of course, are able to command, but if Tempy takes my advice, she will do what is not only for her own and present happiness but for that of us all.'

'I don't know what the deuce you mean,' says the Colonel, testily, and suddenly losing his temper.

No wonder poor John Dymond found himself bewildered. There was Fanny defying him, Caroline frowning, Susy, whom he had seen for all these days, so bright, so radiantly happy, so easily pleased, now standing pale, silent, and repulsed. Bolsover alone came up to the Colonel's expectations; you could always count upon Bolsover. Hitherto John Dymond thought he could have counted on them all. He could hardly believe that this strange, new, terrible Fanny Bolsover, so elaborate and frigid, was the ideal of goodness and amiability which they had all looked up to for years. And Tempy – was this *his* Tempy, so sullen, so changed? Nor did the Colonel find himself much more at his ease when he presently met the intelligent look of his sister, Mrs Bolsover.

'I knew all along how it would be,' said Aunt Car, who had, among other habits, that inconvenient trick of occasionally speaking her thoughts aloud.

'Knew *what*, my dear Car?' said Mr Bolsover, by way of turning off the conversation agreeably; 'that we should all be here – a family party, happily united at last?'

'I little thought how it would all be,' said the Colonel. 'Tempy, you must make your own arrangements with your aunts, and by all means attend to their wishes. But, remember, *this* is your natural home;' and the Colonel, turning very red, and feeling his temper beyond his control, marched out of the room, leaving Tempy still standing as if she was dazed.

Susy ran up again, and put her arms out; Tempy looked at her with strange eyes. 'Tell papa I will come back,' she said; 'tell him it is no want of love.' Her lips quivered; she did not finish her sentence.

'Come, my child, come,' cries Aunt Fanny, suddenly, extremely animated, and swooping down from the other end of the room. 'Car, do not keep her standing; Frederick, you can walk;' and before any one could speak another word or interfere in any way, Miss Bolsover throws a shawl over Tempy's head, motions Mrs Bolsover to the door, and in another minute has urged, borne, carried her niece by main will out of the room. In the hall Miss Bolsover's maid was waiting ready with a bag, the butler was holding open the carriage-door, Miss Fanny, with something of her brother's agility, thrusts Mrs Bolsover into her usual place on the back seat, hurries passive Tempy up with the assistance of the maid, and when the Colonel, after a few minutes' struggle with his temper, came back from the garden, he found the room cleared, doors open, the company gone; Susy had fled upstairs; only Frederick Bolsover remained for a minute, disconsolately standing in the passage, talking in a low voice to Jo.

'Fanny is too abrupt – too abrupt,' says Uncle Bol. 'Means well, of course. Poor Tempy looks wretchedly out of sorts. These family entanglements are always trying, very trying. Charlie is expected back, I believe; there was a telegram to Fanny this morning.'

Tempy's looks had startled her father, even more than they did her uncle. He was deeply hurt by her departure; he had trusted in her sympathy. The prosaic old fellow felt as if he had had a shock, as if all the quiet foundations of his life had been shaken. He nodded to his brother-in-law and son, but he went straight into his study, and began tearing open the pile of bills and letters upon the table. But his hand trembled so much that he threw the whole parcel down upon the table in a heap.

Then he crossed the room to the window, which he threw wide open. As he came back to the table, he saw his own figure reflected in the glass against the light, and he turned away his head. He was troubled – agitated. Could it be that, perhaps, Tempy was right in the main – that she had a right to resent his marriage? He had never imagined anything like this. The poor Colonel's head sank upon his breast. Just then the door opened, and Jo came straggling in.

'Don't you want lights or anything, papa?' said the young fellow, with a touch of real sympathy in his voice. The father did not answer, but held out his hand without looking up. 'Tempy is terribly cut up about Charlie Bolsover,' said Jo, shyly. 'You know he is very fond of her, papa, and they have been constantly together all this time. But these love affairs never last,' says the experienced youth, 'and I'm sure Aunt Fanny had been giving her chloral. Tempy hardly knew what she was about.'

'Love affairs!' says the father, looking up extraordinarily relieved. 'Is that the meaning of it all? Chloral! How very wrong and imprudent of your aunt. Confound Charlie Bolsover! So he's at the bottom of it all, is he? He deserves to be shot!' cries the Colonel.

CHAPTER XVII

JOSSELIN'S STEPMOTHER

It was a valley filled with sweetest sounds,
A languid music haunted everywhere. . . .
From rustling corn and song-birds calling clear,
Down sloping uplands which some wood surrounds,
With tinkling rills just heard, but not too near;
And low of cattle on the distant plain,
And peal of far-off bells now caught, then lost again.

T. MILLER

It was not in Susanna's nature to dwell upon vague and melancholy suggestions. With the morning came a hopeful aspect of things, a burst of sunshine and youthful spirits. Crowbeck, notwithstanding the heavy cornices and hangings, began to look more home-like. The new mistress of the Place was down betimes; her presence seemed already to brighten everything. She went out into the garden for a few minutes before breakfast; as she stood on the lawn in her fresh morning dress the sunshine set her hair aflame. The hills across the water seemed to be also touched with some gentle mood of rainbow light. The green slopes beyond the lake were green, soft, silent as the sward on which she stood. George Tyson and his father came striding up from the boat-house across the dewy fields, trudging upon daisy-flowers with their heavy, hobnailed boots; the little calves ran to meet them with playful starts and caresses. Jock, the sheep dog, leapt a fence and darted off after some imaginary sheep. Then came Jo, advancing from beyond the trees, with his rod and with fish in his basket.

'Good-morning,' said Jo. 'Look here, I caught all these up by my uncle's boat-house this morning. Tempy was out; she is all right again. Aunt Fanny is always making scares about nothing at all.'

Susy longed to ask more about Tempy and Aunt Fanny and life at Bolsover, but she found it difficult to frame her questions. Jo also seemed anxious to explain and yet reluctant to speak; he, too, had something on his mind.

'I am afraid your sister is very unhappy,' said Susanna at last.

'They are both very unhappy,' said Jo; then, with a heroic effort, for he did not like to hurt his pretty, shy stepmother, 'I think,' said Jo, turning red and looking into his basket, 'if you had known more of Charlie you would have advised my father differently.'

'I!' said Susy. 'I never——' then she stopped short. She was a new-made wife and not yet used to her position, was it for her to disclaim all responsibility in her husband's actions? What did wives do under such circumstances? Susy, in her perplexity, fell back upon another question. 'What has your cousin done to trouble your father so much?' she asked, also with eyes cast down.

'He has been a fool,' said Jo. 'He has spent his own money, and he once got me to back a lame horse – papa never could forgive that. I think this is about the worst, except that row at Oxford, when Charlie was caught and the others got off; and – and I'm afraid there was something else in London,' added Jo. 'Papa tells me he was seen drinking, but Charlie was so cut up, poor fellow, he hardly knew what he was about.'

'One can't wonder at your father's anxiety,' said Mrs Dymond gravely. 'I saw your cousin for a moment in London. I felt very sorry for him.'

Somehow, as Jo talked on, little by little Susy began to find her sympathies enlisted on Charlie's side. 'Poor fellow!' she said pityingly, forgetting her own determination to blame.

'There goes Hicks; papa has done his business,' cries Josselin, abruptly disappearing with his fish as the bailiff issued from the study window. The Colonel followed, and seeing his wife, came up to her with a smile.

'Mr Hicks, I want to introduce you to my wife,' said Colonel

Dymond, proudly; and Mr Hicks, a brown, tattered man, who seemed bailiff to many winds and storms and moors, made a clumsy, smiling salutation to the smiling, graceful young lady.

The new family breakfasted as they had dined, in a triangle at the round table.

Susy poured out tea from behind the old-fashioned silver urn. The Colonel looked round, satisfied, dissatisfied.

'The place seems empty without Tempy,' said he 'You saw her this morning, Jo; when is your sister coming back?'

Jo didn't answer; he was not at ease with his father.

'I am afraid, from what Jo tells me, that she is very unhappy indeed,' said Susy, blushing up; 'that is why she keeps away. She cannot bear to – to differ from you. John, don't you think – do you really think – there is no hope at all for them? Is it possible,' she continued bravely, 'that we may have done your nephew injustice?'

'My dear Susanna, my dear woman,' said the Colonel gravely, putting down his paper and looking fixedly at her, 'pray do not let me hear you speak in this way again. Josselin,' with a stern glance at his son, 'has no doubt influenced you. Do you suppose he cares more than I do for his sister's ultimate happiness? It is no kindness on his part or on yours to interfere – to urge me to consent to Tempy's life-long misery. My duty as a father, and as head of the family, is to decide upon what seems to me best and right for my children and for their good. Do you know that this fellow is a gambler, a drunkard? He was seen drunk in a public eating-house in London the very night he had asked me for my child in marriage. Tempy's husband must be a good, true man, one she can trust, an upright man, who will love her and make her happy and respected. You, Susy, know but too well the suffering that a man with a low standard of honour can inflict upon a high-minded lady.' (Susy turned crimson; she could not answer.) 'We all have to face the truth,' said the Colonel. 'I am sorry to speak of my own nephew so harshly, but I look upon Charles as an adventurer and not uninfluenced by mercenary motives. Why should I refuse my consent if I trusted him, or believed him in the least worthy of Tempy?'

'Papa,' cried Jo, hotly, 'indeed you are unjust to poor Charlie. He is desperately in love; he has been silly; he has no interested motives.'

'I beg you will drop the subject, Jo,' said the Colonel. 'Tempy is rich, as girls go. Even without your share of my property, the interest of your poor mother's money now amounts to a considerable sum, and, by the way,' said the Colonel, glad to change the subject, 'I shall have to get you to help me, Jo, as soon as you are of age, to make a provision for Susy here, who hasn't any expectations or settlements,' said the Colonel, smiling and softening, 'and who would be poorly left if anything happened to me.' The Colonel, as elderly people are apt to do, rather enjoyed discussing such eventualities; neither Susy nor Jo found any pleasure in the conversation.

Jo, with an awkward grunt, got up and left the room. And Susy meanwhile sat silent, looking at the walls of the room, at the Landseer stags, the showy Italian daubs, the print of the passing of the Reform Bill, with all our present Nestors and Ulysses as spruce young men in strapped trousers; then she slowly turned her eyes upon her husband, as he stood with his back to the chimney, erect and martial even in retreat. Colonel Dymond was making believe to read the paper which had just come, in reality greatly agitated though he looked so calm.

He was one of those people who, having once made up their minds, never see any great reasons to alter them unless some stronger will enforces the change. When Susy looked up with tears in her eyes, all troubled by his severe tone, her sweet, anxious, shy look seemed to absolve him, and it won his forgiveness; only Susy could not quite forgive herself.

John Dymond was a weak man, kind-hearted, hot-headed, honourable, and both obstinate and credulous, and created to be ruled. For some years after his first wife's death he had constituted Aunt Fanny into a sort of directress – her unhesitating assumptions suited some want in his nature at the time – perhaps of late he had changed in this respect. It most certainly still suited Miss Bolsover that people should do as she told them. She should have been abbess of a monastery, prime minister of some kingdom where women govern the state. She had not imagination enough to correct the imperiousness of her nature, whereas Susanna had too much to allow freedom to her actions, and so to-day again she gave in with a sigh; the power of sulking persistence which some people can wield was not hers. That gift of adaptiveness which belonged to Susanna Dymond, led her to acquiesce in the conclusions of those she loved.

The Colonel went over to Bolsover in the course of the morning; Susy begged to be left at home. She was busy unpacking, settling down, exploring her domain. She had a grand bedroom, with cornices, red damask curtains, and solemn mahogany furniture to match; there were prints of the Duke and Duchess of Kent on the wall, and of the Queen as a pretty little girl with a frill and a coral necklace. The young mistress of Crowbeck looked about, wandering along the passages of her new kingdom followed by an obsequious housemaid, who led her from room to room. Then she came back to her own pretty boudoir, where her prints and her various possessions were lying ready to be set out: among them was that old drawing of Naomi and Ruth from Madame du Parc's; how vividly she could see it all, and the studio and the neglected garden, so unlike the trim lawns at Crowbeck Place.

Josselin came up to her later in the day as she stood complacently among the girlish treasures. He gave a quick, asking look. Susy shook her head – 'Your father is gone over to the Hall to see Tempy – he ordered his horse just now. He *must* know best,' she repeated with some effort; 'we must trust to him, Jo.'

'We can't help ourselves,' said Josselin. Then he added rather gruffly, 'Would you care to come out with me, Mrs Dymond?' (He had elected to call her Mrs Dymond.) 'I shall have to be back at my tutor's tomorrow, but I should like to show you about the Place to-day. Tempy told me she might be over in Tarndale – I could row you across.' As he spoke some breeze came into the room, the whole lake seemed to uprise with an inviting ripple, and through the open window the distant shriek of the railway reached them from the station in the garden of sweetbriar.

'That is the afternoon up-train,' said Jo in a satisfied tone. 'Charlie is gone back in it. I did not like to tell papa, it would have vexed him too much. I thought how it was when Tempy went off to the Hall last night. . . . She knew he would be coming.'

'Oh, how wrong! how could she!' cried Susy. 'Oh, Josselin, why didn't you warn us?'

'He is gone again,' said Jo doggedly; 'it was only to say good-bye, poor fellow.' And, as the young stepmother, troubled, bewildered, began to exclaim: 'Don't you tell papa,' her stepson interrupted. 'You only know it because I thought I could trust you. You will get me into no end of trouble, and poor Tempy has enough to bear as it is. Let Aunt Fanny tell papa. She sent for Charlie, not I.'

This was true enough, but Susanna felt somehow as if the whole thing was confused and wrong, and jarring upon her sense of right and family honour. 'Listen,' she said with some spirit; 'if ever Charlie comes here again, I *shall* tell your father. At present I do not feel as if I could interfere. But even at the risk of getting into trouble, Jo, we cannot all be living in his house, acting parts and deceiving him. It is not for Tempy's happiness or yours or mine.'

'I know that,' said the young man impatiently. 'Come along, I will show you the way to the boat-house.'

CHAPTER XVIII

THREE ON A HILL-SIDE

True that we must live alone,
Dwell with pale dejections;
True that we must often moan
Over crushed affections.
Let in the light, the holy light,
Brother, fear it never,
Darkness smiles, and wrong grows right;
Let in light for ever.

ANON

Meanwhile poor Tempy sits high up on the mountainside, on a spur of the 'Old Man' that overhangs the village, and stares at the distant line of rail in the valley by which Charlie is travelling away. The little brook ripples by her with many sweet contentful sounds and chords, then a fresh breeze stirs the leaves of the oak-trees round about, and many noises come to her with the rising breeze – the clang of the blacksmith's forge from the village below, and the cheerful voices of the school-children striking like a sort of sunshine from beyond the wood; a cock sets the wild echoes flying, then a cow passes lowing across the road from one sloping pasture to another, followed by its calf, hurrying into green safety. The soft full wind of autumn seems suddenly to gain in life and will; it blows up the ascent. Tempy, as she sits there, listless and depressed, can see the village below still bathed in sunshine, and the team of horses winding round the hill, and the water of the lake lying bright and restful, and a boat zigzagging across from the Place. The boat disappears behind an elder bush, and Tempy, high perched, looking *down* upon her own short life, as it were, goes back to that day which will never be over any more, when she, too, rowed in the boat with Charlie – that happy wondrous day, to be so soon clouded and followed by parting. But she had seen him once more, with his pale, changed looks and faithful tender vows and protests.

Meanwhile the boat has crossed the lake, the sculls dip the placid surface of the water, the boat's head thuds against the end of a long wharf. Jo hooks the rusty chain to a convenient block of wood, then he gallantly hands out his white cambric stepmother, who has been sitting in the bow, dreadfully frightened, but prepared to enjoy herself nevertheless. Susy still practised that sensible, youthful privilege of enjoying the present whenever the sun shone upon it, and leaving the shadowy ghosts and omens of apprehension to take care of themselves. Jo led the way across the flat and by the little village built upon the stream. The place seemed deserted; the men were at work in the fields and in the mines, the women were busy indoors. They met no one but Tim and Tom Barrow, who both stared and curtsied, as they had been taught to do by their mother.

'Have you seen Miss Tempy, Tim?' says Josselin.

'I-sâ-err-a-gwoan-oop-t'-Auld-Mann,' says little Tim, all in one word, 'aafter-Mr-Charles-gotten-into-t'-Barrow-train.'

'Can you understand him?' Susy asked, laughing.

'Yes,' says Jo. 'He says she is gone on.'

Susy trustfully followed her new stepson, holding up her white dress. Their way lay through a farm-yard at the end of the village, where cocks and hens were pecking, and some lazy, comfortable cows were bending their meek horns over a trough supplied by the running stream. Beyond the farm was a little climbing wood of ferns and ling – a wonder of delicate woodland – all in motion, all in life.

'What a lovely green place!' cries breathless Susy. 'Jo, please, don't go quite so quickly. Is this the foot of the mountain?'

'Why, you are no good at all,' says Jo, looking round. 'Tempy can go twice as quick.'

'I am very sorry,' says Mrs Dymond, laughing, and coming out of the shadow of the wood, and finding herself in the dazzling brightness of the mountain-side.

The crest of the Tarndale 'Old Man' towered overhead, the shadows of the clouds were crawling along its rocks and heathery flanks, the foreground opened out shining; beautiful boulders of purple rock were lying on the smooth turf, the stream hurried by, the air became keener and more keen, the country changed as they climbed, the nearer hills seemed to shift their place, to melt into new shapes; under their feet sparkled ling, flowers, specks – delicate points of colour. Susanna's cheeks glowed. There was something exhilarating in the sense of the quiet moor all round about, of the wide fresh air, and the racing clouds overhead.

'There she is,' said Jo, suddenly. 'I thought we should come upon her.'

And so it happened, that Tempy, looking down from a rock above, sees the heads of two figures against the sky coming straight upon her from the valley. She cannot escape.

Why will not they leave her alone? All she wants is to be alone, to live over poor Charlie's parting looks and words an hour ago. How can they ask her to be smiling and complaisant and indifferent, they who are all happy and contented and together, while she is lonely and forlorn? and then as Tempy looks down defiantly she sees them close both beside her. There is Jo with his friendly, home-like looks, and Susy, silent, shy, with those appealing glances, which Tempy scarcely knows how to escape.

The girl flushed up, and turned away; she would not meet Susy's eyes.

'Here you are!' says Jo, cheerfully. 'I thought we should find you here.'

'What have you come after me for?' says the girl, at bay. 'Why won't you leave me? I came here to be alone, Jo. I am too unhappy to be able to pretend, that is why I keep away,' says Tempy, trembling excessively. 'Why do you bring Susanna? If it had not been for her, my father would never have interfered – never, never. Oh, it is cruel – cruel!' Then she turned desperately upon Susy herself: 'Tell papa he can prevent our marriage, but what I am, what I feel, belongs to me and to Charlie – not to you or to him,' cries the girl, something in her old natural voice and manner.

After all, it was a comfort to her to speak – to complain, to upbraid, to be angry.

As for Susy, she flushed up and sighed, she did not know how to answer her stepdaughter's passionate appeal. Poor little Tempy!

'O Susy,' Tempy continued, 'I thought you would have helped us – I thought' – she burst into tears.

'You are all wrong, you know,' said Jo quietly. 'Mrs Dymond did her very best to help you. Don't cry, Tempy.'

How different words are out of doors on a mountainside to words shaped by walls and spoken behind doors! Jo's matter-of-fact, Susanna's simple eloquence of looks, of pitiful feeling, touched Tempy more than any elaborate words, to which indeed she could scarcely have listened at first.

'Your father would consent if only he thought it right,' Susanna was saying. 'He knows better than you or I what is best. Ah, you don't know,' she continued, speaking not without that personal feeling which gives so much meaning to the most common-place expressions, 'you must never, never know, Tempy, what it is to be linked with a man for whom you are ashamed, whose life is one humiliation. I have lived this life,' said Susy, turning very pale. 'I know what your father dreads for you, and that even his dread is not so terrible as the reality. I bore it a little while; my mother has lived it ever since I can remember,' her voice faltered. Tempy looked hard at Susy, and now it was Susy who began to cry.

'You don't understand, any of you – nobody can understand anything for anybody else,' Tempy said relenting; 'but I should like to be with papa again, only promise me to say nothing hard of Charlie – not a word – I cannot bear it, I will not bear it.'

'O Tempy, that you may be sure of,' cried Susy, eagerly, 'only come!' and she took the girl's not unwilling hand.

The three walked back in silence, Jo jogging ahead with his hands in his pockets, not absolutely satisfied with this compromise, and sorely tempted to whistle. Susanna and her stepdaughter, hand in hand, following silent, but reconciled in that odd intangible way in which people sometimes meet in spirit after a parting perhaps as silent and unexplained as the meeting.

Some great events had been going on meanwhile overhead, the clouds were astir beyond the crests of the hills. Vapours were rising from behind vapours, strange shrouded figures were drifting and flying across the heavens, steeds and warriors followed by long processions of streaming fantastic forms; while the southern hills were lying in a golden stillness, the head of the valley was purple, black – angry. The summit of the mountain was half hidden in mysterious rolling clouds. Sometimes from one break and another break in the rolling clouds, yellow streams of gold seemed battling with the vapours; you might almost imagine the wonderful, radiant figure of the lawgiver coming down out of the glorious haze.

'We had better make haste,' said Jo; 'it looks like a storm,' and he trudged faster and faster. The cows were whisking their tails and crowding together in the meadow as they crossed by a stile and a short cut back to the farm again. The opposite side of the lake above Crowbeck was calm and bright, with the sky showing through soft mists, midday shining through silver. They come round by the village with its straggling lodging-houses, built of country stone, with slated roofs from the quarries. It is civilised life again after the solemn mountain-side.

Doctor Jeffries dashes by in his gig. 'You must make haste,' he cries, flourishing his whip; 'the storm is coming.'

Then they meet George Tyson from the Place, coming with bread and provisions in a basket.

'Come down and help to shove off the boat, George,' says Tempy, who, as usual, gives her orders with great authority, and so they come again to the sandy shore.

'Ye'll ha'e nobbut time to get hoam before the storm,' says George, pushing them off with a mighty heave.

It took all Jo's strength to get the boat across, for the breeze was freshening every moment.

The Colonel was waiting anxiously at the other end. He helped out his wife with anxious care. 'Jo, you should have come home by the road,' he said severely. He held Tempy's hand for a minute as he helped her out. 'I wanted you home, my dear,' he said.

'Papa, I am glad to come, but I shall never change to Charlie,' said Tempy, looking hard at her father.

The Colonel's face grew set and black – 'I am sorry to hear it,' he answered, and he dropped her hand, and turned abruptly away and walked ahead with Susy. The storm broke before they reached the house.

After her first warm greeting the girl seemed to draw back. She did not sulk, she did not refuse to join them, but every day seemed to divide her more and more from her father and stepmother. She used to go for long walks across the moors and come back tired and pale and silent. She took to sewing, a thing she had never cared for in her life, and she would sit stitching all the evening silent, gloomy; no longer monopolising the talk with cheerful vehemence, scarcely hearing what was said. Miss Bolsover used to come in sometimes, and then Tempy would brighten up a little. One day Susy found them sitting hand in hand by the fire. Tempy seemed to be in tears, Miss Bolsover was wiping them with her lace pocket-handkerchief. Aunt Fanny looked up with her usual flutter as Susy came in.

'You mus'n't mind her liking to tell me her little troubles,' she said.

'Tempy knows well enough I don't,' said Susy, with a sigh.

'She must come and stay at the Hall. We know how to cheer her up,' Aunt Fanny continued playfully.

Susy looked at her. Miss Bolsover turned away with a faint giggle. Generous eyes have looks at times which malicious orbs cannot always meet.

CHAPTER XIX

DAY BY DAY

I vowed that I would dedicate my hours
To thee and thine – have I not kept the vow?

SHELLEY

There are bits of life which seem like a macadamised road. The wheels of fortune roll on, carrying you passively away from all that you have done, felt, said, perhaps for years past; fate bears you on without any effort of your own, you need no longer struggle, the road travels into new regions, time passes and the hours strike on, and new feelings and new unconceived phases arise while you rest passively with your companions. Perhaps meanwhile some of us have left the romantic passes and horizons of youth behind, reaching the wider and more fertile plains of middle life.

Susy, who was young still, embraced the calm of middle age with something like passion. By degrees she took the present in, and realised little by little where she was, who she was, how things were, in what relations the people among whom her lot was cast all stood to one another. She realised her husband's tender pride and affection for herself, and his anxious love for his children; realised the deep pain and bewilderment which any estrangement between Crowbeck Place and Bolsover Hall would be to him. Susy no longer wondered, as she used to do in Paris, that the kind old Colonel had not become more intimate with his son and daughter; he loved them and they loved him, but too many rules and trivial punctualities seemed to stand in the way of their ease. It is as little possible to be quite natural with a person who is nervously glancing at the clock to see if it is time to do something else, as it is to write unreservedly to a friend who dockets and dates your letters for future publication, or to talk openly to a superior whom you must not contradict. For Susy there was rest in these minor details, after her chaotic experience, the order, the tranquillity of all this suited her, and she tried more and more to suit herself to her husband's ways and habits, to show by her life the warm and loving gratitude she felt in her heart. When Susanna Dymond first came to Tarndale as a bride she was not very different from what Mr Bolsover remembered her at Vivian Castle; she was tall and harmonious in her movements, specially when she was at her ease, her face was of changing colour, her eyes were clear like two mountain pools, her brown hair was thick and soft, the tint of the bracken in autumn, as the squire once gallantly said, with all the lights in it. There were two Susannas some people used to think, one young and girlish, with a sweet voice and smile, with a glad and ready response for those who loved her; the other Susanna was Mrs Dymond, stately, reserved, unexceptionable, but scarcely charming any more.

As the days passed on the neighbours began to drive up by basketfuls and carriagefuls to make the acquaintance of the new lady of Crowbeck. Some came in boats, some on foot, some on horseback to pay their respects to the bride. They would be ushered into the drawing-room, with the glimpse of the lake without, with the stuffed birds and gorgeous chintzes within – those remaining tokens of Aunt Fanny's Oriental fancy. Not unfrequently the Colonel would come in from his study, looking pleased and ready to receive his friends' congratulations, 'brushed up' was the verdict passed upon the Colonel. Tempy, who kept out of the way, was pronounced 'dreadfully changed,' and finally the bride herself was to be commented on as she sat there, placid, reserved, in smartest Parish fashions.

Susy puzzled other people besides her neighbours, who hardly knew as yet what to think of her. To please her husband, who liked his wife to hold her own, to be respected as well as admired, she tried to cultivate a stiff and measured manner, something in the style of her own newly-bought silks and laces; she had lost her girlish look of wondering confidence and simplicity, nobody to see her would imagine that she had ever lived in anything but country society of the most orthodox description. Alone with Jo and Tempy, or walking in sunshine by the green shore of the lake, she would forget this lay figure made up of manners and fashions, but at the first sound of wheels in the distance all our Cinderella's grace of youth and gaiety vanished, all her bright gala looks were gone; there she stood in milliner's rags and elaborate tatters, prim and scared and blurred by the decorum which oppressed her.

At Paris Colonel Dymond had laid his old habits and associations aside, but here, in his old surroundings, with Miss Fanny's pink eye to mark anything new or amiss, his idiosyncrasies returned with a renewed force. Meanwhile, however wanting Susanna might seem to Miss Bolsover's ideas, to Miss Trindle's the vicar's daughter, or to Mrs Jeffries the doctor's wife, Mrs Dymond appeared the very personification of calm and successful prosperity. She was handsome without expression, well dressed without much taste. She had been used to consult the Colonel latterly about her dress, finding her own fancies for the picturesque not approved. Her clothes were expensive, her shoes were French, her gloves were always buttoned, her manners were well-made county manners, composed and somewhat starched. This was the Susanna of the neighbours, and many a girl envied her; but this was not the home Susanna, who, little by little, day by day, and hour after hour melted and warmed and thawed the hearts of the two young people who had met her with such scrutinising looks and divided minds. How often Susy in her early married days had suffered from those glances. Jo had relented from the first moment he saw her standing shyly in the drawing-room, but Tempy used to have strange returns of suspicion. And whenever Susy by chance met one of Tempy's doubtful scrutinising looks she would shrink up suddenly into herself. Or if Mrs Bolsover came in severe and incoherent, or, worse still, if it was Miss Bolsover sneering and civil, then the new married wife would turn into a sort of statue. Susanna used to feel the cold strike upon her heart, her blood seemed to creep more and more slowly in her veins, and her voice died away.

She rarely said much in company, for she had lived among talkative people all her life, but with Miss Bolsover present she became utterly silent. Her nature was not an outcoming one, but very deep in its secret fidelity and conviction. She was not timid, and yet she was apt to be too easily impressed and frightened by the minor details of life. She did not hold her own, when other more self-important people were ready to thrust themselves into her rightful place. She could not ignore the opposition which from the very first had met her, but she never spoke of it. She had a curious, instinctive sense of the rights of those she lived with. She dreaded to jar upon them, to be the cause of trouble or discussion. And little by little she got into a habit of always looking to her husband for a signal. He led the way, he started the conversation, he invited the people who came to the house – dowagers from neighbouring dower-houses, well-to-do magnates, respectable rectors and rectoresses, colonels and generals of his own standing. With the

Colonel's old companions Susy felt more at her ease than with any one else. These comrades in arms were invariably charmed with Mrs Dymond's grace and gentle temper; no wonder they lost their hearts to the beautiful young creature, so sweet to look upon, so modest and ready to listen to their martial prose.

'You should just hear her talking about the Punjaub,' says Tempy, in amazement to her brother.

Tempy used to wonder more and more about Susy. She seemed no longer able to understand her. But perhaps the truth was that Miss Tempy had never much troubled herself to understand her at all hitherto. She used to speculate about Susy now with an odd mixture of affection, of pride, and jealous irritation. 'Was she really happy? did Susy really care for her father?'

'What does it matter?' Jo answers, impatiently. 'You and Aunt Fanny are always for skinning a person alive, and I hate talking about people I'm fond of.'

As for the Colonel, he was delighted with everything Susy did, whether she spoke to others or held her peace. Because he loved her so well, because he spent his money so freely upon her, because she was so good a wife, he took it for granted she was a happy one, and indeed Susy never seemed otherwise. She appeared free to do as she liked in most things, or to submit with good will to her husband and her sisters-in-law. When these ladies contradicted or utterly ignored her, she would smile good-humouredly; and yet in her heart she now and then had experienced a strange feeling that she scarcely realised, something tired, desperate, sudden, unreasonable, almost wicked – the feeling she thought must go, and she would forget it for a time, and then suddenly there it was again.

'What is it, my dear, is the room too hot?' said the Colonel one day, seeing her start up. Miss Bolsover was explaining some details she wished altered in the arrangements at the Place; his back had been turned, and he had not noticed Susy's growing pallor.

'Nothing, nothing,' says Susy, and she got up, but as she passed him took his hand in hers and kissed it, and went out of the room.

She hurried upstairs into her own room, she sank into the big chair, she burst into incoherent tears. Then when she had gulped them down she went to the basin and poured water to wash her troubles away – her troubles – her ingratitude! John who has been so kind, John so generous and good, was this how she, his wife, should requite him for his endless kindness and benefits? By secret rebellion, unkindness, opposition? Ah, no, never, never, thought the girl. And the young wife, whose only wish was to spare her faithful, chivalrous old colonel, did that which perhaps must have hurt and wounded him most of all had he known it. She was not insincere, but she was not outspoken, she did not say all she felt, she put a force and a constraint upon herself, crushed her own natural instincts, lived as she thought he expected her to live, was silent where she could not agree, obliged herself to think as he did, and suffered under this mental suicide.

There is something to me almost disloyal in some of the sacrifices which are daily made by some persons for others who would not willingly inflict one moment's pang upon any human creature, how much less doom those dearest to them to the heavy load of enforced submission, to a long life's deadening repression.

'I for one don't pretend to know what Susanna means or wishes,' says Aunt Fanny.

But although Miss Bolsover did not understand, my heroine in the course of her life changed not, and therefore often changed; she was loyal and therefore she was faithless; loyal in her affection, faithless in her adherence to the creeds of those she loved. When she was young she believed and she doubted; when she was older she doubted less, but then she also believed less fervently; but in one thing at least she was constant, and that was in her loving fidelity to those whose interests were in her keeping.

People did not always do her justice. Max du Parc was one of these. During the following spring, to please Mrs Marney, who had written over on the subject, Colonel Dymond (not over graciously it must be confessed) invited Du Parc to spend a night at Crowbeck. The Colonel's invitation reached the young man at the Tarndale Inn, where he was staying. He had come there to make an etching of a Turner in the collection at Friar's Tarndale, one of those pictures which M. Hase had been anxious to include in his publication. Max, who had been hard at work for Caron all the winter, and obliged to give up the volumes containing the London galleries, had still found time to bring out a smaller collection of drawings from country houses, and had come to Tarndale for a few days. He felt some curiosity as to Susy's English home, and did not like to pain her good mother by refusing the Dymond's somewhat stinted hospitality; so he wrote a note of dry acceptance in return for the Colonel's, and walked over to Crowbeck after his day's work, carrying his bag for the night. The party from the Hall had driven over for the occasion, and passed him on the way.

Susy looked forward with some pleasure to entertaining her French guest, to showing him his own etchings hanging up in her room, to hearing of all the events at the villa, and of Madame du Parc, and Mlle. Fayard, and all the rest; but the guest, though brought to Crowbeck, would not talk, he would not be entertained; he came silent, observant, constrained, and alarming; he answered, indeed, when spoken to, but he never looked interested, nor would he relax enough to smile, except, indeed, when Miss Bolsover graciously and volubly conversed in French with him after dinner. Du Parc left early next morning; Susanna was vaguely disappointed, and a little hurt; his shyness had made her shy; she had scarcely asked any of the questions she had meant to ask, she had not shown him the drawings she had wanted to show him, she had felt some curious reserve and disapprobation in his manner which had perplexed her.

'It is no use trying to entertain these foreign artists and fellows,' said the Colonel after Max's departure. 'They want their pipes and their liberty; they are quite out of place in a lady's drawing-room over here.'

'M. du Parc certainly did not seem to like being here,' said Susy, smiling.

'For my part, I like artists,' says Miss Bolsover; 'and we got on delightfully. I asked him to teach me *argot*; he looked so amused.'

'Well, Max!' Mrs Marney was saying, as she sat under the acacia-tree in the little front garden at Neuilly (where the sun was shining so brightly, though its rays were still shrouded in mist by the waters of Tarndale), 'tell me all about it. Have you seen my Susy? Is the Colonel very proud of her? How did she look? Is she very grand? Is she changed? Wasn't she glad to see an old friend?'

'Yes,' said Du Parc, doubtfully, and lighting a cigar as he spoke. 'She was very polite and hospitable (puff), she is looking forward to your visit (puff, puff), she told me to say so; she sent *amitiés* to my mother (puff); she is changed – she is handsomer than ever; she is richly dressed. Her life seems to be everything that is most respectable and tiresome; she gave me a shake hands; that young miss, her daughter, stared at me as if I was a stuffed animal. The son was away preparing for his college. There was an aunt, a *béguine* lady, who frightened me horribly; an uncle in top-boots, a little man to make you laugh. There was a second aunt, a red, old lady, who was kind enough to interest herself in me, to take me for a walk in the park. She was even amiable enough to make some sentimental conversation. They are extraordinary, those English. Ah! It is not life among those respectables! it is a funeral ceremony always going on. I give you my word,' says Max, taking his cigar out of his mouth and staring thoughtfully at Mrs Marney's knitting, 'it seemed to me as if I was a corpse laid out in that drawing-room, as if all the rest were mourners who came and stood round about. Madame Dymond too seemed to me only half alive, and laid out in elegant cere-clothes.'

'Oh, Max, you are too bad!' cries his mother, in English. 'How can you talk in that hogly way, making *peine* to Mrs Marney?'

'No, I don't think it at all nice of you. M. Max!' says Mrs Marney, reproachfully.

'You are quite right, and I am not nice, and I don't deserve half your kindness,' cried the young man, penitently, taking his old friend's hand, and gallantly kissing it.

'Ah, Max would have liked to be before'and,' said his mother, laughing. 'Susanna is a sweet creature. We must find such another, one day, for my son.'

Max looked black, and walked away into his studio.

CHAPTER XX

A WELCOME

Along with that uprising dew
Tears glistened in my eyes, tho' few,
To hail a dawning quite as new
To me as time.

T. HOOD

Before Susy had been a year at Tarndale she had the happiness of welcoming her mother to her new home. The Colonel kept his promise, and, not only the little boys, but Mrs Marney came over for the summer holidays. Needless to say that it was all the Colonel's doing, and that it was not without some previous correspondence with Mr Marney, who, in return for a cheque, duly received, sent off a model and irreproachable letter to announce his family's departure (*via* Havre, not Boulogne, as the liberal Colonel had arranged for), and also to consult with the Colonel about the little boys' future education.

Mr Marney wrote that Dermy had a fancy, so his mother declared at least, for being a doctor. 'Charterhouse had been suggested,' says the correspondent, in his free, dashing handwriting. 'I do not know if you have heard of my late appointment to the *Daily Velocipede*, and are aware that although I am not immediately able, my dear Colonel, to repay you in coin of the realm for that part of your infinite kindness to me and mine which can be repaid by money, yet my prospects are so good and so immediate (the proprietors of my newspaper have written to me lately in very encouraging terms) that I feel I am now justified in giving my boys a gentleman's education, and in asking you to spare no expense (in accordance with my means) for any arrangements you may think fit to make for their welfare. It is *everything* for them both to get a good start in life. I trust entirely to your judgment and experience. I have been too long a vagabond and absentee myself to be *au fait* with the present requirements. I know it is the fashion to rail against the old-fashioned standard of education, which is certainly not without objections, and yet to speak frankly I must confess to you that, much abused as the time-honoured classics have been, I have found my own smattering of school-lore stand me in good stead in my somewhat adventurous career. I am daily expecting a liberal remittance from my proprietors, and when it arrives I will immediately post you a cheque for any extra expense you may have incurred. As for the better part of your help, its chivalrous kindness, and generous friendship, that can never be repaid, not even by the grateful and life-long affection of mine and me.

'Do not hesitate to keep Polly as long as your wife may require her mother's presence. I am used to shift for myself, and though the place looks lonely without the old hen and her chicks, it is perhaps all the better for my work and for me to be thrown on my own resources. A family life, as you yourself must have often found when engaged on' (here Mr Marney rather at a loss for a word had erased 'military' and written 'serious') 'matters, is a precious but a most distracting privilege. May your own and Susanna's present and future prospects continue to afford you all that even your kind heart should require for its complete satisfaction. And above all remember that you are *to keep my wife as long as you need her.* I shall not run over. With all my regard and admiration for your country and its institutions I do not wish for the present to set foot on English soil. I can also understand my poor wife's dislike to her native land after all that we endured while we still lived in London. When I compare this cheerful place, the brightness of the atmosphere, and the cheapness of provisions, with the many difficulties we have had to struggle through before we came, I feel how wisely for ourselves we acted in turning our back upon the "ould counthree." The one doubt we have ever felt was on the boys' account, and this doubt your most wise and opportune help has now happily solved. Believe me, my dear Colonel, with deep and lasting obligation.

'Yours most faithfully,
'MICHAEL MARNEY.'

Mr Marney's letters need not be quoted at length. The Colonel used to read them with some interest and a good deal of perplexity, date them gravely and put them away in a packet. Susy shook her head when her husband once offered to show them to her. One day, not very long afterwards, with a burst of tears, she found them in a drawer, and she threw the whole heap into the fire.

Towards the end of June, Mrs Marney, smiling and excited, in her French bonnet and French cut clothes, and the little boys, with their close cropped heads, arrived and settled down into the spare rooms at Crowbeck. Jo took the little boys under his friendly wing, and treated them to smiling earth, to fresh air and pure water, and fire too, for a little rabbit-shooting diversified their fishing expeditions, so did long walks across the moors. The two little fellows trudged after their guide prouder and happier than they had ever been in all their life before. Susy was very grateful to Josselin for his kindness. Tempy was absorbed, the Marneys coming made no difference to her one way or the other. If the Colonel had not been so preoccupied about his wife he must have noticed how ill Tempy was looking. But almost directly after Mrs Marney's arrival another personage of even greater importance appeared upon the scene, and a little baby-girl lay in Susy's happy arms.

This little daughter's birth brought much quiet happiness to the Place. The Colonel used to come up and stand by the pink satin cradle with something dim in his steel-grey eyes. 'Is Baby awake?' says Mrs Bolsover one day, following close upon her brother and speaking in her deepest voice, 'what a lovely child, John. What shall you call her?'

'I – I don't know,' says the Colonel; 'Frances, Caroline, are pleasing names.'

'I shall call her little bright eyes,' says Mrs Bolsover severely. 'Look here, Fanny' (to Miss Bolsover, who had also come up); 'just look at this dear infant, is it not a lovely child?'

'Excuse me, my dear Car, you know I'm an old maid and no judge of babies,' says Miss Bolsover airily. 'It seems a nice little creature. Here, here, hi, hi,' and she began rattling her *châtelaine* in the child's eyes, woke it up and made it cry, to the no small indignation of the nurse. 'A pretty little thing, but not good-tempered, and dreadfully delicate,' was Miss Bolsover's description of her infant niece. The report came round to poor Susy after a time, and might have frightened her if her mother had not been there to reassure her. Mrs Bolsover's speech also came round in that mysterious way in which so many insignificant things drift by degrees. Susy and her mother between them determined that the baby should be called bright eyes. Euphrasia was to be the little daughter's name.

How happy Susy was all this time; the day seemed too short to love her baby, she grudged going to sleep for fear she should dream of other things. It was no less a joy to her mother to see Susy so happy, though poor Mrs Marney herself was far from happy; she was unsettled, she was anxious, she was longing to be at home once more. Susy felt it somehow, and dreaded each day to hear her mother say she was going, and anxiously avoided the subject lest her fears should be confirmed. Madame used to write from time to time, and her letters seemed to excite and disturb her friend. 'I am not easy about Mick, Colonel,' Mrs Marney would say in confidence to her son-in-law; 'he is not himself when I am away.'

Susanna suffered for her mother silently, guessing at her anxiety, but not liking to ask many questions. She was also vexed by Miss Bolsover's treatment of Mrs Marney, which was patronising and irritating to an unbearable degree Susy thought, on the few occasions when she happened to see them together. Mrs Marney, in her single-hearted preoccupation, seemed absolutely unconscious. Already in those days rumours of war and trouble were arising; they had reached Tarndale, and filled Mrs Marney with alarm. But what did emperors, county families, plenipotentiaries, Bismarck, Moltke, generals, marshals, matter – what were they all to her compared to one curl of her Mick's auburn hair? 'It is not so much his profession that terrifies me, it's his Irish blood, Susy, which leads him into trouble! You English people don't understand what it is to have hot blood boiling in your veins. Your Colonel is not like my husband. I must get home, Susy dear, now that I have seen you with your darling babe in your arms.'

Was it possible that Mrs Marney was more aware of Miss Bolsover's rudeness than she chose to acknowledge? One day, before Susanna was down, when several of the neighbours were present, calling on the Colonel, Susanna's mother, in her black dress, had come by chance into the room, followed by the two noisy little boys, and carrying that little sleepy bundle of a Phraisie in her arms; Miss Bolsover, irritated by her presence and the baby's flannels and the comfortable untidiness of the whole proceeding, began making conversation, politely inquiring after Susy, and asking Mrs Marney whether she and her children were contemplating spending the whole summer at Crowbeck. 'But it must be a great pleasure to my brother having your boys for so long,' says Miss Bolsover.

'It has been a joy to me to be here, and to welcome my sweet little grandchild,' said Mrs Marney, hugging the baby quite naturally; 'and if it had not been for Susy wanting me, and for all the kindness I've met here from the Colonel, I should never have kept away from Paris so long. A woman with a home and a husband should be at home, Miss Bolsover; it is only single ladies, like you, that can settle down in other people's houses. I am thankful to see my child happily established in such a warm nest of her own, but, dearly as I love her, I want to get back. Somehow I seem to know by myself how sorely my poor Mick is wanting me,' she said, with a tender ring in her voice. The whole sympathy of the room was with the warm-hearted woman. Miss Bolsover was nowhere. The little boys, with their French-cropped heads, suddenly flung their arms round their mother's neck, calling out that she must not go – that papa must come and live here too. The Colonel might have preferred less noise and demonstration in the presence of callers. 'Now then, Michael and Dermot, run away, there's good boys,' said he; 'and, my dear Mrs Marney, I think we will ring for the nurse and send baby upstairs to her mamma. The help and comfort you have been to us all this time I leave to your own kind nature to divine.'

As soon as Susy was strong and well again, and the boys had been received at their school, Mrs Marney departed; nothing could keep her, and the good Colonel went up to London to see her safely off, with her

French box in the guard's van, and her friendly, handsome face at the carriage window, smiling and tearful. Poor Mary Marney, what a good soul it is! he thought as he stood on the platform. What an extraordinary and most touching infatuation for that husband of hers!

'Good-bye; God bless you, Colonel. Write and tell me all about the dear babe,' says Mrs Marney leaning eagerly forward from the carriage.

The Colonel was already looking at his watch; he was longing to get home. He had only come up from a sense of duty, and because he had some reason to fear that Mrs Marney had received some slights from other quarters for which he was anxious to make amends. He looked at his watch as the train puffed off with his wife's mother; at his Bradshaw as soon as her white handkerchief had waved away out of the station. He found that by taking the express he might get home that night by midnight instead of waiting till the morning. He was too old to wait away from those he loved, he told himself; he longed to see Susy again with little Phraisie in her arms. The Colonel called a hansom then and there, dined hurriedly at the hotel, picked up his bag, and drove off to Euston Square station.

CHAPTER XXI

ABOUT PHRAISIE

A tiny now, ere long she'll please
To totter at my parent-knees
And crow and try to chatter;
And soon she'll come to fair white frocks,
And frisk about in shoes and socks,
Her totter changed to patter.

And soon she'll play, ay soon enough,
At cowslip ball and blindman's buff;
And some day we shall find her
Grow weary of her toys indeed,
She'll fling them all aside to heed
A footstep close behind her!

LOCKER'S 'London Lyrics'

The sound of children's footsteps pattering about the house is perhaps the sweetest music that has ever fallen on listening mothers' ears, or that their hearts have ever kept time to. When Susanna Dymond first heard her little Phraisie's merry heels stumping overhead her first waking hours seemed to brim over with happiness. The thought of her little one seemed to shine in her face, to beam from her eyes – some indescribable new charm was hers. Small and young as Phraisie was, she seemed to fill the whole big house at Crowbeck from her early morning to her no less early evening, for Phraisie set with the sun in winter and went to roost in summer-time with her favourite cocks and hens. She was a friendly, generous, companionable little soul. As soon as Phraisie was able to walk at all, it was her pleasure to trot up to the people she loved with little presents of her own contriving, bits of string, precious crusts, portions of her toys, broken off for the purposes of her generosity.

'Da,' says she, stuffing a doll's leg into her big sister's hand.

Phraisie was rather bored when poor Tempy suddenly caught her up, hugged her passionately, kissed her.

'A-da-da-dad; no, no,' cries little sister, objecting and tearing out a handful of Tempy's red locks in self-defence.

Fayfay, as Phraisie called herself, was certainly one of the round pegs for which the round holes are waiting in the world – no hard sides, no square ill-fitting corners, but kind, soft nests, already lined with love and welcome. Miss Phraisie, perching on her mother's knee, took it all as a matter of course. How could she, little baby that she was, guess at the tender wild love which throbbed in her mother's heart, at the wonder and delight her father felt as he gazed at his pretty shrine of home and motherhood, at the sweet wife, the round, happy, baby face, and the little legs and arms struggling with jolly exuberance; and even old and wise and experienced as we are, and babies no longer, I wonder which of us could count up all the love which has been ours, all the fond looks, the tender, innocent pride which has been given to us. So Phraisie went her way, unembarrassed by false humility.

Tempy was devoted to the child, and seemed to find her best companionship with that small and cheerful person. She used to carry Fayfay about in her arms all over the place, up into her room, out into the garden again, from the garden to the pigstye, from that fascinating spot to the poultry-yard, where the chickens were picketing round about the châlets where their Cochin China mothers were confined, or to the stables where the puppies were squeaking in the straw. It would be hard to say, when the stable door opened, letting in the light and the crumbs of cake and Miss Phraisie and her capers, whether the puppies or Phraisie most enjoyed each other's society; these youthful denizens of Crowbeck seemed made for one another. She was not very unlike a little curly puppy herself in her ways, confident, droll, eager, expecting the whole world, from her father downward, to have nothing better to do than to play with her, to hide behind doors and curtains, to go down on all fours if need be. Josselin was also among her subjects, but for the first two years of Miss Phraisie's existence he was very little at home. The year and a half after his father's marriage were spent at a private tutor's; then came Cambridge and new interests and new life for the young man, while Tempy lived on still in the old life, and among the old thoughts and prospects. For Tempy time did not efface old feelings, but only repeated those of the past more vividly. Perhaps her father took it for granted that because she was silent all was as he wished and that she had ceased to think of Charles Bolsover, indeed one day he said as much with quiet satisfaction to Susanna, who looked a doubtful acquiescence. But Tempy grew more and more reserved about herself; neither to her inquiring Aunt Fanny nor to her stepmother would she speak any more. I think Phraisie was the only person to whom Tempy Dymond ever made any confidences.

'Don't ty To-to,' said Phraisie one day, 'toz it's vezzy naughty.'

Tempy laughed, and began to play bo-peep behind the sheet of the *Times* which had made her cry; it was a June day *Times*, with Oxford and Cambridge lists in its columns. Phraisie couldn't read, and had never heard of any prize poem, except perhaps 'See-Saw, Margery Daw,' or she might have seen that Charles Bolsover of St Boniface was the prize poet of the year.

It was later in the afternoon of that same summer's day that the Dymond family, tempted out by the beauty of the weather, in company with numerous other families of the earth and the air and the water, might have been seen quietly walking by the field-way towards Bolsover Hall. A message had come up from Aunt Fanny, stating that signs and tokens had arrived from the roving uncle, Peregrine Bolsover. These strange camphor-scented treasures used to appear from time to time, giving some clue to the donor's travels. He hated writing and preferred this means of communication with his friends.

Tempy was even more silent than usual, as she walked along the slope of the field, leading little Phraisie by the hand. At every step the child stooped to pick the heads of the delicate flowers that were sprinkling the turf with purple and white and golden dust.

The Colonel walked on with Susanna. The hour was full of exquisite peace and tranquillity, and summer distance. As they cross the Crowbeck meadows (they lead by a short cut to the garden of the Hall), the soft wind meets them blowing from across the lake and tossing the fragrance which still hangs from every hedge and bank and neighbouring cottage porch into their faces; white roses in sweet clusters, lilies from adjacent cottage gardens, scent the highways; a little stream dashes across the way watering the green meadows on either side, and Phraisie laughing and chattering is lifted over. The June fields are sumptuous with flowers and splendid weeds. Foxgloves stand in stately phalanx, full beds of meadow-sweet are waving, the blue heads of the forget-me-not cover the water's edge. A broad plank crosses the bubbling rivulet, and leads to the upslope and to the Bolsover farm beyond, where the cows are browsing or looking over the low walls that enclose their boundaries; a colony of ducks comes down to the water from under the farm gate, waddling, with beautiful white breasts.

'Dook, dook, pitty 'itty quack-quacks, papa, dook,' cries Phraisie, setting off running after her parents; and the Colonel stops and looks at ducks with an interest in them he has not felt for half a century, while Susy, smiling, stands gazing at her little blue-eyed naturalist.

At Bolsover Hall Miss Phraisie was a no less important member of the family than at Crowbeck Place. The good-natured squire used to waylay her as she was walking up the avenue, and bring her by the back-way into his private room, where he would detain her by many interesting and rapidly following experiments, the click of pistols, red balls from the billiard table, whips, spurs, shiny noisy whirling objects of every possible description, until presently Mrs Bolsover would appear, followed by a couple of Aunt Fanny's dogs, with a 'Baby, baby, don't disturb your uncle;' and then the fickle Phraisie, starting off in pursuit, would forget her uncle's past attentions, and leave him panting, but tidy as ever, to put by all the many charming objects he had produced for her benefit.

It would be difficult to imagine anything less congruous than the squire and his favourite gun-room, where he spent so many peaceful hours. It might have seemed at first view a terrific apartment. A death's head and cross-bones (stuck up by Charlie Bolsover) ornamented the top of the old-fashioned clock. Along the fireplace nothing more terrible than a row of pipes' heads might be seen hanging from pegs, but everywhere upon the walls were murderous weapons shining in their places, revolvers, crossed foils and fencing implements. A great curling sword, all over ornaments and flourishes, hung over the comfortable leather sofa cushions, where Uncle Bolsover loved to doze away the hours.

Day after day Uncle Bolsover used to go peacefully off to sleep over his *Times*, among all these trophies and weapons of destruction. There he lies to-day slumbering tranquilly; the tranquillity, the soothing sunshine, all contribute to his happy dreams. The squire has earned his repose. He has been all the morning unpacking the huge case which has come jogging up from the other side of the world, whence Peregrine Bolsover, having heard of Colonel Dymond's marriage, has despatched an extra crate full of traveller's gifts to his family at home. He had heard the news from his sister Fanny, whose flowing streams of correspondence contrived to reach the wanderer even in those distant countries which he frequented, countries so far away, so little known, that it seemed as if they had been expressly created for his use. The gifts are of a generous, inconvenient, and semi-barbarous character; elephants' tusks, rude strings of teeth, and gold beads for the bride; carved ostrich eggs for the Colonel; a priceless bamboo strung with the spine bones of some royal dynasty for Mrs Bolsover; various daggers wrapped in rough paper, and marked '*poison – very dangerous*,' for the squire; a Spanish leather saddle all embroidered for Charlie, besides several gods of various religions and degrees of hideousness. Gratitude, natural bewilderment, and hopeless confusion raise up mixed emotions in the family on receiving these tokens of their absent member's affection. The squire having conscientiously unpacked the chest, ranged the various objects round the room, and put the daggers safely in the cupboard out of the way, feels that he has earned his afternoon's siesta. As he sleeps the door opens gently, and a pale handsome young man comes in quietly. By his rings, by his black curls, by his shiny shoes and red silk stockings, it is easy to recognise Charlie Bolsover restored to his usual health and spirits, and profiting by his newly-gained honours and by the first days of his long vacation to come off uninvited, and even under prohibition, to the place where he is always returning in spirit.

'Good heavens! Charlie,' says Uncle Bolsover, waking up with a start.

'Aunt Fanny sent me in to wake you, Uncle Bol,' said Charlie, with a smile. 'She says I may stay.'

CHAPTER XXII

UNDER THE CEDAR-TREES

O sweet fancy! let her loose,
Everything is spoiled by use
Where's the cheek that doth not fade,
Too much gazed at? . . .

ANON

The Colonel and his wife had been met at the door, and told that the ladies were at tea in the garden; and without entering the house or visiting the gun-room on their way, they passed by the side gate that led to the velvet lawns, so greenly spread beneath the shade of those old trees which have always seemed to me the rightful owners of Bolsover Hall. The tea-table stood under a cedar which had sheltered three or four generations of Bolsovers in turn, and which had seen grandparents and parents at play before Fanny Bolsover and her sister and her brothers had grown up from children. The eldest of the generation, Tempy's mother, the first Tempy, who married little Jacky Dymond, as the Colonel was once called, was long since dead, and so was Charles, the youngest brother, the father of the present Charles. Peregrine, who came next to the squire, and who once climbed to the rook's nest on the upper boughs of the tallest cedar, was far away, and had returned no more to the old place. And the brilliant Fanny, the lovely spoiled girl who once thought all mankind, all life was at her feet – was *this* what she had come to, this garish, affected woman, with her disappointed ambitions, her limited imaginations, her ostentatious cleverness, and dominating will? The good squire in all his sixty years had scarcely travelled beyond the shadow of his old trees, nor changed in heart since he first came out at the head of the brotherhood, to play hide and seek upon the lawn.

Miss Bolsover advanced to meet the little party – Susanna and Tempy, and Phraisie, running ahead, and Jacky Dymond, now sobered, silvered, settled, and no more like the youth she could remember than she resembled the Fanny of forty years ago. Aunt Fanny was unusually gracious (so it seemed to Susy). She sent the servant for a low table and a baby-chair for Phraisie; she insisted on ordering tea upon the lawn for them; she stirred and mixed milk and water, and divided sponge-cakes and strawberries and cream with extra alacrity; she would not hear of the Colonel going into the house to look for the squire.

'We will leave poor Frederick to have his nap out,' says Miss Bolsover; 'plenty of time, John, to see the presents. Do let us enjoy this lovely afternoon in peace! It is so good of poor dear Peregrine; only I can't conceive what we are to do with all the eggs he sends home. Do look at that lovely effect of light upon the lake, Susanna! So you are going on to the magistrates' dinner at Countyside, John? What time is your train? Shall you call in on your way back? I hear Lord Neighborton is expected to speak. Poor you! you will have to propose his health. Little mademoiselle, where are you running to?' in a high staccato voice. 'Do keep the child quietly here and amused, Tempy dear. More strawberries, anybody? Ah! here comes Car from the schools. Well, Car, tired? What news? When is the terrible inspector to come?'

And Aunt Car wearily sinks down upon a chair, not without a benevolent iron grin of welcome to Phraisie, who runs straight up to her and climbs upon her knee and begins at once to pop strawberries into her mouth.

Miss Bolsover, for some reason or other, seemed absolutely determined that no one should move from the tea-table.

'Well! have you seen the presents, Phraisie?' Mrs Bolsover was beginning.

'Car, Car, don't talk of poor dear Peregrine's horrors just yet!' cries Aunt Fanny. 'You know they are always the same – claws, and teeth, and fusty bison-skins,' and as she spoke the stable clock, soft and clear and deliberate, came to their ears, striking the three-quarters.

'A quarter to six,' says the Colonel.

'Car,' says Miss Bolsover, 'the man was here this morning, he says the clock is some minutes slow.'

'It is all right by my watch,' said the Colonel, looking down at his gold repeater.

'I nearly missed my train yesterday,' Miss Bolsover remarked, absently stirring her tea; 'but most likely – of course your watch is right, John.'

However, to the punctual Colonel this most likely was not to be endured.

'I'll make sure of my train, anyhow,' says he, getting up leisurely. 'Phraisie, will you give papa a kiss? Good-bye, Susy; expect me after dinner. Car, tell Bolsover I'll look in on my way home.'

As the Colonel was walking off across the grass on his way to the station the figures of Mr Bolsover himself and another person might have been seen at the drawing-room window, where the squire stood trying to undo the hasp. Aunt Fanny, who had eyes everywhere, caught sight of the two, for she suddenly seized little scared Phraisie up in playful arms and went flying, and rustling, and panting across the lawn towards the house in time to meet her brother-in-law face to face on the step.

'Here is our dear little Fayfay come to see Uncle Fred and all the pitty tings,' says Miss Bolsover playfully, thrusting the child into her brother's arms. 'Don't come out, Charlie boy, I want to speak to you, dear, most particularly. Come into my boudoir. Frederick, will you take the child into the gun-room? Auntie will come for her directly.'

Presently a servant came out from the house with a message to Tempy under the tree. Miss Bolsover wanted to speak to her. Then Miss Bolsover herself returned again without Tempy, leading little Phraisie by the hand.

'Tempy is delighted with the eggs and things,' says Aunt Fanny to Aunt Car. 'I brought the little one back, Susanna. Your pony-carriage is come for you. I don't know if you are at all afraid of keeping her out too late; I myself know *nothing* about it,' says Miss Bolsover, with her merry tinkle of earrings and laughter; 'but if you would like to go home we will send Tempy home in the T-cart and be glad to keep her.'

'Tempy said she wanted to get back early,' Susanna answered, quite unsuspiciously.

'Oh! we will see to that,' cries Aunt Fanny, affectionately conducting Mrs Dymond to the side gate where the pony-carriage was standing. 'Dear me, you have never seen your beads after all, nor the scalps either. I'll send them to you by Tempy.'

Then Susy nodded and smiled and waved good-bye to Mrs Bolsover, and was more than absorbed in making her little Phraisie kiss her hand and say good-bye too. Phraisie behaved beautifully and did all that was expected of her, and chattered all the way home on her mother's knee.

'Nice gentypan in dere, mamma,' said little Phraisie as they drove off. 'Gentypan kissed Fayfay.'

Susy did not quite understand what Phraisie meant

'No, dear,' she said, 'there was no gentleman only papa.'

'Ozzer ones,' said Phraisie, persisting.

Susy waited dinner, but no Tempy came home, and Mrs Dymond finished her meal by herself. All the bright, dazzling hours of the day seemed passing before her still, shining, crowding with light and life – with Phraisie's busy little life most of all. Susy went upstairs on her way to her own room, and stood for a few minutes by Phraisie's little crib, where all the pretty capers and sweet prattle and joy and wonder were quietly dreaming among the pillows. The child's peaceful head lay with a warm flush and with tranquil, resting breath; the little hand hung over the quilt, half dropping a toy, it was some goggle-eyed, wide-awake dolly, staring hard, and with loops of tow and gilt ornaments, not unlike Miss Bolsover herself.

For once Mrs Dymond had also enjoyed her visit to Bolsover Hall. Aunt Fanny had been gracious. She had spared those thrusts which used to sting, for all Susy's calm imperturbability. As for Mrs Bolsover, Susy had learnt to be less and less afraid of her grim advances. Little Fayfay, asleep or awake, was an ever-growing bond between the two women. Susy had brought Fayfay's nursery down from the upper floor, and she had now only to cross a passage from the nursery to reach her own sitting-room, where she found a green lamp burning and a fire burning. Even in summer-time they used to light fires at Crowbeck after the sun was set. She had no other company than that of Zillah lying asleep by the hearth, but she wanted none other. She settled herself comfortably in her sofa corner, where the lamp shed its pleasant light, and after writing a long, rambling pencil letter to her mother, Susy took up a novel and read assiduously for a time. Then she closed the book. Her little Phraisie's eyes and looks, and her button of a nose, and her funny sweet sayings, seemed to come between her and the print. What chance has a poor author with such a rival? 'Funny gentypan,' who could Phraisie mean by 'funny gentypan'? Then suddenly, as the baby herself might have done, Susanna, happy, thankful, resting and at ease, dropped off into a sleep, sound and long and deep as these illicit slumbers are apt to be. I do not know how long her dreams had lasted; the nurse looked in, and not liking to disturb her went off to bed. The clock struck ten and the half-hour, and suddenly Mrs Dymond started up, wide awake; she thought she had heard a sound and her own name called, and she answered as she sat up on the couch, bewildered. Was it her husband's voice? Was it Marney come home? Susy rubbed her eyes. All seemed silent again, but she had been startled, and looking at the clock she flushed up, ashamed of her long nap. Then she crossed the room to the bell and rang it, but no one came, for the maids had gone to bed and the men were in a different part of the house. I don't know what nervous terror suddenly seized her, but as she listened still, she grew more frightened. Then she thought of calling the nurse, and looked into the nursery again for that purpose, but gaining courage from the calm night-light and the peaceful cradle, she came quietly away; only, as she crossed the passage, she now distinctly heard a low continuous murmur of voices going on in some room not far distant. Then Susy reflected that housebreakers do not start long audible conversations in the dead of night, and summoning up courage, she descended the broad flight of stairs which led to the sitting-rooms below; the voices were not loud, but every now and then the tones rose in the silence. As she came to the half-open drawing-room door (it was just under her dressing-room) she heard a man's voice speaking in eager tones, and then the colour rushed up into her face and once more her heart began to beat, for she seemed to recognise Tempy's low answer. She opened the door. There stood Charlie, who seemed to be destined to disturb the slumbers of his family. There stood Tempy beside him, in the glow of the dying embers – the two sadly, happily miserable, and yet together! Susy could see poor Tempy's tears glistening in the red fire-light, and Charlie's rings and decorations, as they stood holding each other's hands in parting grief.

Mrs Dymond came in like a beautiful fate, in her long white dress floating sternly across the room. She set her light upon the table.

'Tempy!' she said. 'Oh! Tempy, I could not have believed it of you. And how can you come,' Susanna said, turning to Charlie Bolsover, 'how dare you come,' she repeated, 'disturbing us, troubling us with your presence? Tempy has promised – has promised not to see you,' she went on excitedly. 'Why don't you keep away? Do you not know that all our home peace and happiness depend upon your absence? You are not, you will never be, her husband. Do you want to part her for ever from her father?' cried Susy, passionately. 'As for you, Tempy, I thought I could have trusted you as I trust myself. Was this why you stayed behind, why you deceived me?'

Susy might have been kinder, she might have sympathised more, but that her own youth had taught her so sad, so desperate a lesson; the comfortable *débonnaire* vices, easy-going misdeeds and insincerities, seemed to her worse and more terrible than the bitterest and most cutting truths, the sternest, baldest realities. That Tempy should deceive her, deceive her father, should be seeing Charlie by secret arrangement, seemed to Susy unworthy of them all.

Charlie turned round upon her in a sudden fury. Where was his usual placid indifference now?

'If you knew what you were saying; if you had ever been in love,' he said in a rage, speaking bitterly, indignantly, 'you would not be so cruel to her, Mrs Dymond. You part us for no reason but your husband's fancy, and you divide us as if we were two sacks of potatoes – "Go," you say, "forget each other." You don't know what you say. You might as well say, "Do not exist at all," as tell us not to love each other. It may be easy enough for people who marry not for love but for money, or because they want comfortable homes or housekeepers, to part, but——'

'Oh, for shame, for shame, Charlie,' cried Tempy, starting away and pulling her hand from her lover.

'Let him speak, it is best so,' said Susanna very stern, and pale, and uncompromising. 'He has a right to speak.'

'I speak because I feel, while you all seem to me stones and stocks,' cried the young fellow. 'I speak because I love Tempy with all my heart, and you are condemning her and condemning me unheard to sorrow and life-long separation.'

There was something, some utter truth of reality in the young man's voice, something which haunted Susanna long after. This had come upon her suddenly, unexpectedly, but not for the first time did she feel uneasy, impatient with her husband.

A sudden indignant protest rose in her heart; for the first time since her marriage she questioned and denied his infallibility. It might be true that Charlie Bolsover had been foolish, true that he was in debt, true that Tempy was rich and young, but was it not also true that these two people were tenderly, faithfully attached to each other? It seemed a terrible responsibility for the father to divide them; absolutely to say, 'Death to their love, let it be as nothing, let it cease for ever.' Susy thought of the boy's sad wild looks as he rushed past her in the passage of Eiderdown's Hotel.

She looked at him again. He was changed somehow; he looked older, stronger, angrier, less desperate, more of a man. He stood fronting Tempy, not with the air of one who was ashamed and out of place, but as if he had a right to speak. Susy, Rhadamantine though she was, covered her face with her two hands for a minute. She could not meet the young fellow's reproachful look. It seemed to her that it had all happened before, that she had known it all along, known it from the beginning, even when Charlie, exasperated, turned from her to Tempy saying,

'Tempy, I can't bear this any longer, you must decide between us. Send me away, if you have the heart to send me away.'

Still Susy seemed to know it all, to know that Tempy was saying, 'I shall never give you up, Charlie, but I cannot go against my father's cruel will.'

The sound of wheels, of a horse's hoofs stopping at the front door, brought the situation to a crisis.

'Listen! That must be papa,' said Tempy, starting forward. 'Go, Charlie, go! there is still time! You must not meet him!' and she, all in tears, took his hand into both hers, and would have dragged him to the window through which they had entered together.

'Go! Why should I go?' cried Charlie, exasperated, holding his ground. 'I am not ashamed of being here,' and as he spoke Susy heard the hall door open.

'He is right, Tempy,' she cried, with a bright look, and then with a sudden impulse Susanna ran to the dining-room door, threw it open, and called her husband by his name as he came into his house.

'John! come here! Charles Bolsover is here,' said Susy, standing in the dining-room door.

Then she saw that her husband was looking very pale. Instead of coming up to her he stood by the staircase holding to the bannister. He looked very old suddenly, quite different somehow.

'I know Charles Bolsover is here,' he said, looking hard at his wife. 'I heard it just now before you told me. Tell him I will not see him. Tell him and Tempy to carry on their plots elsewhere. You Susy, I can trust, thank God.'

'Dear John, what is it?' Susy cried, running up to him. 'Tempy, Tempy, come to your father! Come and tell him he can trust us all!' Susy cried in despair at her husband's strange manner and looks, and Tempy hearing Susy's voice also came out with her round face still bathed in tears.

'Oh! papa, what is it?' she said gently. 'I didn't know Charlie was to be at the Hall. Indeed I didn't, though perhaps if I had, I could not have kept away. I hadn't seen him for, oh, so long; he walked back with me just now, that is all! Are you very angry?'

The poor Colonel's face altered, changed, softened, the colour seemed to come back into his lips.

'I am not angry with you, my poor child,' he said, and he sighed, and held out his hand. Tempy felt that it was cold like stone. 'I am tired; another time I will speak to you. I cannot see him. I thought – I thought you were all trying to deceive me,' he repeated, with an attempt at a smile.

Tempy watched him step by step till he turned the corner of the staircase, still holding by the bannisters. Long, long afterwards she seemed to see him climbing slowly and passing on.

CHAPTER XXIII

'THE COLONEL GOES HOME'

I falter where I firmly trod,
And falling with my weight of cares
Upon the great world's altar stairs,
That slope thro' darkness up to God,
I stretch lame hands of faith, and grope
And gather dust and chaff, and call
To what I feel is Lord of all,
And faintly trust the larger hope.

IN MEMORIAM

Susanna was not happy about her husband next morning. He seemed unlike himself; though he said he was well, he looked dull and out of spirits. Tempy's heart, too, was very heavy, and she hung her head over her sewing, setting one weary stitch after another as women do. Charlie was gone, she knew not when she should see him again; and her father was there, and yet gone too in a way. She could not bear him to be so gentle, so reserved, so absent in his manner; she was longing for an explanation with him, longing to speak and yet scarcely knowing how to begin. When the play of life turns to earnest, how strangely one's youthful valiance fails – that courage of the young, armed from head to foot with confident inexperience of failure and with hope all undimmed as yet.

The Colonel was busy all the morning, and closeted in his study with the bailiff. He came into Susy's room once or twice, where she was sitting with Tempy, and with little Phraisie playing at her knee. Phraisie was the one cheerful, natural person in the house this gloomy morning. The Colonel's silence did not silence her. Tempy's depression seemed to vanish suddenly when the child came tumbling across the room from her mother's knee; Tempy's black looks (so curiously like her father's) turned into some faint semblance of a smile as the little sister tugged at her dress to make her play.

Susy had left the room when little Fayfay, perching at the window, suddenly began to exclaim something about 'papa and his gee-gee,' and Tempy, who had hoped that the moment for explanation had come, found that her father was starting for his morning ride, and now explanation must be again deferred. The explanation was not then, but it was very near at hand.

Presently Susy looked into the room, with her straw hat on. 'Your father is gone to Ambleside. He has ordered James to meet him there at the station with the dog-cart; they will bring Josselin home. Won't you come out now, Tempy? It will do you good; or will you come with me to Miss Fletcher's after luncheon?'

But Tempy shook her head. She would not come, neither then nor later. She sat stitching away the morning, moping through the hours in a dreary, unsatisfactory sort of way. Susanna hoped that Josselin's return might cheer her up.

'What did papa say to you last night?' Tempy suddenly asked, when she saw Susy getting up after luncheon to prepare for her walk.

'He said that he was glad that we had hidden nothing from him – that we had told him Charlie was here. He said he liked to feel that he could trust us,' Susanna answered, and as she spoke she seemed to see her husband's kind face and his outstretched hand again.

'Trust us, trust *you*!' said Tempy. 'Did Aunt Fanny tell him Charlie was here?'

'No,' said Susy, blushing up. 'It was Aunt Car who told him, she had gone to bed when your father reached the Hall. She came out of her room in her dressing-gown, hearing his voice. Miss Bolsover assured your father it was I who had arranged it all,' Susy went on; and as she spoke two indignant tears flashed into her eyes.

'Don't! don't! don't!' cried poor Tempy. 'My aunt knows how unhappy I am,' and she turned and ran out of the room.

Susy was glad to meet Wilkins and her little Phraisie at the garden gate that afternoon. She was starting for her walk before the travellers' return. Phraisie was armed *cap-à-pie* and helmed in quilted white and starch as a baby should be who is meant to defy the sun. She had picked a bunch of flowers, and was hopping along the path, and chattering as she went something about 'De pussy and a de kitty is in de darden, and de kitty is eaten de petty flowers, and please, mamma, take 'ittle Fayfay wid dou.'

'I should like her to come with me, Wilkins,' said Mrs Dymond. 'I am going to call at the Miss Fletchers'.'

'Oh! very well, mem,' says Wilkins, resigned. She prefers her own company to respectful attendance upon her mistress, but she is a good creature, and allows Susy to see a great deal of Phraisie. Perhaps the thought of Miss Fanny's various paragons hanging by hairs over her head inclines Wilkins to regard her mistress's failings with leniency. Susy felt so sad and so much depressed that it was a real boon and comfort to be led along by the little one and to feel her warm hand in her own. Phraisie was sturdy on her legs, and thought nothing of the expedition.

Their walk ran high up above the roadside, along a bank cut in the shelving slopes, and shaded by big trees, of which the stems were wreathed and wrapped with ivy leaves. Beneath each natural arch formed by the spread of the great branches, lay a most lovely world of cool waters and gentle mountain mist, of valleys full of peaceful, browsing sheep. A strange cloud hung along the crest of the Old Man flashing with light. Susanna remembered it long afterwards; every minute of that day seemed stamped and marked upon her mind. Phraisie went first, still chattering to her mamma, who followed quietly, looking out at the tranquil prospect; then came Wilkins. Once the nurse stopped short, and Susy, who had walked a little ahead, called to her.

'I thought there was a something on the other side of the lake, mem,' says Wilkins. 'There's a boat and a crowd.'

Susy stopped, looked, moved on again after an instant's pause. 'I cannot see clearly across the lake,' she said; 'but the rain is coming, we must not be long,' and she went on her way, still holding Phraisie's warm little hand. The Fletchers lived in a stone, slated cottage high up on the mountain-side; it was homely enough, scanty, but exquisitely clean and in perfect order. The little garden, enclosed by its stone walls, flashed lilac, gold, and crimson, for the cottage flowers were all ablaze – convolvulus, floxes, sweet william, and nasturtium, opening to the raindrops that were already beginning to fall.

Martha Fletcher, the younger sister who kept the school, was standing out in the porch as her visitors arrived somewhat breathless with their climb; and she came forward to welcome them with her smiling, peaceful looks and voice, and, calling to her sister, opened the cottage door and showed them in. There were two rooms on the ground floor, leading from one to another – pleasant rooms, scantily furnished, with slated floors and lattice windows and cross lights, and a few geraniums in pots; both rooms opened to the garden. The first was a sort of kitchen, with a kettle boiling on the hob; the second was a parlour, with a few wooden chairs, an oak chest, and a quaint old cupboard that would have made the fortune of a collector. 'It is old; it were never very much,' said Martha. In front of the cupboard, Jane, the elder sister, was lying back in her big chair knitting, with a patchwork cushion at her back. She looked pale and worn by ill health, but she, too, brightened to welcome their visitors. Both these sisters had the calm and well-bred manners of people who live at peace, in the good company of great and lovely things. Susy herself had not such easy and dignified greetings for her guests, such kindness and unspoken courtesy in her ways, as that with which these two women now met her.

Mrs Dymond had come only intending to remain a few minutes, but from behind the Old Man some sudden storm began to spread, and in a few minutes, swiftly, rapidly, the clouds had gathered, and the rain began to pour very heavily all round about.

Perhaps half an hour went by – a strange half-hour, which ever afterwards Susy looked back to with a feeling half of longing, half of miserable regret. It seemed to her as if some other Susanna had lived it, with its troubled apprehensions, with a heart full of pain, of dull excitement. So long as it had been her own self in question, she had felt no disloyalty in suppressing her own wishes, crushing down the instinctive protest in her heart against the family thraldom and traditional subjection to conventionality. But now that Tempy's happiness and honesty of mind were concerned, it seemed to Susy that the time had come to speak. She could not bear to disagree with her husband, but the sight of Tempy's dull pain stung her into action. Ah! John who was so good, so gentle and forbearing, he would understand her, he would yield to her entreaties, to Tempy's pleading.

Susy sat paying her visit in a curious, double state of mind. The rain had ceased, the cottage garden was refreshed; the floxes, the zinnias, the lupins, the marigolds, the whole array of cottage finery was refreshed and heavy with wet. The birds had begun to fly and chirp again; little Phraisie stood at the door peeping out at an adventurous kitten which was cautiously advancing along the wooden bench. Martha sat erect on the well rubbed mahogany settle, Jane lay back in her big chair with an invalid's gentle eyes full of interest, fixed on their young visitor.

'How comely Mrs Dymond du look,' thinks Jane the fanciful, 'there side-by-side wi' Martha on the settle.'

Mrs Dymond dressed in some soft brown pelisse with a touch of colour in it, her loose country gloves, her lace ruffles, her coquettish brown felt hat with the shining bird's breast, all seemed to make up a pleasant autumnal picture, even more interesting to Jane than that baby-one in the doorway. After all, a tidy, well-dressed child is no prettier an object than any one of the little ones barelegged and rosy and tattered, such as those Jane and Martha were used to teach and have up to play in the garden. But a well-dressed, beautiful lady is an interesting sight to a country woman. Martha from habit, perhaps, kept watch over Phraisie, but Jane's eyes rested gently upon the young mother.

Susy lingered on. There was a sense of peace within as without the cottage, a feeling of goodness, of quiet duty fulfilled, and unpretending refinement. A thought crossed her mind, what a happy life she might have led if only these women could have been her sisters – true ladies indeed they seemed to be – tranquil, courteous in their ways, making no difference between persons, as gentle and as welcoming to the shepherd's wife, who came drenched to the door in her clogs, to report of Mrs Barrow's fourth, as to Susy herself, the lady of the Place. While the neighbours talked on, Susy, girl-like, began to picture a life with John, in a pleasant cottage with a garden full of flowers. She seemed putting off the moment of return and explanation, and trying to think of other things. Susy dreaded going home, dreaded the explanation before her, dreaded the pain she must give her husband if she told him all she felt, and that his decision seemed to her unjust and arbitrary; dreaded concealment of the truth. Some instinct seemed to tell her that Miss Bolsover, whatever happened, would make ill-will between them all, and that trouble was at hand; and yet the heavy indefinable sense which had haunted her all the morning was lighter since she had reached that peaceful home and seen the simple and comforting sight of two contended souls.

These fancies did not take long, a little ray of light came straggling by the lattice. Phraisie leaped and laughed in the doorway at the kitten's antics; suddenly the child came running back to her mother's knee, and hid her face in her lap and began to cry.

'My Phraisie, what is it?' said Susy, stooping and lifting her up. 'Did the kitty scratch you?' but little Phraisie didn't answer at first, then looking up into her mother's face,

'Papa, Fayfay wants papa,' was all she said.

'I think papa must be home by this,' said Susy, going to the door with the child in her arms; and she felt that with Phraisie in her arms she could protest for Tempy's future rights. She could trust that kind and generous heart which had ever been so true to her, to them all. The rain was gathering again; the sisters urged her to stay, but she was impatient – suddenly impatient – to get back. A feeling which seemed strange, indescribable, outside every-day things and common feelings, had fallen on her once more; was it the storm in the air? As she looked at the opposite hills, she felt as if the very line of the clouds against the sky had terror in it. No tangible impression was in her mind, but a restless alarm and discomfort. Susy wondered if she was going to be ill, though she was not given to fancies; her one desire was to get home, and she took leave, hastily gathering up her skirts with Wilkins's help, tucking Phraisie safe into the folds of her pelisse. Jane and Martha looked gravely at her, and did not attempt to detain her. 'Take care of ye'sell,' they said. Martha came with them to the garden-gate, and stood holding it open, and as they were starting, they heard a step hurrying up from below. It was one of the grooms from the Place, who, not seeing Susy, exclaimed –

'Oh! Miss Fletcher, have you heard that there's been a' accident across the lake? The Colonel and Mr Jo have been cast out of t' dog-cart. I am seeking Mrs Dymond.'

'An accident!' said Susy, coming forward, holding Phraisie very tight. 'Are they hurt, James? Is the Colonel——'

'Neither o' the gentlemen had spoke when I came away to seek ye, mem,' said the man, with a pale face; and some wonder at seeing her so composed. 'George Tyson brought them across in t' boat wi' doctor; the parson is there wi' Miss Bolsover. We have been looking for you, ma'am, a long while.'

CHAPTER XXIV

THE DOCTOR AND THE LADY

But the last tune the harp played then,
Binnorie, O Binnorie

The train came in in the early morning, and the great London doctor got out; he had travelled all night comfortably enough in his first-class corner; he was there to see what could be done; he had a confident, cheerful aspect, which gave hope to the bystanders. The porter began to think the Colonel might recover after all; the station-master also seemed to regain confidence. Mr Bolsover, who had come to meet the train, and who liked to take things pleasantly, shook the oracle warmly by the hand. 'I'm afraid you will find things as bad as can be,' he said, as if he was giving a welcome piece of news, though his pale round face belied his cheery tones. 'Jeffries has been up all night. I have brought the carriage for you. We telegraphed to you yesterday when Jeffries thought so badly of him, poor fellow. Get in, please; drive hard, George.'

'Is Mrs Dymond aware of the danger?' said the doctor, as he got into the carriage, after seeing that his bag was safely stowed on the box.

'She is anxious, very anxious,' said Mr Bolsover; 'so are my wife and sister, who are nursing them all most devotedly. You know the boy is hurt too; broken rib – concussion. They were driving home together; they think poor Dymond fainted and fell, the horse was startled, the carriage upset just by the forge. Luckily one of Dymond's own men was standing by; the poor fellows were brought straight home across the lake in the ferry-boat. Mrs Dymond was from home at the time. The boy recovered consciousness almost immediately, but my poor brother-in-law seems very ill, very bad indeed,' said Mr Bolsover with an odd chirruping quake in his voice; then recovering, and trying to quiet himself. 'Do you dislike this?' and he pulled a cigar-case out of his pocket.

'Not at all – not at all,' said the doctor, looking out of the window. 'What a delightful place you have here!'

'It is almost all my brother-in-law's property,' said Mr Bolsover; 'all entailed upon my nephew. We married sisters, you know.'

'Oh, indeed!' said the doctor. 'I did not know.'

'I was not speaking of the present Mrs Dymond,' says Mr Bolsover, hastily. 'The second wife is quite a girl; some of us thought it a pity at the time. Poor child, it will be easier for her now, perhaps, than if they had been longer married.'

The horses hurried on, the gates were reached, the neat sweep, the pleasant shade of trees; the doors of the house flew open, and the servants appeared, as on that day when the Colonel had brought Susy home as a bride. The doctor was shown into the Colonel's study, where a fire had been lighted and some breakfast set out. The master was lying scarcely conscious on his bed upstairs, but his daily life seemed still to go on in the room below. The whips and sticks were neatly stacked against the walls, his sword was slung up, his belt, his military cap, everything curiously tidy and well-ordered. The Army List and Directory, the Bradshaws and Whitaker, were each in their place on the table in a sort of pattern. The bookcases were filled, and every shelf was complete; the writing apparatus was in order, with good pens and fresh ink, for Dr Mayfair to write the prescriptions with. They could do little good now, for all the good pens and paper. The neat packets of letters, answered and unanswered, with broad elastic straps, lay on the right and left of the writing-book; the post-bag was hanging on a nail, with a brass plate fixed above, on which the hours of the post were engraved. Everything spoke of a leisurely, well-ordered existence, from the shining spurs on their stands, to the keys in the despatch-box. The doctor had not long to wait; the door opened, and a lady came in – a fat, florid lady, who seemed to have performed a hasty toilette, not without care. She was wrapped in a flowing, flowery tea-gown, a lace hood covered her many curls and plaits; she had gold slippers, emerald and turquoise rings; she advanced with many agitated motions.

'Oh, doctor! – oh, how we have looked for you! You may imagine what this night has been. How am I to tell you all? A chair. Thank you. Yes – oh, yes! – our darling boy scarcely conscious – his father in this most alarming condition,' and she laid her jewelled fingers on the doctor's sleeve. 'Mr Bolsover will have told you something, but *he* has no conception of what we have suffered, what anxiety we have endured. My brain seems crushed,' said the lady. 'If you felt my pulse, doctor, you would see that the heart's action is scarcely perceptible.'

'You are very anxious of course,' said the doctor, rather perplexed, 'shall I come upstairs at once? Is Mr Jeffries upstairs?'

'He will be here in a minute, if you will kindly wait, and you must be wanting some refreshment,' said the lady. 'Doctor Mayfair, do you prefer tea or coffee? Here are both as I ordered. One requires all one's nerve, all one's strength for the sad scene upstairs – the strong man cast down in his prime – let me pour out the tea.'

The doctor, somewhat bored by the lady's attentions, stood before the fire waiting for the arrival of Mr Jeffries, and asking various details of the illness, of the accident, to which his hostess gave vague and agitated answers. 'I was resting in my room before dressing to drive out, when my maid brought me word of the dreadful report. I lost not a moment, I told them to bring me a cloak, a hat, anything, the first come, to order the carriage, to send a messenger to say that I was on the way. But one has to pay for such efforts, nature will not be defrauded of her rights. You, doctor, know that better than I do.'

'Oh, of course, no, yes,' says the doctor with a vacant eye drinking his tea and looking round: was this the enthusiastic young girl disapproved of by the poor Colonel's relations! 'Mr Jeffries has been sent for, you tell me,' said the great man, politely interrupting.

'I hear him now,' said Miss Bolsover excitedly, and rushing to the door she opened it wide. 'Here, come in here, Doctor Mayfair is expecting you,' said the lady in a loud whisper. 'Oh, Mr Jeffries, you can tell him what we have all endured, you can tell him what a life-long tie it has been between us. How unlike that of a few short months; how much deeper, how much'. . . . Mr Jeffries looked round uneasily, he was followed by Susanna, still strangely quiet, scarcely uttering a word, but with anxious, dark-encircled eyes trying to read from their faces what was written there. She heard Miss Bolsover's speech, and crimsoned up as she turned a quick, reproachful glance upon her; even at such terrible moments people are themselves, alas! and their daily failings do not die when those they love lie down for the last time, but assert themselves, bitter, exaggerated. To reproach her at such a time! Oh, it was cruel, Susy thought, and then she forgot it all – Miss Bolsover's sneers, and the petty pangs and smarts of daily jealousies; she caught sight of a glance which passed between Mr Jeffries and Dr Mayfair, and all her strength and courage seemed suddenly to go, and she sat down for a moment in the nearest chair, while Miss Bolsover followed the doctors out of the room. Susy herself had no hope, Jeffries' deprecating look answered her most anxious fears, she had watched all through the night, and each hour as it passed seemed to weigh more heavily upon her heart. Now for a moment the load seemed so great that she could scarcely bear it, she seemed suddenly choking, and she opened the window and went out into the open air to breathe. There he was, dying, and all the garden was so sweet, so full of early green and flowers. He was doomed, she knew it, and a new day had dawned, and nothing was changed from yesterday; only the beauty of it all seemed aching and stinging instead of delighting her, its very sweetness turned to grief, its peace jarred like misery, a great flash of brilliant pain seemed spread out before her. Why had they ever come there? Susanna thought. Oh, why? How happy she had been alone with him in London. How unhappy she had been among these cruel people. How dear and how kind he had been; how little they knew her. All the spiteful things Miss Bolsover had ever said came into her mind with a passionate exaggeration. Ah! she was not ungrateful, she was not mercenary, she had not married for money and mean things. Her husband had been her kindest, tenderest friend, he had helped her in her sorest trouble, and she had come to him gratefully and with trust. And now all was over; and they would no longer molest her.

Poor Susy wrung her hands in a miserable impatience. She was a young creature still, exaggerated and uncharitable as young warm-hearted people are. The lovely sweetness of the morning, the tender light upon the sky only seemed to sting her to fresh pain. Then she thought of his dear pale face upon the bed upstairs – of his look of wistful love with some sad terror of conviction. She had meant to speak to him that very day, to tell him all her heart, and now it was too late, it was over now. All was coming to an end for ever and she had not half loved him, half told him how she felt his goodness. Reader, forgive her if she with the rest of us is selfish in her great grief, so keen, so fierce, distorting and maddening every passing mood and natural experience. She could not stand. She fell on her knees, poor child, with a sudden overpowering burst of sobbing pain. There was an iron roller somewhere by the wall and she laid her poor head upon the iron with incoherent sobs and prayers for his life, for strength to love him as she ought, for forgiveness for the secret rancour which had poisoned her life. As she knelt there two kind, warm arms were flung round her, 'Dear Susy, don't, don't,' sobs Tempy, who had come to look for her, 'don't, don't, don't,' was all the girl could say; 'be good, be brave, I've come to fetch you.' Susy started up, quiet again, ruling herself with a great effort. Mr Jeffries had also come down hurriedly into the drawing-room to look for her, and as the two women entered through the open casement, pale and shaking still, he looked very grave, and beckoned them upstairs. 'He is come to himself, he is asking for you,' he said to Susy; 'you must be very calm, dear Mrs Dymond.' Tempy was now sobbing in her turn, Susy was white, quiet, composed. Her husband knew her to the last, and looked up with a very sweet smile as she came to his side.

An hour afterwards she was a widow, and the grand London doctor went back to town.

BOOK III

AFTERWARDS

There was a roaring in the wind all night;
The rain came heavily and fell in floods;
But now the sun is rising calm and bright;
The birds are singing in the distant woods;
Over his own sweet voice the stock-dove broods;
The jay makes answer as the magpie chatters;
And all the air is filled with pleasant noise of waters

W. WORDSWORTH

CHAPTER XXV

AFTERWARDS

When the grass was closely mown,
Walking on the lawn alone,
In the turf a hole I found,
And hid a soldier underground.
Under grass alone he lies,
Looking up with leaden eyes;
Scarlet coat and pointed gun,
To the stars and to the sun.

R.L. STEVENSON

Among the many who appeared to show their respect to the good Colonel's memory was Mr Marney, in a shining and easy suit of deepest black, an appearance of profoundest grief tempered by resignation, to which a new hat swathed in crape greatly contributed. Aunt Fanny, strange to say, was somewhat taken by Mr Marney; his frankness (how Susy loathed it), his respectful sympathy, his intelligent grasp of the situation, of the many youthful failings to which, with all his affection for his wife's daughter, he could not be blind, his full appreciation of the good Colonel's strange infatuation, his easy compliments, his amusing little jokes at his wife and family, uttered in a subdued voice as befitted the circumstances, all amused Miss Bolsover, who accepted his odious compliments to Tempy's indignant amazement.

Susy had not asked Mr Marney to come; he was no guest of hers; she was unaffected in her grief, unselfish, anxious to spare others. She would have come down had it been necessary, but hearing of her stepfather's presence, she kept away, upstairs by Jo's bedside, or in her own room, silent, and apart in her sorrow. Some instinct seems to warn simple and defenceless creatures of the dangers of beasts of prey.

Meanwhile, in Jo's absence, Miss Bolsover received the company, gave every possible direction. She was in her element. Pens, ink, and paper, her flowing hand and spreading sheets of platitude, surrounded by broad edges of black, filled the post-bags to the brim. Mr Bolsover, all crushed somehow, sat dolefully dozing or smoking in his cosy gun-room. Mrs

Bolsover came there too for comfort, or moped silent and apart. Sometimes she went over to the Place. Susy liked to have her there. Aunt Car would come in looking old and scared into the little boudoir where Susy sat alone. The young widow used to go to meet her, and without a word would put little Phraisie on her knee.

Charlie Bolsover was present at his uncle's funeral, naturally and unaffectedly shocked and overcome, and yet not unnaturally thinking still more of Tempy than of his uncle, who had dealt hard measure to him and never done him justice. He had but a few hours to remain at Tarndale, and he had determined to come and go without obtruding his own personal feelings either upon Tempy or her stepmother. But man's resolves, especially Charlie's, are apt to be carried by the tide of the moment, and the sight of poor Tempy in her black with her wistful looks was too much for his philosophy. He came up to the house late in the afternoon of the funeral day, hoping for another sight of her. She was alone in the drawing-room.

And then it happened that when Charlie would have gone up to her, Tempy for the first time in all her life drew back, shrunk from him; she glanced at him, and then dared not look again.

'Tempy!' he said.

She did not look up, but she stood pale and frozen, with averted eyes.

'Go, Charlie,' she said at last. 'This is no time to think of our selfish wishes; ours have been selfish. I see how wrong – how wrong I was all along. Go, dear Charlie,' she said, covering her eyes with her hand. 'Go,' she repeated angrily. 'Do you hear me?' Her overstrung nerves were almost beyond her control.

'I hear you,' said Charlie, turning sick and pale; 'you do not mean it, Tempy.'

'Yes, I mean it, I mean it,' Tempy cried. 'Why do you doubt it? Go, I tell you; go.'

Charlie stood as if some gun had been fired at him; he tried to speak; no words came. With one look he turned and walked straight out of the room. Tempy waited for an instant, heard the front door shut, then sank into the first chair. When Susy came to look for her, she found the girl still sitting in the semi-darkness on a chair against the wall. She had not moved since Charlie had left her an hour before. Seeing Susy she looked up.

'You are satisfied,' she said; 'I have done as papa wished. I have sent Charlie away.'

She spoke in a thick, dazed way, which frightened her stepmother.

'Your father wished it,' Susy repeated, faltering. 'Dear Tempy, you could not go against his will;' and Susy took Tempy's cold hand and put her arm round her neck.

'You did not love him as I did,' said Tempy, tearing her hand away and flashing her blue eyes at her young stepmother. 'He loved you, but you did not deserve it, and Charlie loves me and I do not deserve it.' The girl was in a frenzy of grief and despair. 'Ah, papa thought I did not care for him because I loved Charlie,' cried Tempy; 'but I have given poor Charlie up for papa. I let him go, I let him go, and now I am all by myself. They are both gone, both gone; they will never come any more,' and she wrung her two hands.

Susy stood in silence listening to the girl's reproaches. Were they deserved? She did not know; she did not ask. For the first time she felt herself alone, silent, helpless, as people feel who have to learn to live anew, without the strength of long use to hold by.

'O Tempy!' Susy said at last, 'I do honour you; I can only feel you have done right. Let us put all doubts and perplexities away just for the present and wait. In a little time everything will seem more clear.' And Tempy took heart somehow once more. Susy's cordials were more to her mind than Aunt Fanny's chloral.

The next day the blinds were up, Miss Bolsover, in bugles and crape, was still occupied with her own and everybody else's feelings, giving every possible direction in the conduct of affairs. Charlie and Mr Marney had departed. Tempy's tears were flowing; but that explanation with her stepmother had taken some of the bitterness from her heart. She had done what she could. She sat in Jo's room, languid, by an open window, looking across the gardens and the lake, and the beautiful smiling valley. The valley itself, the fringed hills, the moorlands which enclosed them, were all a part of Jo's inheritance.

There are also other things entailed besides farms and country estates which parents leave behind them. They leave their lives to their children, as well as their savings, and their looks and family characteristics. Jo and Tempy inherited among other things their father's directness and simplicity of character, and his upright and honourable name, and the memory of his many kind and liberal actions.

When the will was read, it was found that the Colonel had left a legacy of 5,000*l.* to each of his daughters, and 1,000*l.* a year to his widow during her widowhood. Subject to these charges, and various legacies enumerated, he bequeathed the whole of his property to his son. Jo and Tempy also inherited their mother's property, which had been settled on them at his marriage.

Strangely enough, the Colonel had added a codicil to his will on the very day of the fatal accident, for he had called at his solicitor's while waiting at Countyside for Jo's train. By this codicil, the Colonel executed a power of appointment contained in the settlement made on his marriage with his first wife, and appointed the trust funds in equal shares to his son and daughter; but he made a proviso that the whole of that property should go to Josselin in the event of his daughter Tempy marrying under twenty-one without the consent of her guardian; and he appointed his widow, Mrs Susanna Dymond, to be the sole guardian of his three children.

In the event of Mrs Dymond's re-marriage, she was to give up her right to her jointure as well as to the guardianship of the elder children. This provision, which seemed of little importance, was not in the codicil but in the will, and had been suggested by the family solicitor. The good, loyal old Colonel was indignant at the time at something his sisters had said, and which the family adviser had quoted; and protesting his wife's indifference to money, had agreed to the clause without wasting much thought upon future possibilities. Susy had never cared for money, of that he required no assurance, and as for re-marriage, what should she want to marry again for? she was much better at home at the Place, looking after Phraisie and the other two, thought the Colonel to himself, to say nothing of poor Mrs Marney and her boys. The kind old son-in-law had left Mrs Marney a hundred pound legacy as a token of friendly regard, together with a small sum to each of the boys; and there were legacies to his sister and her husband, and to his sister-in-law. Miss Bolsover was offended by the portion which came to her share. Mr Marney was also disappointed, and made no secret of his irritation. It was a shabby concern, he said, from beginning to end. What is a hundred pounds? A mere nothing; and we owe it all and more too. The boys' 50*l.* won't find them in boots for six months to come. As for Susy and her beggarly jointure, she may marry again and lose it all to-morrow.

'Susy won't marry; she knows there is her brothers' education,' said Mrs Marney, with anxious conviction. 'She has Mikey and Dermy to consider now, and she is not one to forget her own people. We all know the Colonel's wishes, and that he meant them to be properly taught.'

'It would have been more to the purpose if the old boy had written his wishes down on lawyer's paper, with a couple of witnesses to see them carried out,' said Marney. 'I call it a d——d unbusiness-like proceeding – to say nothing of having to pay Madame, as you propose. I'm getting out of patience with her endless——'

'Oh, Michael!' said poor Mary, reproachfully; 'Madame lent me 20*l.* last month; it is not for the rent only!'

Not without difficulty was Mikey's legacy reserved for Madame's just claim. If it had not been for her genuine love for the little boys and their mother, Madame du Parc, the sturdy and methodical, would long ago have got rid of her unpunctual lodgers, but she had grown to love the children, and, above all, the poor lady, whose troubles, little by little, had become her own.

Susy wrote to her mother at once, telling her of herself and of all in her home, promising to provide for the boys' schooling as heretofore. She was to keep house for Jo, and she had no expense and plenty of spare money, she said, and she knew that John in his kindness would have wished her to continue what he had so generously begun. She missed him sorely, mourned him with a tender, grateful heart; she seemed at first scarcely able to live without him, or to have a wish, or to be able to settle the commonest things. He had been a man of methodical habits; he had ruled his household, and drilled Susanna to his own ideas; she had never stood alone. We know she was young and yielding and easy by nature; she had learnt from him to sort out and arrange her life, her events and friends, her feelings and hospitality – to use certain stock phrases to herself, which she thought she believed in. Now that he was gone, it seemed to Susy as if she had become for ever what she had tried to be before.

'*Elle était plus femme que les autres femmes*' has often been quoted, and never too often; surely it applied to my heroine as she sat in her corner by Jo's sofa a few weeks after her husband's death. Jo looked haggard, but he was nearly well. Susy in black and in her widow's cap looked far more beautiful than in her coloured fashionable dresses – younger, gentler, less reserved. The western sunshine was coming in at the open window. Jo had fallen asleep, and in the stillness, as Susy sat in the low chair by his couch, she could also hear the voice of her little Phraisie at play in the garden without, and the hum in the distant field, and the sounds coming across the lake.

Josselin liked to have his stepmother near him. Susanna had that gift which belongs to some people for taking care of sick people. Tempy was too abrupt and nervous from very affection. Miss Bolsover fussed; she also wanted to do too much. Jo found in his stepmother the most comforting of nurses. 'I do believe she's made of sticking plaster,' he used to say. Day by day his strength seemed to return, his burning eyes become clear and soft. He rarely spoke of the accident; but he told them once for all what he could remember of it. His father, who was driving, had suddenly fainted or fallen from his seat; as he fell, the horse was startled; Jo trying to catch the reins, had been thrown from his seat. He lost consciousness; once he revived enough to hear George Tyson saying, 'The boat be there, shall we take them home?' and then all was as nothing once more, until he awoke in his own bed with Tempy hanging over him.

Nobody pretended to be anxious any longer. Jeffries grinned satisfaction at his patient's progress. When Aunt Fanny suddenly appeared with the barouche, announcing that change was now necessary, and that she had come to carry Jo off then and there, broken bones and all, to the Hall, Jo worked himself into a passion. He didn't want to go, he was much better at home. He gave an unearthly groan when his aunt advanced to persuade him in her most dulcet tones.

'You may as well say at once, Jo, that new things have bewitched you, that flattery has divided you from old friends, that your old home has lost all interest for you,' said Aunt Fanny, greatly startled by his noise, and fairly losing her temper and her eternal melodious inflexions.

'I don't want to be tortured all the way from this to the Hall,' cried Jo with condoning crossness. 'Flattery! why, don't *you* flatter me? you and Aunt Car too?' And then Aunt Fanny leaves the room, followed by Tempy in tears trying to soothe her.

Poor Tempy! the tears rose very easily to her eyes now.

'I don't know what has come to Jo and Tempy,' said Miss Bolsover, exasperated on her return. 'The influence she has gained over them is most painful, and scarcely to be believed.'

'Ha! petticoat influence,' says Mr Bolsover rashly; 'we all know what that is – a very powerful thing; I myself could imagine it difficult to resist Susanna at times.' . . .

Miss Bolsover goes into a peal of silvery laughter. 'Another victim! I told you so, Caroline; another of her victims.'

'I don't know about that,' says Mrs Bolsover, speaking to herself, in her odd mumbling way. 'Victims, victims; Fanny has had plenty of victims in her days, now she is too old and too fat to charm people any more.'

'H'm, h'm! A-h'm, my dear!' says Frederick with warning signs.

So Miss Bolsover fortunately kept away from Crowbeck Place, indignant almost beyond words or expression. Mr Bolsover himself did not come very often, but when he appeared it was generally with a chastened look, which suggested vicarious suffering.

Then things settled down in their new state; Charlie returned no more to Bolsover, Jo went back to college; seasons passed on their course, winter followed the autumn. It was a cold and bitter season. Tempy and her stepmother kept indoors and by the warm fires, while the winds whistled shrill and the snow fell upon the surrounding fells and moors. But Phraisie, a frolicsome little breath of comfort and new hope, would come flying to their arms, and when the winter was gone and the soft spring came, piercing the frozen ground, Jo, returning home for the Easter vacation, found Mikey and Dermy also established for their holidays at Crowbeck, and Susy, in some perplexity as to what she should do with them and how they were to be conveyed home to their mother. It was Josselin who suggested something which every one agreed to then and there without discussion. They all wanted change of scene, he said; they all shrank from London and from Wimpole Street. 'You would like to see your mother, wouldn't you, Mrs Dymond?' said he. 'Why cannot we take the boys over?' Even Tempy brightened up and approved of the suggestion.

CHAPTER XXVI

AT A WINDOW

De la Villette
Dans sa charrette
Suzon brouette
Ses fleurs sur le quai,
Et de Vincennes
Gros Pierre amène
Ses fruits, que traîne
Un âne efflanqué.

J'entends Gavotte
Portant sa hotte
Crier carotte,
Panais et chou-fleur:
Son cri se mêle
A la voix frêle
Du noir ramoneur.

'PARIS.' – DÉSAUGIERS

One night, as if by magic, the whole party found itself neatly packed away in a little omnibus coming from the Northern Station at Paris. Mrs Marney had met her boys, and carried them off home to Neuilly in joyful triumph. The rest of the party were meanwhile jogging deliberately over the stones to the hotel, Phraisie asleep in her mother's arms, Wilkins buried beneath the parcels and shawls and umbrellas which well-bred people always carry wherever they go.

Jo and Tempy, with their heads out of the windows, were exclaiming, while the shops seemed to jolt past, and lights and public buildings ablaze, followed by black spaces crossed with lines of lamps. Finally, the omnibus turned into a narrow street out of a wider thoroughfare. How familiar the echo of the wheels between the high houses sounded to Susy's ears!

More lights flash; the omnibus stops; the landlord and landlady appear in the doorway, the newly-arrived company is officiously escorted and assisted up the narrow staircase to its apartments; the cloth is laid, the candles are lighted; Phraisie's room and Susy's room are on either side of the sitting-room; Jo and Tempy find themselves established across the landing, with more tall windows shaded by muslin blinds and red curtains, and all the echoes of Paris without.

The hotel had been recommended by Madame du Parc as quiet and convenient. Their apartments were on the third floor, small enough and shabby enough compared to the splendour of Crowbeck Place; but Mrs Dymond suddenly felt as if she should like nothing so well as to spend all that remained to her of her life in this little noisy place. She had seen her little Phraisie laid snug and peaceful in her bed; she had unpacked some of the many bags and parcels (how many more she had to unpack of different shapes and sizes than when she had first come abroad some four years ago!). Her own bed was in a curtained alcove, with griffin claws to hang the curtains to; a grey marble table stood in the centre of the room; the prints on the walls were of Napleon, and Poniatowski in Polish boots and a blue helmet; the walls were of faded red, shabby even by candle-light. Susanna thought the place a little paradise. Shabbiness is as much of a treat to people overdone with luxury as a silk gown is to a little Cinderella out of the ashes.

Susy opened her casement wide and leant out, gazing straight down the dark precipice of walls and windows beneath her own with the sense of new breath and life which most people feel when they breathe the pleasant foreign air.

With this breath of relief she leant out farther and farther, looking up and down the chattering, half-lighted street, at the people passing by, so indifferent and unconscious of her existence, at the lamps radiating from the broad boulevard beyond. There was some heap of shadowy blackness at the other end of the street, but Susy had to wait till morning light to realise that the black shadow was that of the church of St Roch.

'Susy, Susy, come to supper,' cries Tempy from the next room, where she and Josselin are already hungrily established, and beginning to help the fishes and fried potatoes by the light of the two tall tapers.

Very early next morning Susanna woke again, for she had not closed her window all the night, and the sun was shining in with dazzling rays. All the world's voice seemed calling up to her from the street below; water, fruit, flowers, old clothes, were being proclaimed with different intonations. Now by the bright daylight, as she leant against the wooden bar, she could see into the stone depths below, and the tall houses rising with their many balconies and shutters. The Rue du Dauphin is a sort of sunshine trap leading to the Tuileries gardens, that were all festive with spring behind the railing and set with orange trees, beyond which rose the glittering mansard roofs and pinnacles of the old palace, where the Henrys and Louises ruled so long, now followed by the Napoleons in turn. At the other end of the street the church of St Roch was standing in the early shadow still, like some huge mountain with flaming peaks. Already its doors were swinging, and people were ascending and descending the great flights of steps; the bells were tolling, the clocks were chiming, the people going in and coming out to their work again; the old women were sitting huddled, with their cloaks and their foot-warmers, at the church doors, with chaplets and religious newspapers to sell; the carts and omnibuses had long since been rolling; the indescribably gay and busy chorus reached the travellers in their high lodging.

The little party could scarcely tear itself away from the windows through which so much was to be seen and heard. Mrs Marney had promised to come to Susy, for Marney was starting off on one of his expeditions, and she meant to join her at the hotel with the boys. Josselin went out, but Susy and Tempy, with Phraisie between them (absorbed in the contemplation of another little girl at play on a balcony opposite), spent their first morning looking out of the window. As the day went on the company became more and more varied; they watched the Frenchwomen floating by, walking with quick and pretty steps and with neat black skirts, leading children drolly attired, elaborate and bedizened, and well-mannered. 'Mamma, look at the funny boy,' says Phraisie, pointing to a little fellow with an enormous collar covered with anchors and emblems, who was advancing up the street with a dignified and monkey-like bearing. The country nurses also go by with their *bambinos* and long cloaks and cap ribbons; coachmen jog past with their white oil-cloth hats; a gendarme passes, cocked hat, epaulettes, white gloves and all, arm-in-arm with his wife; finally, up come Dermy and Mikey at a trot. Susy, seeing the little boys down below, followed by her mother, who had stopped to speak to somebody in the street, went to the door and looked over the stairs, as people do who are on a holiday with time to look out for one another. Mrs Marney came toiling up the winding staircase, breathless, but still conversing.

'Do come up. Come up, I tell you,' Susy heard her say. 'My daughter will like to see you, and we can arrange our plans.'

She heard the little boys also joining hospitably from below: 'M. Max, do – do come; you *shall* not go,' from Dermy; and then Mrs Marney, looking up, sees Mrs Dymond on the landing, and calls –

'Here we are, Susanna; we are bringing Max du Parc to see you.'

Susanna retreated gently and rather shyly into the dignified safeguard of her own room, whither they all followed her, chattering and clattering up the wooden staircase. They brought with them Du Parc, who had not meant to come in, but who could not help himself, for Mrs Marney went ahead announcing him, while one boy held firm by his coat tails, and the other by his hand. Susy, willing to please her mother, and to show her guest that she was not unmindful of all his kindness to her family, came forward in her crape and blackness with her hand out. Du Parc, who was shy and French, bowed very low without noticing the friendly gesture and the outstretched hand, and then Susy seemed to remember suddenly how stiffly he had always met her advances. She blushed, withdrew, and turned shy in an instant, and the young man saw with surprise that the colour was rising in her pale cheeks. He had imagined her belonging to another world and phase of life far distant from his own simple estate, and absolutely indifferent to his presence or absence. Was it possible that such blushes sometimes flashed out of marble statues – that such looks sometimes brighten and then die away, when the gods come in presence with mortal beings?

The little party started forth that morning, as so many have done before and since, with open eyes for the new sights and men and manners – Jo, Tempy, Susanna by her mother, and the two boys walking on either side of Du Parc, who was on his way to a bookseller's in the Rue du Bac. What a walk it was across the gardens by the great Place of the Carrousel, with its triumphal mythology; then by the quais and the noble chain of palaces they reach the river, and so cross the bridge to the Quai Voltaire, where Mrs Marney had some mysterious business to transact for Marney at a furniture dealer's. The business began with some discussion on the door-step, it had then to be carried on in private into the dimmer recesses of the store among the bloated chairs, the gilt and ornamented legs of the Capet dynasty, and the prim, slim, stinted graces of the early Napoleonic times. Whatever it was (Susy would not ask what it was), the discussion took a long and confidentially explosive turn, but the young folks waiting outside upon the quai were in no hurry. They watched the river and the steamers and the crowds upon the quai, where the lime-trees were coming into leaf – where the shops were in full flower, and the many twinkling windows were full of varied hues and shapes. Curious, wonderful, century-old stores of goods, scattered from the past, lined these streets and shop fronts. Looking-glasses reflected the blouses and the white caps passing by the place of courtly splendours, there was silent music in tattered covers, and there were timeless clocks, and flower-pots empty of flowers, and uncut books; fans which had been lying asleep for a hundred years still ready at a touch to start into fluttering life, and wreaths of lovely old lace, there were wonders galore to amuse the country ladies. Susy looked with longing eyes at the delicate festoons and ivory-looking heaps of lace. Mechlin, with its light sprays flowering on soft net, carelessly thrown into a china bowl; the point d'Alençon, like jeweller's work, chased upon the delicate honeycomb, devised by the human bees, who had worked at it year after year. Perhaps also some florid scroll from Italy would be hanging from a rusty nail, with careful pattern travelling from one tendril to another.

'What lovely lace!' cried Susanna. 'Look, Tempy, at the shells upon it; how exquisite they are!'

'Shall I ask the price for you?' says Tempy, instantly bursting into the low shop with its dark panes, where an old Rembrandt-like woman sits keeping watch. '*Combien?*' cries Tempy, in her confident British tones.

'Four hundred francs!' '*Bocoo tro!*' cries the young lady, dashing out again into the warm sunshine.

'Did you ever hear of such extortion?' cries Tempy, whose experience of lace does not reach very much beyond her tuckers.

'It is a great deal of money,' says Susanna.

'Quite out of the question, Susanna,' cries Tempy, decidedly, and her stepmother blushed a little at the rebuke.

Sometimes Tempy's voice sounds so like the Colonel's that Susy could almost imagine he was there to control her still.

'Why is it quite out of the question?' says Jo, stopping short; 'sixteen pounds won't ruin the family altogether. What did your new habit cost, Tempy?'

'A habit!' says Tempy, with a laugh, 'that is something one really cares to have; but Susanna will not care to wear lace again, Josselin.'

'Aunt Fanny is all over lace, and stuffed birds, and things,' says Jo.

'She is not a widow,' Tempy answers gravely. 'Jo, you should remember before you say such things.'

Mrs Marney came out of her shop at that minute, and Max du Parc, who seemed only to have waited for her return, took leave of the party. They asked him to come again. He hesitated, and suddenly said, yes he would come, and he walked away with a swinging step along the quai. They saw him disappearing under the lime-trees, looking across the river as he went along.

CHAPTER XXVII

INCENSE AND VIOLETS

Droop, droop no more or hang the head,
Ye roses almost withered,
New strength and newer purple get,
Each here declining violet.

HERRICK

Du Parc came, shyly at first, because they had asked him to do so, but very soon he got into the habit of coming as a matter of course. The English ladies were not used to Paris and its ways. Du Parc acted as their guide and leader, thanks to whom they enjoyed many a pleasant expedition and sight of the old city, many an amusing experience. They had one other acquaintance, a Mr Bagginal, at the Embassy, who was from their own county and glad to be of use to them; but Max knew more of Paris and of its aspects than the young attaché, who moved in fashionable and restricted circles, and brought invitations, and callers, and bouquets, but who was of little use as a cicerone. . . .

How delightful is the dinning sound of a melodious church bell going in the early morning sunshine; it comes floating into the room and seems to be a part of the very morning and of its joy, a hint of other things to heighten the feast of life.

'Well,' says Mrs Marney, who has just come in as usual with her boys and her friend Du Parc, 'what are we going to do?'

An exclamation from Tempy, who is also as usual leaning from the window, replies to this pertinent question.

'Come here! What is this?' she cries.

All along the Rue du Dauphin, from every quarter people are assembling in crowds that gather thicker every moment – youthful white figures led by parents and relations in their Sunday clothes, boys in shiny shoes and white trousers, girls dressed like brides.

'It is the *premièrecommunion*,' says Mrs Marney all in one word. 'Susy, you should take them to see it. Let Wilkins go too, dear, and I will mind Phraisie.'

Phraisie thought herself quite old enough for any amount of sightseeing, but she was never happier than when alone with her grandmother, and she made no objection.

'But all of us in this crowd, mamma?' said Susy, doubtfully.

'Max will take the boys. Won't you, Max, like a good fellow?' cries Mrs Marney, determined that everybody shall see everything that is to be seen anywhere; and so the party, after some further demur, starts off.

Max goes first with the boys, then come Susy and Tempy in their black dresses; then follows Jo, with his hands in his pockets. He wears a Scotch cap, a rough, cut-away coat, a pair of knickerbockers, less commonly worn in those days than they are now. The tidy French people turn to stare at him, ejaculate 'Anglais!' They also look at Susy with more respectfully admiring eyes. Old St Roch had prepared a welcoming benediction for them all, heretics and Catholics alike, that morning. The centre aisle was full of a white snowstorm of muslin figures. The church was crowded from end to end; the altars were lighted, the candles were burning, hundreds and hundreds of heads were bent in childish adoration, the little restless snowy figures swayed and tossed their white veils. The chorister boys were clustering round about the altars, the priests were passing up and down the middle of the church. The old abbé, in his silver and embroidered shining dress, leant from the pulpit and seemed to be calling a blessing upon the eager congregation. By the high altar stood the curé of the Madeleine, a noble looking figure, also in splendid robes. The sisters and nuns who had had the teaching of so many of the children were keeping guard over their flock from beneath their bent white coiffes as they knelt. The priests beat time, processions come swaying from one chapel and another bearing virgins and saints embroidered on satin with golden fringes. The great organ strikes up, and all the children's voices break out into a shrill sweet morning hymn, as the whole dazzling tide sweeps in procession towards the high altar, carrying its thousand lights and emblematic candles, and followed by crowding parents, friends, sightseers. Then after a pause another discourse begins in sing-song from another pulpit. A monk, in his Benedictine dress, stands up to address the assembled congregation. His words are full of affectionate warnings, exhortations, incitements to religious life in the midst of the world and its temptations. He raises his worn hands as he appeals to his listeners – to the pale motionless sisters, the rosy awe-struck children. It struck one man present strangely and sadly to hear these passionate warnings from those who had not lived, to those whose life was not yet begun. He looked round at the sea of faces, at the blooming company of youthful postulants, at the nuns who stood with bent coiffes and folded hands by the column where he was standing. Poor souls! what hearts had they wounded, what unfair advantages had they grasped from the world? What had all this to do with them? . . . And a sudden revolt rose in his mind, an indignant outcry against the creed which superadded these cruel mortifications and sufferings to the stresses and starvation of daily life, where the poor day by day are expiating the ease of the rich. He thought of Caron's teaching, of his wider horizons, some strange impatience came over him, he would wait no longer in this atmosphere of artificial light and smoke; the incense stifled him; he had an odd feeling that if he stayed he should find himself standing up protesting against the golden pulpit. What was that written up on the wall, *Mene, mene*? Was the church feasting in pomp while multitudes were dying of hunger and ignorance? There stood his English friends in a shy group, the beautiful young mother with eyes full of tears, the young lady with an odd scowling expression; let them look on; how could they know the meaning of it all, or realise the commonest truths of life? 'May they never know,' Du Parc repeated to himself. 'Go to your sister,' he said, suddenly, to the boys. 'I will wait outside.'

Susy saw Du Parc go; she was not surprised; but she was glad nevertheless to find him still waiting in the doorway when she came away followed by her little court. Her eyes were dazzled, her ears ringing with the music and the voices of the people: the great clouds of incense, the thousand lights of the tapers, all intoxicated and excited her. Her heart beat, she looked up with almost childish delight. Du Parc looked grave, impenetrable, very handsome as he stood in the shadow of the arch. As Susy turned to Tempy, who was following, she wondered to find her cold, with a look of something which was almost disgust in her face. Good old Wilkins herself could not have seemed more scandalised by 'them popes and virgins,' as she called them. Jo followed, he had been well amused, admiring and scrutinising the ceremony from a more artistic and dilettante point of view; now he was staring at the church, at the people, at the crowds in the street. Susanna stood for a moment on the steps looking out. Not long afterwards she remembered this minute, so strangely to be repeated by a grim freak of chance. Here were peaceful crowds in a fanciful excitement and ecstasy, in a rapture of white muslin and candlelight, shaken by the echoing organ-sounds. The next time she stood there, she was watching these same people fighting for their lives, flying from death – worshippers at another shrine, fiercer, more terrible, and yet not less remorseless in its expiations and demands.

'Here you are!' said Du Parc, with a sort of impatient cheerfulness. 'Well, now you have seen the great ceremony and the abbé and his eleven hundred virgins. They call him l'Abbé des Demoiselles in the Quartier.'

'Why did you go away?' Susy asked.

'I cannot stand it – the smell of incense always disagrees with me. You, madame, look as if you did not mind being half suffocated; but you will like the lilacs down in the gardens better still.'

'It seemed to me very beautiful,' said Susy, with dancing eyes. 'My daughter here disapproves of it as much as you do. It seemed all so wonderful to me – so beautiful, so full of interest.'

Tempy looked daggers. She had a vague idea Susanna was going over to the Roman Catholic persuasion, that Du Parc was a Jesuit pretending indifference, that the whole thing was a plot got up to influence and persuade her too-yielding, too-persuadable stepmother. She too came down step by step with the crowd, following the stream of people. Some seemed still in a sort of dream, some, on the contrary, wide awake and most keenly alive to the dignity of the moment, to the splendour of their sons in varnished boots, with fringed ribbons on their arms, of their daughters in white muslin, with veils and white caps, and a general unction of new clothes and new blessings. And indeed there can be but one feeling when the boys and girls at the outset of life come up one by one with beaming faces to ask a blessing upon their future from the old time-worn bishop and pastor, whose own life is so nearly at an end. This was what Susy said as they walked down the crowded street which led to the Tuileries garden, when Du Parc again made some bitter joke. 'I am like the *gamin*, who put aside the faith of a Pascal with a joke,' said Du Parc. 'I'm afraid it is no use talking to me.'

The little shops were bristling with their treasures, the people were standing in their doorways to see the company disperse, the carts and carriages cumbering the road. They passed a flower cart standing in a gutter; a country woman with a red handkerchief on her head was changing the beautiful bunches of fragrance into halfpennies and pennies. It was another version of the old lamps for new. Many of the flowers were delicate, such as we grow with elaborate care in greenhouses and hothouses – white lilacs, and pink carnations with their long blue stalks, some sort of early flowering poppy, pale and feathery, and then narcissus and roses in heaps, and white daisies in their modest garb, looking as if they too had been to their first communion. The violets in their fragrant heaps were piled together, all their sweetness tied with a wisp of straw. Susanna stopped, exclaiming, but Du Parc hurried her on. 'Pass on, pass on, madame,' he said almost impatiently; 'you are stopping the way.' Again Tempy drew herself up with a look of absolute amazement and impatience; what did this man, this drawing-master, mean by speaking in this imperious tone to her stepmother? She deliberately stopped and began to ask the price of the flowers, and bought a bunch of somewhat faded rosebuds which the flower woman thrust into her hand; the others waited while she bargained, not that she cared for pennies, but from an Englishwoman's sense of duty.

'Why didn't you get violets?' said Susy; 'they seemed so sweet.'

A minute after they were crossing the Rue de Rivoli to the side gate of the Tuileries gardens.

'One crosses at the risk of one's life,' said Susanna, smiling and turning to speak to Du Parc, – but he was gone. When he rejoined them a minute after at the iron gate he was carrying a huge bunch of the sweet violets Susanna had liked.

'I ventured also to add some lilies of the valley; such flowers were created for you,' he said.

There was something indescribable in his tone which startled her; she looked up, she saw a look of such bright admiration, such pride and homage combined, that her thanks suddenly failed her.

'Violets and lilies,' said Tempy, wanting to say something to break the momentary silence, which seemed almost significant; 'violets are not so nice as roses.'

'Unhappy France has heard more than enough of them, mademoiselle,' said Du Parc, recovering himself quickly, but with a very well-pleased expression still showing in his dark eyes. 'This is the first time for years I have cared to buy any; but to-day they have seemed to me emblems of peace and sweetness, instead of greed and wicked rapacity.'

Susy could not answer all this. She, a mother, a widow who should have known life, to be silenced suddenly, confused like a very school-girl, it was not to be endured.

CHAPTER XXVIII

ST DAMIAN AND OTHERS

. . . that silver sphere
Whose intense lamp narrows
In the white dawn clear.

SHELLEY

All their time was not given to Paris, delightful as Paris was; it was a pleasure to escape the city on those glorious spring days. Marney was still away, and Susy and her children often found their way to the Villa du Parc, and from thence to the Bois de Boulogne or the outlying country places. Little Phraisie used to remain with her grandmother; the others would stroll further afield, and Du Parc, who so rarely left his work, who never allowed himself a holiday, now seemed to have nothing better to do than to escort his mother's friend and her companions. One afternoon he took them to a village about a mile off; he led the way with his big stick along the high road for a time, then across a cabbage-field, then by a country cross-road leading to a village not far from the Seine. There was an old church, one of the very oldest in the neighbourhood, that he wanted them to see. He had done an etching of it for the 'Beaux Arts.'

The lamp was burning dimly in the little church before the high altar, where a black verger stood in his robes. There was a silver dove hanging from the middle of the roof, and a gilt sun, with brassy rays like an organ, which shone upon the altar. Little pictures, bright-coloured, miraculous, covered the bare walls with representations of benevolent marvels – heavenly hands and protruding arms interposing from the clouds to prevent disaster here on earth; runaway horses arrested, falling houses caught in the act. There was a huge black crucifix with a coloured figure of Death – a somewhat terrible and striking reminder to the living of the future and the past. More cheerful tinselled ornaments were piled upon the altar, whose fine cloth was guarded by a chequered linen top. The wooden pulpit was painted to look like precious veined marble, so was the battered old confessional with the thumb marks of the penitents. Outside the little church, in the Place, the cocks and hens cackled, becketed in the grass; a stream ran close by the opened door with a pleasant wash of water. They had passed the curé's house close at hand, with its laburnums, and the field beyond where the linen strips were bleaching, and the children squatting in the dust, and the man with the wooden shoes and the oilskin hat and the torn blouse, breaking flints in the sunshine. Everything outside looked hot and bright and delicate and business-like, while everything inside was dark and dreamily fervent. To people accustomed from childhood to Catholic chapels, the scent of the lingering incense seems to be the breath of the prayers and hymns of the pious who have lingered here generation after generation on their way from the streets and the sunshine outside, to the quiet churchyard across the field.

Max looked round to-day with friendly eyes at his old playmates, St Cosmo and St Damian, those favourite martyrs – at St Dominic in his black robe, St Catharine with her pointing finger, St Barbara with her wheel, good St Ursula with a detachment of maidens, standing by the well-remembered sketch of the Day of Judgment, where six or seven just persons escorted by two virtuous little angels were being trumpeted up to heaven, while over a dozen wicked were being swallowed then and there by a huge green monster. All these quaint familiar things hung undisturbed as they had hung in the young man's recollection for the quarter of a century he could look back to. The bright silver hearts and tokens, the tallow candles peacefully smoking on the triangle – all meant childhood and familiar faces and everyday innocent life to him. He did not feel here in the little village church as at St Roch on the day of the great celebration. There he had chafed and revolted. Tempy herself could not have felt more repelled than Max du Parc; but this was his whole childhood, one of his simplest and most intimate associations. How curiously the same emblems affect different minds. To Tempy they meant terrors and superstition; to Jo a picturesque and characteristic episode of foreign travel; and to Susanna they meant something like a strange dream of reality, like an image of all that was in her heart just then. There was the charm, the intense attraction of that which was not and must never be her creed; and also a terror of that remorseless law which spared not, which accepted martyrdom and self-renunciation as the very beginning of the lesson of life – of that life which since the world began had been crying out so passionately for its own, for its right to exist, to feel, to be free. This afternoon Mrs Dymond seemed to have caught something of Du Parc's antagonistic mood that day at St Roch's; she was thinking how these pale saints had turned one by one from the sunshine and the storms of daily life, from the seasons in their course, from the interests and warm fires of home, to a far-away future, of which these sad tapers, winking and smoking, these glittering silver trinkets, were the symbols; they had given earnest and passionate prayers in the place of love and living desires and the longing of full hearts; they had taken pain and self-inflicted sufferings in place of the natural submission and experience of life, and the restraints of other's rights and other's needs.

'I can't think how people can endure such superstition,' said Tempy, flouncing out into the porch. 'Come, Jo, it makes me sick,' and she nearly tumbled over an old couple who had been kneeling in the shadow of the doorway.

Susy blushed up, as she often did, for Tempy's *brusquerie*, and looked anxiously at Du Parc, who had caught the young lady by the arm as she stumbled.

Tempy seemed to rouse some latent opposition in Max du Parc.

'Take care,' he said in English; 'go gently, and don't upset those who are still on their knees. After all there are not many people left upon their knees now,' he added as they came out together, 'and I don't see that much is gained by having everybody running about the streets instead.'

'At all events it is something gained to hear people speaking the real truth, and saying only what they really think, as we do in our churches,' said Tempy, with one of her stares.

Du Parc made her a low bow.

'If that is the case, mademoiselle, I shall certainly came over to England and get myself admitted into your religion by a reverend with a white tie.'

Tempy didn't answer, but walked on.

Jo burst out laughing. Susy didn't laugh; she was in this strange state of emotion, excitement, she could not laugh. Something had come to her, something which in all her life she had never felt as now, a light into the morning, a tender depth in the evening sky, a meaning to the commonest words and facts. There is a feeling which comes home to most of us at one time or another; philosophers try to explain it, poets to write it down only, musicians can make it into music, it is like a horizon to the present – a sense of the suggestion of life beyond its actual din and rough shapings. This feeling gives a meaning to old stones and fluttering rags, to the heaps and holes on the surface of the earth, to the sad and common things as well as to those which are brilliant and successful. Had this supreme revelation come to Susanna, now? or was it only that in France the lights are brighter, the aspects of life more delightful – that with the sight of all this natural beauty and vivacity some new spring of her life had been touched which irradiated and coloured everything?

But it was not France, it was the poetry of to-day and the remembrance of yesterday which softened her sweet looks, which touched her glowing cheek. It was something which Susy did not know of, which she had never guessed at until now, widow though she was, mother though she was.

Susanna for the last few years had been so accustomed to silence, to a sort of gentle but somewhat condoning courtesy, that it seemed to her almost strange to be specially addressed and considered.

Tempy could not understand it either. Once or twice Susanna met the girl's surprised half-laughing, half-disapproving glance, and the elder woman would blush and look amused, appealing; she seemed to be asking her stepdaughter's leave to be brilliant for once – to answer the friendly advances of the French gentlemen who called with red ribbons, and the French ladies with neatly poised bonnets. One or two invitations came for them through Mr Bagginal. Sometimes Susy, animated, forgetting, would look so different, so handsome, that Tempy herself was taken aback. Mrs Dymond's black dignities became her – the long lappets falling, the silken folds so soft, so thick, that moved with her as she moved. She had dressed formerly to please her husband, who, in common with many men, hated black, and liked to see his wife and his daughter in a cheerful rainbow of pink and green and blue and gilt buttons. Now that she was a widow she wore plain long dresses, soft and black, suiting her condition and becoming to her sweet and graceful ways. She had bought herself a straw hat, for the sun was burning in the avenues of Neuilly, and with her round hat she had given up her widow's cap. A less experienced hand than Max du Parc might have wished to set this graceful blackness down for ever as it stood on the green outside the little chapel that summer's day. The children were still playing, the geese were coming up to be fed, the dazzle of light and shade made a sweet out-of-door background to the lovely light and shade of Susy's wistful pale face as she stood facing them all, and looking up at the carved stone front of the shabby little church.

They walked home slowly two by two. Tempy, who had not yet forgiven Du Parc his religion or his bow, took her brother's arm.

Two figures that were hobbling along the path a little way in front of them, stopped their halting progress, and turned to watch the youthful company go by. They were forlorn and worn and sad, and covered with rags and dirt; the woman carried a bundle on a stick, the man dragged his steps through the spring, limping as he went.

'Yes,' said Max, answering Susy's look of pity, 'one is happy and forgets everything else, and then one meets some death's-head like this to remind one of the truth. Think of one man keeping all that for himself,' and he pointed back to a flaming villa with pink turrets beyond the field, 'and another reduced to such shreds of life.'

'I don't think people in England are ever quite so miserable,' said Susy.

'You think not?' said Max. 'I have seen people quite as dirty, quite as wretched in London. I remember one day at Caron's lodging in Brompton'. . .

Susy wondered why he stopped short in the middle of his sentence. Max had suddenly remembered when it was he had seen two wretched beggars thrust from a carriage door, and by whom. 'And in Soho near where you lived,' the young man continued after a moment, speaking in a somewhat constrained voice and tone. 'Any night, I think, you might have seen people as sad and wretched as these. I used to go to a street in that quarter for my dinner very often, and while I dined they walked about outside. Once,' he added more cheerfully, as another remembrance came into his mind, 'I met a member of your family, madame, at my dining-place, Monsieur Charles Bolsover. Poor fellow,' said Max, returning to his French, 'I hope he is in happier conditions than he was then – he had a friend whom I met afterwards and who took me to see him. He seemed in a doleful state.'

'Were you then present on that dreadful occasion?' said Susanna, turning pale. 'Oh! Monsieur du Parc, he had been drinking to forget his trouble!'

'What, madame, even you,' said Max, 'do you find nothing kinder to say of the poor boy? Drinking! He had not been drinking any more than I had – he was ill, he was in a fever for a week afterwards. I used to go and sit with him in his friend's lodgings. . . . They told me the story.' . . . Max glanced at Tempy, who was walking ahead laughing, and twirling her parasol – 'Forgive me,' he said, 'I am meddling with what is not my concern!'

'But it concerns *me*, Monsieur du Parc,' said Susy, trembling very much. 'It concerns me very very nearly, if Charlie has been unjustly accused – if he was ill, poor boy, and we did not know it.'

'It is a fact, madame,' said Max, dryly; 'if you were to ask his friend, the Reverend White, he will tell you the same thing. Your nephew is not the first of us who has been overcome by an affair of the heart. I gathered from him that your . . . that you disapproved of his suit.'

'My husband was afraid to trust his daughter's happiness to any one of whom we had heard so much that was painful,' said Mrs Dymond coldly, and remembering herself.

Max civilly assented.

'A father must judge best for his child,' she continued, melting as he froze, and speaking with an unconscious appeal in her voice and her eyes. Why was it that she felt as if Du Parc's opinion mattered so much? She could not bear him to misjudge things; to think any one cold, or hard.

'Of course you have to consider what is best,' said the young man, softening to her gentleness; 'but believe me that is not a bad young fellow. Poor boy, it was a heart of gold. I can scarcely imagine the young lady having inspired such a devotion,' he said, for a moment forgetting the near relationship between the two women; 'but to me she seems strangely fortunate.'

'Ah! You don't know her,' said Susy eagerly; 'you don't know how noble she is, how good, how lovable.'

'What would you have, madame?' said Du Parc laughing. 'Of you I am not afraid, but of the Miss I am in terror, and she detests me too. Ask madame your mother.'

They had come to the gates of the villa by this; Phraisie appeared in the doorway with Madame to welcome them back. Mrs Marney's voice was heard calling from within. Max was not over-pleased to see a visitor under the tree waiting the ladies' return. It was their north-country neighbour, Mr Bagginal from the Embassy, who had been making himself agreeable to Madame in the meanwhile. He had a scheme for a walk in the wood at St Cloud, and a dinner. The court was there, and the gardens closed, but the young man with some pride produced an order of admission.

'Thank you, we shall like it very much indeed,' says Tempy.

Susy looked at Du Parc. 'Shall you have time to come, too?' she asked.

'Monsieur Caron is in the studio waiting for you, Max,' said his mother; 'he has got his pocket full of proclamations, as usual,' and without answering Mrs Dymond, Du Parc slowly turned and walked into the studio.

CHAPTER XXIX

ALMSGIVING

In that new world which is the old.

As the actors pass across the stage of life and play their respective parts, it is not difficult at the outset to docket them with their different characters – a soldier, a parson, an artist, a lawyer, a lover, a heroine, a law-giver, a widow, and so forth.

But presently, after the play has gone on for a little while (on the stage of life it is not the play that ends, but the actors who come and go), we begin to see that, although some of us may be suited to our parts, there are others whose natures are ill-fitted to their *rôle*, and very often we find the performers suddenly playing away in their own natural characters instead of those which they are supposed to represent, to the very great confusion of the drama which is going on.

Here is the lawyer making love to his client instead of drawing up her will; the parson fighting his bishop instead of guarding his flock; the soldier preaching sermons; the actor taking his part in serious earnest, and blessing his people with unction. A hundred instances come to one's mind of fiddlers and tailors set to rule great kingdoms, with what tragic ill-luck, alas! we all remember. Was not one mechanician born to a throne, whose life paid for his idiosyncrasies? And, again, have we not heard of a Spinoza patiently at work upon his lenses earning his daily pittance, a true king among men, one whose wise and noble thoughts still rule the succeeding generations? Other instances will occur to us all, of travesties still more incongruous. A priest serving his king before his God, a poet, with wilder blood and genius than his compeers, sitting with them at St Stephen's upon a dusty cushion, which he presently flings in their faces, and, in generous wrath and excitement, goes off to die, fighting for liberty, under the blue sky of Greece.

When Max du Parc, the son of a dreamer and of a downright and practical woman, found himself started in life in the little studio at the end of his mother's garden, he was certainly to blame in that he did not keep with peaceful devotion to the career into which Fate had launched him, with so little effort on his own part. His engravings were excellent, but still more so were his etchings, boldly worked out, remarkable for their force, their colour (and such a term may often be used with justice even where black and white alone are used). He had received his red ribbon with the rest of them for work done during the last two years, for medals gained at exhibitions for etchings, some of which were now hanging in gilt frames at St Cloud among the eagles. Among others he had worked for money as well as for love. The day before Susanna, seeing one of his most successful prints in a shop window, had blushed up painfully and looked away. Du Parc saw her turn crimson; he guessed that she had recognised his work; he felt as if he could gladly tear the picture with its insolent Bacchantes from its place and destroy it then and there for ever.

Susy guessed what was passing in his mind.

'I have never lived among artists,' she said. 'I know there are many things I do not understand; but I have lately learnt,' she added, gently, 'how beautiful, how wonderful it all is; and I shall always be grateful to you for teaching Jo.'

And Du Parc turned a searching look upon her, though he did not answer. Perhaps if his art had meant less to him it might have led him further still; it was something beyond colour, beyond form that he wanted, in his work as in his life, which haunted him at times and made him ashamed of mere clever successes.

All this moralising equally applies to my heroine, Susanna, a woman of natural aptitude and impressionability, placed by no unkind fate in a peaceful and prosperous position. And now the moment had come when she was to play her touching part of a mourning Dido no longer, and lo! flinging away the veils and the dignity of widowhood, wiping the natural tears, she found herself true to her nature – not false to her past; alive, not dead, as she imagined, existing still, not having ceased to feel, a human being, not an image in a looking-glass; not remembering only, but submitting to the great law of life, which is stronger and less narrow than any human protest and lamentation.

Once more Mrs Dymond was leaning from her high window,

impatiently scanning the figures coming and going along the pavement. Why did he keep them? The day was passing, the hours were waning. She was the most impatient of the party. There sat Jo, absorbed in his painting. He was trying to copy the great blue china pot he had brought home from the Quai, and the pink poppies that Tempy had stuck into it, with their blue shadows and their silver-green leaves; Jo had a natural taste for still life. His stepmother was grateful beyond words to those squares of colour, to those never-failing interests of form, of light, of arrangement, which interested him; she herself had no such natural gift; she was all the more glad when Jo, under Du Parc's guidance, had tried his hand at art. Mrs Dymond was less pleased when she heard her stepson announcing that he had also adopted some of Monsieur Caron's doctrines. Jo had met Caron once or twice at the studio, where the good old man used to call with the various handbills and tricolor announcements which he was having printed to herald the coming book.

Tempy, who had wanted to start half an hour before, now sat half asleep upon the red couch with its red cushions. The faint aroma of the poppies in the sunlight seemed to taint the drowsy air in the little room, where time passed to the slow ticking of the clock, and where Apollo in his car was for ever galloping beneath his crystal dome. Little Phraisie was in the next room, also sleeping, on the bed with drawn curtains. When the heat of the day was over, Henrietta Wilkins was to take her into the Tuileries gardens close by. It was her pride to sit there at her work, and to hear the people admire the 'little Cherubim,' while she piled her gravel pies at her nurse's knee.

Mrs Dymond had insisted on waiting for her mother and Du Parc. As the flood of people passed on down below in vain she scanned the figures – seeking for the persons for whom she looked. A vague sense of uneasy disappointment came over her. So absorbed was she watching the endless procession that she did not hear the door open, nor become aware that Du Parc was in the room, until Jo's loud cries of 'Mrs Dymond! Mrs Dymond!' made her look round.

A dark figure was standing in the doorway. Tempy started up, Jo put down his brush, and Susanna, with a sudden sense of ease and tranquillity, turned from her window and faced her new friend, blushing a little, looking more beautiful than he had ever seen her.

'Madame,' said Du Parc, bowing very low as usual.

'How do you do, M. Max?' said Mrs Dymond, welcoming her visitor. 'Where is my mother? Is she not coming?'

'I was not able to see her when I called – Madame Marney was in her room. She sends a message,' and Du Parc brought out a folded scrap from his waistcoat pocket:–

'My Darling Susy,

Do not wait for me; I had rather not come. I am keeping the boys, for I expect their father home.

'YOUR LOVING MOTHER.

'P.S. – I will call if I can, and see the darling baby in the course of the day.'

The note was disappointing, but it was no use delaying any longer.

'We are late,' says Tempy, starting up. 'We ought not to have waited so long. Mr Bagginal will be quite tired out.'

'I have been with M. Caron. I am sorry you delayed for me,' said Du Parc, as usual only addressing Susanna, who was giving Wilkins some parting directions as she took her cloak and her parasol from her faithful attendant.

Max seemed preoccupied at first and unlike himself, as they all walked along the street to the Quai, whence the steamers started.

Susanna and the pursuit of pleasure were not at this moment the great preoccupations of his mind; other things less peaceful, less hopeful were daily closing up around him. There was a terrible reality to him in his apprehensions, all the more vivid because from his artistic qualities he belonged to the upper and more prescient classes, while from experience and birth he was near enough to the people to understand the tones of its voice, the wants of its daily life, its angry rising, and its present mood.

But by degrees, being in Susanna's company, he brightened up. Love requires time and space, if it is not able to accomplish absolute impossibilities, but it certainly makes the most of the passing lights and moments of life.

'M. Caron detained me over the proofs of his book,' said Du Parc.

'You need not explain. We have nothing to do but to amuse ourselves, you have your work to attend to,' said Susy gaily.

Susanna had felt of late as if her relations with Du Parc were changed, and it seemed quite natural that he should give her details of his day's work. Max, too, realised that he was some one in her life, not a passer-by, but a fellow-traveller. The two might very well have walked out of one of the galleries of the Louvre hard by. She with her Grecian goddess looks, he of the dark, southern head with the black hair, that beaked nose, the dark, sudden eyes, so deeply set, eyes that were hard and soft by turns. And now at this moment, not for the first time, a sense of his reality, of the importance of his presence, of his good-will, of his approbation and acquiescence with her conclusions came over her. There was a curious simplicity about Du Parc which impressed people; either he said what he meant, or he let you see that he mistrusted you and was silent. He had great powers of work and a gift for enjoyment as well, which is perhaps more rare, and as he walked along by Susy's side, with his bright looks and his odd swinging gait, he had seemed the very impersonation of a holiday-maker, of a man at one with the moment. They were crossing the great court of the Louvre when a shadow came from behind a statue, and a frightened woman, starting out into the sunshine, suddenly put out a trembling white hand for alms. Susanna and her young people, from their English training, were passing on, they had a vague idea it was wrong to give to casual beggars, but Du Parc stopped short.

'Why are you begging, Madame Lebris?' said he roughly. 'Are you ill?'

'I am dying,' said the woman quietly; 'my children are starving.'

'Where is your husband?'

'You know better than I do,' she answered.

'Go home at once,' said Du Parc. 'I will come and see you this evening.'

He thrust a napoleon into her hand. She took it with a weary look, and he nodded and hurried after the others. They were all standing a few yards off waiting for him.

'I know the woman, she is the wife of a man who has worked for me,' he said in French, looking vexed and confused. He had paid away his last gold piece, and he had but a few sous left in his pocket. How was he to go on with them and pay for his share of the dinner? Max had hardly recovered himself when he saw Mr Bagginal. 'Ah!' said he, 'there is your friend!' and, as he spoke, our attaché, with an umbrella, a grievance, and a flower in his button-hole, came up to meet them from the steamer-steps.

The holiday of the year had begun, and with the sunshine the shores had quickened with green, with song, with the stir of spreading life. There were two or three young men and women and some children on board, one or two experienced excursionists, some housekeepers, carrying their baskets, a village wedding, returning home after the ceremony; as the steamer stopped at each landing-place in turn, the company passed off the boat, scarcely any one remained by the time they were nearing St Cloud. Jo was practising his French upon the man at the wheel. Tempy, much amused by the smoothly talkative and attentive Mr Bagginal, sat somewhat mollified and relenting on a bench, red hair and Parisian checked cotton dress and her big white ombrelle open to shade her pink cheeks. Susy, at the other end of the same bench, sat smiling, watching the lights and the shadows, listening to the song of the birds and the wash of the ripples, answering a word now and then when Du Parc, who had been smoking at the other end of the boat, came up to speak to her.

At first, conscious of impecuniosity and also under the restraint of Mr Bagginal's presence, he had kept silent and aloof. Now he began to talk again; he told her stories along the shore, pointed out the prettiest walks, the pleasantest *châlets* where the Parisians go on summer afternoons, and dine and enjoy the sunsets in the sky, while the fish come leaping from the river into their plates, and the white wine flows into the glasses which the damsels bring with serious smiling looks, and the white boats glide by, and birds fly home to rest, and the glorious sunset says, 'Come, clink the glasses and quaff the golden wine.'

'Ah! do you know that place?' interrupted Mr Bagginal, as Max pointed out a restaurant with wide balconies standing by the water's edge. 'I'm told it is first-rate; shall we dine there?'

'You will find a very good dinner,' Max said.

The steamer travelled on between the shores in the new sunshine. It was so early in the season that but few people were on board. One of those glorious bursts of spring had overtaken them.

Susy saw villas amid budding sycamore trees, with fringing poplars, whitewashed walls, terraces, gardens breaking into flower, high roads, whence people hailed the steamer with friendly signs. She watched the pale blue spring sky, the high floating clouds.

'Are you not afraid of being burnt?' said Du Parc.

Susy opened her sunshade, though she loved the sun. Was she awake or asleep; was this herself, the sad, harassed, bewildered, lonely widow, this happy being basking in this delightful, invigorating present? Vivid admiration is a disturbing element sometimes, we thankfully absorb the hour tranquilly, exist to the uttermost while it lasts, scarcely understand it all. So sits Susanna while the water beats fresh against the sides of the big boat and the warm sunlight comes quickening; everything flows into the very soul of the hour, that mysterious natural soul, which people share with one another, with place, with time.

They travelled on peacefully in this floating companionship and sympathy, while the new life stirred along the banks.

CHAPTER XXX

ST CLOUD BEFORE THE STORM

Amidst th' Hesperian garden, on whose banks,
Bedewed with nectar and celestial songs,
Eternal roses grow and hyacinth,
And fruits of golden rind, on whose faire tree,
The scaly harvest-dragon ever keeps
His unenchanted eye.

COMUS

'I wish my mother had come with us,' said Susy, as the steamer stopped at the landing-place of St Cloud, just where the public place and the barracks and the terraces all meet, while beyond these slate roofs and balustrades, the tufted green and lilac, and silver and gold of the lovely hanging garden rise, and the white walls and windows of the palace. A flag was flying, for the court was there, the Emperor, the Empress, the young Prince Imperial, and their attendants, and indeed as they landed, the soldiers were presenting arms to some smart open carriages, which were rolling by with glittering outriders, a flashing of harness, a waving of plumes, a click of arms; it was a pretty, brilliant sight.

'Shall we dine first, or walk first?' said Mr Bagginal gaily. 'M. du Parc, you know the place better than I do.'

Du Parc hesitated.

'If *ces dames* are not afraid of a long walk,' said Du Parc, 'we might stroll back through the woods to Sèvres; and I can recommend that little restaurant you were looking at just now for your dinner,' he said, finishing his sentence to Susanna herself.

Susy agreed at once. She was in childish spirits, and behaving like a child, thought Tempy severely, somewhat in Mrs Bolsover's frame of mind.

Jo stared at Susanna, he too did not know her; he too liked her best in her old subdued condition, though he was glad to see her happy.

There was a pretty little girl in a village night-cap on board, about little Phraisie's age, and as the steamer started, Susy stood looking after the child, and thinking of her own with some natural maternal solicitude; then she turned and found Max as usual waiting by her side and watching her with something the same expression as that with which she had looked at the departing child.

'I should like to have made a sketch of that child,' he said, a little confused at being surprised. 'No wonder women are pious,' he added, 'when they have pretty *bambinos* of their own to worship. I should think for you, madame, the difficulty must be, not to believe, but to keep rational in your convictions.'

Then Max moved on again and joined the others, for he had seen, though Susy did not notice it, a somewhat gloomy exchange of looks pass between Tempy and her brother as they stood waiting on the slope above.

It was a general holiday of sunshine, lilacs, lime-trees; dazzling, blossoming flowers on every slope and terrace. The steep sides were heaped with colour; the wrought-iron railings were overhung with garlands, with ivy and laburnum and sweet flowering bushes pushing through the bars. Whitsuntide had come with an exquisite burst. All these French people, natural lovers of beauty and sunshine, were out basking in the flood of sudden happiness. At the gate of the great court stood a girl, with a half-penitent, half-laughing face; she had stolen some overhanging branches of lilac and May blossom, and had been called sternly to account by one of the old veterans in uniform and metal buttons, guardian angels of this earthly paradise.

The girl, undaunted by the buttons, looked up with merry, entreating eyes, the brave old veteran, unconquered in a hundred fights, seemed hard put to it now, for all his stripes and gold braid. Just overhead from a second terrace, bordered by scrolled iron rails and ivy creepers, hung an anxious audience of girls, also provided with the plunder of spring, and wondering what their own chance of escape would be.

'She will come over him,' said Mr Bagginal laughing. 'Look, he is yielding.'

Max shrugged his shoulders in an irritating way.

'Why do you look so angry?' said Susy.

'She will get as a veniality what is her natural right,' said Max. 'That is how morality is taught in our schools.'

'But if you think everybody else has a natural right to pick everything there will be only broken stalks for you and me,' says Mr Bagginal with his usual drawl.

'I don't know about you,' said Max laughing, 'I myself have long ago made up my mind to broken stalks,' and as he spoke he flung a little spray of lilac he had picked over the railings of the terrace.

'M. Caron should be here,' said Jo. 'What is it he was saying in the studio last night, that an equal subdivision of material was an absurdity – that all gifts should be spiritual . . . and capable of infinite division?'

'I don't suppose even Caron could tell you the difference between material and spiritual,' aid Max, shrugging his shoulders. 'He certainly doesn't practise his precepts, but I suppose *the Patron* meant that if you give a man a fish he is hungry again in an hour. If you teach him to catch a fish you do him a good turn. But these very elementary principles are apt to clash with the leisure of the cultivated classes. Will Mr Bagginal now produce his ticket – the result of favour and the unjust subdivision of spiritual enjoyments?' said Du Parc, with a smile.

Mr Bagginal stared at Max for a moment. Max stared back. Du Parc had a quiet, confident manner, which had not, however, always put people at their ease.

Mr Bagginal's order was produced, and the veterans unlocked the gates and admitted these wanderers into deeper and sweeter glades and beauties. They skirted the avenues, advancing by the stately green arcades, walking under the chestnut-trees in flower, climbing from one ivy-bound terrace to another – from stone flight to stone flight, from avenue to avenue again, and so onward through the glorious spring into greener and yet greener places. The larks were singing overhead, nightingales and thrushes were answering from end to end with notes so sweet, so loud, so mellow that all these human beings, with one accord, ceased talking to listen to the sweet pertinacious melody. After a time they found themselves coming out into an open place where a lake lay glistening in the spring.

'There is a terrace somewhere near this,' said Mr Bagginal. 'Who knows the way to it?' And Du Parc went to inquire of some women with flowers in their hands, who stood smiling, and pointing out the road.

'One certainly gets a capital panorama of Paris here,' says Tempy, breathlessly, and ascending the steps of the terrace, and talking in her loud, cordial voice to Mr Bagginal. 'I should like to sketch it, but I'm not good at sketching! Jo could do it, couldn't you, Jo?'

'Would you also like to see me stand on my head on the dome of the Invalides?' said Jo gravely.

'What *do* you mean, you silly boy?' said Tempy. 'You sketch beautifully; doesn't he, Monsieur du Parc?'

But Max didn't answer. He had not yet reached the others, and stood leaning against the lower end of the stone parapet by Mrs Dymond, and looking out at the wondrous circle of hills. Susy lingered for an instant, she had almost forgotten that such happiness was possible – such a moment, such a spring-tide; the whole air was full of a wonderful perfume, the very branches of the trees all seemed to be singing and flinging their incense upon the air.

As Mrs Dymond stood, flushed and motionless, a new sense of the universal community of life reached her, was it her sorrow that died away in the flame of the sunshine? Her black gown turned to purple in the light. Suddenly she seemed to know that she was young, that she belonged to the world in which she was breathing, to *now*, not only to the past; that the present claimed her, that the past was past.

'Come up this way. Come! come!' cries Jo, looking back, and in a sort of dream Susanna moved on, still followed by Du Parc. At their feet spreads Paris in its sober robe of white, with its thousand domes and roofs and spires, pale, shining and beautiful, delicately outlined and shaded; while the hills lie like a charm enclosing all, and the silver turns of the river are flowing on into the very heart of the great city, as though to wash away every shadow and stain from its stones.

There are some things can scarcely be remembered, much less written down; among these is the quality of moments which come to us now and again, the complexity and multiplication of happiness and beauty which can give these life.

'And what about dinner?' says Mr Bagginal. 'How does one get away from here?'

'There should be a path somewhere through this wood,' says Max, looking about him.

He found the way presently, along the shade and the sunshine under the trees, past a sunny glen where some milk-white goats, like creatures out of an idyll, were disporting themselves. Pan was perhaps hidden among the bushes or Actæon was sleeping among the ivy. The little wood led down hill to iron gates.

CHAPTER XXXI

À LA PÊCHE MIRACULEUSE

Pour être au ton de vos musettes,
En vain je cherche de l'esprit. . . .

MOREAU

As they came jogging gaily along the lane Jo leaped up in the air, broke a branch of lilac from one of the over-hanging trees, and coming up to his stepmother flung it to her.

'Take it home for me,' said Jo; 'put it in your parasol. I'll try and paint it when I get back,' and he hurried past her to overtake the others.

'Don't you think he has great talent?' said Susanna, with a thoughtful look, which brightened as it fell on Jo's red shock head.

'He must work on and find out for himself what he is capable of,' said Du Parc, looking not at Jo but at Susy herself with unconcealed kindness and admiration.

Even for Susanna, or perhaps because it was Susanna (to him the sweetest, fairest woman he had ever known), he could not say more than he felt. Her concerns seemed to him next to his own the most important things in all the world. Perhaps his own also gained in importance from her coming, her interest in them. They were reaching the gate where the sentry was standing, armed to the teeth, and Susy, with a woman's disregard of lawful authority, drew a fold of her dress over the lilac blossom.

The iron gates led by a lane to the village green of Sèvres, where the children were at play and where many people were coming and going, while old people talked in the sunshine. The green led to the river, spanned by the bridge soon to be the scene of so many desperate encounters, of unavailing appeals and hopeless parleys, the boundary line between victory and defeat. Who could have realised that day the piteous tragedy, already near, while the children danced and the peaceful elders rested at the end of their long day's work, and the young people advanced gay with the mirth of the hour?

Neither Jo nor Tempy as they went along noticed a strange-looking figure, who, however, seemed greatly interested in them. It was a tall, pale man, in a workman's dress, with long fair hair reaching to his shoulders. He had been resting on a bench; he got up, seeing Du Parc, and laid his hand heavily and familiarly upon his arm.

'Ah! at last. I hoped we might meet,' he said, drawing him a little aside. Then quickly and excitedly, 'Hast thou heard the news? The police have paid a domiciliary visit to Papa Caron: they found nothing except some of thy caligraphies. Happily art is privileged. The commissaire was told that thy "Goddess of Liberty" was the portrait of the late Madame Caron. I have seen Lebris,' the stranger went on. 'He tells me Dombrowski is in Paris. He will be in the Rue de la Hotte to-night, are we to expect you? *Mademoiselle vous es'cusera*,' said the long-haired man somewhat familiarly, with a stare at Susy.

Du Parc looked at his acquaintance with a very haughty air, which took him of the long hair somewhat aback.

'Lebris had much better be looking after his family than meddling in things he does not understand,' said Du Parc, and turning away without a further answer he rejoined Mrs Dymond and almost hurried her away.

'Is that an artist?' said Susy, rather awe-stricken.

'An artist, no; that is one of our rising politicians,' said the young man, with a shrug of the shoulders as they walked on. 'I confess that if it was not for M. Caron's sake I could gladly knock him down for his impertinence to you. His name is Jourde, he is one of the best of them. But – ah! the whole thing seems like a bad dream now as I walk along by your side,' cried Du Parc, suddenly forgetting his reserve and realising the utter gulf, the absolute distance, the impassable barrier which divided him from the sweet and gracious being whose looks rested so kindly on his, whose voice filled his ears, whose every word and motion seemed to him touched with peace, beauty, good-will upon earth, some harmony almost more than human.

And was all this to be put aside, thrust away, for what? For a hopeless cause, a nightmare, for these dirty hands holding out a grotesque semblance of liberty and justice. Then he thought, with a bitter pang of self-reproach, of his dear old master and friend, of that life-long sacrifice and devotion, that patient following of Truth in its many disguises, and that aspiration after greater things than tranquillity and ease. Suddenly shaken and stung back to the reality of life Max put a hard and dogged control upon himself for the rest of the walk; he would not let himself think, and yet he could not enjoy the present any more. Mrs Dymond wondered what had come to him. His manner, his voice, his face had changed, he seemed no longer her friend and companion, but one strange and far removed from their simple merry-making.

The others saw no difference, and came up laughing and in high spirits, when Max called to Jo to hasten, or they might not got their table at the inn where they were to dine. They turned down along the river-side again, the Pêche Miraculeuse stood at a silver turn of the Seine, and the hungry excursionists were coming up from various sides to the many tables which were set ready, some in the dark dining-rooms down below, some on a broad balcony or terrace from which the river could be seen, floating into those glorified distances, where the sweet resounding woods and visions through which they had been passing lay hidden in the sunset.

The lady in the camisole sitting in the little lodge below smiled an affable welcome, and put out five ivory counters for her guests.

'Will you take your entrance tickets?' said Du Parc, holding out four of the counters.

'And what will you do?' says Mr Bagginal, rather relieved to find Max was not to be at the dinner.

'I am not coming. I must go back,' he answered.

Susy exclaimed in disappointment.

Max heard her exclaim as, lifting his hat, he turned away quickly. He could not explain to them all that when he had thrust his last napoleon into Madame Lebris' trembling hand he had given his share of the feast to the poor woman who had appealed to him as they started. At the time he had regretted the sacrifice, now he was glad to get away – his mood had changed. He was in no difficulty about his meal. There was always a loaf of bread and a bottle of wine in his mother's cupboard at home, and he now started to walk back to the villa and to partake of this frugal repast before visiting his *protégée* on his way to joining Caron at the appointed place.

Dombrowski had been sent on some mission – Du Parc knew not what, only that it was of vital importance to the cause, so, at least, Caron's friends affirmed. Max himself had little faith in these mysterious expeditions and conspiracies. He was ready to do his part, even to go on missions if need be; at all events, to help those that wanted help, to send a share of his own strength and good-will to others, but he had no fancy for plots and secret societies; and it may as well be explained at once, that, although he lived in the company of schemers and plotters, he himself belonged to no secret societies. His godfather had promised the sturdy Madame that Max should not be involved. Caron was scrupulous to keep his word and his promises. He was absolutely trusted and respected; introduced by him, Max was welcomed, although bound by no promises. He was even courted by many of those who were able to see his utility to their cause if he once heartily joined any one of the many cliques and brotherhoods which were secretly growing round about. But, in truth, his mind just then was full of other thoughts and preoccupations, and one's own experience perforce comes before that of others however unfortunate. As he walked along in the dusk by the river-side towards home, something seemed calling to him – calling from the little eating-house where the lights were beginning to kindle up. 'She is going from you,' said a voice. 'Who knows she might remain, she might be yours; but she is happier as she is, and you would not have things altered.' He knew enough of the world to realise that Susy and her surroundings were utterly unsuited to him and to his life. Max was not over-diffident; modesty was not one of the qualities with which nature had endowed him, and something in Susanna's eyes and voice and manner told him that to her he was beginning to be no less interesting than she had long been to him. Poor child! she had better go before she knew the truth, return to her home, her comforts, her religion, her friends, the reverends in their white ties, to her narrow prejudices, her well-mounted household. Hie thee to a monastery! What had induced this lamb from the flock to come in innocence and thrust itself into his *gueule de loup?* Dear woman, she should go as she had come. She should not know how near he had been to asking her to make the sacrifice of peace and home, and country, and consideration, 'for she might accept me. She is a woman just like any other.' So reasoned Max, who was himself a man just like any other.

Meanwhile Susanna sat silent in her darkening corner, also changed and silenced, disappointed and angry with herself for the difference she found in everything; wondering why Du Parc had left them so abruptly, where he was gone, what his going meant. The western light shone on still, but with long radiations; the fisherman's boat, catering for the guests, pushed out across the river to the reservoir of trout, the oars flapped with a sad, chilling sound. Tempy's spirits rose as Susy's fell, and she and Jo, and Mr Bagginal joked and laughed with an extra gaiety and noisy enjoyment which jarred upon poor Susy, sitting lonely and motionless, with all the fading glory of the sunset for a background to her depression. It was the same thing on board the steamer in the evening grey, where their youthful sports offended not only Susy but a little French couple sitting by the wheel. '*Anglais*,' said the man, '*Barbares*,' hissed the pretty little lady, to Jo's immense amusement.

CHAPTER XXXII

SUSANNA'S CORRESPONDENCE

We let false whispers, breeding hidden feares,
Break gentle sleepe with misconceived dout.

Susy came home still, tired, and dispirited. She left the others to their cheerful interminable leave-takings down below, and hurried up the stairs to her own room. As she passed through the sitting-room she saw some letters lying on the round table, and she carried them with her candle into her own room to read. It was nearly dark, the light was dying out of the sky, and she untied her bonnet and sat down in the chair by her bedside with some sense of rest and peace. The first letter was from Mrs Bolsover, and in her own handwriting:–

'Bolsover Hall, April 22nd.

'My Dear Susanna,

We are all glad to think the time for your return is so near, though I am afraid you will find us very humdrum after your foreign friends and amusements. I only write to say that we are expecting you. News concerning such old fogies as we are is generally nothing but a catalogue of ills, more or less tiresome. Happily we are all much as usual, with nothing more to complain of than when you left the Place. Aunt Fanny has been up in town, and has brought back a couple of white rats, which Phraisie will approve of.

'The squire is very well satisfied with his lambs and the look of the spring crops. He goes over to the Place on Tuesdays, and says all is as it should be. He brings us back cartfuls of fruit and vegetables, which the gardeners might otherwise appropriate.

'Our nephew Charles has been staying with us, and left us this morning. He is thinking of trying for the Civil Service. I was delighted to get your letter contradicting the unfavourable accounts which had reached us of his conduct in London, and which, as you know, I never believed. I was glad to tell him how completely you had justified him.

'We are rather anxious at the last accounts from Paraguay, where my brother Peregrine is now living. The country seems in a very unsettled state. He has written us a very long, and, no doubt, interesting letter on the subject of the last ministerial changes there. He promises to send us another box of curiosities before long.

'Pray remember us very kindly to your mother and her family. Give our fond love to Jo and Tempy, and with a hug to the precious child, believe me, my dear Susy, ever your affectionate old sister-in-law,

'CAROLINE BOLSOVER.

'Tell Phraisie we shall be looking out for her by the end of the week, and that we shall keep the rats till she comes for them.'

The second letter was also stamped with the Bolsover crest, but it bore the London post-mark, and was directed in a dashing and blotted handwriting at which Susy wondered as she opened it. Then she began to read attentively, and having finished she read the letter through a second time; and then, still holding it in her hands, she sat motionless trying to think, to realise how much it might mean. The words were simple enough, and to the point:–

'D—— Street, Soho, April 23rd.

'My Dear Mrs Dymond,

Many months have passed since I have troubled you, either by writing or by coming. When I last saw Tempy, I felt she would prefer that I should absent myself for a time. I think, however, it will be better for all our sakes to get to a definite understanding. My time at Oxford is at an end, and it is necessary to make some plans for the future. My Aunt Fanny has been in town, visiting Jamrach's and the spring exhibitions, and kindly exerting herself on my behalf. A former admirer, she tells me, has promised her to give me a nomination for the Foreign Office, and this, with what my uncle allows me, will enable me, I trust, to pay my washing bills, and keep me not only in crusts but in cigars. My Aunt Caroline has also shown me a letter which you have been kind enough to write, contradicting a report which I never heard of till now, and which certainly confirmed my poor Uncle John in his prejudice against me. I will not dwell upon this unexpected *éclaircissement*, for although in this particular instance appearances were hard upon me, other facts (that I am heartily ashamed of now) may not have reached his ears, which would have undoubtedly seemed to him good reasons for opposing my marriage with my cousin Tempy. But at the same time I protest that I was hardly dealt with on the whole; if he had lived I should have appealed once more to him, to his sense of justice, to his great affection for his daughter. He is gone, leaving you her guardian in his place, and I come to you. If you could see my heart you would understand that I am sincere, you would see how truly I love her. I also think that no one else could ever make her so happy as I could. If she still loves me, I will come at once and meet you anywhere you like; to *her* I would rather speak than write. Meanwhile, I can only ask you to believe me.

'I am yours very sincerely,
'C.P. BOLSOVER.'

As Susy sat there her mind was quickly made up; something in Charlie's letter rang true and seemed to find a ready answer in her feeling. Ah! she knew now as she had never known before what it was to divide yearning hearts. John would forgive her even if he did not approve; but he would approve; true himself, generous, considerate for others, how could he not approve? Why should she mistrust his unvarying goodness? . . . As she sat there she found herself almost speaking, almost appealing to her husband, and a feeling of *oneness* with him in her wish to do right seemed to set her mind and her heart at ease, her eyes filled with tears, her hands trembled with excitement.

Her dreams of the past and of Tempy's future were not altogether dispersed by the voices coming into the next room. Jo and Tempy, having taken leave of Mr Bagginal, had come upstairs after her.

'It would have been a delightful day if it hadn't been for that tiresome M. du Parc,' said Tempy very loud and cheerfully, dropping down once more on the red divan which she had left some eight hours before. 'I can't think what Susy finds in him. He is a thoroughly disagreeable man, and so are all his friends. He has scarcely the manners of a gentleman; do you think so, Jo?'

'I don't know; I like him and I like his friends,' said Jo, lighting the candles. 'They are rather rough to be sure, all except Monsieur Caron; but I don't care so much about manners. You like superfine cream-laid people, like Bagginal and Charlie.' Jo said all this walking noisily about the room looking for matches, soda-water, opening windows, &c., as people do after a day's absence. 'Mrs Dymond likes them rough,' he went on, 'without too much polish, like me and Du Parc.' He looked up and stopped short, for 'Mrs Dymond' had come back, she was there, she had heard what they said. She was blushing crimson and waiting in the doorway.

Jo gave one glance at Tempy, then another at Susy, as she stood quite still looking down, and nervously smoothing the ribbons of her cloak which she had not laid aside, then he took up his hat and was preparing to go out again for an evening pipe in front of the house.

'Don't go yet, Jo,' said Susanna, in an odd voice. 'I have something to say to you and Tempy. Something which has been on my mind for some days.' Tempy sat bolt upright on her sofa, and wondered what on earth was coming.

'M. du Parc, whom you dislike, Tempy, so much,' said Susy, with a touch of severity in her voice which Tempy had never heard before, 'has done us a service for which we ought all to be grateful. He has cleared away a cruel injustice. Do you not both remember the things which were said of your cousin Charlie, that sad time when – when he first spoke to your father? They were all false. Monsieur Max knows it was all untrue about the drinking. Your father never knew it, and now I too have heard from Charlie – the letter was here when I came in. Tempy,' said Susy, trembling, but recovering herself and speaking more quickly, and looking very sweet, 'it is for you to answer the letter. I should no longer feel I was doing right if I continued to oppose your marriage. I think – I cannot say for certain – but I *think* your father would agree to it now. He used to say,' and Susy turned to her stepson, 'that her husband must be a good man, Jo, a man to be trusted and that she could depend upon – and surely Charlie has proved himself faithful and to be trusted.'

Susy's voice failed her from sheer emotion and excitement, her eyes were full of tears, she felt terrified by the responsibility she was taking, and yet she had no doubt in her mind. She came up to the divan, and sitting down by Tempy, in her excitement she caught her hand in both hers, but Tempy started to her feet and shook off the gentle fingers which Susy had laid upon her own. The letter between them fell to the ground.

'You will not oppose! You want to get rid of me, that is what you mean,' cried the girl in a sudden jealous fury, speaking with volubility and vehemence. 'You want to be free to marry that Frenchman – and you expect me to be grateful to him and to you – for months and months you have looked on at my misery, and now because that man tells you to change your mind, to forget my father's wishes, you – you – Oh, Susy, Susy, I don't know what I am saying,' cried Tempy breaking down suddenly, flinging herself back upon the cushions and bursting into wild passionate sobs.

Susanna sat, scared, terrified, too deeply wounded to speak or to show any sign. Jo, greatly embarrassed, came forward and stooped to pick up Charlie's letter which was lying at Susy's feet.

'Yes, read it, Jo,' said Mrs Dymond, in an odd chill voice. 'You can show it to her when she is more reasonable. You can tell her that I did not look on unfeelingly; I have tried to be sincere with your father and with his children. Tempy ought to trust me, and to know that I have no secret reasons – though I understand better than I did once, perhaps, what she has had to suffer.'

As Susy spoke the meaning of her own words seemed to overcome her. She started up. She was wanting to get back to her own room, to be alone, to hide her agitation, to rest from her fatigue and exhaustion of spirit. Her tears were gone, but as she stood up, suddenly everything became dim to her eyes. In one instant life's perplexities, joys, and agitations ceased for Susy Dymond, except, indeed, that in some utter depths of unexplored darkness, something was still struggling, amid strange and distant clangings and reverberations, struggling and floating back towards life – a something which became herself once more as Susy opened her eyes to find herself in Tempy's repentant, loving, trembling arms, dabbed and fanned, sprinkled and dribbled over by tears, eau de Cologne, and wet sponges. Jo was rubbing her hands, Wilkins was present. Susy found herself lying back in a chair by the open window, the moon and stars were looking in at her, a soft wind was blowing in her face. The windows of the opposite balcony were lighted up, a chance spectator in a white waistcoat leaning over the rails was watching the incident with interest. This was the first trivial fact which impressed itself on Susy's reviving senses.

'Another sup of water, mem,' says Wilkins, sympathetically. 'Them expeditions is too much for her! Ah! your colour is coming back, let Miss Tempy fan you.'

'Darling, sweet Susy,' whispered Tempy, in a tender voice, like a child's treble. 'Oh, my Susy, I nearly killed you.'

'Well,' said Jo, who looked still quite white and frightened, 'I thought you had, Tempy, and no mistake.'

CHAPTER XXXIII

SUSANNA AND HER MOTHER

I drink it as the fates ordain it,
Come fill it and have done with rhymes,
Fill up the lonely glass and drain it,
In memory of dear old times.

BALLAD OF BOUILLABAISSE.

Early next day Susy was standing at the gate of the villa. After the events of the night before, they had all come to the conclusion that it would be best to go home at once. And Tempy, agitated and surrendering, had written to her lover to meet them. Susy knew that her mother would approve of the engagement, but she was doubting how she could best break to her the news of their approaching departure. She herself was loth enough to go. Her heart was not light, she could not feel as Tempy did, whose new life was waiting for her on the English shores. Whereas it seemed to Susy as if she was leaving all hers behind – her true interest, her truest self; as she drove along she wondered whether she should see Max presently, and be able to tell him of all that had happened, and of the great determination they had come to. She wondered what he would say, how he would look – approving? disapproving? Would he be in the same mood as when he had left them the night before? She found no answer to her question. The villa was silent and deserted, and as she crossed the garden she saw that the studio windows were closed, as well as Madame's kitchen doors. She went in at the passage, passed through the Marney's dining-room, where the breakfast things were still upon the table, and so came into the little sitting-room, where she found her mother. Mrs Marney was lying on the old yellow sofa; for once she was not at work. Mikey and Dermy's piles of underclothing lay ripped unheeded, seams opening wide, upon a chair. Their mother was leaning back with her hands upon her lap, a pair of horn spectacles and a newspaper lay upon the table.

'I think I am better, dear,' said Mrs Marney peacefully, like a person going on with a sentence already begun. 'Madame has been in to sit with me. She has been reading to me. I have heard all about St Cloud. Max du Parc came for a minute last night, and brought me news of you all. What a lovely day you have had for your walk! Marney is at the Tuileries today. Yes, indeed, M. de Morny sent for him. You don't know how much they all think of his opinion. Nobody knows more about politics than he does; I wish he understood his own affairs half as well as those of Europe,' said Mrs Marney, with a sigh and something of her old manner. As Susy stood in the summer light, against the green of the windows, with all her black rippling round her, the mother looked fondly and proudly at her daughter. 'What a beautiful cloak that is, my child, how well your widow's mourning becomes you.' Susanna blushed up crimson.

'Oh, don't, mamma, don't say such things.'

'Why, the Colonel always liked you to look well and becomingly dressed,' said Mrs Marney. 'I used to tell him it was he, not you, that cared for the bonnets. I myself like pretty things, I can sometimes think of your clothes, Susy, when I can't look at my own for worry. I was upset yesterday; the police came just after Max was gone. Madame was in a terrible taking, and talked some nonsense about Marney.'

'What nonsense, mamma?' Susy asked.

'Oh! we have made it up,' Mrs Marney said, taking Susy's hand and stroking it. 'Max, like a good fellow, brought her in this morning. Well, what have you got to tell me? I see there is something by your face.'

When Susy began, with no little reluctance, to break her own news she found that her mother received it better than she had dared to hope. 'So you have made it all right for the poor girl. I am glad of that, my Susy; it's ill work parting those whom God has joined together. I shall miss you sorely; but promise me to come back if ever I want you. Promise, Susy, and I shall not fash over the parting,' and Susy eagerly promised. 'Oh, mamma, any time, any time.'

'I can keep the boys a few days longer,' Mrs Marney continued. 'Caron is going over to England next week, and he will leave them at school for me.' Mrs Marney was very tender, very motherly, but absent in manner. 'Is that Madame's voice?' she said uneasily. 'Don't wait, Susy, you must have so much to see to.' But almost as she spoke Madame appeared upon the threshold, concentrated, forbidding in aspect. When she saw Susanna standing near her mother's sofa Madame stopped short, stared fixedly, and immediately turned and walked away out of the room. Mrs Marney flushed up, then laughed at Susy's look of bewilderment. 'I did not want her to see you here, Susy.' And when Susy asked what it meant, 'She has got some nonsense in her head – people trouble themselves too much about other people's affairs,' was all Mrs Marney said, and then she kissed her daughter's face, holding it between both her hands and looking into her eyes as tenderly as if Susy had still been a child depending on her for everything. Mrs Marney promised to come up with the boys, and to say good-bye next day in the afternoon, when Marney was gone. Susy would gladly have remained longer, she hoped to have seen Max before she left; she wanted an explanation with Madame; but her mother seemed only anxious to hurry her away; for one moment at the door did Mrs Marney detain her wistfully, and in that moment Susy found courage to say in a low voice, 'Mamma, you will tell M. Max we are going. We expect him, to say good-bye.' Then Mrs Marney flung her arms around Susy's neck and began to cry.

'Ah, poor Max! he will miss you, but not so much as I shall. Oh! remember, I must always count on you for my boys, Susy; you are young, but no younger than I was when I was left a widow, and I took my own course, and it has been a hard life, but indeed I would not change it,' said the faithful inconsequent woman. 'Go, darling, go.'

Poor Susy drove home disappointed and perplexed by her visit, and wondering at the meaning of it all. She was used to her mother's ways, used to the mysteries of that household from which she had so thankfully escaped, she could imagine, alas! what good reason her mother might have to try to avoid a meeting between Mr Marney and herself, but Madame du Parc's behaviour distressed and troubled her. Some crisis had occurred, of that she was assured. They were all against her, her mother and Madame and that hateful Marney. People in an excited and abnormal condition are quickly suspicious, and Susy crimsoned at the thought that it must all have to do with her friendship for Max. Ah! what business was it of theirs. If only she could have seen him once more. If only he had come to her. Then she felt that everything would have been plain.

Mrs Dymond found active preparations for their departure going on when she reached the hotel, and a general confusion of Wilkins among the bandboxes, of parcels without number, and milliners-in-waiting. Tempy was writing in the drawing-room, and looking up with a face so changed, so radiant with transient beauty and happiness that Susy could scarcely believe that was the Tempy she had known all along. 'I have had a telegram,' said Tempy. 'Charlie will meet us at Folkestone the day after to-morrow;' and, 'Oh! Susy, Mr Bagginal came this morning and Monsieur du Parc. I was very civil indeed, and nice to them both. They want to take us somewhere to breakfast to-morrow, and M. du Parc is coming on to the Louvre afterwards, so he will have all day long to say good-bye, as we don't leave till after dinner.'

Susy didn't answer. She sat down rather wearily, he had been there, she was glad of that, even though she had missed him; but at the same time she had an odd feeling of some intangible, unrecognised trouble at hand, one to be avoided, not faced, to be fled from, never to be realised. All day long the thought possessed her while she packed and paid and parted, and settled the various details of their going.

Du Parc saw Susy again that evening though she did not see him. Susy and Tempy, with Phraisie between them, were driving at foot pace along the Champs Elysées. They were rolling home from the Arc, behind which the sun was setting, a huge dropping globe of limpid fire. Max had been staring at the glories that were lighting up the Arc, and its stony chariots, and heroic memories, while the triumphal clouds above were heaped in a present apotheosis of splendour and commemoration. The victors and victoresses of this present generation were complacently driving out in the soft evening air, after the heat of the day, and issuing from their houses, or strolling leisurely or resting on the benches along the way. Many of the passers-by looked up at the two English ladies in their equipage with the pretty blue-eyed child between them. Among these came Max du Parc, trudging home from M. Caron's with a portfolio under his arm containing his completed work. Susy did not see him, but he saw her, and the prosperous serenity of the little party struck him painfully, and the carriage seemed to him somehow to be rolling and rolling away, right away out of his life.

CHAPTER XXXIV

SAYING 'GOOD-BYE'

Farewell, thou art too dear for my possessing,
And like enough thou knowest thine estimate.
The charter of thy worth gives thee releasing;
My bonds in thee are all determinate.

Mr Bagginal was also of the farewell party. They were to breakfast at a certain old-fashioned café near the Panthéon, which Du Parc had recommended, and to adjourn to the Louvre for one last morning in the galleries which already seemed so familiar. That last day in Paris, the lights, the streets, the café with its shining tables and deep windows and criss-cross shadows, the blazing gardens without, long haunted Susy, who was destined to live so many of these hours again and again, in other scenes and other surroundings. She had met Max with an effort, trying to be calm. Alas! her effort to be wise and calm only revived for him the memory of that stiff, doll-like Susanna who used to seem so meaningless once. Now he knew better, he did not think her meaningless; on the contrary, he attached too much meaning to her coldness.

As they all sat at their table with the snowy cloth by the grated window, Mr Bagginal and Jo kept up the ball; Tempy was too happy, Susanna was too sad to talk very much.

'I shall be coming over to see my people in a few weeks,' said the attaché. 'I hope I shall find you at Crowbeck, Mrs Dymond.'

'That is all right,' said Jo. 'You must come and see us, and you too, Du Parc. When shall you be in England again?'

But Du Parc did not respond very warmly. He felt some jar, some constraint in this semblance of a meeting. 'I don't like making plans,' he said abruptly; 'plans are for landed proprietors and diplomats; we working men are obliged to take things as they come.'

'Here come the cutlets,' cried Bagginal, who thought Max's sallies not in the best taste. Susy, too, was vaguely vexed by his roughness. Things mended a little when they reached the Louvre. The work of great men, which makes a home for us in strange places, is often not unlike a living presence, influencing us, just as some people do, calling something that is our best selves into life.

There is something in the highest art which is like nature, bringing people into a different state of being, sweeping away the reticences, the hesitations, of the different grades of life. The different manners and ways of men and women are realities in their way, but they scarcely count when the greater truths prevail.

Max walked ahead, suddenly more at home and more at ease; he led the way from room to room, from one eventful picture to another, and yet all the time as he went along the voice of that night before was haunting him still, and even while he was speaking he sometimes broke off abruptly to listen to it. 'She is going from you,' this voice still said; 'she might be yours, she might remain.' Perhaps some vein of English blood had taught Max to feel for women some deeper, more tender sentiment than the passionate ferment of romantic admiration and excitement which seems to play an all-important part in France (if we are to judge by its yellow and bilious literature); some gentler and more noble instinct was in his heart than that strange emotion which, according to these same observers, belongs to any one but to a wife – to a passing dream, to a flaunting venality. . . . Whereas (according to these same records) for the mothers of their homes, for the companions of their life, a family lawyer's acquiescence, their parents', their grandparents' approbation is to be considered first and foremost, human nature, instinctive feeling, last and least.

But Max was but half a Frenchman, after all, as he walked along by Susy's side through the long galleries. They came down from the glowing pictures into the cool, stony halls below, and passed from one century to another with a few lingering steps. The tombs of Egyptian kings and warriors lined their way; then came the tokens and emblems of the great Roman empire, with all its pomp of funereal rite; followed by the bland and lovely emblems of the Greeks, those stately figures still treading the earth in some immortal fashion, while the present waves of life flow on, washing away the relics of the past as they flow.

Max looked at the woman he loved, as she stood before the statue of some bygone nymph. The young man, who was an artist as well as a lover, made a mental note of the two – the stony, impassive nymph, the noble human being so wistfully radiant. Susy felt his eyes upon her, and as some feel the sunshine kindling their chilled veins, so to her unacknowledged perplexities that bright odd glance, part sympathetic, part scrutinising, seemed to bring reassurance and to give life to her very soul. That one moment was the best of all those moments; almost immediately a look, a something, a nothing, seemed to come between them again.

Long after, an *eau forte*, signed Maxwell, had a great success, and was for a time to be seen in the window of every art shop in London. It was very slight, but also very complete. They stony statue was faithfully copied, its grace and solemn life were repeated as it stood upon its pedestal with its finger on its lips; and a woman, also draped in flowing folds, also bare-headed, and with a strange likeness to the marble, stood with innocent eyes gazing up at the stone that recalled her who once was a woman too, who was now only a goddess, but still somehow whispering of the beauty and of the love of two thousand years ago.

Mr Bagginal, loth to go, had to say good-bye presently, and return to his embassy. His departure scattered them all. Susy felt a strange impatience of this long-drawn leave-taking. She wanted to get it over, and to escape from Tempy's eyes and Jo's; she was not herself, her nerves were irritated, and the restraint she put upon herself only added to this nervous impatience.

'Shall we walked home through the gardens?' said Mrs Dymond with an effort, in her stiff and formal manner; and without a word Du Parc turned and led the way to the entrance gates. The great doors let a blaze of light into the cold marble galleries; the cocked-hat of the *suisse* was resplendent and reflected the fine weather as it flashed in the doorway; the great *place* without looked like a triumph of summer; the rearing stone horses and chariots rose high against the deep blue of the sky. Short black shadows marked the arches and the pedestals, and Susy breathed deep as she passed out, followed by Jo and Tempy. Opposite was the piazza of the Louvre, where the lovely lights were floating from pier to pier, while high overhead one or two diaphanous clouds were mounting in the air.

As they came out of the shade of the portico they seemed almost blinded by the glaring sun; the *place* was burning with scorching heat; it flashed from every arch and pinnacle and window.

'It is a furnace,' said Tempy; 'hadn't we better wait another hour in the gallery?'

'I have to go home,' Susy said hurriedly. 'Tempy, I cannot stay longer, I have to pack. Don't come; you will find me at home. Jo will come with me.'

But Tempy clutched Jo fiercely by the wrist. She did not want to be left alone with Du Parc in the gallery.

The heat seemed to confuse them all. Susy found herself crossing the burning *place* alone, as she thought, but when she looked round, Du Parc was striding by her side, while she hastened to the more shady gardens of the Tuileries. It was the ordeal by fire through which they were passing.

'Everything seems on fire,' said Susy, looking about. 'See, we shall escape over there,' and she pointed with her hand.

The young man was unconcerned by the heat, and chiefly conscious of the cool shadow of her presence. He remembered her words and her action one day long after, remembered them for an instant amidst the flash of fiercer conflict than that which stirred him now; and yet at the time he scarcely seemed listening when she spoke, and now and again forgot her presence in the sudden realisation of what her absence would be to him. He had imagined once that she understood him – cared something for him. It must have been a mistake. How quietly she spoke of her departure. 'These English-women are made of tougher stuff than a poor Frenchman is aware of,' Max thought bitterly.

The sentry in his shady box stared at Mrs Dymond and her companion quickly passing in the burning silence. They reached the gardens, almost deserted in the midday heat.

If it had not been for Tempy's jealous words the night before, Susanna might have parted from Max naturally with regret, sadly, but without this cruel pang, this self-reproach. As it was, she could not trust herself to be sorry; she must take leave coldly. She must not allow herself to feel.

Then she looked up suddenly, just once to remember him by when she was gone, when this cold unmeaning good-bye had been said; and she saw Du Parc's keen brown face turned upon her with a look which seemed somehow to stab her, and she started as if she had been hurt.

'What is it?' said Du Parc. 'What is it, madame?'

Susy's heart began to flutter oddly. She could not answer. Her face had been pale before – was now burning with her self-betrayal. Was the final decision to be made already? Was there no escape from it? It seemed to her as if Tempy had cruelly taken down the shutters, and let bright daylight into a darkened room. Now for the first time Susy seemed to know that the daylight was something so clear, so beautiful, that all other lights and flickering tapers were but as shadows before it.

Susanna's changing looks touched Max with some odd mixture of pity and alarm. He had been angry with her for her coldness all the morning. But this was no cold indifference. Had she, too, felt this estrangement? If it was so he forgave her, took her into his confidence, once more began to speak naturally.

'Yes, madame, this vile good-bye has come already,' he said, 'and yet too late for me. Good-byes come most easily to those who, like you, take everything with them – almost everything,' he repeated, with a sigh. 'I cannot pretend to know how it all may seem to you; we belong to different worlds. It is best we should part. Ah! you could not face poverty,' he went on suddenly. 'You are not made for sufferings; you belong to the wealthy, happy, placid people, not to us who are struggling for our lives.'

Susy felt hurt by his strange tone. 'What do you mean?' she said. 'I have been poor too.'

'You have been poor,' he said, looking hard at her, and smiling coldly; 'but you have never known what it is to suffer, nor to be bound and helpless watching others day to day, condemned by their race, and dying from sheer incapacity for the struggle of life. Pass on – pass on,' he said, almost fiercely.

Susy's eyes filled up suddenly, and again her tears softened his mood. 'You have courage and you have heart, but you cannot help these things any more than I can,' he went on more gently. 'To have known you is a possession to those you leave behind. When I remember you after you are gone, it will be with a thought of peace in the midst of noise and confusion.'

Susy, as many a woman before and after her, stood listening, scarcely taking in the words, only the sense of the moment. All she knew for certain was that they were parting, that he was there still, that he was unhappy, that presently she should see him no more. They had reached one of the stone benches of the Tuileries, which stood in the shade of a tree, almost opposite a little gate that led to the Rue du Dauphin.

'I must go,' said Susanna, speaking very quietly; and he nodded, and yet detained her, absently holding her hand, which she had given him.

'Ah, yes,' he said, suddenly dropping it, 'it is indeed time we parted.'

She did not dare to answer or to comfort him; she did not dare tell him that for her too the parting had come too late.

'Good-bye,' she said, still in the same quiet everyday manner. As she moved away slowly he sat down upon the bench.

The time had come, as she had known it would, and she walked on as she had drilled herself to do; with what sad steps she climbed the street none but herself could tell. She walked till she reached the door of the hotel, where the waiter was standing. He asked her some trivial questions about her bill, and an omnibus. She looked at him without understanding what he said. Then she mounted the wooden stairs, up and down which they had so often happily clattered on their way in and out. She might have been kinder, this was what she kept thinking over and over again; she might have been kinder; how sad and stern he looked, was it her fault she had only thought of herself, not of him, in all she left unsaid? Every sound, every touch seemed to jar upon her nerves and to reproach her. As she opened the sitting-room door, she was met by a loud discordant crash. Little Phraisie was passing the long, hot morning by thumping on the keys of the piano in tune to her nurses's packing.

'I'se playing,' says Phraisie, triumphant.

'O Phraisie, Phraisie, don't make such a noise,' said her mother irritably, stooping over the child and trying to lift her down from the chair.

'I'se not done,' protested Phraisie struggling.

'Leave off, Phraisie,' Susy repeated; and the child looked up surprised by her mother's tone. She ceased struggling instantly.

'Mamma,' said she, 'are I so very naughty? is that why you's crying?' and then Susy found that her own eyes were full of tears – she had been selfish and unjust to Phraisie as she had been to Du Parc.

Wilkins came in hearing the discussion, also heated and cross with packing, and asking one question after another about her overflowing boxes. Susy could scarcely force herself to listen; Du Parc's wild sad looks were before her eyes, his bitter words in her heart; she might have had the courage to speak the truth to him. She might have been kinder – was it even yet too late? 'Phraisie, darling,' she said suddenly, 'you may play a little bit longer. I have forgotten something, Wilkins; I shall come back. I – I am not feeling very well, I must leave the packing to you.' And before Wilkins could ask another question she was gone again, hurrying as she went.

'Madame! Madame!' cried Auguste, flying after her with his napkin; but Susy did not turn, and only hastened out into the street, tying the long ribbon of her silk cloak as she went. She thought she heard her name called, she would not look back. She must see him once more, if only to leave him more happy, if only to tell him that she was not ungrateful for his friendship. It seemed to her as if he was wanting her, as if it was her least duty to go to him, to say to him, 'Ah, you do me injustice. It is not that I am rich, and prosperous and heartless, but because I am poor and have others to think of, others depending on me that I leave you.' Yes, others to whom she was bound by a thousand ties;

but in her secret heart she knew that never again would she feel for any one what she felt for this stranger.

Surely two less propitiously matched people never came together than this man and this woman, who seemed to suit each other so well. She, tender, practical, humble and yet exacting, as diffident people are who are not sure of themselves and require constant convictions and reassurance. He, reserved, over confident, with a courageous power of self-command, perhaps somewhat blunted to the wants and pains of others by circumstance. For him the real material wants of life existed chiefly. The hunger for affection, the thirst after sympathy was a fancy not worth considering. He was suffering now; but he also knew – perhaps better than Susy did – that his pain would pass in time. . . .

He was still sitting on the bench, he had not moved since she left him. He was not conscious of the minutes which had passed. He loved her. He knew it. Whether or not she loved him seemed to be but a secondary thing. A man loves; a woman longs for response. Max had not stirred except to light a cigar. For a few minutes he had gloomily puffed at the smoke, then he took it out of his mouth and sat holding it between his fingers. Then he heard her quick step advancing, he did not look up or turn his head, but when she came close up and sat down on the bench beside him, he turned at last. He was all changed, Susy thought. It was as if an east wind had passed over some landscape. She was not shy now. She was not thinking of herself any more, only of him, and her sweet eager face was lighted with solicitude and kindness.

'Won't you speak to me?' she said, after a moment, forgetting all her dignity, all her gentle pride; 'I want to say a real good-bye – since we must say good-bye. I came back, for I could not bear to part as we did just now. I am like you, I am not free, to think only of my own happiness. I – I wanted to tell you this. I have my mother, my brothers, my children depending on me. I should forfeit all means to help them if I married again. I too have my duty. I want to hear you say you forgive me,' she went on more and more agitated. She spoke in her pretty English-French. He was silent, and she turned very pale as she realised how little her words must mean to him.

He looked up with dull eyes and spoke at last.

'I have nothing to forgive,' he said; 'I do not complain; you have judged wisely; you are perfectly justified. There is nothing to regret, nothing to forgive.'

'Oh, Max!' she said reproachfully, unconsciously calling him by his name, 'when you speak to me like this how can I answer you; how can I feel you are my friend? What am I to say to make you understand?'

She wrung her hands with sudden pain, for indeed his pain seemed to her harder to bear than her own, his happiness seemed to her to matter far more than hers could ever matter. She felt herself in some way accountable for this man's happiness. The thought was almost more than she could bear, but he would not help her.

'Yes; I understand well enough,' he answered; 'and you have also to understand me,' he continued, in a hard, commonplace voice. 'Don't you know that graves have to be dug? Do you expect me to grimace and make phrases while I am digging a grave?'

Then he looked up at last, and his eyes met hers for one moment. Then, still dully and wearily, he rose from the bench.

'Your stepfather is coming,' he said, 'and his family. I cannot stay here any longer.'

And as Susy looked up, in that bitter moment, she too saw Marney advancing, and the little boys running towards her, and her mother following through the iron gate by which she herself had come into the gardens but a moment before.

Max du Parc had got up deliberately, without hurrying; he stood for an instant still looking at her; then he took off his hat without a word, and turned and walked away. The clocks were clanging four o'clock; he crossed the stiff shadow of the orange-tree, and with long swinging steps reached the shade of the avenues beyond, he was gone. She had longed to help him; she had only disgraced herself, she had done nothing for him – nothing, nothing. Was it the sun's heat sickened her? Was it some overpowering sense of shame, of hopeless regret, that seemed to burn into her very heart?

Some children who had been watching eagerly from behind the orange-tree came running up and established themselves upon the vacant bench and began to play an eager game with stones and sticks, while the Marney party cheerfully closed round Susy, the little boys were specially loud in their demonstrations. 'Sister! Auguste told us you were here, Didn't you hear us calling? We knew we should find you.'

'I am only come for one moment, just to take leave, Susanna,' said Marney, with extra heartiness, advancing with both hands extended; 'but here is your mother for the rest of the day. Is not that Du Parc going off? I may as well catch him up. Well, take care of yourself, my dear girl, and don't forget to write.'

Susy was still in a sort of dream; she scarcely returned her stepfather's easy salutations. She met her mother, but without a smile. The poor woman had lingered behind. Had she guessed something of what had happened?

Mrs Marney more than once looked anxiously at her daughter as they walked back together to the hotel. As the day went by the elder woman seemed silently to be asking Susy's forgiveness. She took up her daughter's hand and kissed it.

'Don't, mamma,' said Susanna, pulling her hand away.

All the same she was glad to have her mother near her until the moment of departure came. They sat side by side on the old red sofa, saying little, but grateful to be together. Once they heard a man's step in the passage outside, and Susy wondered whether Max after all had come back again for a few last minutes, but it was only Mr Bagginal with some flowers and bonbons for Phraisie. Then the train carried them all away, and Susy looked from her sleeping child to Jo peacefully nodding in his corner, to Tempy sitting absorbed and radiant, and then, something within her suddenly cried out, in despairing protest, in tune to the wheels of fate as they carried her away. To have so much, yet to be so utterly disheartened and alone; to have felt as if the world itself could scarce contain her happiness, and now it seemed to her that the worst of all was yet to come. What would he be doing? Who would he be talking to? Of what would he be thinking? It was well for her that she did not know what the future had in store.

BOOK IV

SUSANNA'S CONCLUSION

O air-born voice, long since severely clear,
A cry like thine in mine own heart I hear;
Resolve to be thyself, and know that he
Who finds himself, loses his misery

M. ARNOLD

CHAPTER XXXV

WAR AND RUMOURS OF WAR

For the angel of Death spread her wings on the blast.

To all of us who were safe at home in 1870, the distant sound of the cannon, the cry of the ousted, sorrowful inhabitants of a country but a couple of hours' journey from our own shores came, softened by distance, and by that stultifying sense of our own safety. It was not indifference; our neighbour's trouble was present to us and keenly realised; but we know that the good Samaritan himself, after walking by the ass and upholding his sick and wounded neighbour, left him to recover alone at the inn. With the first alarm Michael and Dermy appeared in Tarndale, sent by their mother, to finish their holidays, in safety. Mr Marney, whose trade was flourishing for the moment, forwarded a letter by the boys, in his dashing handwriting. 'I send the boys, my dear Susanna, trusting to your sisterly care. I cannot bring them myself. This war gives absorbing occupation to men of my trade. I am trying to persuade my wife to pack up her boxes and also rejoin you in your luxurious home. Poor Polly has some impression that her presence at the Villa du Parc acts as a pledge for her unworthy husband's safety. "Think of the Prussians!" says I. "Let them come on," says she. "I will not desert my post." Though what good she can do me here, and I at the other end of France, is past my comprehension. "Your home will be always ready," says she. "You can come back at any hour of the day or night," and when I represent to her that I can do that anyhow with a latchkey and a couple of sovereigns, she bursts into tears. Madame du Parc being of a less valorous constitution, has chosen the better part under present circumstances, and discreetly retires to her vineyard near Avignon. Seriously speaking, my dear Susanna, I do entreat you, who have more influence over Polly than most people, to persuade her that there is no advantage to me whatever in her remaining here, only great inconvenience. Even though the Prussians should not advance beyond the frontier, there are all sorts of ill-looking adventurers and Francs-Tireurs hanging about the place just now. . . .'

Poor Mrs Marney! she scarcely knew how to withstand the united commands of her husband and her daughter. Crowbeck seemed so far away, so utterly out of reach. There was no one there, not even Susanna, to whom she could speak of Marney. What should she do there? If he was ill or wounded, Susy would never let her go, she would keep her from him. The poor thing wandered about the empty villa, pale, anxious, huddled in an old cloak, wistfully watching Madame's independent arrangements as she prepared for her own departure. Torn with terrors of Marney, unable to decide for herself, Mary Marney was utterly miserable and wearying to others. Susy's letters, full of entreaties and of the preparations for Tempy's wedding, only elicited a faint return from her mother. Phraisie's printed messages, the boys' round-hand, seemed alone to bring some gleam of interest to the poor soul. She studied the papers for news; she cross-questioned everybody. Marney had been ordered to the front to join the emperor's head-quarters at Châlons, to be in the triumphant train of the journey to Berlin. Marney used to shrug his shoulders when his wife appealed to him as to his probable destination.

'I don't mind taking the odds against setting up my quarters in the Royal palace at Berlin, if that is what is what you mean, my dear,' he said. 'Heaven knows where we shall all be this day month. You will be more in the way of news at Crowbeck than anywhere else. They take in the *Velocipede*, don't they? – county bigwigs, as they are, crowing on their dung-heaps.'

Mrs Marney only turned away to hide her tears. One day, Madame, at once touched and irritated beyond measure by her friend's imploring looks, suddenly said, emerging from a huge *caisse* of cooking utensils, which she was carefully packing,

'I believe you would be happier, after all, if you came with me, Madame Marney. If your husband joins the camp at Châlons, you will be nearer at Avignon than anywhere else, not that you need fear anything for him. He is not one of those who get drowned or shot,' mutters Madame, with her head in the saucepans again.

But Mrs Marney did not care what Madame muttered; she clutched at her offer as a child might seize upon a toy. Marney, who was absolutely indifferent to his wife's movements, did not oppose the scheme, except by the usual shrug.

'You know your own mind best,' he said.

When he took leave of her soon after, her beautiful sad eyes, her mute, tender, passionate farewell touched him. 'Poor Polly,' he thought, as he turned away, 'what the deuce possesses her to be so fond of me?'

Marney actually took the trouble to write to his wife once or twice during the first few days; and when his letters came, Mrs Marney, radiant and delighted, would send on long quotations to Susy at Tarndale.

For once Susy was thankful to receive news of Mr Marney, and to know his whereabouts, and that he was prospering. For this also meant that her mother's mind was at ease and able to rest. When Marney took the trouble to write to his wife, he would send brilliant accounts of his own doings, and graphic descriptions of the events as they occurred. Others news there was which Susy read quietly, turning a little pale as her eyes followed the straggling lines of her mother's correspondence, which was not all confined to chronicles of her husband's doings. Madame du Parc was, it appeared, actively engaged in a lawsuit with a neighbouring proprietor. She was indignant with her son for leaving her to bear the brunt of it all alone. 'Why did he stop away among all those cutthroats and conspirators?' The first news of him came from Tours, where he had joined General d'Aurelles. Then Mrs Marney wrote that he had been sent back to Paris with a regiment of Mobiles in which he had enlisted.

How many things happen to us up in the air! Whole seasons of life seem to pass not on the ground, not ruled by hard tangible things and details, such as events, and chairs and tables, but overhead in some semi-mysterious region, where we turn to the vague inscrutable fancies which belong no less to our lives than its facts and statistics; where amid the chimes and the song of birds, or among storms and clouds, so much of our secret life is passed. Susanna Dymond was a timid woman in some way; half educated in the art of feeling, of living beyond. She would not let herself face the thoughts which she could not always dispel, nor dared she try to measure the load of anxiety at her heart, with which she lived through all the long months of that glaring summer-time, with its cruel, arid hours dividing her from the soft dreams of the spring. Those past days had been so lovely, so natural, and easy, and now it seemed so unnatural to be unhappy. From day to day, from hour to hour, she never knew what the fate might be of that one person who had changed her life's secret course. What was it that had come to her, a sense of the nothing in life, a bitter impatience of that terrible decree by which time after time we are swept away from our nearest and truest. . . . And then there would dawn for her the sense of possible happiness, of companionship which might have made a heaven for her of all those anxious days and heavy hours, and she dared not even think of it; she must not even realise the tender blessing. Every material comfort was hers. Tempy's affection touched her deeply. She had means to help those she loved; she had been faithful to her husband's trusts. All round about her were grateful sights and sounds, his legacy of comfort and happiness. The beacons of golden gorse lighting along the high moors; as the sun sets, the sky turns to gold and Crowcrag to purple. Suddenly a great burst of evensong comes from the birds overhead. All is peace except for the melodious din of whisperings and chirrupings and sweet repeated notes. She can hear the church bell across the lake ringing for evening service; it is a strange confusion of light and sound, of rest and life. But nature is often like the children piping in the market-place. There are times when beauty only jars, and aches, and stings. No one seeing Susy all through these months could have guessed at the hard fight she made, struggling to put aside vain regrets, to live in that wholesome hour the present, which is so much better for all of us than the past moods and future tenses to which so much of our life is strained. No one seeing her calm and smiling on Tempy's wedding-day would have guessed at the longing strange pain and self-reproach in her heart. Indeed, some of the neighbours could not help contrasting her coldness with Miss Bolsover's warmth of overflowing tears and feelings.

Tempy's wedding had been fixed for the 4th of September, a day peaceful and of good omen for the inhabitants of Crowbeck Place, one full of terror and alarm for the dwellers in a city not twenty-four hours distant from Tarndale.

While Tempy put on her travelling dress with Susy's help, a weeping woman, standing among other women, also in tears, overwhelmed by disaster upon disaster, by desperate news of armies flying and broken, terrified by the angry cry of the gathering populace outside the windows, was also taking leave of her home for ever. Her attendants came up one after another to kiss her hand; one of them hurriedly tied a black hood over the lady's beautiful hair, helped her off with her gold embroidered mantle, and flung a darker wrap upon her shoulder; then, followed by one of her faithful women only, the empress came out of the golden gate of the palace, trembling, because some passing urchin called her name. Meanwhile the Tarndale bells were ringing across the lake for Tempy Bolsover's wedding-day, and the young couple were speeding northward on their happy wedding journey; Aunt Fanny, in garments gorgeous beyond compare, stood taking leave of the wedding guests; good Mrs Bolsover sat subdued and emotioned in a corner. Jo had gone off for a solitary walk over the hills, and when the last of the company was gone, including Uncle Bolsover, who had lately started a tricycle, and who departed zigzagging along the road, Susy went upstairs to her own room and changed her silk dress for a grey country gown. She called the children, Phraisie and the little brothers, and crossing into the wood beyond the road, she took the woodland path leading upwards to the moors. Phraisie, trotting along the lane, looked like a little autumn berry herself. The leaves were turning brown upon the trees and sparkled, repeating the light; tiny leaves of gold amber-brown, crimson, or lingering green overhung the winding way. Presently they came to a little pool of all colours – gold with the reflection of the ash-trees, crimson where the oak-trees shone – into which the boys flung their stones and then set off running ahead once more. Susy still followed in silence; Tempy's happiness had warmed her heart, and she was thankful to be quiet in the unconscious company of the happy children; glad to be recalled from her sadder world by their happy voices.

From the shade of the wood, with its nuts and birds and squirrels, they come out upon the moor, whence they can see the silent tumult of the mountains beyond, crest and crescent, and sweeping ridge and delicate sunlit peaks silent and very still, yet shifting perpetually and changing with every minute's light. As Susy stood there the old cruel feeling which she had hoped to subdue suddenly came over her again. Everything seemed so confused, so short, so long; so many things to do, so many to undo; there were so many words to say, so many to unsay. Ah! why had she ever tried to explain to one who would not understand? Ah! how gladly she would have waited for years had he but agreed to it. But with him it was a man's strong passing feeling, with her it had been a new self only then awakened. Now she knew what it all had meant as she went back in mind to those early spring days, remembering the new light in the sky, the beauty of the world, the look in people's faces, the wonder of common place. She understood it all.

'Susy,' cries Dermy, 'come! come! Phraisie wants you!'

Little Phraisie had tumbled into a furze bush, and refused to be comforted by her uncles; and her mother, suddenly awakening from her dreams, now hurriedly ran to pick her up, to kiss away her tears, and wipe her wet cheek with her handkerchief.

CHAPTER XXXVI

THE BLACK SHADOWS

Like as the waves make towards the pebbled shore,
So do our minutes hasten to their end,
Each changing place with that which goes before.

As disasters thickened and closed in, Mrs Marney's letters became more scarce. She was still alone with Madame, whose chief anxiety was for Max, little as he deserved it. 'All those friends of his were *drôles*, and he should tell them so,' said the old lady, who seemed to think that this was the way to settle matters at once. Then came the news of the siege of Paris. Max was there shut up with the rest of them, but Mrs Marney wrote in happy excitement, for that same post had brought a letter from her husband. He was safe at head-quarters, and day by day the readers of the *Daily Velocipede* might trace his brilliant career. Emperors, princes, marshals, diplomats, Marney seemed to be the centre, and the leading figure of them all.

It was not till January was nearly over that the confirmation of the surrender of Paris reached Tarndale. This news was followed by rumours of every sort, and finally by a long rambling letter from Mrs Marney, full of many laments. She had seen but little of Marney, who had been at Châlons and Metz most of the time, and who was returning to Paris now that the siege was being raised. Did Susy know that poor Max had been wounded at Champigny? They had had a letter by a balloon from Mademoiselle Fayard, who had seen him in the Wallace ambulance. Madame du Parc also was determined to nurse her son, and planned returning to the house at Neuilly, which she heard was safe and scarcely injured.

'Do not be surprised if you see me after all,' wrote Mrs Marney. 'I cannot stop here alone with all I love so far distant from me. Ah! Susy, I should have done better to come to you, as you wished, but with my husband in danger how could I leave the country?'

Susy was full of alarm at the thought of her mother's dangerous journey through such a country at such a time. She wrote at once to Neuilly and to Avignon, imploring Mrs Marney to wait until things were more settled, promising to meet her later in Paris if need to. To her letters she received no answer; and a week passed full of anxiety. Jo was at Cambridge, she had no one but Mr Bolsover to consult. She might as well have talked to a looking-glass as to the sympathising little man, who invariably reflected her own expression of face. One day Susy thought of telegraphing to Neuilly to ask if her mother had arrived; the answer came sooner than Susanna had dared expect it, early next morning before she was up: –

'Madame du Parc, Neuilly, to Mrs Dymond, Crowbeck Place, Tarndale.

'Your mother is here very ill; pray come.'

Susy did not wait to consult Mr Bolsover again; she wrote a line to Mrs Bolsover, sent her little Phraisie to the Hall with the nurse, and started at once by an early train to town.

And thus it happened that at three o'clock in the morning, awakening out of a common-place dream, Susy found herself on board a steamer nearing the shores of France; with the stars shining through the glass in the roof of the cabin. A lamp is swinging, some of the passengers are preparing to land, wrapping rugs and parcels together. There are dull sounds and tramplings overhead, a couple of low voices are whispering to each other such things as people whispered in that disastrous year of 1871, when all voices were telling of changes and death, and trouble, and people gone away and families ruined and separated. 'We shall be in directly,' says the first voice, that of the stewardess, 'but I don't think you will find one of them left as you expect.'

'Ah! those Prussians!' says the second speaker in that whispering voice which people use in darkened places and at night; and still the steamer paddles on. Susy's own thoughts are too anxiously travelling ahead for her to take so keen an interest as she might have done at any other time in this new and unexpected phase of life. Is her journey too late she wonders, is her mother still alive, still calling for her, and wanting her? Susy is superstitious, as anxious people are. The two melancholy voices depress her, and seem like an echo of evil things to come; the look of her own hands lying listless in her black lap frightens her. She starts up impatiently, and begins to hope again as unreasonably as she had feared. Is everything changed, is nothing changed? Can it be that she shall find it all as in old days when troubles were not, nor wars to call men from their quiet toil to join the ranks of devastating armies? Presently they reached the French coast, it is time to go up on deck with the rest of the passengers. Susy keeping to the protection of the other two women comes up on deck and sees the dark line of the quai; lights go by, ropes are hauled in, and once more Susanna hears the familiar French sing-song of the people exclaiming and calling to one another. The voices sound melancholy, but that may be her fancy, or because it is a cock-crow sort of hour. Mrs Dymond carrying her hand-bag walks along to the hotel in company with her fellow-travellers. She had come across by chance with a party of Cook's tourists availing themselves of the escort of the great circumnavigator of our days, whose placards and long experience seemed to guarantee the safety of his adventurous followers. The only other ladies of the party were Englishwomen like Susanna herself, and also evidently travelling with a purpose. One, the friend of the stewardess, an old bedizened creature belonging to the race of the wandering British spinster, walked ahead still bemoaning herself as she went, the other a handsome young woman, of sober dress and appearance, stopped short suddenly as she crossed the quai by Mrs Dymond's side.

'Look!' she said, 'a German!' and with a thrill they recognise a brazen spike and the gleam of a helmet as the sentinel passes steadily up and down under a lamp-post in front of a garish-looking restaurant of which all the doors and windows are awake and flaring with gas, and evidently expecting guests.

Susanna for all her sad preoccupations stopped short with the rest of them, and experienced a curious thrill seeing the first ripple of that brazen tide which had overspread the desolate country of France. There the whole story seemed told as she watched the spike of the helmet and the big boots steadily pacing the pavement. She wondered at the courage of the English girl who went straight up to the sentry and asked him in abruptest German, 'How soon was he going back to Berlin?' The helmet stopped and answered good-naturedly enough, 'He didn't know, the King was at Rheims, they expected to leave in a day or two.' He was a big tawny young fellow with a handsome heavy face. Mademoiselle Célestine, the waitress at the Hôtel et Restaurant des Étrangers pouring out her *cafés-au-lait* told the passengers that he and his companions were *très gentils*, they had done no harm. They had good appetites, but the mayor paid for all they ate; she didn't believe the stories people told. They were there with the general and his staff. . . . Mademoiselle Célestine would have gone on blessing her enemies at greater length, but people from above, from around, from below, from within, from without, began calling out '*Garçon, garçon!*' bells rang violently, Cook's tourists shouted, and Britons demanded their suppers.

The house was so crowded, so noisy and uncomfortable, that Susy and her two casual acquaintances, after listening for some minutes to the landlady's glowing descriptions of blazing fires and velvet sofas at the railway-station close by, started boldly into the night to find this haven, and to await the six o'clock train there.

A few gas becks were flickering at the station, where they found looking-glasses and velvet sofas according to promise. In the first-class waiting-room a group of officers in white uniforms with many accoutrements were dozing away the time, with their boots and swords extended upon the chairs and couches.

Susy looked at them and instinctively left them to their slumbers, and went into the second-class waiting-room with her companions and sank down into the first-come seat.

A lady and a little girl were already sitting upon the wooden bench beside her. It was too dark to see their faces, but not too dark to hear the lady's plaintive voice – 'What a journey! what nervous terrors! what delays! after six months' enforced absence to return to a country in such a state – no lamps, no omnibus, no trains to depart, Germans everywhere.' (Two tall jangling officers with great cloaks and boots come in from the next room, look round and walk away.) 'Ah!' shrieks the lady with fresh exclamations of alarm, 'and I without a passeport! I could not get one where I was, at Vittington, a little village in the Eastern Conté; nor have I one for that child, who only yesterday was studying her piano at a school, for why should she lose her time because her country is being ravaged?' And so the poor lady talks on unheeded, finally nodding off to sleep. The time passed slow and strange and chill, the dawn began to grow, Susy was sitting by a window looking on the platform. A veil of early dew was upon everything, and figures began to move like dreams across the vapour. At last a train arrived with snorts and clamour about five o'clock, conveying among other passengers some wounded Prussians. Then for the first time, Susy, forgetting her own preoccupation, realised the horrors of war; and as she looked again she saw that these were the victors, these wounded, wearied men, scarce able to drag themselves along. Some were carried in their companions' arms, some sick and languid came leaning on their guns, some again were loaded with spoil and bags. One soldier passed the window carrying a drawing-room clock under his arm, and a stuffed bag like an old-clothes-man's upon his back. The wounded were to change carriages, and went hobbling from one train to another; among the rest came a poor Prussian soldier, pale, wasted, with one leg amputated, slowly, painfully dragging on a single crutch, with another man to help him, and in the crowded rush the crutch slipped and the soldier fell to the ground half fainting. His companion tried in vain to raise him; not one of the shadowy figures moved to his help. Susy with a cry of pity started up; but the glass door was locked and she could not get out. It was a Frenchman, at last, who came forward and picked the poor fellow up, helping to carry him, with looks of aversion and deeds of kindness.

And then, at last, the way being clear, the weary Prussians having departed, another train drew up in the early morning light, and Susy found herself travelling towards Paris and her journey's end. The light grew, and with it came the thought of the coming day, what would it bring to her, of good or evil? This much of good it must bring, that she should be with her mother. And Du Parc, did she hope to see him? She could not have answered or acknowledged, even to herself, what she hoped. From her mother she hoped to hear something of Max's doings, and to get news of that one person in all the world who seemed most to exist for her. She longed to see him, to speak to him once more, to get some certainty of his well-being, to be reassured by one word, one look. She dreaded the meeting, its inadequate explanation, its heart-breaking, disappointing silence. . . .

The English girl opposite had taken off her hat and smoothed her long plaits of hair, and now, with a Testament in her hand, was reading her early orison. The morning grew, the sunrise touched the wide country, they passed orchards in flower, green spring shining upon every cottage and pleasant garden and spreadings fields. One little orchard remained fixed in Susanna's mind, pink with blossoms, and in the midst upreared the figure of a Prussian soldier in full uniform, stretching his arms while the children of the household clustered round about him, and the rays of the rising sun flashed from his brass helmet.

As they travelled on, stopping at the various stations, more passengers got in, all with the same miserable story, sometimes piteous, sometimes half laughable. An old lady with frizzed curls described her home as she had found it after eighty Prussians had inhabited her house, the linen, the crockery, the clocks, all stolen and spoilt, the flowers down-trampled. 'They even took my son's cigars, which I had hidden in my wardrobe,' said the poor lady, waxing more and more wrath; 'and the monsters left a written paper in the box, "*Merci pour les bons cigares!*" Ah! that emperor,' says the old lady, 'to think what he has brought us to, with his flatteries, and his vanity, and his grand army.'

Another woman, dressed in black, sadder, more quiet, who seemed to be returning home, utterly worn out, now spoke for the first time.

'One thing we must not forget,' she says, 'we have had twenty years of peace, and yet only one man in France has had the courage to adhere to the fallen emperor.'

Susy's heart failed her as they neared their journey's end, for they came to a desolate country of broken bridges, of closed houses, of windows and palings smashed, of furniture piled in sheds along the line; and as they neared Paris, to a wide and devastated plain across which the snow was beginning to drift. The plain spread dim and dreary, sprinkled with ghosts of houses, skeletons of walls that had once enclosed homes, now riddled and charred with burnt beams, and seams, and cracks, telling the same sad story, reiterated again and again, of glorious conquest and victory.

CHAPTER XXXVII

THREE MILES ALONG THE ROAD

With what sharp checks I in myself am shent
When into reason's audit I do go,
And by just counts myself a bankrupt know
Of all those goods which heaven to me hath lent,
Unable quite to pay even Nature's rent,
Which unto it by birthright I do owe. . . .

SONNETS

When Susy stepped out of the train and looked around, she was struck by the change in the people standing all about the station. They had strange, grave, scared faces; they were more like English people than French people; every woman was in mourning, which added to the sadness of the place. A cold east wind was blowing up the silent street and across the open place in front of the railway. A man came to offer to carry her bag; when she told him she wanted a carriage to take her to Neuilly, he shrugged his shoulders – 'A carriage,' said he; 'where am I to find a carriage? the Prussians have made cutlets of our horses.'

Susy looked round, there were porters and trucks in plenty, but not a carriage was to be seen. It was a long weary tramp after a night spent in travelling; but there was no help for it, and after a minute's hesitation, Susy told the man to take up her bag. She had walked farther in old days when she was coming and going and giving her music lessons.

The man trudged in silence; it was a good three miles' walk across the boulevards, and by streets and shops; some were open, some were not yet reassured enough to let down their closed shutters. One of the very first sights which met Susy along the road was a dispirited, straggling regiment marching into Paris from the frontier, torn, shabby, weary, the mud-stained officers marching with the men. These men were boys, for the most part half grown, half clothed, dragging on with a dull and piteous look of hunger and fatigue, while the piercing wind came whistling up the street. 'They are disarmed, that is why they look so cold,' said the porter stopping for a moment to look after them. 'There is one who can keep up no longer;' as he spoke one of the poor fellows fell out of the ranks too much exhausted to go on any farther; a halt was called, and many of them sank down on the pavement just where they stopped.

The way seemed longer and longer; more than once she was obliged to rest upon the benches along the road. It was now about twelve o'clock, the sun had come out bright though without warmth, and it somewhat cheered the shivering city. They reached the Arc at last, still swathed in its wooden shields. Susy thought of her last sunset drive, and of the glories in which the stony heroes of the past had then brandished their spears. Here Susy saw an empty carriage coming out of a side street, and she told the porter to secure it.

The man thanked her for the money she put into his hand as she sank tired out into a corner of the coach. The driver leant back upon his seat, and seeing she was tired and prepared to pay, began to make difficulties.

'Villa du Parc, Avenue de Neuilly?' says the coachman; 'you will not find any houses standing in the Avenue de Neuilly. The Prussians have taken care of that. I will drive you if you like; but you will have your course for nothing.'

'Pray drive on,' said Susy wearily, 'I will tell you when to stop.'

'When I tell you that there are no houses left to drive to!' persists the coachman, 'but I must be paid all the same, whether the house is there or not.'

'Yes, of course you shall be paid,' said poor Susy, utterly tired, frightened, impatient, scarcely knowing what to fear or to expect.

Madame du Parc's letter had been dated from the villa, but Susanna's heart began to fail her as she drove on. They drove past blackened walls, by trees half destroyed and charred, and breaking out into pale fresh green among the burnt and broken branches; and by gardens all trampled and ravished.

Susanna was almost too weary to think, too sadly impressed to be frightened. She seemed to herself to have gone through some great battle, some long and desperate siege, and now again, when the victory had been so sorely won, the enemy repulsed with such desperate resolution, now that she was so tired, so worn, came a fresh assault more difficult to withstand than anything that had gone before. Should she see him again, would he be there at home once more, was he well of his wound, was it – was it Max or her mother that she had come for? she suddenly asked herself with an angry, desperate effort. Mrs Dymond, absorbed in her own thoughts, had driven past the house without seeing it, and the coachman had stopped of his own accord in a sunny, windy corner, where three ruined streets divided from the broad avenue.

'Well!' says he, 'I told you how it would be.'

She looked blankly up and down the road; she scarcely knew where she was. Then, as she looked again, she remembered once seeing Du Parc coming up one of these streets in his workman's blouse.

'Am I to turn up these roads – am I to go on?' cries the coachman, again stamping his wooden shoes upon the box to warm his feet.

'I will get out, follow me,' says Susy, suddenly remembering where they had come to, and she sprang out and walked back along the avenue to the villa, which was not far distant. It seemed like a miracle to see the old green gates actually standing, and the villa unaltered in the shaded garden. The gates were splintered and half broken down, the garden trampled over, but the house was little changed and stood in the cold spring sunshine, with no sign of the terrible wave of war which had passed over the village. Even the weathercock was safe, glittering and quivering changefully, for the east wind had gone round to some warmer quarter. A sick woman, propped up by pillows, was sitting out in the garden, a stout old lady was trotting backwards and forwards from the house with wraps and bottles and all that miserable paraphernalia of sickness. (How well one knows the look of it, one could almost believe that pain and suffering and sleepless nights came in those bottles and round china pots. Nervous miseries, brown studies, blue devils, pink, yellow, white decoctions, there they all stand waiting to be taken at bedtime or dinner-time, or whatever the proper time may be.)

Poor Mary Marney was looking wild and worn, and strangely changed in these few months.

'The wind blows chill,' she was saying, querulously. 'If only I could get into that patch of sunshine, but I can't move, I can't get there,' she cried, suddenly breaking down.

'La! la! la! la!' says Madame du Parc, extra noisy, trying to be cheerful. 'What is there to prevent you being in the sunshine. *Aïe!*' adds Madame, 'if it was not for this rheumatic arm I could carry you there myself. Denise! what are you about?'

Susy stood frozen in the gateway for a moment, too shocked to move.

Was this her mother, this her busy hard-working mother, thus changed, thus terribly altered in so short a time?

While she paused, Mary, looking up, saw her daughter, and gave a faint cry. Madame also looks up.

'*À la bonne heure!*' says the one cheerful, unemotional person present. 'You see she come at once, and I was right,' cries the old lady, rushing to the front, and bestowing two hearty kisses on Susy's pale cheeks.

All Madame's preventions were gone, Susy was in her highest favour.

'You are a googirl to come,' she reported, pronouncing it as if it was one single word.

'Mamma, my dear!' Susy whispered, kneeling down by her mother's side; for she could not stand. 'I have come to fetch you, I have come to make you well again, mamma! mamma!' She hardly knew what she said in her low, tender whisper; but Mary saw her looks of love, felt her warm, panting breath, and the quick beat of the pulses, and asked no more.

Madame took Susy upstairs after a while. The house had been used as an ambulance. There were beds everywhere – in the dining-room and the drawing-room. Most of the appliances of the ambulance had remained.

Susy followed her hostess into one of the rooms; it had been the little boys' nursery; it was now full of empty iron bedsteads.

The old lady made her sit down on one of them, as she told her, not without kindness, but plainly enough, what the doctor had said.

'He had declared Mrs Marney to be suffering from an aneurism; her very life depended on perfect calm and quiet – Calm! quiet! I ask you how that is to be procured? And that vile husband! Oh! I could tell her how deceived she is in him, but she will not hear reason;' and Madame, in that peculiar voice in which people repeat scandal and bad news, assured Susy that Marney was not far off, he was comfortably established in the neighbourhood, and absenting himself on purpose. Max had heard things in his ambulance. A wounded man there had had dealings with Marney. 'We will go together,' says Madame, 'we will make inquiry. When we are chased from this, as my son declares will be the case, your dear mother must not be abandoned. I must go back; I have no rents, nothing to depend upon here. In the south Max has a little farm, which will keep us both. I sent for you, my poor child, when I heard the doctor's terrible announce, and we will arrange presently what we should do. Here is your old room; the doctor of the ambulance has been living here; you see nothing is new. It is all the same.'

There is something which appeals to most imaginations in places scarcely altered, when those who inhabit them are so changed. Susy looked round as she sank wearily down upon the old creaking wooden bedstead. How often before this had she cried herself to sleep upon it. She looked at the whitewashed walls, at the shadow of the window bar travelling across the tiles; then a curious shock reminded her of the difference of the now and of the time to which she had travelled back again. . . .

She came down to find her mother impatiently waiting for her. Mrs Marney had been carried into the sitting-room, and Susy's hope sank afresh as she looked at the changed face turned to the door, and expecting her so eagerly. One little crisp, familiar wave of curly hair beneath her cap seemed the only thing which remained of Susy's mother as she had been but a few weeks ago.

Poor Mrs Marney was worn by many sorrows and anxieties besides her illness. Of Marney she knew scarcely anything, and that was the chief of her many pains.

'Oh, Susy! I would not trouble you with my troubles,' she said, 'but I have gone through more than I could bear. After the first weeks at Avignon he scarcely wrote; he scarcely gave one sign, and I knew not what to fear. I have been mad to see him. Madame has said cruel things which I seem to have no strength to hear. I wrote to him when I first came here. And now I hear nothing, I know nothing.'

Susy turned scarlet; but she soothed her mother again, with many gentle words and caresses.

CHAPTER XXXVIII

ADIEU LES SONGES D'OR

Oh! how shall summer's honey breath hold out
Against the wreckful siege of battering days?

Things come about simply and naturally which seem very terrible and full of emotion beforehand. Here was Susanna, after all that had happened, standing with Madame du Parc by Max's bedside, and neither of the three seemed moved beyond their ordinary looks and ways. Had they parted yesterday in a garden of roses they could not have met more quietly, though they met with disaster all about, among omens and forebodings of worse evil to come. For a moment the room seemed to Susy to shake beneath her feet, but it was only for a moment. The sight of his pale worn face, so sad and strangely marked with lines of care, and yet so familiar withal, called her back to the one thought of late so predominant in her mind: what she could do for him, how she could help him best. Of sentiment and personal feeling she could not think at such an hour.

Great events carry people along into a different state of mood and being, to string them to some greater chord than that of their own personality. In all these strange days and stirring episodes Susanna seemed to herself but one among the thousands who were facing the crisis of their fate, a part of all the rest, and yet at the same time she knew that every feeling she had ever known was there keenly alive, unchanged by change.

'Ah! we have had a narrow escape,' said Madame. 'They got the ball out of his chest; a little more and it was in his lungs. But he is well now, and he was able to save his man. Eh! Max?'

'Save my man, mamma?' said Max, smiling faintly. 'There was not much of him saved, poor fellow. I pulled what was left of him from under his horse, then some one helped me up. By the way, can you arrange for Adolphe to return to the villa to-morrow? Caron will bring a carriage for us.'

'Why, of course, *comment donc*. I will speak to the sister at once,' said Madame du Parc, jumping up. Then she paused. 'Susy has something to ask you,' she said. 'Who was it, Max, who saw Marney at St Cloud? Who can give us his address?'

'It was Adolphe,' said Max, shortly. 'You had better leave Mr Marney to his own affairs.'

'I wish it were possible,' Susy said with a sigh; 'but my mother cannot rest day or night. I am driven to look for him. It is only to help her that I am here.'

'You will find Adolphe in the next room,' said Du Parc, looking disappointed. 'My mother will guide you. Good-bye; do not stay now,' and he put out his hand.

He spoke advisedly. He was still weak from illness. This meeting was almost too much for his strength, and he dreaded one kind word from Susy, lest, like a woman, he should break into tears. These were not times for tears of sensibility. There had been too many tears shed, Max used to think. Statesmen wept when they should have resolved; made speeches where silence would have been more to the purpose; and Du Parc felt that for the present, for Susy's sake and for his own, they must be as strangers together. His was a somewhat old fashioned creed, but one which, after all, has kept the world going in honour and self-respect since the beginning of all honour, and Du Parc, having made up his mind, was not in the habit of wasting his time by undoing it again. He was but half a Frenchman, but he loved his country, its welfare, its good name beyond all other things. For the last four weeks he had lain patiently waiting for his wound to heal, now that his strength was returning he longed to be at work once more. It was little enough, but it was something. One more pair of arms to help to keep order in the chaos, one more recruit on the side of justice and of law.

Max followed Susanna's tall retreating figure to the door with his sick man's wistful looks. She stopped for a moment, looked back, faintly smiled, and passed on. The two were in deeper sympathy in their silent estrangement than in any romantic protests and explanations. The next room had been a grand lady's boudoir once. It was still hung with a few smart pictures and ornamental glasses. A young soldier, in undress, with a wounded shoulder, who was standing in a window, greeted them cheerfully and immediately began fumbling with his good arm at his red trousers pocket.

'Good-morning, Madame du Parc,' he cried. 'Your son told me he was expecting you. I want to show you this.' And he produced a purse, in which, with some coppers, was a piece of his own bone wrapped up in newspaper.

The next man to him who was bedridden brought a bit of his knee-cap from under the pillow. He had a handsome brown face, and lay looking up wearily; he couldn't sleep, he was never at ease, he said; his comrade had been writing home for him. 'He won't tell them of his wound,' cried the man in the window. 'He made me say that he had a slight sprain in the leg,' and the good-natured young fellow roared with laughter at the joke. 'Never mind, we shall see thee a captain yet, Jean!' he said gaily.

'A captain! not even a corporal,' answers poor Jean.

Some other men who were playing cards and dominoes at a table in the centre of the room looked up and greeted Madame du Parc, who seemed to know them all. One poor fellow, who was looking over a comrade's cards, came striding forward with both hands in his trousers pockets. This was the Adolphe whom Max had saved at the risk of his own life. He was a sergeant, a superior sort of man, with a handsome face. He had been a carpenter when the war broke out. He had been wounded in the side. He had a wife and three little children, he told Susanna. He was going home to them, 'but I shall never be able to work for them again,' he said sadly, and Susy could hardly repress a cry of compassion as he showed her his stumped fingers – they had been clean cut off both hands.

'*Tu vivras de tes rentes*,' cried one of the card-players cheerfully, and again the poor fellows all laugh, not heartlessly, but with the real courage and humility of endurance, which is more touching than any bitter complaints. Adolphe, who had been taken prisoner, had seen Marney at Versailles in the Prussians' head-quarters, and it was Marney who had helped his escape, giving him money and also certain commissions to execute in Paris. Adolphe, being questioned, told Susy of a place where Marney was always to be heard of; he had often carried letters for him there – a café at St Cloud, it was easy enough to find. While they were talking, Madame, who hated being quiet, was walking round the room with her basket on her arm, distributing various things which she thought might be useful to the patients. She offered a newspaper to one of them, who refused it gaily with thanks.

'I never read them,' said he, 'since the war began, they are nothing but lies. Holloa! Who wants the last number of the *Fausses Nouvelles?*' he shouts.

A few beds off lay a poor Englishman. He had enlisted in the line. He had been with General Failly at Lyons. 'He has been very ill, poor fellow,' said Madame, as Susy joined her. 'John Perkins! here is an English lady come to see you!'

'See me! There is not much of me fit to see,' muttered poor John Perkins, wearily, pulling up the sheet over his face.

The sister-in-charge now came up. She was dressed in her sister's dress, with a white coiffe and loose grey sleeves. She had a fine and sensitive face, and spoke like a person of some distinction, but she seemed distressed and over-tasked.

'Your son has a home to go to; he is ready to go, the doctor tells me. So many of my patients would be the better for a change, but I have nowhere to send them. Everything is in ruins. Our convalescent hospital has been wrecked; the furniture has been given for ambulances. All is gone, all is destroyed. We do all we can for them. Mr Wallace says they are to have anything they want.'

It was a handsome house, polished and shining, there were Englishmen to wait, carved ceilings, tall windows, and yet it was a sad place to think of. Susy came away haunted by pain. Madame was not a comforting companion, the consciousness of all this suffering rendered her morose and irritable. She was anxious about her son, and she had the fate of her old friend, Mademoiselle Fayard, on her mind. Mademoiselle Fayard, after being driven from Neuilly, had lodged over an undertaker's shop in the same street as the hospital, and thither Madame insisted on going.

The young undertaker received them in the uniform of the National Guard. 'Mademoiselle Fayard and her brother were gone,' he said, 'but their address was always to be had at the convent of the *Petites Soeurs*.' In reply to inquiries about himself, he answered blushing, that he had volunteered. He had been in three battles, and had got his discharge; he had been wounded. His wife had given him up for dead. He found her in mourning for him when he got back. . . .

It was but a few hours since Susy had left her home, and already it seemed to her natural to hear all these histories, to see ruin and trouble on every side, and incongruous things which no longer surprised her. A few minutes later she was standing with Madame du Parc in the old courtyard of a convent. A pile of knapsacks was heaped against the old grey wall, some soldiers were coming in at the gateway, and two nuns were advancing to receive them. The soldiers looked well pleased, and the nuns, too, seemed amused. They were all on the best of terms. The nuns smile and fold their hands, the soldiers laugh and nod and scamper upstairs to their allotted cells. 'Poor fellows! they would have had to sleep out of doors all night if we had not taken them in,' said the nuns. 'We had one ward of the infirmary empty, and the Superior said the soldiers might occupy it.' The sister went on to tell Madame du Parc how they had kept their infirmary open almost all through the siege until one morning when a poor old fellow had gone out early to get a drink at the fountain in the garden, and an obus fell and killed him, 'just there where the sun is shining,' said the Soeur Marie Joseph. 'All of the nuns wanted to go to him, but Bonne Mère ordered us down on our knees and went alone. The Prussians seemed to have got the range of our convent, for the shells fell at intervals all that day, and we moved the old men, not without difficulty and danger. We had hardly got them out when a great bomb came crashing into the infirmary. You can see for yourself,' said the sister, opening the infirmary door.

All was restored again, the holes were mended in the floor with squares of new wood, the orderly beds were in their places, and the old men safe back in their beds.

'Nothing happens to us,' said an old fellow, with a long white beard, sitting up in bed; 'here we lie, tied by the leg!'

'I have been to Prussia,' says another, in an arm-chair, beside him, with a white nightcap pulled over his ears, talking on continuously whether anybody listened to him or not, 'I have pillaged, too, in my time, but, thank God [*Dioû marchi* he pronounced it], we are not bad men like those Prussians. We used to take to eat because we were hungry. We didn't pillage for nothing at all. No, no; we are soldiers, not bandits,' says he bringing his hand down upon his knee. 'If we hadn't been betrayed we should have smashed those Prussians.'

'Yes, we should have smashed them!' cries a third old feeble fellow on his pillow just beyond.

A lady in black was sitting by his bedside, a sweet-faced woman. A *dame de charité* they called her, an Englishwoman, living in Paris, who gave herself up to visiting the poor. When they asked the nuns about Mademoiselle Fayard, they said she too was well known at the convent, and often came to read to the old men. She was lodging close by with her brother, next door to the Carmelite convent in the adjoining street. Mrs Dymond was longing to get home to her own sick woman again, and Madame du Parc promised that this should be their last visit. Susanna could not help thinking of Dante's journey as she followed Madame's steady steps. They came out into the street, and presently found themselves standing in the Rue d'Enfer in front of an old grim house, with grey and silent walls, against which came the beating sleet and the cutting winds. Two men were at work in the yard carting away a heap of stones and plaster. A little girl was standing at the door, too much engrossed by the bombshells to understand what they said at first. 'Look! they are removing the ruins from the chapel, the bombs fell just there, mesdames, piercing right through into the cellar beneath. The director of the ladies escaped as by a miracle. We only came home yesterday. Our lodge is in an indescribable state.' By degrees the little girl was made to understand what it was they wanted, and after consultation with her mother, who was at work indoors, she came back with the news that Mademoiselle Fayard was at home, upstairs at the very top of the house, and Susy and her old guide now climbed flight after flight of stone steps, bound together, as in old French houses, by wrought-iron banisters. At the very top of the house, under the skylight, they found the door to which they had been directed, and rang a bell, which echoed in the emptiness. Presently they heard steps, and the door was opened, and Mademoiselle Fayard, the shadow of herself, so thin, changed, worn, limp, opened the door. Madame's grunts of compassionate recognition nearly overcame the poor lady as she fell weeping into her old friend's arms. She flitted before them exclaiming, and hastily opened the door of the room where she had been sitting with her brother. It was a long, low room in the roof of the old house, littered with books and packing cases. They had prepared to fly at one time, Mademoiselle Fayard explained, and had commenced to pack.

'Brother! brother! here is Madame du Parc,' cries the ghost of Mademoiselle Fayard to the skeleton of her brother, who was sitting in an old dressing-gown by a smouldering stove in the semi-darkness of the room. The old lady had already lit up her lamp, and as they came in she hospitably turned it up with her trembling hands, while he disencumbered two chairs for the ladies. 'Oh! my poor frens,' says Madame, sitting heavily down. 'What have we all suffered!' Susy could only look her pity as she listened to the sad reiteration of cold, hunger, hope deferred, darkness and anxiety.

The Fayards were both speaking together; they described their past alarms, their weary waiting, how the food and the fuel failed first, and then the light; they used to go to bed at seven o'clock, and lie awake the long hours listening to the boom of the guns; how towards the end of the siege the bombs began to fall in their streets and upon the houses all around them; the old lady and gentleman felt the crash of the first that fell into the linen-closet of the ladies of the Carmelite convent next door; the *pompiers* had hardly put out the fire when another bomb broke into the chapel. The *petite soeur tourière*, who was arranging the altar, stood alone and unhurt in the midst of the falling timber and glass, but the pulpit was destroyed, and the marble columns were injured, the sisters could not escape because of their vow, and had to remain in the cellars. For a whole fortnight, every day, the priest went down to say mass, though it was dangerous to cross the court, for bomb after bomb kept falling there.

'Once we went away,' said Mademoiselle Fayard, in her extinguished voice, 'but we had to come back for food. Our ticket was of no use in any other district, and we thought it best to remain at home. Many days I have waited for three hours in the pouring rain to obtain our daily allowance of food. We could hardly cook it, we had no fuel left. Oh! it was bitter cold,' said she; 'we have endured very much; and if only it had been to some good end we should not have felt our sufferings.' The old people promised to come over very soon. They asked affectionately after Max. Mademoiselle Fayard had been to see him in the ambulance as soon as she heard of his wound. He, too, had been to see them during the siege. He had brought them a couple of new-laid eggs 'as a present,' said the old lady. 'I know he paid fifteen francs for the two. Oh, madame, the price of everything! Cabbages were five francs apiece! Elephants, monkeys, cats, all were at exorbitant prices.'

As the two women turned homewards, the streets were full of people in black, with sad faces; they passed soldiers and more soldiers, all disarmed and ragged to look upon, and Francs-Tireurs in top-boots lined with old newspapers. As they passed the Luxembourg Gardens they could see the tents of the shivering soldiers sleeping within. Many of them were sick, just out of ambulance, some had not even tents.

Madame du Parc walked on steadily, and Susy hurried after. They were both anxious to get home, but as they passed a bookseller's shop on the quai, Madame du Parc went in for one minute to ask some questions about M. Caron, who was a friend of the shopkeeper. M. Caron was down near Corbeil looking after his mills; he was coming up next day; nobody was doing any business. The bookseller himself had only opened his shop for company. He directed them to a coach-yard close by, where they now went in search of a carriage, and thought themselves lucky to find one. Their journey home was enlivened by the coachman's remarks. What did they think of his horse? It was one of three left out of a hundred and fifty. The man stopped of his own accord before the Column of Victory. A flag was flowing from the top, garlands had been twined about its base. 'A *mirliton*, that is what it looks like,' he cried, cracking his whip gaily.

As he spoke a little cart was slowly passing by, in which sat two women dressed in black.

CHAPTER XXXIX

ST CLOUD AFTER THE STORM

Or of the church-clock and the chimes
Sing here beneath the shade
That half mad thing of witty rhymes
Which you last April made. . . .

Max and Adolphe came back next day in the carriage M. Caron had sent for them. They were a pale and depressed-looking couple. As their strength returned day by day, in common with many of the wounded they seemed to feel their country's cruel wounds more and more keenly. Bourbaki was not alone in his despair and passionate regret. Many men committed suicide, many lost their senses, but others pulled themselves together and bravely by degrees began to reconstruct their lives once more. Max tried to make a rally when he came in to see his old friend Mrs Marney. But he could not put away the lines in his face, the hollow rings round his eyes; he laughed, but it was only a melancholy echo of long-past gaiety.

'Why, Maxwell, ye look thin and half-starved, and yet none the less handsome for that,' said Mrs Marney, smiling faintly, and indeed what she said was true enough. As he stood there in his torn and shabby uniform, he seemed to the three women more stately than any general in brilliant orders and triumphant prosperity.

'We must keep him with us, and make him strong and fat!' says Madame, who was the least changed of the party as she stood beside her son in her Rembrandt-like old age.

'Are ye a general, Max, or only a colonel?' said Mrs Marney. 'I wish you would tell them to cease firing their cannon and to leave us in peace!'

'I am neither a general nor a colonel,' said Max gravely, 'and as for telling them to leave off, I might as well speak to the winds and the seas.

Our troubles are not over; you must let your daughter take you to her home, madame; this is no place for women. There is no time to lose. She should be away from here.'

And yet he was glad that Susy had come; he had doubted her at one time, tried to do her cruel injustice, to put her away out of his thoughts with some hatred mixed with his feeling, some angry resentment for those very qualities for which he had loved her. Now they met with an abyss between them, but he could not see her unmoved even at such a time as this, and as Max went on packing, ordering, arranging, the thought of her was in all he did; she looked worn and tired, the worst had not yet come. Max stopped to consider what would be best for them all. His mother must go into safety, and chance had favoured him there. Susy must be sent back without delay, taking her mother with her.

But Mrs Marney would not hear of going away, she almost screamed when her daughter gently and tenderly suggested it, and repeated what Max had said. The mere hint of a move threw her into a state of such hysteric grief, that Susy feared she might die then and there in her arms. 'Go without seeing Mick, Susy, are you made of stone? Don't you know that he is my husband, my love, my life? Go home yourself, – and indeed your child must be wanting you, – leave me, only leave me, in peace to die. Madame *must* go, I know that well enough; has she not said so a dozen times a day? I only ask to be left; my husband might come back and find me gone, I who never failed him yet.' It was all so piteous, so incoherent, so tragical, that neither Susy nor her old friend knew how to reason with it.

Madame du Parc was preparing to start at once, her 'affairs' were weighing on her mind. 'If I delay there are those who are ill-disposed, who are hungering to lay their 'ands on our property. I must have a 'ome for Max.' In despair, and scarcely knowing what to suggest, Mrs Dymond determined to go and find Marney himself, if he could be found. He would be the best person to persuade his wife.

Madame du Parc had been talking to Maxwell's coachman. It happened by chance that the carriage Caron had engaged belonged to Versailles, and was returning that afternoon. Carriages were rare, and Susy, finding that she could hire this one, after a couple of hours' rest for the horses, determined to set off on her quest without loss of time. Denise was left in charge of the sick woman; Madame, availing herself of the opportunity, proposed to accompany Mrs Dymond.

'Max is at home,' she said; 'your mother is used to him; he will go up if he is wanted, and that Adolphe is very handy, poor fellow.' It was Adolphe who saw them off, and who told the coachman where to drive when they reached St Cloud. So they started along the desolate road. Madame's grunts, groans, and exclamations seemed the most lively and cheerful sounds by the way.

'Oh! Oh! Oh! Only look at the ruined houses! That is poor Mademoiselle Fayard's apartment up there, right up there.'

Mademoiselle Fayard's late apartment was now nothing but a sort of hanging grotto in the air, and consisted of three sides of a blackened room, of which the floor was gone, the ceiling was gone, although by some strange freak of chance and war the gilt looking-glass still hung upon its nail in which Mademoiselle Fayard had been used to crimp her curls. All the rest of the tidy little home had crumbled and fallen away.

'Ah! Susy – I must call you Susy still – how terrible it all is. Only just now I say to my son, "Let us go together, Max; come away to the south – bring your tools and your work and let us live rational lives once more," But he will not. He say to me, "Go, mother; you go, I will follow when my work here is done." His work, what is it, I ask you? He have finished M. Caron's book, and now, when I go into the studio I see nothing on the walls. Why does he not come away? If only your dear mamma could travel with us she too might enjoy the peace, the beautiful clime of Avignon. But she have you now; you are a better cure than an old *patraque* like me; you must take her to your home, and make her happy with you.'

Susy looked away, her eyes were heavy with tears, she felt that no nurse, no care could ever make her mother happy again. Madame went on talking and exclaiming; when Susy could listen to her again, she found she had gone back to the war, to her terrors, to her joy, when she found her house spared as if by miracle. They had floated the ambulance flag over the roof, and those abominable Prussians did not dare fire the villa. 'And now they say there is still danger, and we must go. It is horrible.'

So the voice monotonously droned on, and meanwhile they drove their way by a desolate road, a Pompeii of the nineteenth century, past deserted houses, open to the winds, past fallen walls, between the blackened homes, all alike forsaken and abandoned. The pleasant country seats, the schools, the shops were all empty and wrecked. Here and there they passed soldiers leading horses; and carts, loaded with household goods, slowly labouring along the way. Men and women came slowly dragging trucks piled with what few possessions they had saved from the storm.

At last they reached St Cloud itself, and once more Madame exclaimed in consternation. Overhead the sky shone blue and the clouds were floating gaily, but the village of St Cloud looked like a pile of children's bricks overthrown by a wayward hand, so complete was the change and confusion. The stones were heaped in the streets, only the shells of the tall houses were standing still, with strips of paper fluttering from the ruined walls. Here and there were relics and indications of the daily life of the inhabitants. In one place a bird-cage was found hanging unharmed among the ruins. At the corner of the principal street (how well Susy remembered standing there little more than a year before with Max, when the Imperial carriages rolled by and all seemed so prosperous) a tall pile of ruined houses upreared their black walls. High up overhead a kitchen range, with its saucepans, was still fixed, and some toppling chairs were wedged into a chimney-stack. At the foot of the ruin, three women in country cloaks were standing together looking up vacantly at the charred houses. They had but just come home to find their homes gone and utterly desolated.

A few steps farther on Susy saw a child playing battledore and shuttlecock in front of the blown-up houses. High up against the sky she could see the gutted *château*, still standing on its terrace, while the sky showed pink through the walls. Some sightseers were standing looking about. '*Papa, monte par ici, si tu veux voir quelque chose de beau*,' cries a boy, springing up on a heap of bricks, and pointing to a falling street. Although the whole place was thus ravaged and destroyed, by some odd chance the spire of the church and its bells remained untouched.

The café was also little harmed, and some people were sitting as usual drinking at the little tables in front of the windows.

For once the presence of these indifferent philosophers was reassuring, one of them, who had already imbibed more drink than was necessary to prove his philosophy, began a song with a chorus in which two or three of his companions joined.

'Listen to them,' said a workman going by; 'they drink and sing while their country is in ruins.' And he flung some common word of disgust at them, and trudged on his way.

Madame was looking at the address Adolphe had given her.

'This must be the very place – see, "Café de l'Empire" is painted outside. Here, *garçon*!' and she beckoned to the waiter.

The waiter professed to know nothing of M. Marney. He had never heard the name; no Englishman was staying there. In vain Madame harangued and scolded.

Madame was not be repulsed by a little difficulty. She slipped a five-franc piece into the waiter's hand.

'Try and find out Monsieur Marney's address within,' said she, 'and I will give you a second piece.'

'His wife is very ill,' said Susy, bending forward; 'he is sadly wanted at home. We have come to find him.'

'Can it be the capitaine you want?' said the waiter, suddenly relenting, as he looked at her entreating face; 'a fine man, not tall, but well dressed, and well set-up, curly hair, moustache *en croc*?' And as they assented, 'I did not know his name; our patron sends all his letters to Versailles. Wait!' And the man ran back into the house.

'Ah, you see, he knew very well,' says Madame du Parc, with satisfaction, and in a minute the waiter returned with a paper, on which was written, in Marney's writing, '15 Rue des Dominicains, Versailles.'

'Ah! That is just what we wanted; and now the coachman must take us on quickly,' said Madame. 'Good-morning, young man.'

The waiter refused the second five-franc piece that Susy would have given him as they drove away.

'One is enough,' said he. 'If the captain comes I will do your commission.' And spreading his napkin wings he flew back again to his work.

CHAPTER XL

AT VERSAILLES

Even kings and kesars biden fortune's throws.

The carriage rolled on along by the banks of the river, by more ruin, by desolation in every form; a few people were out, a few houses and shops were opening once more; the gardens bloomed with spring, and lilac, and laburnum; the skies were bright, and the ruins black.

The coachman stopped at a village to give his horse a drink. A great pile of crockery stood in the middle of the street; all about houses, wine-shops, wayside inns, alike abandoned, a blacksmith's forge, empty and silent, a great seared barrack standing gaunt and deserted. It was one continuous line of desolation all along. Here and there a face looked out of some rifled home, and disappeared into the ruins. A cart went crawling by, piled with household goods. Out of one big broken house, with shutters flapping and windows smashed, issued a grand carriage, with a coachman and groom in full livery, and twinkling harness, and horses looking strangely smart and out of place. A little farther on was a china shop that seemed to have escaped by miracle; its broken panes were mended with paper. Then came children two by two. They reached Versailles in less time than they expected. It was barely five o'clock, the sun was sinking in a warm and cheering stream of light. As they drove into the city, they heard the distant sound of a military band. Great changes were taking place, not the least being that the Germans were leaving. As they came up the street they met a company, spiked and girt, tramping out of the town. The soldiers marched past the old palace that had sheltered so many dynasties with stony impartiality, bearing in turns the signs of each invading generation. The noble gardens were flushed with blossom and growing summer; the shops were all open, the children were at play in the streets. On the walls were affixed papers in French and German, sales of horses, of camp furniture. Susy read of the approaching departure of the ——Company of the Hessian Division, with a notice requiring any claims to be immediately sent up, and a list of the articles to be disposed of by public sale. As they waited to let the soldiers pass by, some more Germans came out of a stable across the road, carrying huge bundles of straw upon their backs and talking loudly to one another. How strange the echo of their voices sounded, echoed by the stately old walls of Versailles!

The soldiers were gone; they were driving on again along the palace gardens, when Madame leant forward with a sudden exclamation. 'There is Marney!' she said. 'I see him; he turn in there at the palace gate.' And the old lady, leaning forward, loudly called to the coachman to stop. 'We will go after him,' she said to Susy; 'there is no time to lose.'

Susy did not say a word. It had to be gone through, and she silently followed Madame, who was crossing the great court with heavy rapid steps in pursuit of the figure she had recognised. They met with no opposition. The guardian of the galleries stared at them as they hurried by; the place was nearly empty; they saw a distant figure rapidly retreating, and Madame hurried on in pursuit from one echoing floor to another, past the huge pictures of Napoleon and his victories, past a great gilt frame boarded carefully from view. One or two people were passing and re-passing along the gallery, but Marney (if Marney it was) vanished suddenly, and was nowhere to be found. Madame severely questioned a guardian standing by a doorway, He had seen no one pass within the last few minutes, but there were many exits; there was one door leading to the great hall, which had been turned into an ambulance, and people were constantly going out by it. The officers were gone, he told them; a few of the men still remained, and one young lieutenant, whose sister had come from Germany to nurse him. Susy had hardly patience to listen during Madame's various questions and observations, to which the custodian, being a cautious man, returned guarded answers. 'That was a portrait of the Queen of Prussia, boarded over by command; now that the Prussians were going it was to be unboarded, by order.' 'Yes, he had been there all the time. He had faithfully served the Emperor. He was prepared as faithfully to do his duty by any one who came.' A Coriolanus could not have uttered sentiments more noble and patriotic. At last, finding it was hopeless to inquire further, they got into the carriage once more, and drove to the address in the Rue des Dominicains.

'No. 15! This must be No. 15,' says Madame, stopping before a low white house, with a high roof and a door opening to the street. She knocked with two loud decided raps, raising the heavy scrolled knocker. In a little while the heavy door was opened by a stupid-looking girl in a white cap, who seemed utterly bewildered by her questions.

'Yes,' she said, 'Mr Marney lived there. He was not at home; he was gone to St Cloud.'

'When will he be in?' says Madame in her loud voice. 'I will wait for him. I am Madame Marney's friend.'

The girl looked more and more stupid. 'Madame is here, I will call her,' she said, and she went into a ground-floor room.

Almost immediately a woman, with strange glittering eyes and yellow tawny hair, and some sort of a pink dressing-gown, flung open a door upon the passage. 'You are asking for Madame Marney?' she said with a defiant air. 'What do you want?'

'I *come* from Madame Marney,' said the old lady looking very terrible. 'She is ill, seriously ill. She wishes to see her husband at once, and I must insist——'

But before the old lady could finish her sentence the woman screamed out to the girl, 'What are you doing, Marie? Turn out these German spies,' and, with a look of furious hatred, she sprang forward, violently thrusting poor old Madame backwards out of the doorway and banging the heavy door in her face. Susy, who had not come in, had just time to catch Madame du Parc or she would have fallen. It was a horrible scene, a hideous degrading experience.

The old lady was a minute recovering her breath; then the two looked at one another in silence as they stood together outside the closed house.

'Oh, what abomination!' said Madame, shuddering and putting up her hands. 'Oh, my poor, poor fren'! Oh, Susy, my poor Susy, I have long feared how it might be; I have now the certainty.'

Susanna, who had turned pale, rallied with a great effort. She would not acknowledge, even to herself, much less to Madame, what a miserable revelation had come to her in that brief moment. 'That woman had been drinking,' she said very coldly; 'she seemed half mad. Dear madame, we will go no farther. Mr Marney is sure to receive my mother's message from one person or another, and perhaps, to make sure, you will kindly write to both his addresses when you get back. Let us go home now, mamma will be waiting.' And then, telling the man to drive them to the station, they drove away slowly in the rattling carriage, with the tired horses, scarcely speaking another word.

The wreck of her sweet mother's generous love and life's devotion seemed to Susy sadder and more terrible than any crash of war, any destruction and ravage. What were broken stones, what were overturned walls and fortunes, so long as people could love and trust each other? Once more that idea came into her mind, which she would never let herself dwell upon, a thought of what two lives might be, even tried, even parted, but with trust and love and holy confidence to bind them together.

They were too soon for the train, and had to wait some few minutes at the station; as they stood there in the sunset, two deputies were walking up and down the platform talking gloomily.

'So! the young men of Metz and Strasbourg are to wear the Prussian helmet,' said one of them as they passed; 'it is of a piece with all the rest.'

'I don't know what there is left for us now,' said the other, speaking with emotion. 'Where is our safety? Paris is at the mercy of the first comer. I have seen as many as two hundred young men in a week passing in a file through my village to avoid conscription.' And the voices passed on.

The train arrived at last, puffing along the line, and Susy and Madame got into the first vacant carriage. There they found a trio – a father, a mother in a smart bonnet, a son, a pink-faced youth holding a huge cane and tassel. All these, too, were talking eagerly – they paid no attention whatever to the entrance of the two women.

FATHER. 'Yes, yes, yes! talk to me of change! what does change mean? A Revolution. Quick, add 2,000,000 or 3,000,000 to the national debt. Do you know what the debt was thirty years ago when the minister of finance proposed to pay it off? Now it is just four times the sum! Give us another revolution and we double it again. Liberty! Oh yes! Liberty, or every man for himself. As for me I vote for the man in power because I love my country, and I wish for order above all; I voted for the Emperor and now I shall vote for a Republic, and believe me the only way to preserve a Republic is to take it out of the hands of the republicans.'

SON (*angrily*). 'But, father, our armies were gaining, if only we republicans had been allowed to have our way.'

FATHER (*sarcastically*). 'Yes, everybody gained everywhere, and meanwhile the Prussians advanced.'

MOTHER (*shrilly echoing the father*). 'Pyat! Flourens! these are your republicans, Auguste. They are mud, do you hear, mud, mud, mud.'

Enter an old lady, handed carefully by the guard. 'Ah! sir! many thanks! Madame! I thank you. I am a poor emigrée returning after six months' absence. Alas! I had hoped to be spared the sight of a Prussian, but that was not to be.'

MOTHER (*proudly*). 'We, madame, remained. When one has a son fighting for his country, one cannot leave one's home.' (*Son looks conscious and twirls his cane.*)

OLD LADY. 'Alas! you have more courage than I have. For my part I am grateful from my heart to Trochu for his surrender, for sparing useless slaughter.'

FATHER. 'What could he do alone? he was driven on by your so-called patriots. This is the result of your free press.'

SON. 'But, papa, give us progress, you would not refuse us progress.'

MOTHER (*vehemently echoing the son*). 'Yes, progress and liberty of discussion. . . .'

FATHER (*desperately*). 'I give you progress, but I do not give you leave to talk about it. Progress comes best alone. When people begin to talk nonsense, and pass votes in favour of progress, they show they are not ready for it. . . .'

Sad and preoccupied as Susy was, she could not but listen to the voices on every side; they interested her though they were anything but cheering. When she and Madame du Parc reached the villa, tired and dispirited, a figure was standing at the gate, and evidently looking out for them. It was Jo, only a little more dishevelled than usual, and bringing with him a feeling of home and real comfort of which poor Susy was sadly in need at that moment.

It was the simplest thing in the world. He had started off then and there, hearing that Susanna was gone to her mother; he had come to see if he could help to bring Mrs Marney back; he had left his bag in the train. . . . While Susy walked on with her arm in his, listening to his explanations, Madame du Parc poured out her pent-up indignation to Max, who also came out to receive them. He had been at home all day finishing a couple of sketches ordered by M. Hase for his pictorial newspaper; he had been up once or twice to see Mrs Marney, whom he thought very ill.

'You must tell her nothing, except that you failed to find Marney,' he said compassionately, 'but for God's sake, mamma, leave this place and try and get your friends to go. The sooner the better for us all. The Federals are sure to come down upon Neuilly, another day and it may be too late. I must go back to my work now, for I have no time to lose.'

CHAPTER XLI

RED COMES INTO FASHION

With your hands and your feet and your raiment all red.

MACAULAY

Du Parc was still at his work late that evening when he heard a knock at the door, and he cried 'Come in,' without looking up.

He was bending over his plate with the gas jet flaring above his head, his black curly hair was in the light, his brown face in shadow. He had taken off his worn uniform and was dressed in an old velvet coat, shabby enough for any Communist. His dog was lying at his feet.

'What is it?' he said, looking up half blinded: 'Is it you, mother?'

'It is I, Susanna Dymond,' said Susy, standing in the doorway and hesitating to come in; 'I want you to help me, M. Max. I am in great perplexity, and I want you to advise me,' and as she spoke she came forward into the light. 'I have been expecting Mr Marney, but he has not come yet,' continued Susy, with a faltering voice. 'I fear it will kill mamma outright to be moved to England, I think it will be best to take her somewhere into Paris, where she can be safer than here; and meanwhile your mother must not be delayed by us.'

'My mother had better go,' said Maxwell, after a moment's thought; 'I will see to that. I would not urge Mrs Marney's departure; but if the Federals make a stand at Neuilly, this place may be in flames at any moment. You know I am in their councils,' he said with a shrug. 'You see I am working all night to finish up my plates. I have already tried to talk to Madame Marney,' he continued, putting down his point and rising from his seat. 'You must act for her, pack everything in readiness, and I will make arrangements and have a carriage here to-morrow. I know of a house in Paris where she will be safe for the present. And we must get hold of Marney,' he added.

'Thank you,' said Susy. It seemed to ease her heart to say the words which are so meaningless, but which sometimes mean so much – almost everything, at some moments.

Susy lingered still. She had said what she meant to say; but there was something more she longed to say, as she stood with her true eyes fixed upon Max, while the words failed her.

'Why do you look at me like that, madame?' he asked smiling gravely, and yet not without some feeling perhaps of what was in her mind.

'Ah! Max!' she answered in a low voice, 'I am trying to find courage to ask you to come away. You tell us to go and we are going; why do you yourself remain? What can you do? These Communists are no fit associates for you. I have here learnt enough in the last few days to know something of the truth. What part can an honest man take in this terrible confusion except that of his own simplest duty? Oh, leave these mad people! Your mother is your first duty now. For her sake, for my sake, if my wishes still touch you, come away.'

'Your wishes must always touch me,' he said, simply and gravely; 'but you do not understand; my mother can get on without me. I mean I am not necessary to her,' he said, looking steadily at Susy as he spoke; 'but my poor mother-country wants me. It is true I am only one man in a stupid crowd; but if I go with that crowd I may hope perhaps to lead it in some measure, or to help at least to lead it. For I ask you, madame,' and his eyes began to flash as he went on, 'if all the honest men continue to desert their posts, to take their tickets by every train, as they have done for the last few days, leaving Paris at the mercy of the undisciplined mob, who will be to blame for whatever desperate encounter may arise? I should like *you*, at least, to think of me as an honest man, and not as a coward, even though I tell you I am afraid to go, afraid to abandon a party where I imagine my presence may be of use, for another faction whose acts and deeds I reprobate with all my heart. Caron has elected to stay, and my convictions will not let me abandon him, alone, to face the storm which is ready to break. Our place is here at our posts, even if we cannot keep back the horrible burstings of the floodgates, the hopeless reprisals, which must follow.' He had almost forgotten Susy's presence; he was growing more excited every moment, while she turned paler and paler, and at last sank down trembling on one of the overturned cases.

'I have frightened you,' he said, stopping short, melting. 'Ah, forgive me. There is nothing for people to fear who are doing their duty as best they can. You are in the same danger as I am. You are not afraid for yourself,' and as he spoke he took her cold hand in his. She could not answer; her reluctant sympathy, her utter good-will, her generous love were his; but never, never again should she speak of her feeling to him. She could only faintly press his hand; and then she got up from the wooden case, and walking slowly across the room opened the door upon the garden, dim with the night and starlit; then she stopped – 'Ah! what is that?' said she starting. The muffled sound of a distant gun came bursting through the darkness with a dull vibration. It was followed by a second and a third.

'It is the cannon from the Batteries of Chaumont,' said Max, following her to the door and looking out; 'the fight has begun.' As he spoke two or three figures came up crossing the dark garden. 'Good-night, madame, be without fear; all will arrange itself,' said Max, speaking very loud and distinct. He pushed Susy away with a gentle violence as he spoke, so anxious did he seem that she should go at once.

She went back agitated but calmed by her talk. It was not what he had said which comforted her, but his voice, his bright dominant looks breaking through the occasional glooms and moods she knew so well, the sense of capability and restrained power he threw into the most trivial details, all seemed to her full of help and life. He was no visionary, no utterer of professions; of such men she had an instinctive horror. But he had told her his meaning, his aims, his thoughts, about which he was generally silent, and his looks spoke the truth from his honest heart.

'We are all suspect, we upper classes,' says Mademoiselle Fayard next morning, as she sat there in her skimp gown and limp gloves, clasping her old split parasol; the victim of the German Empire. She had come up to take leave of Madame du Parc, to talk over the horrible news of the outbreak, of the dreadful report of the murder of the generals. 'So Susy and her mother were also going? Had they secured their passports? It was as well to have passports in such times,' said Mademoiselle Fayard.

'Mr Jo must go and ask for them,' says Madame, pouring out the coffee, and shaking her head continually.

But where was Jo? No one had seen him since the early morning. He had been up betimes and had started for the station to look for his bag, so Denise reported.

'I would offer to go for your *passeport*, madame,' said Mademoiselle Fayard, 'but they will see at a glance that I am not a British subject.'

'I am a British subject,' cries Madame with dignity, 'I will accompany Susy.'

'Your complexion alone, madame, is enough to convince them of your nationality,' says Mademoiselle politely. Max came in while they were all discussing their complexions over their breakfast; he looked fagged and anxious, and seemed more and more preoccupied; he also came in to ask for the missing Jo.

'Ah! those yong men!' cries Madame du Parc, 'they are always onpunctual; he leave me and his mamma to get the *passeports*. Why do you not come with us, Max? I am going on to see Caron afterwards.'

Max looked doubtful; 'he could only accompany them as far as the Barrière,' he said, 'if they would start at once;' and they accordingly set out walking along the broad avenue that leads to the Arc. Madame du Parc and Mademoiselle Fayard were ahead. Once more Susy found herself walking beside her friend, but he seemed busy, hurried, scarcely conscious of her presence. A double supply of soldiers were mounting guard at the gates of Paris, and an officer, followed by an orderly, came forward to interrogate them. To this officer Madame immediately addressed herself with dignity.

'We come to demand passes, monsieur,' said Madame; 'I am the proprietress of the Villa du Parc, where I have dwelt respected for nearly thirty years, and now that I am driven from my home by those who . . .'

But here her son hastily interposed, fearing lest one of his mother's outbursts of eloquence might bring them all into difficulty: 'This officer is busy, mamma,' he said, interrupting and laughing at the same time; 'he has not time to listen to all your reasons for leaving home. Madame is residing in Paris,' Max goes on, pointing to Mademoiselle Fayard, 'and is returning to her domicile, and madame,' says he, pointing to Susy, 'is English; she is going to the English Embassy, to demand a *passeport* for herself and her mother, who is ill. I will answer for these ladies. You know me, my lieutenant.'

'Pass, mesdames,' says the officer, politely saluting, and he turns away and goes into his little wooden hut.

As he was turning away, Maxwell came close to his mother, and said in a low voice, not laughing any more –

'Mother, I conjure you to remember that if you say things to people in the street you will not only bring trouble upon yourself, but endanger every one of us. Be silent, I beseech you.'

'This is a pretty country, indeed,' says Madame, with a grunt, 'where sons can impose silence on the mothers who brought them into the world. So much for your liberty.'

'Come along, dear madame,' said Susy, slipping her arm into the old lady's.

Max looked after them for an instant as the three walked away, the sturdy old mother still protesting; the limp one-sided member of the upper classes fluttering vaguely after her; and Susy, straight, majestic, walking steadily on with her long black folds flowing round her upright figure. They turned a corner and were gone.

The streets of Paris seemed strangely changed to Susanna from that chill morning only a few days ago when she first arrived. The city seemed suddenly awakened to an angry mood, noisy, excited. The sad women in their mourning were still coming and going about the streets, but there were also others whom she had not seen before – strange-looking figures, like old-fashioned pictures of Jerome or Horace Vernet.

'How the red has come into fashion; how much it is worn,' said Mademoiselle Fayard, stopping, breathless, to look about. Indeed, it was remarkable that so many people should have suddenly changed their looks and their mourning clothes.

Men and women too wore bands of crimson round their waists and across their shoulders; one or two people passed in red pointed caps of liberty, and presently coming up the street appeared a figure like one of Gillray's caricatures. A huge man, with a long tufted beard, with an enormous necktie tied in a huge bow, swaggering along as if all Paris belonged to him, with wide coat flaps, a tricolour rosette in his peaked hat. Into his sash he had stuck two pistols and a dirk, in his hand he carried a cane with a long tassel. As he advanced puffing and strutting up the road, Susy pressed Madame's arm, in terror lest she should address herself to this imposing apparition.

'Oh the abominable monkey,' mutters the old lady between her teeth.

The man scowled at her as she passed, but fortunately did not heed what she said.

They parted from poor Mademoiselle at a street corner; she had various commissions of her own on her mind, and Susy and her companion went on to the Embassy in the Rue St Honoré. A friendly Union Jack was hanging over the British lion upon the gate. The tall English porter, with his brooms and pails, was washing out the courtyard.

There was a peaceful and reassuring aspect about the place, which restored their somewhat troubled spirits. The porter pointed up a narrow staircase leading to the 'bureau,' in a side lodge.

'The clerk would be back immediately,' he said, and he left them in a little inner room with a stove and a pen and a half dried-up inkstand.

It was an entresol; the low window opened to the yard, so that they could see nothing of the streets outside.

When the clerk came in at last, the two ladies immediately told him their business. He said he must consult a superior. Mrs Dymond, of course, could have a passport for herself. He thought there would be no difficulty about her mother. As for Madame du Parc, he did not know how far she was still entitled to be considered a British subject. He would inquire.

'Is Mr Bagginal still here?' Susy asked. 'He knows my name.'

'Mr Bagginal is away on leave for a few days; he left immediately after the siege. We expect him back daily.'

Then the young man signed to them to come into the second room, of which the windows looked upon the street.

How quickly events arise when the time is ripe for them!

In those few minutes while they waited in the back room, the whole place had been transformed; the dull street was now crowded and alive with people; every casement was open and full of heads, women peeped from the garret windows, men crowded to the shop doors. Where was the gloom of yesterday, the mourning sadness of a conquered nation?

Mr Bagginal's representative entered the room at this minute with Susanna's card in his hand. He was another young man of the Bagginal type, well dressed, well bred. He knew Mrs Dymond's name, he said, while Madame, as usual, began her statement; she gave a retrospect of her past life, her marriage, her early difficulties; she was proceeding to give her views upon the politics of the day, when a sudden cry from the street distracted the polite attaché.

Madame exclaimed, and left off in the midst of her harangue and ran to the window, and Susy turned pale as she followed her.

Up the centre of the street came a mad-looking, dancing procession. A great red flag was borne ahead by a man in a blouse and a scarlet Phrygian cap. Then followed a wild bacchanalian crew, headed by a dishevelled woman also crowned with the cap of liberty, and dressed entirely in red from head to foot, followed by some others dancing, clapping their hands, and beating time to a drum and a tambourine; half a dozen men, with pistols in their belts, with huge boots, and a scarlet figure, carrying a second flag, wound up the procession. The whole band swept on like some grim vision; it was there, it was gone, the window closed up, the street was empty again. The sight seemed so ominous of past terror, of new disaster, that even Madame was silent for once.

'Oh, come, my child,' she said to Susy, who was now standing with her *passeports* in her hand. 'We have much to do; we must not delay. This city is no place for quiet people.'

CHAPTER XLII

ONE OLD FRIEND TO ANOTHER

A comfort of retirement lives in this.
SECOND PART OF HENRY VI

Madame had very much at heart her desire to say good-bye to Monsieur Caron. 'He and I are old people, we may not meet again in this world,' she said. 'He has filled my son's head with many mad ideas, but he has shown himself a good, true friend. Are you afraid to come, Susy?'

She looked pleased when Susy said she should be glad to go with her, she was not afraid.

Monsieur Caron lived some way off in the Rue du Bac, and Mrs Dymond, seeing a chance carriage in the road, signed to it, and got in with her friend. As they rolled along, they passed the head of a second procession coming up some side street, and preceded by a blue flag carried by a man like a beadle.

This procession, unlike the other, was not on tip-toe; it came steadily and quietly along, and consisted almost entirely of well-dressed and respectable-looking people, civilians, National Guards, and others, walking five or six abreast, with folded arms and serious faces, talking as they went.

'That is a deputation going to parley with the Federals,' shouted the coachman, turning round upon his seat. 'Everybody has a procession; you will see the Federals with their barricade in the Place Vendôme; these gentlemen are going to mediate; that is why they are not armed.'

The carriage jogged on, and presently they passed two stacks of guns, piled at the entrance of the Place Vendôme, where the column still rose supreme above the heads of the encamped Federals.

'Do you see the cannons?' said the coachman, a little old man, who seemed of a military turn of mind. 'Oh, they are strong, *ceux-là!*'

'It is all nonsense,' cries Madame, very angrily, 'all childish nonsense.'

One of the sentries looked up at her as she spoke.

It was a glorious spring morning, and the sweetness and the sunshine seemed to be on the side of peace and happier promise. The stacked guns gleamed, the mediators and the soldiers alike seemed enjoying the beauty of the morning.

A few minutes afterwards they were crossing the Pont Neuf, from whence they could see all Paris and its glories shining along the river banks, and soon they reached Monsieur Caron's house on the far side of the Seine, where he lived in a high-perched lodging.

The coachman would not wait for them; they paid him and let him go, and walked into the stone-paved court, where a porter, as usual, was collecting the broken fragments scattered by the Prussian bomb-shells. The house in which Caron lived was well known to the world. Many messengers of good and evil tidings had passed up its stone flights. Chateaubriand had once lived there, faithful to his poor blind, beautiful friend of earlier days. Madame Recamier had lived there, and her friend and disciple. Wise men had climbed those flights, and mighty men belonging to the world of action; there had come the Ampères and Mathieu de Montmorency – that loyal gentleman – all the shifting splendours of those early days, and ministers, and kings, and queens deposed, and courtiers in the ascendant: the place still seems haunted by those familiar ghosts of the first half of the century.

Madame, who knew the way, panted up, followed by Mrs Dymond. They rang the bell of a door, which was presently opened by an old woman-servant in a country dress, who nodded recognition, and showed them through the dining-room to Caron's study.

How peaceful it all seemed, after the tumult of the streets full of the signs of war, of party strife, and confusion. The old man sat reading the paper in his dressing-gown and velvet toque. He sat with his back to the warm flood of light that came from the open window. He rose to meet them, looking surprised but pleased at their visit: his bright blue eyes shone like a young man's beneath his grey hair. 'How good of you, mesdames, to take the trouble,' said he, courteously, in his pretty slow English, 'and to find me out in my nest. It is a long way up, as I fear you have discovered. Will you have some refreshment – coffee or sirop? Madeleine will be proud to serve you.'

'Oh no, nothing of the sort,' says Madame, putting up her hand. 'We come to take leave, Monsieur Caron. I did not wish to go without seeing you once more. You and I are too old friends to part without a good handshake, although our opinions differ, and you know that I shall always detest yours.'

Caron smiled. 'And so you are driven out?' he said. 'It is hard on you, my poor lady. It would take a great deal to tear me from my quiet corner here. You see the Prussians have had some grace; they sent an enormous cannon-ball into our courtyard, but it has done no great harm. Those are Chateaubriand's trees,' he said to Susy, who was looking about with some interest and surprise. 'He used to walk there in that avenue, and compose his sentimental poetry, his impossible idylls. Will you like to come out on the balcony?' and as he spoke he stepped out into the sunshine. A sweet, peaceful sight met their eyes; the old gardens were shining green among walls and gables and peeps of distant places far away. As Susy leant over the rails the twitter of the birds was in the air, and with it all the sweet spring fragrance of the hour. 'That is the priests' garden next door,' Caron said, pointing to a beautiful old garden, with lilacs, beyond a wall. 'They have just come back with their seminarists; there is one of them reading his breviary. He is dreaming away his time, poor fellow! I fear he does not know what an awakening is before him.'

Alas! the old man spoke prophetically, not knowing what he said. Only a few weeks more and the silent young priest was heroically giving up his life for his bravery.

'One can hardly realise that this is also Paris,' said Susy, 'as one comes in straight from the streets, and from hearing the clamour and cries of those horrible people.'

'Ah! my dear young lady, do not call them horrible people,' said the old man, with a sigh. 'They want good things, which pleasant and well-mannered people withhold from them and their children. They are only asking for justice, for happiness. They ask rudely, in loud voices, because when they ask politely they are not listened to.'

'Excuse me, Monsieur Caron,' cries Madame, stoutly, 'I cannot help contradic. They imposes on you; they asks, they takes, they gets rations, they runs away, but they will not work, they cannot learn, they will not fight; you will never teach them anything except to drink and shout. . . . But I forgot; I did not come to argue, I came to shake your hand,' said the old lady, with a touch of real feeling. 'I go to-morrow, Max will follow as soon as he has despatched his work. He will come after me if you do not detain him. Caron, my old friend, I am here to ask this of you – do not keep him from me, do not lead him into dangers.' Two tears stood in her little grey eyes, winking with emotion. 'Would that you, too, were coming into safety,' she said; 'that you were coming with me – or even with Susanna – she go back to England, and there you would be safe.'

'Will you come?' Susanna cried, blushing up eagerly, 'Dear Monsieur Caron! Jo and I would, oh so gladly! bring you home with us. Indeed our house is always open to you – any time, any day.'

The old man looked touched and pleased by her eagerness. 'I thank you warmly,' he said, 'but my work is here. Dear lady, what would you think of me if I abandoned it – my *ateliers*, my *employés*, my half-finished schemes?' Then he turned to Madame du Parc, and took her old brown hand in his with the same gentle, courtly respect that he might have shown to a princess, to a beautiful lady. 'You must trust me as you have always done hitherto,' he said. 'Max shall run no danger if I can help it – none that I do not share myself,' and as he spoke a bright and almost paternal look was in his face. 'Only you must remember,' he added gravely, 'there are some chances which an honest man must face in times like these, and Max is an honest man.'

His words struck Susy; they reminded her of her own talk with Du Parc.

Madame turned red, snorted, jerked, tried to speak, failed, choked. 'Where is Madeleine?' she said at last. 'I will ask Madeleine for some sugar and water,' and she left the room very quickly.

Caron shook his head gently as he looked after her; then he turned his blue eyes on Susanna, who stood silent with her pale face. Still without speaking Caron went to a table, opened a drawer, and came slowly back to her, holding a packet in his hand.

'I have something to ask of you,' he said. 'It has just occurred to me that I have some papers here which I should be glad to know of in a place of safety. Will you take them back to England with you? and if anything should happen to me send for Max, and he will know what to do with them. They are papers relating to my works,' he added, 'and some private memoranda for my friend Max. I left another parcel in my old lodging in the Brompton Road, with Mrs Barry,' he added, smiling. 'It is only an unfinished article about my society, but Max may like to finish it some day.'

Susy knew that for some time past Caron had been trying to apply his socialism to his paper-mills, and that he had turned the whole concern into a company, of which the shareholders were the workmen themselves. It was a society conducted on the same plan as that of Leclair, which had proved so successful. The workmen gave zeal, care, thrift, as their share of the capital; Caron administered the whole, and re-invested the profits in graduated shares at the end of the year.

'You have heard of my factories,' he continued as quietly as was his wont to Susy. 'Do you know the story of the slave who fell with the bowl of grain, and of the swallows who flew to fetch each other to share and share alike? My work-people are my swallows, and if anything were to happen to me, Max must be able to supply them with grain. Do not look distressed, my dear lady,' said the old man, shrugging his shoulders, 'death must come to us all. I care not by what name it comes; but I want to know that my children are provided for. I know that I can trust you, and for the present will you keep my little confidence?'

'You know you can trust me,' Susy said with a sigh, and as she spoke, Madame came back with hurried steps and with red eyes. 'Well, then, good-bye, Monsieur Caron. Madeleine gave me all I wanted,' cried the old lady. 'Come, Susy, come.'

Caron followed them in silence to the door. 'Good-bye; good-bye, take care of yourself, Monsieur Caron,' Madame kept repeating, as she stumped down stairs.

CHAPTER XLIII

PAST THE CHURCH OF ST ROCH

Higgledy-piggledy packed we lie,
Rats in a hamper, swines in a sty,
Wasps in a bottle, frogs in a sieve.

R. BROWNING

They came away into the street again, and walked in silence for a time. Madame went ahead, incoherently grunting and grumbling to herself, quieting down by degrees, and finding some comfort in checking off her many plans upon her fingers. 'Luncheon, necessaries for the journey, a carriage to be commanded, then the omnibus, and so home.' They crossed the bridge and went into the Tuileries gardens. The first thing that struck them was that the sentries had been changed since they passed before. Two hideous little men, with straw in their boots, were keeping guard, and as they crossed each other in their zigzagging lines they occasionally stopped and whispered together. A dirty-looking officer, with a calico sash tied round his waist, came strutting up, and rebuked the sentries in a loud, familiar voice. Many people were about, staring at the strange-looking soldiers established in the customary places. Most of the shops seemed to have put up their shutters again. Madame's purchases preoccupied her, and she crossed the street to one of the few shops which still remained open. Just as she came up to the counter, the shopwoman suddenly put down the handful of things she was folding away and looked at the door. There was a crowd of voices outside, a murmur rather than a cry; one or two people came rushing by the swinging glass door; a man burst in, whispered something across the counter, and the woman, with a pale scared face, turned to Madame.

'They are shooting down the people in the Place Vendôme,' she said quietly; 'we must put up our shutters. Will you remain?'

'Oh, no, no! Let us go home to mamma,' cried Susy, running to the door with a first terrified impulse of flight, and in an instant she and Madame found themselves in a tide of human beings flowing along the street. A minute brought them to the turning up the Rue St Roch, that narrow defile where, near a century before, the young Napoleon, Dictator, had ordered his troops to fire on the mob; along which the young communicants had crowded that day last year. Susy thought of it, even at that moment, flying with the flying stream – children, women in their mourning dresses, couples arm-in-arm. An omnibus, turning out of its way in the Rue de Rivoli, began madly galloping up the steep ascent, along which every door, every shop, seemed closed already, whereas the great church gates flew open wide, and something like a black wave of people came sweeping down the great flight of steps into the street below, flowing and mingling with the crowd. One or two people were standing outside their doors, watching this flight.

'Let us get out of the crowd,' said Madame, coolly, as she hurried along. 'Once across out of the Rue St Honoré we shall be safe enough.'

Susanna in those few moments of time seemed to see more of life than in as many years of an ordinary existence. The people running, the groups rallying, the terrified woman dragging their children into shelter. She saw a group of hateful young dandies leaning over a balcony with opera-glasses in their gloved hands, and laughing at the diverting sight of fellow-citizens flying for their lives. She saw a man in plain clothes suddenly attack a little man in a National Guard's uniform, clutch at him by the collar, with an oath: 'Ah, you hide away in your shops and corners, and this is why we are abandoned to these wretches!' cries the assailant. Then a few steps farther on, a door burst open, a middle-aged man, dressed in the uniform of the National Guard and evidently prepared for action, sallies forth to be as suddenly dragged back by one of those huge and powerful *mégères* for which Paris is famous. 'Do you think that I shall let you go?' she shrieks, as she hurls her husband back, and the door bangs upon the struggling pair. As they were crossing the Rue St Honoré Madame said 'Ah!' in a peculiar voice, and a couple of bullets whistle by. The insurgents were still firing from their barricade at the unarmed masses, at the formidable children, the dangerous nursemaids and servant girls. Once across the Rue St Honoré, as Madame said, they were in comparative safety; but one more alarm was reserved for them. In the street leading to the Boulevard they suddenly found themselves surrounded by soldiers. In a moment they saw that these were not insurgents, but National Guards belonging to the party of order, with broad blue sashes round their waists. One of them, a big, fair young man, stopped short, and stamped his foot in furious helpless rage and indignation as he looked up at the lounging young men in the balcony overhead. 'The country in ruin, and not one of you cowards to answer her call,' he cried, shaking his fist at them with impotent fury. An older officer said something, pointed somewhere, and the little band hurried on, glittering clanking, helpless against the great catastrophe.

On the Boulevards everything was quiet and silent. The place seemed almost deserted; a few people were resting on the benches, the sun shone, the surly women were selling their newspapers in the little kiosks, upon which the various placards and appeals of the day were fluttering. Susy saw one despairing cry from a friend of order, headed –

'LIBERTY, FRATERNITY, EQUALITY.

'I appeal to the manhood, to the patriotism of the population, to those desiring tranquillity and respect for law. Time presses; a barrier is absolutely needed to stem the tide of revolution; let all good citizens give me their support.

'(SIGNED) A. BONNE,
'Captain Comm., 1st Company, 253 Batt.'

Alongside with this, and indefinitely multiplied, were the Federal manifestos in their official type and paper –

'Citizens! the day of the 18th of March will be known to posterity as the day of the justice of the people! The government has fallen, the entire army, rejecting the crime of fratricide, has joined in one cry of "Long live the Republic, long live the National Garde!" No more divisions; perfect unity, absolute liberty are before us.' . . .

'Come, come; do not waste your time upon that *barbouillage*,' cries Madame; 'here is our omnibus.' And as she spoke she hailed a yellow omnibus that was quietly jogging in the direction of Neuilly.

Everything was as usual when they got back to the villa, but Susy found to her dismay that Jo was still away. Max came in almost immediately after them; he seemed to have been chiefly concerned for their safety.

Jo could take care of himself, he said roughly. He must follow them later in the day if he did not get home before they left. The carriage was ordered and the *concierge* of the house they were going to had been forewarned.

CHAPTER XLIV

FUNERALIA

Seul avec sa torche.

V. HUGO

There was a great deal to be done before the time which Susanna had agreed upon with Max when her mother was to be removed into Paris. Everything had to be quietly prepared; but the boxes were packed, and all was in readiness at the time appointed. Adolphe was outside waiting to help to carry Mrs Marney in his strong maimed arms, Susy anxiously came and went, looking out for the carriage. She gathered a last bunch of lilac and brought it up to her mother's room. She felt her heart sink as she thought of the pain she must give.

'Let me tie the flowers up for you,' cried Denise, meeting her in the doorway, and anxious to show her good-will.

'Susy,' said Mrs Marney, as her daughter came into the room, followed by Denise carrying the lilac, 'come and sit down here beside me, dear. Michael has been here. He is coming again.' She spoke gently; a very sweet expression was in her face.

'When was he here, mamma?' said Susy, surprised. 'I have only been away a few minutes.' And then in a moment she knew that it was all a sick woman's hallucination.

'He left as you came into the room. He wanted to see me. He came and stood by my bedside,' said Mrs Marney. 'He comes when I am alone. I tell him he must not neglect his work for me; but he knows I like him to come.'

Her expression was so sweet, so strange, that Susy was still more frightened – she took her mother's hand; it was very cold.

'How sweet those lilacs are,' Mrs Marney went on. 'The hot weather is here; I have been thinking the boys will be wanting their summer clothes. Susy, will you see to them when you go back? You must not stop away any longer with me, dear. It is a rest to my heart to know my boys are in your care.'

Susanna could not speak. She heard the wheels stop at the gate outside, and the thought of tearing her dying mother away seemed to her so cruel, so unnatural, that suddenly she realised that, whatever happened, Mrs Marney must be left in peace. It was at this moment that the door opened, and Du Parc came in quietly, followed by Adolphe, prepared to carry the poor lady away. Susy put up a warning hand as they approached.

Mrs Marney smiled, seeing Max. 'Ah, Max,' she said, 'have you come for us? Take her away; take care of her. I have no strength to go with you, my dears. I shall stay quiet now, Susy,' she said, putting out her hand. As Susy caught her in her arms she gave a deep sigh, and her head fell upon her daughter's shoulder. Max sprang to the bedside.

'She is gone!' said Adolphe, in a whisper. 'Poor lady! poor lady!'

She was quiet at last, lying with closed eyes, with her hands crossed above the heart which ached no more. Susanna had sat all that long night by her mother's bed. She had ceased to weep when morning came. She sat almost as quiet as her dead mother. Only yesterday, as it seemed to her, she had watched by another death-bed. Here again the awful hand had come across her path, dividing those living still from those who had lived. Susy was a child to no one any more – all her past, all her childhood, was gone. The room was in order. Madame and Denise had helped to put it straight; there were more flowers out of the garden, a mass of spring blossom, which Max had brought to the door in his arms and given to his mother. Everything was put straight for ever. There would be no more work done, though the work-basket was still heaped; no more travelling, though Mary's boxes were packed; no more talks, no more troubles. Marney's strange trade of pen and ink had travelled elsewhere; so had the cheerful noises and shouts of the little boys their mother had so loved to hear. Mary wanted nothing any more. She had longed for her husband, and she had seen him, though he had not come to her; her daughter was by her side and held her hand, and death cannot seem anything but peaceful to a mother with her child to tend her to the end.

A sort of altercation on the landing outside seemed strangely at variance with the stillness of the room. Madame's indignant 'Oh! no, no, you cannot pass like that,' aroused Mrs Dymond. She went to the door and opened it quietly. 'What is it?' she said as she did so, and, not for the first time in her life, she came face to face with Marney, heated, excited – strangely excited.

'I have travelled all night, and this old devil would keep me away from my poor Polly,' he cried. 'She wants me, alive or dead, my poor, poor Polly! and that is why I am here,' he went on. 'D'ye hear, Mrs Dymond? For all your money and grandeur, ye didn't love your husband as your mother loved me. Don't bear malice!' he cried, more and more wildly. 'You can give me a kiss, though you always hated me,' and he caught Susy in his arms, and then pushed her roughly away, and went up to the coffin with a reeling step. 'Polly!' he said, 'why didn't you wait for me? – you knew I should come if I could! Ah! it's the first time you ever failed me, my poor girl! I travelled all night. I could not have got through the night but for a dram,' he cried, excitedly.

While he was still speaking thus incoherently, standing by the coffin, the sound of music outside came into the room through the open windows. It was the funeral march of a military band following some famous patriot to his grave. To Susy, in her highly-strung condition, the sound seemed almost supernatural. She laid her hand on Marney's arm, then, with one look at her mother's face, she burst into tears, and went out of the room. She met Max on the stairs hurrying up with a pale face; the thought of her trouble quite unnerved him.

'My mother sent me for you,' he said. 'Is Marney there? Has he frightened you?'

She put her hand to her head. 'No,' she said, 'but I cannot stay with him alone.'

They could hear him walking up and down excitedly, talking and calling piteously for some one to come to him. Then the steps ceased, the music went dying up the street, other steps came sounding on the wooden stairs. Madame's friend the young undertaker and his man came tramping up the wooden stairs, and all the dreary preparations for the funeral went on.

The patriot's procession, meanwhile, travelled on its way, the car, covered with flags, slowly winding through the streets of Paris; people looked on or fell into its train. For two hours it paraded thus, amid cries and shouts, and in time to the beat of the muffled drums and to the crashing music of a band which was conducted, so it was said, by the great Bergeret himself. It was late in the afternoon before it reached the gates of Montmartre, where the women were selling their wreaths and *immortelles*. The great funeral had hardly passed on its way when a second humble procession appeared – a bier, drawn by a single horse, and driven by Madame's friend the young undertaker, followed by a carriage with some travelling cases on the top. Marney was sitting on the box by the driver of the carriage; Madame du Parc, her son, and her servant and Susanna were inside. The carriage drew up by the roadway; Adolphe, who had come upon the bier, now joined them, and they all passed in together along an avenue of graves and lilacs. The place was looking beautiful in the setting sunlight – for miles around they could see the country lighted by its rays. They came to the quiet corner where poor Mary's grave had been dug under the golden branches of an acacia-tree. As they all stood by the open grave, united together for the last time by their common feeling for the woman who was gone, the muffled drums and funeral strains from the patriot's grave still reached them from a distance. When Mary Marney was laid to her last rest, and the prayers were over, the officiating clergyman turned aside, pulling off his surplice and carrying it on his arms, and went and mingled with the crowd round about the hero's grave. The end of his funeral eulogium was being pronounced – his last words had been '*Vive la Commune!*' said a man in a black tail-coat and a red sash, and suddenly all the people round about took up the cry. Susy heard them cheering as she stood by her mother's grave, she was still very calm, awe-stricken, and silent; she had stayed alone after the others had all gone on. When she reached the iron gates by which they had come in, she found her step-father waiting for her. His hat was over his eyes; it may have been the light of the setting sun which dazzled him. He did not look round, but he spoke as she came up to him.

'You will go and see the boys and tell them,' he said. 'I know that for her sake you will be a good friend to them. As for me, do not fear that I shall trouble you. You can write to the office if you have anything to say. I will send remittances from time to time, if necessary. But they will have their mother's money now. I shall give orders for it to be paid to you, it is little enough, but it will be enough for them.'

'Do you wish me to take care of the boys altogether?' Susy asked.

'Just as you like,' said he, turning away with a sigh. 'Your mother would have wished it so. You are more fit than I am.' A minute more and he was gone. It was the last time they ever met. Susy parted from him with something more like charity in her heart than she could have believed possible. He had made no professions, he had left his boys in her charge; and while Susy had Dermy and Mikey to care for she still seemed able to do something for her mother. Madame du Parc, who had stood waiting a little way off, now also came up to take leave.

'I, too, must say farewell, my child,' said the old lady with some solemnity; 'I can delay no longer, and you are returning to your home. My son will see you off. Ah! Susy, we shall miss you sorely.'

Susy could not speak; she bowed her head, took her old friend's hand in hers, and suddenly flinging her arms round her neck she burst into tears.

'God bless you, my dear child. Write very soon and tell me of yourself, of your safe return,' said the old lady. Then looking about for the coachman, 'Ah! it is insupportable! That man is not there. I shall miss my train;' and Madame, with renewed animation, trotted off towards the crowd. She came back a minute afterwards, followed by the coachman and her friend the undertaker. Max and Adolphe arrived at the same minute with a second carriage for Susanna, which they had been in search of. As the undertaker helped Madame into the carriage, there came a parting cheer from the friends of the fallen patriot.

'Listen to them,' said the man, shutting the door with a bang, 'as if it were not better to die one's proper natural death (*sa belle mort naturelle*) than to be shot and shouted over like this!' Max had delayed a moment to say a word to Susanna.

'I must see my mother off,' he said. 'It is more than likely you may find the Neuilly road blocked up; if you cannot get home, drive to this address, and wait till I come,' and he wrote something on a card and gave her a key. 'It is the house to which I hoped you might have taken her for safety, it is that of a friend; you will find no one there,' he added.

Susy was anxiously hoping to get back and to find Jo at the villa, but when they reached the Avenue de Neuilly, she found that Max's warning was well advised. The way was impassable, a barrier had been erected; the Federals had established themselves; it was hopeless to try to return to the villa.

'Don't fear, madame. I will get through the line,' said Adolphe, seeing her look of disappointment. 'I will find Mr Jo and bring you news of him later.' And when Susy faintly exclaimed, 'I show them my hands, and they always let me pass,' said the poor fellow laughing ruefully, and before she could say another word he was gone.

CHAPTER XLV

IN AN EMPTY APARTMENT

Then go live his life out; life will try his nerves
When the sky, which noticed all, makes no disclosure,
And the earth keeps up that terrible composure.

R. BROWNING

The house to which Du Parc had directed Susy was at the corner of the boulevard and the Rue Lavoisier, near the mortuary chapel which Madame du Parc had once promised to visit with her.

In this strange house, with the occasional roar and rush of the boulevard close at hand, the hours passed like some strange nightmare, so slowly, so long, so stifling in their silent oppression, that Susy could scarcely believe that another hour was gone when the gilt clock struck. The apartment belonged to unknown people who had fled hastily, leaving their clothes and their possessions in confusion; shoes and papers, packing cases half packed, a parcel of silver spoons was lying on the table. The linen cupboards were open with the neat piles disordered and overturned, the clocks were going, but the beds were not made. At first Susy set to work straightening, making order in confusion, preparing a room for herself, another for Jo in case he should arrive. She swept and folded and put away, and made the rooms ready for the night. She put by a lady's smart bonnet, a child's pair of little boots. Had she been in any mood to do so, she might have pieced together the story of those to whom the home belonged; but she was dull, wearied out, only wanting news of Jo.

As Mrs Dymond worked on the time passed; then when the work was done, when she had established herself in one of the two bedrooms, when all was straight and the linen piled afresh and the doors of the cupboard closed, though the clocks still ticked on, time itself seemed to stop still. She was quite alone now, neither Jo nor Adolphe rejoined her, nor did Max come as he had promised.

The rest of the house was also empty; the *concierge* was down below in his lodge, but except for him no one remained in the sunny tall building lately so alive, so closely packed.

There was one lady still remaining of all the inhabitants, the *concierge* said, an English lady – a *dame de charité*, who would not leave her poor; but she was gone away for a day to visit a sick friend.

Susy went downstairs towards evening to ask if no letter had come for her. She even went out, at the porter's suggestion, bareheaded, as people do in France, and bought some milk and some food from an adjoining shop, and then came back to the silent place.

It was a most terrible experience, one which seemed so extraordinary that Mrs Dymond could hardly believe that it was not all some dream from which she would presently awake. She waited till long past midnight and fell asleep at last on her bed; but towards four o'clock the sound of the cannon at Montmartre awoke her, and she sat up listening with a beating heart. There was a crucifix at the foot of the bed; in her natural terror and alarm it seemed to her that the figure on the crucifix looked up in the early dawn. There was a picture beneath the crucifix of a Madonna with a burning heart. A longing, an unutterable longing came to poor Susanna for her own mother Mary's tender, comforting, loving arms round her own aching heart – surely it was on fire too. How lonely she felt, how deserted. Max might have come last night, as he promised. It seemed to Susy that she understood now for the first time what the secret of Mary Marney's life had been; a secret that Susy herself had learnt so unwillingly, so passionately, so late in life's experience. If she had had any one to speak to everything might have seemed less vaguely terrible. As she was listening with a beating heart came a measured sound from without, that of a drum beating with a measured yet hurried roll; the rattle came closer and closer, and finally stopped under her very window. She started from the bed and ran and looked out. The dawn had just touched the opposite houses, another shutter opened, then a door creaked, and a man came out hastily buttoning his clothes, then a second stood in the doorway in shirt sleeves, but he did not move. Then the drum rolled away again, and, with two men only following, passed down the street to the boulevard. The sound came fainter and more hopeless. Then the distant cannon began to boom once more, and some carts with soldiers galloped by.

While Susy stood helplessly looking from her window the inhabitants of Paris were awake, and receiving the sun, as it at last dispelled the heavy morning fogs, with loud cries of '*Vive la République!*' Drink was being distributed among the National Guards assembled in the Place de l'Hôtel de Ville. Many of the bewildered soldiers who had been poured into the town all the preceding days were looking on and sharing in these festivities. Others, who had been out all night, were still wandering about the streets asking the passers-by where they were to go for shelter. A band of armed patriots, crossing the Place de la Concorde, where shouting out '*À Versailles!*' with the same enthusiasm with which their predecessors had cried '*À Berlin!*' a few months before. Those whom they met along the road take up the cry; the women assembling in the streets and doorways were uttering fiercer, vaguer threats of vengeance against tyrants, against Versailles, and the police, and, indeed, before many hours had passed the first of their unhappy victims was being hunted to his death along the Rue des Martyrs. Alas! he was but the first of the many who were to follow, and whose nobler blood was destined to flow upon those cruel stones.

Reading the papers of those days we see that an imposing deputation was preparing to visit the Place de la Bastille, carrying a red Phrygian flag before it; that the new self-elected government was gloriously proclaiming that 'Perfect Unity, that Liberty entire and complete,' of which we have heard so much, for the people of Paris had nobly shaken off the despotism which had sought to crush it to the ground. 'Calm and impassive in its force, it was standing (so say Billoray, Varlin, Jourde, Ch. Lullier, Blanchet, Pougeret, &c., &c.), and incontestably proving a patriotism equal to the height of present circumstances.'

What were all these echoes to Susy at her window, looking out with her heavy anxious heart? Jo! Max! where were they? what were they about? Ah! would these terrible hours never pass?

She dressed very early, lit a fire, and prepared a meal with the tin of milk which she had bought the day before. It was an unutterable relief to hear the door bell ring about eight o'clock in the morning. She found the *concierge* outside bringing up water from the pump below, and a note which had been left very early in the morning before he was up. Susy tore it open. The note was in Max's writing; it had no beginning nor date, but its news was new life to poor Susy. It was in English. '*I have tidings of Jo. Marney, by good fortune, heard of him, and sent me word. He is in custody, and I have gone after him, and hope to bring him back safe to you. Meet us to-day at one o'clock at the station by which you came. Adolphe will conduct you safely there.* – M. DU P.'

Susy burst into tears of relief, and sank into a chair. The *concierge* looked on compassionately at *la petite dame* as he called her, carried his pails into the kitchen, and returned on tip-toe, so as to show his friendly sympathy.

How the morning passed Mrs Dymond could scarcely have told; at twelve o'clock Adolphe appeared with a porter's knot upon his strong shoulders to carry her bag and her parcel of shawls. He had been vexed to fail her the night before; he was coming off when a messenger from Du Parc had met him with a parcel of letters, which he had been obliged to deliver. He had been about the streets till one o'clock at night. 'It was a real *corvée*,' said Adolphe. 'But it was apparently in your service, madame,' he continued, politely. 'It is necessary in these days to make one's plans beforehand, and if people won't agree to reason, one must use a little compulsion.'

Susy did not understand very well what he was saying. She walked by his side, questioning him about Max and Jo. He could tell her very little, except that Du Parc had sent him on these errands. As they were walking along, side by side, suddenly a quiet-looking woman in a white cap and black dress crossed the street, and came up and caught Susy by the dress.

'Oh!' she said, 'why do you stay here? You are English. What do you do here? It is not your home. Go home, go home; you don't know what dangers are about you here.' Then she pushed Susy from her, and hurried on wildly, wringing her hands as she went.

'Curious woman,' says Adolphe, imperturbably. 'She is not so far wrong. Come, madame, we must not be too late. There don't seem to be many people left anywhere,' he said, looking about him.

'How strangely empty the streets are,' said Mrs Dymond. 'The railway *place* is quite deserted, and the station, too, looks shut.'

CHAPTER XLVI

AT THE TERMINUS

. . . Bar we the gates!
Check we, and chain we, and each chine stop,
That no light leap in at louvre nor at loop;
And thou, Ashtaroth, hoot out and have out our knaves. . . .
Brimstone boiling, burning, out-cast it
All hot on their heads that enter nigh the walls,
Set bows of brake and brazen guns
And shoot out shot enough. . . .

W. LANGLEY, 'Ward's English Poets'

The station was shut, the doors and windows seemed closely barred, but as they looked they saw a side-door which was held cautiously ajar. Adolphe kicked with his foot, and in a minute they were let in. . . .

Within was a strange scene of crowded confusion and excitement – baggage in piles, people in groups clinging together, women wringing their hands and weeping, men gesticulating. In one of the waiting-rooms there was a crowd round a wounded man, in another a woman in hysterics.

'Did you see nothing?' cried half a dozen voices as Susy entered, following Adolphe.

'We saw nothing at all; we met nobody anywhere,' said he. 'What is the matter with you all?'

Then they were told by a dozen voices of a fight which had taken place only a few minutes before in the open *place* outside the station. Some of the Federal prisoners were being brought up to the station to be taken to Versailles to be judged. It was a grave affair. They were accused of participation in the murder of the generals. The Federals had made a desperate attempt to deliver their men from the hands of the escort. The escort had driven off the attack, and fought its way into the station. The prisoners were all now safely shut up in the railway carriages and doubly guarded; the Federals had retreated – whether for good or whether they had only gone for reinforcements it was impossible to say. Adolphe's face fell, though he tried to look pleased.

'They are all on a wrong scent,' cries a man in his shirt sleeves. 'They have got hold of Papa Caron among others who never touched a fly. I saw the man who struck down Clément Thomas. I should know him again. He is not one of these. The old man was lying on the ground; they struck him down with the butt-end of their guns.'

There was a murmur of horror all around, as the narrator, a natural dramatist, as most Frenchmen are, threw up his arms and re-acted the dreadful scene. Susy turned sick with horror.

'Your train will be starting in about ten minutes,' her companion was beginning, when suddenly his tone changes. 'Take care! take care! this way, madame,' cries Adolphe, suddenly thrusting himself before her. 'Up! up! on the seat!'

With a sudden cry the crowd began to sway, to fly in every direction; the great centre door of the station trembled under the blows which were being struck from without. There was a brief parley from a window, a man standing on a truck began to shout –

'Let them in! They want to deliver the prisoners! They will hurt nobody.'

A woman close by screamed and fainted. As Susy was stooping and helping to pull her up upon the bench the two great folding doors suddenly burst open, letting in the light, and a file of Federal soldiers marching in step and military order. Adolphe, who had thrust Susy into a corner of the *salle*, now helped to raise the fainting woman, with Susy's assistance, as she stood on the bench, out of the rush of the crowd, while he and his *hotte* made a sort of rampart before them.

'Don't be frightened,' he said, 'no one will fight; the prisoners' escort will see it is no use making a stand against such numbers. *Pardie*, they are off!' he cried excitedly, for as he spoke the engine outside gave a shrill whistle and started off upon the lines. Susy, from her place by the window, could see the train slowly steaming out of the station. There was a wild shout from the spectators. What was it that Susy also saw through the barred window by which she stood (half a dozen other heads below were crowding against the panes which looked to the platform)? She saw a figure, surely it was familiar to her, it could be none other than Max who was flying down the lines to the signal-posts, and in another minute the train, still snorting and puffing, began to slacken speed, then finally stopped, then backed, then stopped again.

'The danger signals are all up. They don't dare advance!' cried some of the men at the window.

'That is it, *bien trouvé*. Look out, madame. What do you see?' cried Adolphe eagerly from below.

Meanwhile the detachment of Federals, still in good order, still advancing, came on, lining the centre of the hall, spreading out through the door on to the side of the platform along which the Versailles train had started. There was a second platform on the other side of the station from which Susy's own train to Rouen and Havre was also making ready to start. It was curious to note how methodically common life went on in the midst of these scares and convulsions. Suddenly Susy, with a sinking, sickening heart, realised that the moment for her own departure had almost come; again she thought of Max's note and of its promise. Alas! alas! it had not been fulfilled – no Jo was there. If she went, she must go alone! all was too rapid for her to formulate either her fear or her hope, but while she hesitated there was a fresh stir among the crowd, and a functionary's voice was heard shouting, 'Passengers for Rouen and Havre *en voiture!*'

'You see it is all right!' said Adolphe, cheerfully. 'You had better go, madame; I will wait here in case your son should come, to send him after you. He is big enough to travel alone,' said the young man, nodding to reassure her, though he looked very pale, and his face belied his cheerful words.

She was in utter perplexity; she knew not what to do – what to determine; of one thing and one only was she sure, Max had promised to find Jo, to save him, and he would keep his word. Yes! it would be better to go on; her presence was but an incumbrance; Max could help Jo; that much she knew; what could she do but add to their perplexities. The fainting woman was already reviving, Susy sprang down from the bench with Adolphe's help, and as she did so she heard another shout, a loud cheer. The crowd swayed. Between the ranks of the soldiers came the triumphant procession of Federals with their red scarves, returning from the platform, and at the head of it Caron borne in triumph on some of his own workmen's shoulders. Half a dozen liberated prisoners were marching after him, shouting wildly and tossing hats and handkerchiefs.

Caron, who had been a prisoner among the rest, was smiling, undisturbed and quiet as ever, and bowing and softly waving his hat. To be safe mattered little to him, but his heart was overflowing with grateful pride and pleasure at the manner of his release; the rally of his friends, the determination with which his workmen had united to defend him against his enemies filled his heart with peaceful content.

Mrs Dymond, speechless, open-eyed, was still looking after him with breathless interest and surprise, when her own turn came, her own release from cruel suspense. A hand was laid on her shoulder, she was hugged in two strong arms and fairly lifted off the ground, and Jo, grinning, delighted, excited and free, was by her side once more.

'I am going back with you, Mrs Dymond,' said he; 'it's all right. I've got my return ticket.'

'He has given us trouble enough!' cries Max, coming up behind him breathless and excited too. 'For heaven's sake carry him off at once now you have got him. It is time you were in the train. The troops may be upon us again. He is not yet safe!'

'Nonsense! I was safe all through,' said Jo laughing, 'but we know Caron has enemies. Lucky for him Max remembered the danger signals.'

All the time Jo spoke Du Parc was hurrying Susanna along towards the platform from which the Rouen train was starting. It was approached by a turnstile, where they were met by an excited functionary who let Jo and his return ticket through the turnstile, but angrily opposed the passage of Adolphe and the luggage. It was no use waiting to discuss the matter, the man was terribly excited and time was pressing.

'Take the bag and find some places,' Max cried, handing the things over the barrier to Jo.

Susy paused for one minute. 'Good-bye, Adolphe,' she said, 'I shall never forget your kindness – never, never.' Then she raised her eyes, looking steadily into Du Parc's face. All the passing flush of success was gone from it. He was drawing his breath heavily; he looked anxious, harassed. Susy, too, was very pale, and she held by the wooden barrier.

'I – I can't leave you in this horrible place,' she said passionately. 'How *can* I say good-bye?' and as she spoke she burst into uncontrollable tears.

He took her in his arms, then and there, before them all – who cared? – who had time to speculate upon their relations?

'I shall come to you; don't say good-bye,' he said; 'we are not parting,' and he held her close and breathless to his beating heart, and then in a moment more he had put her away with gentle strength, and pushed her through the gate. The wooden turnstile was between them, his pale face was immediately lost in the sway of the crowd, a dozen people came between them; she found herself roughly hurried along, thrust into the first open carriage. Jo leapt in after her; the door was banged. Afterwards Susy remembered it all, at the time she hardly noticed what was happening. There were other people in the carriage – some sobbing, some talking incoherently, all excited, exasperated, incoherent. '*C'est trop! c'est trop! c'est trop!*' one man was shrieking over and over again; 'I can bear no more. I am going – yes, I am going! I am leaving this accursed city.' Another young fellow, leaning forward with his face in his hands, was sobbing audibly, he was oddly dressed in the fashion of the first Revolution, with a high Robespierre hat, and big flaps to his coat. Jo was very silent, and sat for a long time staring at his fellow-travellers. It was not till they reached Rouen, and the reassuring German helmets came round about the carriage windows asking what had happened in Paris, that Josselin began to talk to his stepmother. He had met Caron that morning after he left them at the villa, and was walking with him from the station, when they had both been suddenly arrested, together with a young man who had only joined them a few minutes before. They were not allowed a word. They were hurried off, and all three locked up in a guard-house, where they were kept during the two days. Late on the afternoon of the second day they were moved to a second *corps de garde*. On their way from one place to another they fortunately passed Marney in the street. 'I shouted to him,' said Jo, 'for I knew he would let you know, and I knew he had been at work, when Caron received a message through one of the soldiers – they were most of them half Federals – that we were to be rescued. I don't think he or I were in very much danger,' Jo added, 'but the third man had been a soldier, and would have been shot, so Caron told me afterwards. He was a fine fellow – half an Englishman; they called him Russell, or some such name.'

'O! Jo, I have got *you* safe,' said Susy, beginning to cry again, 'I can't think – I can't speak – I can't feel – any more.'. . .

'Why should you?' said Jo, practically. 'Give me your ticket, for fear you should lose it,' and then he settled himself comfortably to sleep in his corner, smiled at her, and pulled down the blind. Susy could not rest; she sat mechanically watching the green plains and poplar-trees flying past the window. She was nervously unhinged by the events of the last two days; the strain had been very great. She longed to get back to silence, to home, to the realisation of that one moment of absolute relief. She felt as if she could only rest again with Phraisie in her arms, only thus bear the renewed suspense, the renewed anxiety. But she knew at the same time, with grateful, indescribable relief, that her worst trouble was over now, even though prison bars, distance, a nation's angry revenge lay between her and that which seemed so great a portion of her future life. Circumstances were changed from the day when she thought she had parted from Max for ever. Tempy was married, her poor mother was gone. The boys were no longer dependent upon her for everything. Jo was a man now and able to make his own life good.

They reached home on the evening of the second day. The carriage was waiting at the station with Phraisie in it. The drive did Susy good after all these tragic, distorted days, during which she had been living this double life. Little Phraisie, blooming and happy, was her best peace-maker.

A gentle wind blew in their faces, a gentle evening burnt away in quiet gleams, the sky was grey and broken, the soft golden gates of the west were opening wide, and seemed to call to weary spirits to enter into the realms of golden peace. The hedges on either side were white with the garlands of spring. The dogs, who had been set loose, came barking to meet them, as the wheels turned in at the familiar home gates. The servants appeared eager to welcome. Jo silently gave the reins into the coachman's hand, and sprang down and handed out his stepmother with something of his father's careful courtesy. Little Phraisie, delighted to be once more at home, went running from room to room calling to Jo and to her mother as she went. It was home, Susy felt, and not only home but a kind tender home, full of a living past, with a sense of the kindness that was not dead.

Phraisie was put to bed; dinner was laid in the library for the young man and his stepmother. Jo sat, still silent, revolving many things in his mind. From a stripling he had grown to be a man in the last few weeks. His expedition, his new experience, Tempy's marriage, his own responsibility – all these things had sobered him, and taught him to realise the importance of the present, of other people's opinion, of his duty to his neighbour; his neighbour at that moment was his stepmother sitting in her accustomed place.

'Here we are beginning our life together again, Mrs Dymond,' said he at last. 'We get on very well, don't we?'

'Very well, dear Jo,' Susy said, smiling, 'and so we shall until some one who has more right to be here than I have comes to live at the Place.'

'What are you talking about?' says Jo, blushing up. 'I don't mean to marry for years to come, if that is what you mean.'

'Ah, my dear,' said Susy, with some emotion, 'make no promises; you do not know; you cannot foretell. One can never foretell.'

He looked hard at her. He guessed that Susy had not come back to them as she went away. She turned a little pale when she saw his eyes fixed upon her. It seemed to her as if her story must be written in her face. She might have told him – she need not have been ashamed – but she felt as if his father's son was no proper confidant.

Long after Jo had gone to bed she sat by the dying fire, living over and over those terrible days, those strange momentous hours.

CHAPTER XLVII

CARON

Fear no more the heat o' the sun,
Nor the furious winter's rages;
Thou thy worldly task hast done,
Home art gone, and ta'en thy wages.

We must refer those of our readers who take any interest in the subsequent adventures of Max and his contemporaries to the pages of the *Daily Velocipede* for some account of those days which followed Susy's departure from Paris. Marney's eloquent pen, dipped in dynamite and gunpowder, flashing with flame and sensation, became remarked beyond the rest, and brought readers by hundreds to his paper. He was everywhere, saw everything, so graphic were his descriptions, so minute, so full of enthusiasm, that it was impossible for more experienced newspaper readers than Susy to say how much he wrote from his own observation, or what hearsay legends he translated into his own language, which, whatever its merits or demerits, did not lack in vividness. Susy scanned the columns day by day with anxious eyes for more and more news. She found so much that she was almost bewildered by it, and scarcely knew what to believe; as for direct intelligence of Max, scarcely any came to her, though Madame sent letters from time to time from her farm at Avignon. But Madame's letters chiefly described her olive-trees, her cow, her pig, her eggs, and her tomatoes. Max delayed; he did not rejoin her as she had hoped he might have done; he left her to do it all, to engage the man, to contract with the hotels for her eggs and butter. Susy wrote to Madame from time to time, telling her about little Phraisie and the two boys, who were doing well at their school. In one letter Susy also described a domestic event, of which the news had reached Tarndale soon after her return from Paris. Uncle Peregrine Bolsover had died suddenly from the effects of a snake bite. He had left no will, but Charlie became undisputed heir to the Bolsover estates, and Uncle Bol now transferred to him the allowance which Peregrine had hitherto enjoyed; but this news did not interest Madame du Parc in the least. The price of butter had fallen, and her mind was preoccupied by more present contingencies.

As the events multiplied in France, as the storms raged more and more fiercely, those who had remained, hoping to stem the waves, felt every day more helpless; the sea was too rough, the evil blasts too high – what voice could be heard? What orders could prevail? Captains and leaders were powerless now. For the first time Caron lost courage and confidence. The murder of the hostages seemed like a death-blow to the dear old man, who could not believe in the wickedness of men whom he had trusted and loved with all his threescore years, during which he himself, though he did not know it, had been as a hostage for good and for truth among the irrational and ignorant people. He moped, his blue eyes were dim, his steps were slow. Max hardly recognised him one day when he met him coming out of his own doorway in the Rue du Bac. He was carrying some letters to a post-office hard by; he seemed glad to take Du Parc's strong arm.

'I am tired; I feel ill,' he said. 'I feel disgraced and utterly ashamed; this is no liberty, no republic any more. This is tyranny, monstrous wickedness; these crimes of the brutal ignorant have only the excuse of ignorance. If I, if others before me, had done our simplest duty in life, such blank ignorance would not now exist.'

Max felt his heart sore for his old friend. He himself had hoped less of his fellow-creatures; he was more angry and less crushed than Caron.

'If these brutes had listened to your teaching,' he said, trying to cheer him, 'and to that of sensible men, it might have all turned out differently. They will still have to learn before they can cease to be brutes.'

'I have no more strength to teach,' said Caron. 'Max, do you know that I have left you all? – all my theories, my failures, my ineptitudes, my realities, *mes chères vérités*,' he said. 'You must make the best use you can of it all. You can ask for the memoranda and papers. I gave them to your friend, *la douce* Susanne. They will be for you and your children, my dear son. If you escape from this terrible catastrophe, go to her. I think that with her you will find happiness.'

Max, greatly touched, pressed his old friend's arm. 'One can scarcely look forward,' he said, 'from one hour to another, but you have guessed rightly; if happier times ever come for me, they could only be with her.'

Caron's eyes lighted up.

'That is well,' he said with a bright smile. Then, giving him the letters, 'I had been about to post them,' he said. 'Will you leave them for me?

They will be safer if they go by hand. You have done me good,' he added. 'I shall return home quietly.'

Max left him at the turn of the street.

Is it chance, is it solemn fatality – by what name is one to call that flash of fate suddenly falling upon men as they journey on their way, that lightning flash which falls, without warning, irrevocable, undreamt of, rending the veil of life for ever?

While Caron turned slowly homewards to his quiet study, where old Madeleine was at work against his return, a mad crowd had gathered in an adjoining street, and was pursuing with cruel rage a wretched victim who flew along a narrow alley, and came rushing across the pavement upon which Caron was walking.

The victim, a *gendarme*, torn, wounded, bleeding in the temples, ran straight against Caron, and fell helpless at his knees, pursued by the yelling mob.

The old man seemed suddenly roused to a young man's strength of indignation, and flung himself before the victim.

'Stop!' he cried to the mob. 'What are you doing? I am Caron. You know me. Let this man pass!'

For a moment, startled by his voice, his fearless, commanding look, they hung back; but out of the crowd a huge, half-drunken Communist came striding up, and putting out his hand with a tipsy chuckle tried to pull forward the poor fainting wretch.

Caron pulled an official scarf from his pocket, and holding it up in his left hand, struck the man in the face with it.

'That man is drunk,' Caron cried, appealing to the crowd; 'and you people – you let yourselves be led by such as he?'

The people looked at the scarf, hesitated, began to murmur and make way, but the drunken leader, still chuckling and stupid, seized the miserable victim again.

'Let him go, I tell you,' said Caron. 'It is the will of the people.'

'Silence! or I shoot you too!' cried the brute, pulling out a pistol, and aiming it at the fainting heap upon the pavement.

With the natural impulse of one so generous, the old man sprang forward to turn the arm, but he was too late. The pistol went off, and Caron fell back, silent indeed, and for ever.

The murderer, half sobered, stood with his pistol confronting them all, as Caron had done a moment before, and then began to back slowly. The crowd wavered, and suddenly dispersed.

'Silence!' cry the blasphemers to those who from generation to generation, by love, by work, by their very being, testify to the truth. And the good man dies in his turn, but the words of his life and the truth he tried to live, live on. There is neither speech nor language: but their voices are heard among them, their sound is gone out into all lands: and their words into the ends of the world. . . .

Susanna was spared the shock of reading the news of Caron's death in the paper. Marney wrote to her, telling her of the event as he had heard it, simply, and without the comments he afterwards added in print.

To the papers this was but an incident in those awful times; the readers of M. Maxime du Camp's eloquent and most terrible volumes will find many and many such noted there; they will also find an episode curiously like one in which Max du Parc was (according to the *Daily Velocipede*) concerned, and which happened upon the last of those terrible nights during which the flames raged and fought on the side of madness in furious might and irresponsibility. 'Was this the end of it all – of the visions of that gentle old teacher of a gospel which was for him indeed, but not for frenzied demons and desperate madmen?' thought Max, as he tried a short cut across the Carrousel, round which the flames were leaping madly. The gate into the Tuileries, by which he had come with Susanna once, was closed: he had to turn back and fight his way along the crowds and the ramparts of the Rue de Rivoli again, to the Ministère de la Marine, whither he was bound. Some weeks before, Caron's influence had appointed Max to some subordinate place under the Commune in the Ministère de la Marine. In his first natural fury and heart-rent grief at his old friend's death, Du Parc's impulse had been to wash his hands of the whole thing, and the guilt and wicked confusion, and to come away with the rest; then came the remembrance of that life-long lesson of forbearance and tenacity; that strange sense – which some men call honour only – awoke; the strange sense of secret duty that keeps men at their guns, faithfully fighting for an unworthy cause in the front of an overwhelming force. Was it also some feeling of honest trust in himself which impelled Caron's disciple to stand to his post? He remained, protesting, shrewdly and intelligently using every chance for right. He had been to the Central Committee just now to protest in vain against the destruction of the building where he had been left. He represented that it was full of sick people; the lower rooms were used as hospital wards. 'The sick people must be moved,' yelled the chiefs; but the fiat had gone forth. The Versaillais had reached the Rond-point of the Champs Elysées; they should find Paris a heap of charred remains before they entered her streets.

Max got back through the wild saturnalia of the streets, where dishevelled women were dancing round the flames, and men, yelling and drunken, were howling out that the last day had come; he reached the Ministère at last, to find that a band of officials with signed orders were deliberately smearing the walls and staircases with petroleum, in readiness for firing; while down below, with infinite pains and delays, the sick were being slowly moved from their shelter into the street. In vain the Communists swore and raged at the delay; slowly, and more slowly, did the doctor and his nurses get through their arduous work. Max saw at a glance what was in their minds, a hope that the delay might be long enough to save the place, for the Versaillais were within a quarter of an hour's march, and once they were there all danger would be over. 'Good God!' said the poor doctor in an undertone, wiping his perspiring brow; 'why don't they come on? Will they wait till Doomsday?'

Max shrugged his shoulders as he stood looking on for a moment. The band of incendiaries, having finished their preliminary work, had adjourned to a small room or office on the first floor, where they sat gloomily drinking round a table and awaiting their summons, and the news that the hospital wards were evacuated.

Du Parc passed on and climbed the stairs, and went and stood upon a flat terrace on the roof, from which he could see the heavens alight with the lurid glare of the flames now bursting from every side. To the right the Rue Royale was burning; to the left, on the other side of the waters, which repeated the flames, the whole of the Rue de Lille was in a blaze. Close at hand the offices of the Finance were on fire, while the Tuileries were an ocean of flame. At his feet was the Place de la Concorde, silent, deserted, covered with wrecks, with broken statues and monuments; beyond the Place de la Concorde lay the sombre green of the Champs Elysées, showing here and there some faintly twinkling bivouac fire.

Suddenly, as he looked, his brain reeled, then he put his hands to his head, and tears came into his eyes and seemed to save him. The clock below struck the hour; for a moment he hesitated, then his resolution was taken. He made certain observations, and down the stairs by which he had come hurried back. When he reached the door of the room where the Communists were still sitting, he passed his fingers through his hair; he tore open his shirt; he had deliberately smeared his hands in some black cinders lying in a heap on the roof, and with his fingers he now blackened his face, and flinging violently open the door, hurried in, crying out the terrible password of those sad times, 'We are betrayed! We are betrayed! The Versaillais are upon us; they have surrounded us. Stop! not that way! I will lead you,' he cried, as the men rose half scared, half drunk, looking for an exit. 'Follow me,' he cried, flying up the stairs once more and followed by the gang, and turning by the upper passages to the lofts and back garrets, he left them suddenly, promising to return. Then, shutting a heavy door upon them, he double-locked them in.

When he hurried down to the ground floor, he found that three wounded men only remained; they were lying on the ground, ready to be carried out.

'You can take your time,' he said to the doctor, 'the incendiaries are upstairs, under lock and key.'

The doctor immediately gave the word to his assistants, and the wounded, who had been carried out with infinite pain and patience, were now brought back again, and were lying in their usual places when the Versaillais marched in an hour later.

L'ENVOI

With the London hubbub,
Over-tired and pestered,
I sought out a subbub
Where I lay sequestered.

'THE IDLER,' W.M.T.

When the flames were extinguished, when the great panic was subsiding, then came the day of reprisals, and the unhappy Parisians, who, after enduring so much with patience, had broken out in their madness, now fell under the scourge once more. Perhaps nothing during the war, not even the crazed monstrosities of the desperate Commune, has ever been more heart-breaking to hear of than the accounts of the cold-blooded revenge of the Versaillais.

But for this again we must refer our readers to the *Daily Velocipede*, in the columns of which Max was reported to be among the condemned prisoners, but Susy was surprised and reassured by an ambiguous letter, which reached her at Crowbeck Place, from no less well-informed a person than Mr Bagginal of the English Embassy.

'I have executed your commission,' so it began. (Susy had not given Mr Bagginal any commission, and she turned the letter over in some surprise.) 'I am sending you the photographs of the ruins and of Paris, that you wished for, in its present changed aspect. I hope also to have some pen-and-ink etchings to forward at the same time. They are by our companion of last year, who has been doing some very good work lately, though he complains of the light of his present studio; he hopes, however, to be able to remove before long to some more commodious quarters. If you should like any more of his drawings, you can always find them at a toy-shop in the Brompton Road, which I believe you and Miss

Phraisie are sometimes in the habit of patronising. Pray present my compliments to that young lady, and tell her I shall bring over some bonbons when I next come. They are making them now of chocolate, in the shape of cannon balls and of shells, filled with vanille creams, which I assure you are excellent. Believe me, dear Mrs Dymond, always most faithfully yours,

'C.E. BAGGINAL.'

The photographs arrived by the next post, and with them a sketch of the well-remembered studio in the villa, and another very elaborately finished drawing of a dark box-room in Mr Bagginal's lodgings, where the artist must have spent a good many hours; the third drawing was a slight sketch of the little shop front in the Brompton Road, with Mrs Barry's name over the doorway. Susy recognised it at once, for she had been there and had often heard of the place from Max himself.

Two days afterwards Susy, with Caron's packet in her hand, was driving along Knightsbridge towards the little shop; in a strangely anxious and excited frame of mind she got out of her hansom, dismissed the man, and stood for an instant in the doorway gathering courage to go in.

It seemed to her as if all the toys were feeling for her as she stood there – the dolls with their goggle blue eyes, the little donkeys and horses, the sheep with their pink and blue ribbons. They all seemed sympathising and to be making mute signs; she saw the little trumpets in their places and the sugar-candy stores; she could have bought up the whole shopful, but the small assemblage would not have seemed the same to her in any other place. Here in the suburban street, with the carts passing and repassing, and the hospitals and buildings, the quiet little shop haunted by the children's smiling faces seemed to shrink away from the busy stream outside; as Susy stood there all the dolls seemed to put up their leather arms in deprecation, crying, 'Don't come in here, we belong to peaceful toy-land, we have to do with children only, not with men and women with grown-up hearts.' The woman who kept the shop had left the parlour door open, and Susy could see the window and the old London garden beyond, the square panes with autumn creepers peeping through.

As Susanna entered Mrs Barry came out from her parlour, and Susy with faltering lips asked her if she could give her any news of M. du Parc, 'I have some papers which I want to send him,' said Mrs Dymond.

'I will call him, ma'am,' said the woman very quietly; 'he came last night;' and almost as she was speaking the door opened and Max was there. . . .

Clap your pink arms, oh goggle eyes, ba woolly lambs, play musical boxes, ring penny trumpets, turn cart wheels, and let the happy lovers meet!

Two more people are happy in this care-worn world; they are together, and what more do they ask!

Du Parc had escaped, although his name was on the list of those attainted. Mr Bagginal could, perhaps, if he chose, give the precise details of the young man's evasion from the back room where he had spent so many dull days. Mr Bagginal sent him over with a letter to Mr Vivian, that good friend of art and liberty. I know not if it was Sir Frederick, or Sir George, or Sir John to whom Mr Vivian in turn introduced Du Parc on his arrival, and who received him with cordial deeds and words of help and recommendation. He was bade to leave his toy-shop and take up his abode with the Vivians for a time and work and make his way in the London world. His admirable etching of Mrs Vivian and her two daughters first brought him into notice and repute: it was followed by the publication of that etching already mentioned of a beautiful young woman gazing at a statue. Du Parc was able, fortunately, to earn from the very first; later he had more money than he knew what to do with, and his old acquaintance in Soho, Mr White, more than once had occasion to acknowledge with thanks communications which passed between Max and Susy and his own particular branch of the Society for the Organisation of the Relief of Distress.

The papers, of which Maxwell du Parc had not at first realised the importance, and which Susanna brought him, contained, besides many theories and verses half finished, a duly signed will which very materially affected Max's future prospects. Caron had left him his heir and executor, his trustee for his works and his men. It is true the old man's fortune had been greatly reduced by late events and by the expenses of his establishment, but his houses were standing still, his machinery and his work-shops were still there – most of the workmen had clung to the enterprise in which they had a personal stake – and though it was not possible for Max, an unwilling exile, to return to France, yet Adolphe was found capable and able to replace him for the time on the spot. Mikey and Dermy, it was hoped, would be in time able to take their share in the management of the works.

When the general amnesty was proclaimed about four years ago Max was once more free to return to France. Susy most certainly would not like to leave England altogether, but she is glad to go from time to time to the low white house with the shutters among the willows and poplar-trees in the little village near the paper-mills. 'Les Saules' is a happy meeting-place for her English friends, and there upon the iron bench by the shining glass ball in the garden sits old Madame du Parc from Avignon admiring her northern grandchildren.

They come up in a little file headed by Phraisie, who is perhaps also dragging a little Bolsover by the hand.

Promenons-nous dans les bois,
Pendant que le loup n'y est pas;

sing the little voices taking up in their turn that song of childhood and innocent joy, which reaches from generation to generation, which no sorrow, no disaster, will ever silence while this world rolls on.